I0534844

Roll Them Bones
Danielle Gomes

Edge Weaver LLC

Roll Them Bones

Edge Weaver Realms is an imprint of Edge Weaver LLC

Copyright © 2025, Danielle Gomes

Book Design: Marie Ito

Kindle ISBN: 978-1-968100-12-4

Paperback ISBN: 978-1-968100-13-1

Published in the United States of America

Edge Weaver LLC
19360 Rinaldi #681
Porter Ranch, CA 91326-1607

Dedication

To my parents, my heroes! Thank you for giving me the most love-filled, fun childhood!

Contents

The string of pearls appear.
Hope held in every breath.
Liquid memories, forgotten names.
A culture of false promises and doomed dreams.
Dawn breaks with oppressive weight.
The lights fade with disillusionment and markers left
unpaid.

Chapter 1

"Ma'am . . . Ma'am . . . you have to wake up." The pungent scent of artificial flowers overtakes the aroma of stale coffee. I push air through my nose and groggily lift my head. My neck cramps forcing me to rest my too-heavy head back against the seat.

"Ma'am. We've landed and you're the last passenger on board."

My eyes won't open. They feel glued. I try again and they finally budge—a fraction. Nothing's in focus. I lift my eyebrows and by default my lids lift a fraction more. The dull gray fabric of the seat in front of me blurs into the open luggage containers as I turn to the source of the voice. "Sorry," I croak. My throat is so dry, I must've slept with my mouth open. I try to stand, but my head spins, leaving my legs feeling like Jello, and I drop back into the seat.

"Are you all right?" the flight attendant asks, her frosted blonde hair pulled back from her face.

"Yes," I whisper, finding my balance. "I'm just exhausted." The plane is empty bar the cleaning crew.

She hands me my bag and smiles beneath a creased brow. I can't tell if she's being sympathetic or judgmental. Probably both.

I trudge my way through the seemingly endless terminal. Thanks to the Xanax, my emotions are tamped down to a manageable numbness, but moving through the airport takes effort. Concrete seems to fill my legs as I drag them past gate after gate. I don't remember Newark Airport being so ridiculously big. People rush by me in every direction. I wish I had someplace I wanted to go to that badly—I'd rather be anywhere than here but have nowhere specific in mind.

By the time I make it to baggage, my flight's luggage is already tumbling down to the carousel. My head spins again while an angry nerve pounds from the inside. The last thing I want to do is watch suitcases whirl by, but I lost the luxury of *wanting* along with everything else. With no seats in sight, I find a column to lean against and fight back a tide of nausea as bag after bag drifts past. *Not mine. Not mine. Definitely not mine.* Then the carousel stops. I do a loop around the empty carousel and double check the screens, making sure my flight number matches, then drag myself to the baggage counter. A middle-aged woman with an accent I can't place waits for me to hand her my baggage claim ticket. The corner of her mouth pulls up, primed for the next complaint she'll have to deal with. I finally dig out my tickets and place them on the counter.

Minutes later, after incessantly tapping keys on her computer, she looks at me. "Lost."

"What do you mean?"

"There's no record of your bags anywhere in the system."

"How is that possible?"

"I'm not sure." She scratches her temple. "It's extremely unusual."

"Everything I own is in those bags. That's all I have. I sold—" Tears sting the corner of my eyes, threatening to spill over.

"I'm sure we'll find them. Probably a glitch. Here, write your number and the address you'll be at."

I turn and cough, quickly wiping my tears before anyone notices. I complete the form, ticking tiny boxes for my tiny life that just got tinier now that my belongings are gone. Lost. I pass it back.

"Hey." She leans in. "I'm not supposed to tell you this, but the airline will give you money for delayed bags. Give 'em a call, ok?"

I nod and step away from the counter, not sure what to do next. My eyes settle on my toes, and I don't care that my sneaker is untied. I'm more bothered by the large, tan stain on my jeans. No amount of wiping helps. It's dry.

"It doesn't hurt to smile."

"Excuse me?" I ask, looking up.

"Go ahead and smile, it'll make you feel better," a paunchy, balding, little old man tells me. On a good day, I hate being told to smile.

"I'm having a bad day."

"Then I'll let you borrow mine." He grins at me.

I force myself to politely smile so I can end this exchange as quickly as possible. "Excuse me, I have to find my ride." From this close, this old man smells like a combination of Aqua Velva and musk; it's just pungent enough to turn my already wobbly stomach.

"See? You're even more beautiful when you smile."

I nod, irritation roiling in my diaphragm, and attempt to continue past.

He steps slightly to block my path. "Are you single, by any chance? I have a very successful son about your age. He's got a big job in the city."

"No, sorry," I say and hold up my left hand.

"That's one lucky guy you have there, and I can tell by that rock he knows it."

"Thanks," I say and push my way past him as quickly as possible.

How pathetic am I? Still can't take the ring off. Even though every time I look at it, I see his left hand, his empty ring finger where I was going to slide his ring on and the tattoo on his forearm—the only part of his body still recognizable as he lay on that cold metal table. The tattoo was just a symbol, nothing more than bold black inked circles and lines, but it meant something to him so I was drawn to it. I spent hours in his arms, tracing my finger along the design. I'm exhausted. Can't walk anymore. So, I sit on the first bench I find and rest my forehead in my hands.

"Lilith Layne Umbra?"

A sigh of frustration escapes me and I look up at a smiling, salt-and-pepper-haired man. Short and a little chubby, he's not wearing a United Airlines uniform, so I know he hasn't found my bags. "Yes?"

"I'm Tony, your driver. I've been looking all over for you since I saw your string of pearls."

"String of pearls?"

"It's not what you're thinking, not the necklace—"

"I know," I interrupt. "It's the lights on landing planes."

"Hey, whatta youse . . . trying to ruin my lines?"

I just stare at him.

"I'm joking," he continues. "You're the first person I ever picked up at the airport that's known that. It's my line. I didn't really see your string of pearls." He laughs. "I have a cell phone."

"My uncle designs airports. I know the lingo."

"Can I take your bags?"

"They're lost."

"They'll find 'em, don't worry." He pats my shoulder. "Follow me. I'm not parked far."

Tony leads me through a nearby set of automatic sliding doors. The moment we cross through the second set, the cold hits my exhausted body like a defibrillator. My comfortable numbness is shocked away, replaced with painful goosebumps that sting like a thousand tiny needles. Blaring car horns assault my already aching skull.

"I'm across the street and to the left," Tony says.

The crosswalk signal turns green, and we obey its command. Cement stretches out in every direction as cars swarm in and out of the gloom. The smoggy gray landscape rolls on and on like the industrial desert it is, completely void of anything natural except the humans that rule over it. The attempt to tame nature's unpredictability with concrete convenience has left the entire city of Newark, New Jersey miserably drab, at least from this vantage point. Even Tony seems gray in this light. His black SUV sits nearby in the limo lot.

"You look a little woozy. Want to sit up front?"

I nod.

He opens the front door for me and I melt into the seat, glad the car is still warm.

"You want a bottle of water?" Tony asks. "I have Coke, too."

"Coke, please."

Tony twists the cap to loosen it and passes the bottle to me. It's ice cold. The syrupy bubbles are exactly what my stomach needs.

"So, who's your uncle design airports for?"

"He's a consultant now, but he used to work for Howard Hughes."

"Howard Hughes! No shit. He basically built my favorite city. Las Vegas. I mean, everyone knows the mob started it, but Hughes turned it into a destination mecca."

I nod, then dig through my bag for my Xanax. I probably shouldn't take another one, but I can tell this is going to be a long ride.

"If you ask me," Tony continues, "the mob buried too many bodies in the desert. Some without their heads." He winks at me. "Hughes was one of the first to show corporate America what the gaming industry could offer, and they bought in big time. I'm not saying those corporations didn't have their own types of collateral damage, they're just a lot cleaner."

"On paper, anyway," I say. "You know a lot about Las Vegas." As we wind through a nest of highway ramps and overpasses, I hope this conversation fizzles out fast. I still haven't seen a color other than gray.

"I go at least three times a year. More if I can swing it. You ever been?"

"Born and raised. That's where I live . . . used to live."

"You're leaving Las Vegas? I thought you smelled familiar." Tony laughs.

"What?"

"*Leaving Las Vegas*, the Nicholas Cage movie. He's an alcoholic."

"I smell like an alcoholic?"

"I'm kidding with you. You don't smell like an alcoholic, just booze. I drink a ton whenever I go to Vegas, too, especially on the flight. You're in good company." He nudges me playfully with his elbow. Something about his frankness is strangely comforting.

"Any chance you have some gum in here? I'm going to my parents."

"Oh, parents? Now I get the booze. Take the whole pack." He tosses me the gum.

I throw the packet in my bag and a Xanax in my mouth.

"You gamble?" he asks.

"A little, but I worked in the casino business."

"No way! To me, a night in a casino is unlike any other experience in the world. It's a night of excitement. An escape from the humdrum. Everyone's a VIP. Even me, a limo driver from Newark."

"That's a good way to look at it. Las Vegas should use you in a marketing campaign." I hope the Xanax kicks in quickly. The weight of dread increases with each mile as we near my parent's home.

Tony laughs. "I just love it. I love casinos. Always seen gambling as a lot like life. It requires balance and restraint. A mix of strategy and luck." He gestures above the steering wheel like a magician performing sleight of hand. "Sometimes you win. Sometimes you lose. But those moments between placing a bet and being dealt your hand are so filled with hope. Win or lose—the wager is worth it."

"Are you always this upbeat?"

"I try. In life, as long as you're willing to step up to the table, you'll eventually win."

Part of me wants to tell Tony he's wrong. There are some tables you don't want to step up to, but I just stare out the window.

A moment of quiet settles over us before Tony clears his throat. "So what d'ya do in Vegas?"

"I worked in casino marketing."

"Worked?"

"Yeah, I'm currently unemployed."

"Sorry. Feel like talking about it?"

"Life got in the way." I take another sip of my ice-cold coke.

"I know how that goes. But youse don't even know. If I could do it all over, I'd work at a casino."

"Are you always so talkative?"

"Nah, only when I like someone."

I attempt a small laugh, but it comes out sounding more like a cough.

"Did you like your job?"

"I used to."

"I bet you were really good at it."

"I got results." The ghost of a smile tugs at the corners of my mouth, stuck somewhere between nostalgia and sadness.

"What's your secret? What got you results?"

"I don't know . . . I guess I always had a knack for reading people. Or I used to." I let out a deep breath, an unintentional sigh.

"I'm not sure what you're going through, but it'll get better. Promise. You'll find another job."

My tongue feels heavy and thick. I can't talk anymore. As silence returns to the car, I stare out the window. The sun has just gone down. The lights from New York City begin to flicker to life. There's barely enough daylight to still see the imposing skyline towering over me. It's like a mammoth limestone cliff on the verge of collapse. Ready to crush the air from my lungs. I'm reminded of how small and inconsequential I am as the curtains close on another day. The meds kicks in and I drift to sleep.

Chapter 2

I haven't been back to Cold Spring since I was a kid. Mom grew up here and my parents moved back full time a few years ago. Standing outside the iron gate to my parents' historic stone Georgian, I prefer the brutal discomfort of frigid temperatures to the even more brutal judgment waiting inside. I'd done my best to disguise the smell of alcohol. But now my jaw aches from chomping on three sticks of minty gum. And I stink of bergamot and sandalwood from the cologne Tony'd given me.

With a wave, Tony drives off, and I intend to give myself a few minutes to air out. I catch the neighbor across the street staring at me from their brick colonial. We make eye contact, and she quickly pulls her curtains shut. I see old Mrs. Stanke hasn't changed. Nothing ever changes here.

Just sixty miles from New York City lies Cold Springs, where my parents, like many residents, make the commute a few times each week. My mom—a former supermodel who's still gracing runways in her sixties—cast a long shadow growing up. Being the daughter of someone that beautiful wasn't easy on my self-esteem. Don't get me wrong, I'm comfortable with my looks; people often remark on my striking combination of light blue eyes and black hair. But I'll never have Mom's showstopping presence. It wasn't until I decided to follow Dad's path that I finally made peace with that.

Dad cut his teeth as a Vegas oddsmaker before building what would become the world's largest publicly traded sports betting company. Not long ago, I was blazing my own trail—the golden girl of casino marketing, my face splashed across every magazine on the Strip. Finally living up to the family name. Now here I am, jobless, homeless, crawling back to my parents' doorstep. Being their only child and their only failure cuts deep. For a moment, I consider turning around, but I'm too exhausted for pride. Too exhausted for any of it.

I take a few deep breaths. The exhale condenses into an icy fog, enclosing my face in mist. The iron gate creaks loudly as I push my way through onto the uneven brick path lined by rich green shrubs of holly that leads to the front door.

Everything about the frontage is so perfectly imperfect, it seems more like a movie set than a home. I imagine accidentally tripping on an out-of-place brick, knocking myself out after tumbling to the ground like a discarded puppet. It sounds preferable, frankly, to knocking on that dark-wood craftsman door.

Still, I do exactly that. There's no response. I knock louder. Nothing. A glance at the neighbor's house, and Mrs. Stanke's plastered to the window again. I wave. She pulls the curtains shut once more. Another bang on the door. Still nothing. Their door chime hasn't worked in twenty years. It's an antique they refuse to replace with something new, something inauthentic. I bang so hard it hurts my hand, then pull my foot back, ready to kick, and the door swings open.

"Sweetheart," Mom says, wiping her hands on a white dish towel. "I'm sorry, I was in the kitchen cooking dinner and your father is listening to his jazz in the study. Where are your bags?"

"Lost."

"Oh, darn. But that's okay, I've been shopping and got you some things," she says. "You look freezing. Come in." She steps back into the foyer, and I follow. Melodic string music drifts from the study down the hall.

I close the heavy oak door with a thud, and Mom reaches past me and twists the deadbolt, clicking it in place. A small auditory reminder that there's no turning back, she's locked in, the metal bars have slid into place.

"Dinner will be ready soon. Would you like a glass of wine?" she asks.

"I'm okay," I say as Dad joins us in the parlor.

"You look terrible," he says and hugs me. "I think you've had enough alcohol."

"Thanks, Dad. Good to see you, too." I clench my jaw. "Actually, I will take that glass of wine."

"It was a long flight," Mom says. "Why don't you shower and clean yourself up, and I'll have your wine waiting."

Dragging myself up the oak stairs to my childhood summertime bedroom, my fingers trail along the banister's familiar grooves. The door creaks open and there it is—a crochet duvet with tiny pink bows, pristine and untouched since I was fifteen. I run my hand over the scratchy fabric, remembering how on hot summer nights, with sun kissed skin, I'd roll myself up in this blanket, pretending it was a wedding gown. God. Justin Bieber's, my future husband's, face beams down at me from a yellowed Tiger Beat poster, his 2010 swooped hair forever frozen in time. I grab a corner and rip—the tear loud in the quiet room. Pale-yellow paint flakes drift to the carpet like dandruff.

The attached all-white bathroom is just as revoltingly bright and cheery. I crank the shower on—as hot as it will go. It steams up the cold room. Wiping the fog off of the mirror, I get a look at myself. Dad is right; I look awful. Dark circles under hollow eyes. Oily hair matted to my scalp. He's always right.

The shower feels good. The layer of grime accrued in my travels swirls down the drain as the hot water relaxes my tired muscles. If I didn't want to get this first dinner over with, I'd stay longer.

There's a fully stocked closet. Nothing I'd buy for myself, but clearly how my mom thinks I should dress. I settle on a fuzzy sweatsuit that sits folded on the shelf, knowing this is the most comfortable I'll be for at least the next couple of hours. Before I head downstairs, I search my bag for another Xanax. I should be fully present when I deal with my parents, but that possibility passed when I met my maximum daily dosage a pill ago My fingers close around the smooth tablet. Insurance policy. I slip it into my pocket.

I find Mom in the kitchen, opening a bottle of wine and pull up a seat at the counter. The kitchen is immaculate.

"Did you cook dinner or are we going out?" I ask.

"Dinner is in the oven."

I look at the oven. "It's not on."

"Oh," she says and smiles. "I set the dining room. Help me carry the wine."

I grab my glass and the bottle of pinot noir, then follow her. She has candles lit and empty plates set with the fine silver. I pour myself a large glass, take a sip. Mom fills the other glasses, then goes to get my dad. After another big gulp of wine, I take my seat.

"Dinner looks incredible, darling," my dad says as he takes his seat at the head of the table, my mom stationed at the opposite end.

"Dinner?" I laugh nervously. There's no food on the table. "Am I missing something?"

"Thank you, darling," Mom says to Dad, as if I'm not even there.

My glass finds its way to my lips once again. It lingers there as I breathe in the fruity smokiness between gulps.

"Liiiiilllllly, whaaaaaaattttt'sss yoooouuuurrrr . . ." My dad's voice warps and stretches, like a record player struggling to track. Why is he speaking so out of tune or is it time? My head becomes a bowling ball, too heavy for my neck—it lolls back against the chair. My arms dissolve into useless tendrils, and something warm seeps between my fingers. The wine glass that was in my hand isn't anymore. Red bleeds across the white tablecloth.

I try to tell them I spilled my wine, but my tongue lies thick and numb in my mouth. The room rocks on a carousel gone wrong, tilting and spinning in slow, nauseating circles. My dad rises, his shape stretching and folding like smoke as he moves toward me. White static gnaws at the edges of my vision, eating inward . . .

And then nothing.

"Lilllllyyyy, Liillly, LILLY!" Mom calls my name, but I don't want to open my eyes. The darkness is bliss. "Lilly!"

I finally force my eyes open.

Mom hovers above me, a blur sharpening to focus. "This is Dr. Teufel. She's going to check you out."

Dr. Teufel leans in, her skin luminous as polished bone. Her dark eyes bore into mine, pulling me deeper until the room dissolves at the edges. That severe bun draws her features tight, impossibly perfect—a porcelain mask I can't look away from. My mouth opens but my apology crumbles to dust. A penlight pierces my pupils, white explosions that fade to reveal the flat-screen mounted on dark walnut, anchoring me. I'm on the den sofa. The how escapes me.

"She's perfect," Dr. Teufel tells my parents with such deep, resonant, authoritative tone more akin to that of a grand dame of old Hollywood than a doctor. There's so much power behind her voice that I'm not sure if she actually said those words or willed them directly into my head. She grabs my chin and angles my face towards her. "Lilith, I need you to focus. I'm going to put a pill in your mouth, then give you some water. I need you to swallow it. Can you do that?"

I attempt to nod—my head drops but doesn't come back up. She grabs my chin again. When I open my mouth, she places a large pill on my tongue, then brings a glass of water to my lips. I force it down and darkness sinks its claws in as my world goes black.

When I come to, I'm in my bedroom. My brain feels foggy. I don't know how much time has passed, but I do know how sick I am about to be. My body shivers uncontrollably and I struggle from the sweat-drenched sheets, barely making it to the toilet before my stomach empties in painful heaves.

The sweating won't stop even as I shiver on the cold tiles. The shakes border on convulsion, my bones rattling against porcelain until I think I chip a tooth. My stomach continues to spasm, forcing up hot, yellow bile that scorches my throat. It's physical torture. But I'm strangely distant. Don't feel much of anything. I'm not worried. Not sad. Just watching myself from somewhere far away till rest takes hold.

I awake with a gasp and feel surprisingly good. Better than good. Relieved. Like the moment you wake from a nightmare and realize you're safe in bed. My mind is clear. My stomach is fine. I look around the room, not sure where I am. It takes a minute to register. What the hell happened? I'd popped a few extra Xanax on the drive, but nothing more than my usual lately.

My phone is nowhere to be seen. The digital clock on the bedside table reads 7:15 am. The room is cool, so I pull the comforter back up to my chin, taking in the warmth for an extra moment. I'd like to stay here forever, but I should get ready. Every minute I'm up here is another minute mom and dad have to judge me. I let out an uncontrolled sigh and force myself to climb out of bed and shower.

Hot water flows from my scalp and down my spine. I lather my body in a coat of suds so I can appear clean and fresh when I face my parents. Instead of sweats, I opt for black jeans and a maroon sweater.

The warm, caramel scent of freshly brewed coffee, followed by the sputtering whistle of their old-fashioned percolator hits me before I even make my way downstairs. My parents are in the kitchen, steam billowing off their mugs. The morning sun makes everything seem so bright and cheery. I admit, it's refreshing.

"Sweetheart! You must be feeling better," Mom says.

"I am, Mom. Sorry about last night. I don't know what happened."

"Just a little bout of food poisoning, that's all," Dad says as he looks up from behind his newspaper.

"Was there a doctor here?" I ask.

"You don't remember?" Mom says.

I shake my head. "Not really. I remember her giving me something, then getting really sick."

"You were already sick," Mom says. "So, we had Dr. Teufel come to check on you. She gave you something to help stop the vomiting."

Dad licks his finger and turns the page of his paper. "You looked terrible when you showed up, barely recognizable."

I don't reply; I know how bad I looked.

"She's the best," Mom says. "Said you were fine. You probably ate something bad at the airport and needed to get it out of your system. Coffee?"

"Please." I take a seat at the kitchen counter.

"Your stomach can handle it?" Dad asks.

"I told you, I feel fine."

"Totally fine?" His brow creases with doubt.

"*Totally* fine."

Mom slides a still-steaming cup of coffee across the counter. Somehow, everything seems better. A switch has been flipped, taking me out of sleep mode. My body feels strong, energized. I'm thinking clearly. More like myself again, not a shadow going through the motions. The sadness of this past year feels like a faded dream wrapped in the haze of sleep. I focus on inhaling what feels like my first ever cup of coffee.

"I needed this." I smile and look down at my fingers wrapped around the warm mug. My ring is missing. "What happened to . . . ?" I lift my hand and point to my fourth finger.

My parents exchange a quick look.

"I don't think that's healthy," Mom says.

"Maybe you're right," I reply, ignoring the ache in my heart. "But where did you put it?"

"I will keep it safe for you." Mom smiles and points to a small keepsake box on display in a curved Victorian glass cabinet along the back wall of the kitchen. The box sits beside an antique leather book, its red cover barely visible between her collection of brightly-colored Murano glass.

"She looked horrible when she got here," Dad repeats, looking at my mom.

"You said that already," I snap. "Twice," I add for emphasis.

Dad continues to scowl at Mom for a moment too long, then directs his attention to me. "What's your next move? Think you'll stay here?"

"You made me come here. Want to get rid of me already?"

"You couldn't pay your mortgage."

"Hard to do without help," I say.

"We are helping you," Mom says. "But we weren't going to pay for you to sit around feeling sorry for yourself. Don't you think it's time you got back to work?"

My mouth drops open. Been here twelve hours, and already they want me out of their hair. "You do want to be rid of me."

"Lilly, stop being so sensitive," Mom adds.

"Do you understand what I've been through? He's dead. He's fucking dead and I . . . I can't—" Tears sting at the corner of my eyes.

"Petal, we understand." Dad hasn't called me that in years. He gets up from the counter and places a warm hand on my shoulder. The comfort comes as a shock. "It's been months, and it's time to pull yourself together."

"Months? We were planning our *lives* together. You don't get over that in months."

"Sweetheart, we all cared about him, but you need to move on. He's dead. You're not."

"You don't think I realize that? That's exactly what I think about every single day." I wipe the tears from my cheeks with the sleeve of my sweater.

"You've had enough time," Mom says, impatience in the flatness of her tone.

"She's right," Dad adds. "You need to get back to work. It will help."

"I don't know if I can," I say, but I can't go on like this either.

Dad gives my shoulder another squeeze. "I have a friend in banking who's buying a casino in Atlantic City. I told him about you."

"What do you mean?"

"They're looking for a V.P. of Marketing and Advertising. What do you think?"

"I'd never get that job."

Dad huffs a laugh. "They'd kill for someone with your Vegas background and experience."

"But Atlantic City?" I grimace. In Vegas, Atlantic City is known as Glitter Gulch's ugly stepsister.

"Sweetheart, Atlantic City is beautiful," Mom says. "We've gone every few months since we moved here. It's only about a three-hour drive."

"Seriously?" I'm shocked they've lowered their standards. Mom nods with her wickedly charming smile. No wonder no one ever said no to her.

"You don't have to decide now," Dad says. "But I have work there this weekend. Our new sportsbook at Rise is underperforming. I booked an extra room for you."

"Rise?" I ask.

"I haven't told you about Rise?"

I shake my head. Has he forgotten how little we talk?

"It's Atlantic City's newest property. It's beautiful. We took over their sportsbook a few months ago."

Mom's smile widens. "They have a wonderful spa. I booked us some treat–"

"Do I have a choice?" I ask, cutting her off.

"You're an adult. You make your own decisions," Dad says.

"Well," Mom says, "except you can't stay here." She holds both arms out. "These old walls are getting a fresh coat of paint while we're away."

"Fine," I say, with the huff of my pre-teen self, I wouldn't have stayed by myself anyway.

"Great," Dad says. "Go pack. We're leaving in fifteen minutes."

The immediacy catches me off guard. "Fifteen minutes? Wha–"

"No questions," Dad says. "Pack."

"Wait," I say. "Is my phone down here?"

"Here you go." Mom opens the kitchen junk drawer, pulls out my phone, and hands it to me. It's turned off, but the display shows less than half the battery remaining.

As I turn to leave, I glimpse the still open drawer. A direct-mail flier sits inside with a $100 free play offer for Rise Hotel Casino Atlantic City. The ad is beautiful, silver glass reflecting the blue of the ocean as it stretches to the sky. "Is that the casino your friend is buying?"

"Oh, no," Dad says, the slightest look of disgust raising the corner of his mouth for a fleeting moment. "The casino he's buying is special." He pauses briefly. "The Golden Sands."

"Wasn't that Atlantic City's first casino?" I ask.

"Yes." Dad's eyes widen. "You've heard of it?"

Mom cuts in, "Sweetheart, it's fabulous. I can't wait for you to see it."

"Fabulous?" I say. "It's famous for being a dump built at turn of the century, I can't believe it's still standing."

"Don't be snobby," Dad snaps.

I just look at him, stung by his response and the disappointment in his eyes.

"Lilly," he says, breathing out as his brief bout of exasperation flees. "This property's historic, not old."

"It's *culture*, Lilith," Mom adds.

Dad's scowl makes my jaw tighten. "Your mother is right."

"I didn't mean . . . it's just." I let out a huff. "You're the one that told me the industry changes so quickly. To be successful in gaming, a casino needs to set trends, not follow them. Older properties have a harder time keeping up. Why do you think Strip properties are always getting imploded?" I raise an eyebrow. "I'm not sure I'd even know how to market it."

"You misunderstood. It's not about being new," Dad says, returning to his paper. "It's about standing out." He lets the paper drop once again. "Where's my girl that could sell ice to Eskimos? Can't you give it a chance?"

"Yes, sweetheart." Mom squeezes my shoulders from behind as she walks by, urging me into the hall. "Give it a chance."

"Fine. Let me pack *your* clothes." I roll my eyes as I head to the stairs.

Back in my room, I find my charger and plug in my phone. The screen has a new crack. I turn it on. I didn't expect any notifications—my friends faded from my life one by one. Not that I blame them. I was so focused on work—and him—that I didn't really have time for friends. I wasn't surprised—not a single text or missed call.

Then my phone rings—as if to disagree.

Notification: Victoria Alexander.

I answer. "Hey, Tori."

"Oh my God, you're alive! Where have you been? I've been calling and texting you!"

"I had food poisoning. Sorry, my phone was off." I check the screen again and there are definitely no texts or missed calls.

"Are you okay?"

"Yeah, much better."

"That's good. You sound good. I was worried about you."

"I'm okay."

"What happened?" Tori asks.

"What do you mean?"

"Well, I heard you quit your job and sold your home. Little out of nowhere, right?"

"What do you mean, out of nowhere? The accident, Tori, I . . . I fell apart. I couldn't stand to go to work without him. They let me go and I had to sell my home."

"What accident?" The question throws me. Did I really forget to tell Tori about everything?

"Lilly," my dad yells from down the hall. "I want to be on the road in ten minutes. Are you packed?"

"Sorry, Tori," I say, frowning. "That was my dad. We're going to Atlantic City for the weekend, and I have to pack."

"What accident?" she repeats.

"*His* car accident." I can't bring myself to say his name.

"Who?"

"My fiancé."

"Wait. You were engaged?"

The words knock the air from my lungs. Images flash through my mind—the ring, the dress fittings, Tori helping me pick out floral arrangements—but they feel strange now, like memories from someone else's life. Or a dream so vivid I convinced myself it was real. My hand instinctively moves to my empty ring finger, to twist a band that's not there.

My frown deepens as irritation sets in. "You *knew* that. You were going to be at my wedding, right?"

"Lilly, let's go!" Dad yells.

"Sorry, I have to go."

"Wait, what the hell is going on? I didn't know you were engaged."

She didn't know? I shake my head, suddenly unsure of anything. "I guess, maybe, I was going to tell you? I had all these plans. I don't know, everything is such a blur. I lost it for a little bit after the accident."

"I mean, it's only been a few months *at most* since I talked to you," Tori says. "I knew you were into that guy from work, but engaged? I never even met him."

My mind struggles to wrap around memories that seem to warp and fade every time I reach for them.

"Are you sure you're okay?" Tori asks again.

"Yeah, we were engaged and living together. I loved him, Tori. More than anything."

"I'm sorry. I didn't know any of that."

"I'm sorry, too."

"Lilly, now!" Dad bellows. It's like I'm fifteen again.

"I have to go, Tori. We'll talk soon. Are you doing alright?"

"Yeah. The same, still waiting to hear from Princeton. Call me this weekend, please."

I agree, then hang up. I stand frozen, phone still in hand, as the walls of my childhood bedroom start to feel like they're closing in. Dad's voice thunders up the stairs again, and I mechanically throw things in a bag, trying to ignore how the room, the ring—everything—feels somehow different. Could I have had some sort of psychological break? Could the trauma of his loss have caused me to mix up reality with what we had planned for the future? Whatever's happening, I need to move forward. I need a new start. I need to get my legs back underneath me. Can I find that in Atlantic City?

Chapter 3

Sitting in the back seat, I'm thankful for my parents' inclination to ride in silence as they listen to their podcast—some historical examination of the Knights Templar. The narrator has the most monotone British accent I've ever heard. If I wasn't rested, I'd be asleep.

A move to Atlantic City from Las Vegas solidifies the fact I'm a failure. Staring out the window sinks my mood even lower. Dead winter woods are nothing more than a dreary taupe blur as we pass, accenting my descent in life. And I can't stop thinking about the call from Tori. How did she not know I was engaged? Had I been so consumed with work, with building my life and future with him that I didn't talk to one of my closest friends? She was going to be in my wedding, but . . . but I can't remember asking her. When I try to pull up clear memories from the past year or however long it was, I can't. I force myself to say his name on not much more than a breath, "Kai." I whisper it again. "Kai."

Nothing. Nothing solid, anyway. Just a distant sadness. The memories are there, yet each time I grab at a specific point in time, it slips through my fingers like sand. Could the medication and drinking have damaged my brain? Was I that much of a disaster? The weight of guilt squeezes tight, and I inadvertently loosen my seatbelt—like that would help.

"Lilith! Stop chewing your lip. It's going to bleed," Mom says, and I catch her critical eye in the rearview mirror.

I didn't realize I was chewing, but I accept the admonishment nonetheless, and dig through my backpack for my book. *Lord of the Flies* was my favorite growing up and the only one still in my room.

A mistake is only a mistake if I don't fix it. A sweet college advisor told me that after my first and only bad grade. I want to believe that. I want to believe in redemption. Though deep in the back of my mind where hope lives, guilt has jailed it with bars built from the knowledge my entire life will be punctuated by my one breakdown. I welcome the distraction that Jack, Piggy, and Ralph bring on the well-read pages of my book.

We make our way into Atlantic City through the expressway, which crosses over a portion of marsh and bay. Like much of the drive here, late-winter's gloom has turned everything a pale shade of brown. The drive through the city isn't any better. Exactly how I imagined Atlantic City. We take a side street uptown that's dotted with a series of mismatched homes and businesses—mainly liquor stores. The occasional condemned home solidifies the fact this might as well be a forgotten city. It's old, beat-up and beat-down. Not someplace I want to live.

One right turn and everything changes.

The moment we turn on Massachusetts Avenue, Rise dominates the horizon—a behemoth of angles and curves, a modern fusion of metal and glass that pierces the heavens. The ramp spirals upward, each turn revealing more of the tower's gleaming supremacy over the coastline. It spits us out in the porte cochère, where the sprawling Atlantic stretches endlessly before us. In the winter sun, the cloudless, periwinkle sky meets deep blue ocean like two halves of a perfect whole. White waves repeatedly kiss the soft beige sand, hypnotic and eternal.

"Nice view, huh?" the valet asks as he opens my door.

"I wasn't expecting this."

"First time in Atlantic City?"

I nod, still enthralled by the view. A harsh gust of winter wind blows through my jacket, sending tiny daggers of cold straight to my bones. I follow my parents to the glass doors, overtaking them as I go.

"You must be Ms. Umbra," the doorman says as he opens the door. "Get in here and warm up." Then he adds, "Mr. and Mrs. Umbra, it's great to have you back."

The smell hits me first: it's bright, flowery, fresh, and tells me in unmistakable terms that I'm on vacation. Unfortunately, I'm in on the secret behind this bit of scent-magic. At ONE, the casino I worked at on the Strip, we studied ten different scents to identify which had the biggest impact on consumer behavior. Scent affects the brain's limbic system, which is responsible for processing mood and emotion—motivation, fear, and pleasure. Happy customers are much easier to handle; they also spend more money. That's the theory, anyway.

An executive at ONE thought this was manipulative, but I argued we were crafting a complete experience. Something like seventy-five percent of memories are tied to scent, and it's one of the most powerful tools to create an unforgettable experience. At ONE, we settled on a scent that incorporated notes of leather and money with birch tar, to remind guests that they were on the verge of winning a mountain of cash. We added notes of jasmine to alleviate stress and anxiety—to relax inhibitions—and citrus to energize the mood. We never did a formal study, but based on observations, it worked incredibly well. We received sixty percent fewer complaints, our positive reviews increased, and our casino revenue boosted twenty percent. Yet despite seeing behind the curtain, this aromatic ploy still lifts my mood as I breathe it in.

Glass in every shade of blue melts from the ceiling and only stops when it hits the sharp white of marble. Behind the front desk is a wall-sized tropical fish tank filled with everything from tiny, bright reef fish to small sharks and stingrays. Soft, classical music plays in the background but in the distance is the faint yet unmistakable *ding ding ding* of slot machines. I melt into this moment, an anchor to hold onto, but then the other feeling barrels in. Like a wrecking ball, I'm hit with the sensation that I'm living in a nightmare about to wake up to an even worse reality. The memories from the past year feel distant yet fill me with a pool of swirling dread. My pulse quickens and my stomach drops.

"Here's your key," my dad says. "Are you okay?"

"Yeah, fine. Why?" I force a smile as an exclamation mark and quickly wipe the beads of cold sweat that have formed on my forehead.

His eyes sweep over me for a moment, one eyebrow slightly raised before he decides to move on. "I have a few meetings, but the spa is expecting you." He hands my mom and me each our own envelope. Then he heads through a camouflaged door to the back of the house—home to the employee areas, offices, vaults, and count rooms—and I get a peek into Rise's real heart. The beige linoleum floor, white walls, and fluorescent lighting are familiar. Regardless of how luxurious a casino is, the back of the house is always basic, industrial . . . and by most standards, ugly.

"Let's drop our things off at the room and change," my mom says as she leads the way to a bank of elevators.

Our room is on the top floor, and she has to scan her keycard to gain access that high. When the doors slide open, I'm not at the casino anymore.

I'm at the hospital, stepping onto the elevator that will take me to the morgue.

To identify his body.

A loud bang shocks me back to the present. An older woman has tripped and fallen right next to me.

"Are you okay?" I ask, unwilling to admit I'm grateful her fall has pulled me from the unwelcome memory. When I bend to help, her lips twist into a scowl so filled with venom I almost expect her to strike. I step back, blink, and then her gaze is soft and she's smiling.

"Thank you, dear. I'm fine. This handle broke on me and I stumbled over the darn thing."

I gather the box that tripped her—a brand-new robot vacuum, a gift from the casino. We'd given the same one away more than two years ago as a casino incentive.

"Let me fix it for you," I offer, then readjust the handle on the box. Based on this gift, I can tell that she spends about two-hundred, maybe two-fifty each trip to the casino. Casino player's clubs give away gifts usually a few times a week—a reward for regulars to lure them in during slower times. An arcade ticket shop for adults.

I return the robot vacuum with the handle securely reattached.

"Aren't you the sweetest? We came in just to get these vacuums. I've wanted one for the longest time," the old woman says and smiles right at me. She may have even winked. Her short, dyed-red hair is teased and set in big rolling curls, and she wears full makeup with lots of costume jewelry. Buried in the pile of gold and silver resting on her collarbone, there's a strange symbol I vaguely recognize. Something about her makes me wary. Something I can't quite place.

"That's a nice model," I say. "We gave the same one away at the casino I worked at in Las Vegas."

"Really? Las Vegas?" Her rising tone solidifies her genuine excitement.

"Yeah, the Robovac was a hit."

"Ohhh, I have something that was a hit in Vegas. Whoo-whoo!" She wiggles her shoulders, and I notice her necklace again. A clump of wavy arrows I've seen before.

The elevator door slides open to her floor.

"Thanks, doll, you made my day." As she turns and shuffles off, I think she winks at my mom.

"You sounded professional," Mom says once the doors close.

"I guess." My eyes drift to the ground. "I . . . I'm having these weird feelings, like anxiety and—"

"You need to get back to work. Too much free time is not good for the mind."

My eyes meet hers as I hope that's all that's wrong. "Yeah."

She smiles and her eyes narrow, lingering on me for a moment before the elevator door opens.

There are only a few doors on our floor. All-natural wood, all double. I know we're in a suite before I even step off the elevator. While I've been in countless suites on the Strip, they can't compare to this. As the door opens, all I see is ocean and sky. It's breathtaking. Floor-to-ceiling windows frame azulene that stretches to the horizon. Living in the Vegas Valley has given me an appreciation of the mountains. Though, when you look out over mountains, you see a wall. A beautiful wall, but containment, nonetheless. They don't move, they don't change. They hold you in. Some find comfort in this.

For a while, the Vegas Valley and its mountains felt safe. But when you look out over an ocean, you see movement, you see freedom, you see life. You see change.

And at this moment, there's nothing I want more than change.

Chapter 4

When I come out of my room, Mom's standing near the bar.

"Drink some water before we go." She cracks open a glass bottle of Voss water and pours it into two tumblers, then takes a small glass dropper and adds a few drops of liquid to each glass.

"What's that?"

"Hibiscus, St. John's, ashwagandha, holy basil, and some other herbs. It'll be good for you." She hands me a glass. "Clear your mind, help with the anxiety."

"Okay." Since I don't have anything stronger.

The only reason I haven't tried to find a stray Xanax this morning is that I'm haunted by months of lost memories. Imagine waking from a night of drinking and realizing months have passed and all you can piece together are a few pixelated snapshots of horrible memories. I don't think I'll ever take another prescription med, though a glass of wine would be nice.

The elixir is slightly sweet with a bitter aftertaste. I guzzle it down and catch the drips with my sleeve. Mom takes a dainty, elegant sip and leaves the glass barely touched. It's little things like this that remind me I'll never be as perfect or controlled as her.

Gulping down those thoughts, I follow her out of the room and into a waiting elevator.

"How are you so perfect?" I ask as the elevator descends.

"Lilith, no one is perfect." She looks up at the numbers on the display.

"You never make mistakes."

She lets out an annoyed breath. "Everyone makes mistakes."

"That's not true. I've never seen you make a mistake in my entire life."

"Have you ever seen a dancer fall?"

I shake my head; and I went to hundreds of shows in Las Vegas.

"Well, they do fall. You don't notice because they get up quickly, quietly, and gracefully." My mom scowls at me. "You, on the other hand, are like a Vaudeville act. You make a show of falling down."

"That's not true." I look down at my feet. "Everything just goes your way."

"Lilith, look at me." She waits for my gaze to meet hers. "Every morning, the first thing I do is look in the mirror and say: you are powerful, you are beautiful, the world bends to your will. It's a mantra. You need one of your own. Then maybe you can stop being the victim you so desperately want to be."

On cue, the elevator slows and the doors open. My phone vibrates in my jacket pocket. It's Tori again; I'll call her later.

Once we enter the spa, Mom's quickly swept away to her massage. Left alone to change, I appreciate the solitude set to the tune of new-age music and a soft lavender-vanilla redolence. Wrapped in a soft robe, I weave past steam rooms and saunas to the waiting area. Byzantine tiles in delicate shades of gold combined with soft lighting and salt-water pools transport me to a Turkish bathhouse. Every detail screams relaxation to the point it makes me uneasy. Maybe it's because I'm not used to this. Or maybe it's because I should find this soothing, but don't.

I find a quiet, empty room to hide in. It's the Dead Sea Salt Grotto—an entire room made of blocks of crystalline salt from the Dead Sea. Before I can take my phone out to call Tori back, Alana finds me and leads me back into the treatment rooms.

As I lay on the table, Alana's hands rubbing each tense muscle, I realize I haven't been touched by another human being in so long. That epiphany is both painful and euphoric. I melt into the carnal pleasure of human touch and thoughts of him rise. His body is the first concrete memory I've been able to recall since leaving Las Vegas and I grab onto it. The moment I try to think about our life together—dates we went on, our home—the memories turn to smoke. They're there, but the closer I get, the more they dissipate. I have an understanding that I miss him, but it feels so far away. What is *wrong* with me? A pang of panic tugs on my stomach.

"You're so tense," Alana whispers. "Let me know if the pressure's okay."

"It's . . ." My voice cracks and I cough to clear my throat. "Good."

I exhale and force my mind to clear. Focus on Alana's touch. My muscles soften. I take a deep breath, heavy with lavender, and try to let go.

"How was that?" Alana asks.

"It's over?"

The door to the room opens.

"Yes, but don't worry, Tosh is here for your facial."

"Thank you," I say to Alana and Tosh gets to work on my face, spreading a cool cleanser across my skin. I went days without even washing my face.

"Your mother asked me to clean up your skin and your eyebrows," Tosh says. "I will be as gentle as possible, but it may be a little uncomfortable. Okay . . ." Her voice trails off and I'm not sure if that was a question or a statement.

"Umm, yes," I reply through a slightly clenched jaw. When my parents decided to move back to Cold Springs, I wasn't upset. Having always lived in their shadow, it was nice to stand in my own spotlight, though short lived. Now, I can't even make decisions on my own face.

"Leave my eyebrows," I add as a small act of rebellion.

"I won't overpluck."

Tosh flicks on a painfully bright cosmetic light with a large magnifying glass attached and places two cool, damp pads over my eyes, forcing them shut.

"This eye mask will make you look completely rested," she chirps.

I yelp as she rips a stray hair from the middle of my brow.

"It will get less painful as we go."

Just when I think I can't stand any more of the pinching pain torturing my face, things get worse. Tosh pinches the skin on my cheek and digs in.

"Ouch," I say. Less confrontational than: what the hell are you doing.

"Your skin is very congested. I'll try to be as quick as possible, but it's got to be done."

My nose is the worst. She digs so hard it feels like it might break. My eyes well with water underneath the cotton pads.

"I'm done," I say and try to sit up, but Tosh pushes me back down.

"Almost," she coos. "Just try to relax."

She plows into my chin, sending a sharp jolt of pain into my jaw.

"There, much better," she says and pulls the cotton pads off my eyes. A thin smile lifts the corners of her mouth, and I can't help but think she enjoyed my pain.

"Thank God that's over," I say and start to get up.

"Not quite." She lifts an eyebrow and pushes my shoulders back into the treatment table. "I still have to exfoliate and moisturize. This may tingle a bit."

She paints a solution on my face. The top layers of skin begin to dissolve with acidic pain, like thousands of little gnats are gnawing away the dead skin. I want to scratch my face, but Tosh remains on guard. Finally, she scrubs it off with a rough cloth. Paints something else on. Then blows steam into my face.

In the haze of steam, he comes back. The muscles of his shoulders and the shadow of his body. It seems to hook and hold another memory. A movie. We went to the movies for our first date. It was the new *Exorcist* and I held a huge container of popcorn. It spilled when I buried my face in his shoulder during the scare scenes and he laughed. I was happy. Then . . . Tosh pushes the steam away.

"You look amazing," she says, pulling me from my trance. I try to hold onto the memory, but the harsh breath of reality blows it away.

Tosh jams a small mirror up to my face. My skin is dewy and plump, my eyes bright.

"Maybe the torture was worth it," I concede with a crooked smile as I get to my feet.

"After you're dressed, go next door to the salon. Your mom will meet you there." Tosh smiles then holds the door open for me.

I quickly dress in the locker room, where a group of middle-aged women are drinking champagne. Their loose robes reveal much more than I care to see.

The salon is very close to the spa and easy to find. My mom is getting her precise hair bobbed even more precise.

"How was your massage and facial?" she asks as I take the chair next to her.

"The massage was good. The facial was a bit brutal."

"A little pain is good for the soul."

"I'm glad it's over."

"Look how relaxed you are. That's from the pain, not the massage. Pain releases endorphins. It makes you think more clearly."

I don't notice the hairdresser until she's standing over my shoulder. "So, what are we doing today?" she asks.

My mom answers before I have a chance to respond, "Just a trim, wash and blow dry. Give her a deep side part and some soft waves, think old-Hollywood glam."

She smiles and nods. "Follow me."

The stylist leads me back to the shampoo bowl. My phone vibrates in my pocket and when I get back to the salon chair, I check it—Tori again. I text her.

Me: Can't talk now. Getting my hair done. What's up?

Tori: I got into PRINCETON!!!

Me: Congratulations! I'm so happy for you!!

Tori: Thanks!

Me: I'll call you later.

Tori: Make sure you do. I need to catch up with you.

"Who are you texting?" Mom asks.

"Tori."

"You're still friends with her?" I catch her rolling her eyes as she admires herself in the mirror.

"Yes, but it's been a while since we last talked. She didn't even know I'd been engaged."

"Never liked her. You're better off not talking."

"That's not true," I snap.

"As far as makeup," the stylist interrupts, "natural, glam, or somewhere in between?"

"Gla–" Mom begins.

"In between," I insist.

The stylist looks to my mom, who nods her approval, and starts painting my face. It's been so long since I wore makeup that I'm not sure what she's doing at any given moment. She has me open my eyes, then close them. Look up, then down. Smile. Don't smile. I do as I'm told, all while trying to swallow the lump of irritation sitting in my throat. Tori is a good friend but there's an ounce of bitter truth in what my mom says. How could she not know I was engaged when I'm sure I told her?

"You look gorgeous," the stylist says as she spins me towards the mirror.

I take a sharp breath, not recognizing the face looking back at me. My first instinct is to wipe my hands across my face, to take off the layer of makeup but the more I look, the more a sense of ownership takes over. Hints of confidence build in my gut and rise into my chest. I put my shoulders back, look at myself again and grin. A slight turn of the head; left then right. There's a hint of wickedness in my smile, but I like it, this mask. I like feeling like someone else. Someone beautiful. Someone who demands attention. Not myself . . . and that's a good thing.

"I love it," I tell the stylist.

"You look beautiful. I hope you have plans tonight," she says.

"Let's go find out what our plans are," my mom says as she stands from her chair, looking equally glamorous. But that's nothing new.

I stand to follow her. "Thank you so much," I tell the stylist before rushing to catch my mom.

When we get back to our suite, the sun is setting behind us, but it lights the sky on fire. It's different than a West Coast sunset. The sun doesn't sink below the ocean, gently pulling the color down with it. Instead, there's no sun, at least not in our view of the ocean, but the entire sky is ablaze. In the sun's absence, crimson wages war with fuchsia for dominion over the heavens before darkness takes hold.

Dad is waiting with a chilled bottle of champagne.

"What are we celebrating?" I ask.

"What aren't we celebrating?" Mom grins and hands my dad three crystal champagne glasses. "How did your meetings go, darling?"

"Great. The sportsbook is already in the black, six months ahead of projections. All we did was put our name on it."

"You're amazing." Mom kisses his cheek. He leans into her for a split second before pouring the effervescent wine.

"And," Dad pauses, looking at me for a moment, "my friend, Amon, closed on the Golden Sands casino property today. We're going to have dinner there, with him."

"Tonight?" I ask. "I'm not ready for that."

"Ready for what, Lilith?" Irritation prickles his tone.

"Meeting people."

"We're having dinner with our friends."

"Sweetheart, drink some champagne," my mom says, passing me a glass.

As much as I want it, I hesitate, the newly primped 'me' suddenly undecided. "I don't know. Do you think it's a good idea?"

She looks at me, one eyebrow raised. "Yes." She pushes the crystal flute to me. "Relax. Enjoy the pleasures of life."

"I think I might watch a movie and order room service."

"No, you're not," she snaps.

I roll my eyes, reverting to a stupid teenager too easily.

"You need to get back to work. You're coming to dinner," my dad says.

"I don't have anything to wear."

Mom waves toward the bedroom. "Look in your room."

I turn to peek into the open bedroom door. Draped over the corner of my bed is a black garment bag. "What if he doesn't want to hire me?"

"Your resume impressed him. The job is yours. All you have to do is go to dinner."

"Fine," I say on an outrush of breath.

"Will Mara and Aleister be joining us?" Mom asks.

"Of course."

"Who are they?" I ask.

"Amon's parents, Mara and Aleister Asra," Dad says. "We've known them forever, since before you and Amon were even born."

"Is it strange that I'm going to work for your friends?"

"Why do you have to question everything?" Dad's exasperation is clear, and it claws at me.

"Sweetheart, of course it's not strange," Mom says with a smile.

"If I doubted your ability, I wouldn't have recommended you. Amon's lucky to have you," Dad says, then holds his glass up. "Cheers to our brilliant Lilith."

"Cheers," Mom says and clinks Dad's glass.

Both stare at me, waiting, glasses raised. I don't believe them, but I don't have any other options. I'm in a new place. No one knows me. I can start over.

"Cheers," I say, then clink their glasses.

Mom smiles at me. Dad looks down. There's something bothering him. My guess is that I disappointed him. Now, he's bailing me out. The weight of guilt from being someone else's failure is crushing, and I promise myself that I will never let them down again.

I raise the champagne to my mouth and bubbles tickle my nose, activating my senses before the cool liquid even hits my lips. The first sip stings slightly as the bubbles burst, awakening my palate. But the second sip is crisp, dry, and perfect. The sun's fleeting colors make our entire suite glow a rosy hue. After a few more sips, looking out at the unending view of the sea, I feel like I'm floating, wrapped in a cocoon of bubbly comfort.

"It's beautiful here," I say, topping off my glass.

Dad nods. "I told you."

"It's not what I expected."

"We should get ready," Mom suggests. "I don't want to be late."

I finish my champagne and take one more look at the fading sunset. Shades of navy have begun to snatch at the horizon and night is near.

"Here," my mom calls after me. "Drink another glass of water while you're getting ready."

She adds a few quick drips of herbs from her dropper then hands me the glass.

Lying on my bed is a black satin wrap dress with bishop sleeves and an asymmetric ruffle hem. The pure silk is soft against my skin. The dress fits tight around my now too-slim waist. I can't remember the last time I got dressed up, yet I'm amazed by the power physical appearance has on my mental state. If only I had tried this months ago, maybe I could've saved it all. My job. My home. Myself.

Looking in the mirror, I get such a strange feeling, almost like I'm looking at someone else, someone I could've been. It's a jarring sensation, not quite out-of-body, but close. Hanging next to the dress is a long, black mink coat—one of my mom's—and a pair of black studded Gucci booties. As I slip on the shoes and pull on the coat, I decide to step into this new version of me and leave the other one behind.

We walk to dinner on the boardwalk. It's cold, but the fur is warm.

Then I see it, right next door to Rise. I thought Golden Sands was old, but this property is huge and it at least looks new. Rock music blares from the resort inviting every passerby into the party. Excitement replaces the seeds of caution I had sowed not long ago.

"Dad, I thought you said it was old. This casino looks great."

"That's not it. Trump used to own that. Golden Sands is there." He pulls his hand out of his pocket to point to the next building.

This property is steeped in shadow. The entrance is empty, dark, and forgotten. A relic. "That's open?" I stop walking.

"Sweetheart, it's beautiful inside," Mom assures me and grabs my arm to pull me along before dropping it to take my dad's arm.

"It has great bones." Dad points at the building. "Just needs the exterior freshened up. Amon already has workers lined up to start the historical renovation this week."

The seeds of caution split their husks and sprout into dread. I worked at the nicest casino on the strip; it was new, luxurious, and people wanted to go there. Who would want to go to this place?

I walk a little slower. I'm in no hurry. The entire block around Golden Sands is quieter and darker than the rest of the boardwalk. I imagine that in the 1920s, this section with its bank of archways, was a beautiful open breezeway for glamorous ladies in their cloche hats, pearls, and flapper dresses; gentlemen in their three-piece suits and straw hats. Now, even in the moonlight, I can see chunks of paint peeling off the once white brick exterior and imagine the same is happening to me—chips of my past revealing the person I had become this last year. Something a coat of makeup can't hide. I linger on the sidewalk.

Dad opens the center door and holds it for my mom. She pauses inside and turns back to me. "Come on, Lilly."

My stomach wraps itself into a knot that sinks to the base of my spine. I don't want to go inside. There's something terrifying about walking through this door. Maybe I don't want to accept how far I've fallen.

"Lilith. Come. In," Mom orders. "It's cold."

I let out a breath, accept I've hit rock bottom, and cross the threshold of Golden Sands.

Chapter 5

The inside catches me by surprise. Historic is not the right word. It's more . . . otherworldly. I've toured plenty of historic castles, homes, and museums, all over the world. Without exception, time has stopped in those places. Vestiges frozen in the era of their origin. Golden Sands is different. Time is very much alive here. There's something active in the atmosphere. I hear the ding of slot machines in the distance. A group of girls with drinks in hand—maybe a bachelorette or birthday party—rush past and disappear down a hall. Their high-heeled shoes click on the graceful marble that crawls up a few steps and opens to a large vestibule. Elegant plaster walls with ornate moldings whisper secrets from another era and tell me in unmistakable terms that Golden Sands is not like any casino I've ever encountered. These thick, solid walls tell a very different story. They make modern casinos seem almost flimsy, like a movie set that's not meant to stand the test of time. This structure, bones and all, isn't going anywhere and, now, I understand what my parents meant when they described this property. A chill wraps around my ankle, creeps up my leg and stirs up a mix of tingles that takes root in the small of my back. I'm either nervous or excited.

"I didn't expect this," I say.

"I told you," Mom says and grabs my hand, her eyes wide.

"Naomi, love, I am so happy to see you."

I turn to a woman coming down a small bank of steps from the casino floor. She may be the first woman I've ever seen whose beauty comes close to my mom's. She's very tall and impossibly thin, her silky chestnut hair cropped into a long pixie cut with a wave of bangs that sweeps over her black, almond eyes.

"Mara, darling, it's so good to see you. This is Lilith." My mom holds my hand up and presents me.

Mara kisses each of my cheeks, then places her elegant hands each side of my face. "Lilith, I have heard so much about you from the moment you were born. It's a joy to finally meet you in person. My, you are even more stunning than the pictures. Your eyes . . ." Mara takes a deep inhale, then releases me and kisses both cheeks of my mom and dad.

"Follow me. Aleister and Amon are waiting for us at the restaurant." Mara momentarily pauses and lifts her hand. A bellman appears from a nearby hall. "John will take your coats. Thank you, love," she says to John, and she affectionately brushes his shoulder with her crimson-tipped fingers. He nods.

"Thanks," I say as he takes my heavy fur, then my mom's, and disappears back into a nearby hall.

Mara leads us up the short bank of steps. At the top, I pause for a moment and take in the sprawling view of the casino floor. A strange remix of electro swing music fills the air. It mixes weirdly well with the *ding ding ding* of the slot machines and gives the entire space a wild mood. The table games run down the middle of the hall with banks of slot machines spreading out in every direction. Dealers stand at a third of the tables; the rest are closed. While some slot machines *ding*, the majority sit empty. The casino floor is filled with games but lacks many players. I smile—potential.

"Lil," Dad calls. He nods towards my mom and Mara. They've taken a turn and are waiting at the top of another small set of steps. Mara leads us through a mirrored hall, then to elevators and on to a small escalator that tunnels to the second floor. As I walk by the mirror, I catch a glimpse of myself. The light shimmers off of my dress as it flows with the curves of my gait.

The escalator opens to a hall of ballrooms, a theater, and a group of restaurants and bars.

"I'm stopping in the restroom," I announce.

"Okay, love," Mara says. "We will wait for you at the bar inside Flame. It's right around the corner."

I make a quick stop in the bathroom, a moment alone to take everything in. As I'm washing my hands, my breath catches in my throat when Robovac lady from Rise, walks out of a stall and washes her hands next to me.

"Hi," I say. She looks over. "Aren't you staying at Rise?"

"How do you know that?" she asks, her eyes narrowing.

"I helped you with your vacuum." I smile, realizing I sound a bit crazy.

"Oh, my goodness, yes," she says. "Didn't recognize you all dressed up. Aren't you beautiful."

"Thanks. What brings you here?"

"This is our favorite property in Atlantic City but their management is awful. We don't even have a host here. They don't give out anything, no comps, no gifts. Our host at Rise is so nice, they gave us a free room and the vacuum . . ." She shakes the water off her hands.

"That is definitely a problem."

"The Golden Sands is beautiful, though. We still wanted to come here for dinner and to play a bit. We spend so much money here." She sighs. "It should be run better. Such a shame."

"It is a beautiful property." I look over at her as I dry my hands. She's dressed up but has taken off the pile of jewelry. Now, she just wears the necklace I noticed earlier with the unusual symbol. With a clear view of it, I realize why it looked so familiar to me. The tattoo. The tattoo I used to identify his body; the only thing still left intact.

The image crashes into me like a semi-truck. Unlike my other memories, this one's solid and almost knocks me off my feet. I stumble back, staring at the necklace. A circle framing a straight post with a swirl in the middle and wavy arrows that come out in different directions. I see it on his arm. The bloody mess to which his arm was attached. His tattoo was all I needed to know it was him.

"Oh, my necklace." She smiles after noticing me staring. "Do you like it?"

I nod, unable to form any words. With a deep breath, I find there's something strangely comforting about having a solid memory to hold to. It's a concrete point in time. Allows something in my mind, in my past, to feel real. An awful anchor of sorts.

"This is an ancient Mesopotamian symbol. It means rebirth. A little reminder to keep your eye on the future, even for an old lady like me."

"I like that." A sense of comfort washes over me. It has to be a sign from him, a way of telling me I'm on the right path. What else could it be? It's too big a coincidence to ignore.

Another memory rushes back. We're sitting on the couch at our home. He's telling me about his tattoo as I brush my fingers along his muscled forearm. We have wine and he tells me it's a symbol of his heritage, a reminder to keep his eye on the future. He used those exact words.

"I'm off to my favorite slot machine, the Cleopatra," the old lady says, speaking the name as if the machine were something to be worshiped. "Wish me luck!"

"Good luck," I say as the door closes behind her.

I can do this. Then pull open the bathroom door.

Dark hardwood columns hold up a black iron awning that frames the entrance: Flame. My parents and Mara stand at the heavy oak bar, their backs to me. They must sense my approach because they turn, creating a space that frames who I presume to be Aleister and Amon. My mouth drops open just a hair and I quickly catch it. Amon looks as if he was picked out of a fashion magazine. He's tall and his thick, dark hair is coiffed into a perfect wave. His deep brown eyes bore into me as his full lips curve into a warm smile revealing perfect teeth and two small dimples. *God, why?* Warmth blooms in my cheeks before I've even opened my mouth.

"Aleister, Amon, I'd like to introduce Lilith Layne Umbra," Mara says.

"It's nice to meet you," I say.

"The pleasure is all ours, darling," Aleister says and kisses both cheeks.

Amon takes my hand in his, slightly bows his head, and smiles. "It's very nice to meet you, Lilith." He has the distinct throaty hint of an accent, though I can't quite place it.

"You too . . . I mean it's nice to meet you as well." *Oh no I'm repeating myself.* I sound like such an idiot, yet I keep talking. "You have a slight accent. Where are you from?" I feel sweat soak my armpits and I pray that it's too dark to see these mortifying pit stains. I tuck my elbows down a little tighter.

"Very perceptive," Amon says. "I was born in New York, but we moved to Germany when I was about twelve then came back to New York in my early twenties." He turns to the bar where he has a bottle of Dom Pérignon chilling in a crystal ice bucket.

"We have a lot to celebrate," Mara says. "Most importantly, our two families finally have a chance to come together."

"Hear, hear," Aleister says. "And to future endeavors."

"Yes, may we all keep an eye on the future and good fortune in our lives," Amon adds.

Eye on the future . . . again. I've heard people say there's no such thing as coincidence, but this is impossible to ignore.

"Cheers," Mom says and raises her glass to me as if punctuating my last thought.

"Cheers," I say, careful not to lift my glass too high.

We all clink glasses, then are shown to our table. As we make our way to the table, I trail behind and check my dress. It's not as bad as I thought, no sweat marks at all. Aleister and Mara each sit at a head, my mom and dad on one side and Amon and myself on the other. Food arrives immediately. Charcuterie boards, bread baskets, and bottles of wine come first. Then it's raw oysters and caviar Bellinis.

"Love," Mara starts. "I hope you're not vegetarian or gluten-free like so many young girls are these days."

Shaking my head, I reach for an oyster, topping it with a spoon of mignonette and a little horseradish before slurping it down and reaching for another. Someone, I can't remember who, told me that eating an oyster is like a kiss from the sea, and I can't describe it any more perfectly than that. Amon moves the platter of oysters on ice a little closer to me and I have another.

"I've heard a lot about you," Amon says as he leans over. "I feel a little self-conscious."

Oh no, what has he heard? "I hope it wasn't too terrible."

"Terrible? No," he looks at me, head tilting slightly, "but I have to admit, you know much more about casinos than I do. I read every article about you. 'Girl on Fire'."

I inadvertently roll my eyes. It seems like so long ago and feels like someone else.

"Don't roll your eyes," he says, sounding exactly like my mother.

The metallic taste of dislike singes the back of my throat.

"I mean . . ." Amon bites the corner of his lip; he's backpedaling. "It's something to be proud of. It impressed me."

I let the dislike go a touch. "I was always slightly embarrassed by that article. It portrayed the gaming industry as a wild, cut-throat, male-dominated business, and I was the young girl shaking things up. It got a lot wrong and was terribly cliché."

"You shouldn't be embarrassed. It told a great story. And it didn't get any of your accomplishments wrong." Amon pauses and sips his old fashioned, and I know he's about to double-down. "It's not the article that embarrasses you, but your humility. It's refreshing to meet someone so beautiful, smart, and humble. That's rare."

Heat once again rises up my neck and burns my cheeks. I wash down the remnants of distaste with a gulp of champagne and feel my shield slowly melting, even though I'm not ready to feel like this. "What brings you to the casino business?" I ask, seeking to change the subject.

"I've always been a gambler, but my background's in banking."

I smile. "So, is the Golden Sands a gamble?"

"Touché." He chuckles. "No, I don't think so. I've been a fan of Atlantic City for a long time. When this property came on the market, it was too good of a deal to pass up. I'm not going to lie, it's been struggling for a few years, but it has potential, especially at the price I got it at. After some minor negotiations, it was practically free."

"So, you hedge your bets?"

"I like to guarantee my win."

I finish the last of my champagne and grab another oyster. The waiter immediately comes over. "Red or white?" he asks. I point to the red and he fills my glass.

"You think you'll want to work here?" Amon asks.

"Are you interviewing me?"

"No, I'm offering you a job."

"I . . . I . . ."

The waiters come to my rescue, giving me a moment to think about my response. Their trays are loaded with platters of colossal sliced steaks and plates of sides—asparagus to Brussel sprouts, creamed spinach, mashed potatoes, French fries, and even onion rings. The steak is flame-charred on the outside but bloody and rare on the inside. A waiter places a few slices on my plate. I take a bite and the juice drips down the side of my mouth, which I quickly catch with my tongue. It's so tender, I wish I hadn't eaten so many oysters. The waiter tops up my wine glass with Opus One. I haven't had a meal like this since I was a kid. We would meet my dad at whatever casino he was working at and have dinner in their gourmet rooms. I always ordered bananas foster, flame-cooked tableside. There was one waiter, Julien, who would let me light the skillet.

"What are your salary requirements?" Amon asks, pulling me from the grip of nostalgia.

"What?"

"Your salary requirements?" he asks again.

"Oh, ah, I wasn't prepared to talk about salary. I'm not even sure what the cost of living is around here."

Amon laughs. "I was thinking two hundred and fifty thousand to start, with a fifteen thousand signing bonus. You should have no problem living off that."

"I made one-seventy-five in my last position. I wasn't expecting more than that," I stupidly blurt out, thanks to the champagne and the refilled wine glass.

"I appreciate your honesty." Amon smiles. "But you're my secret weapon. I want to pay you well. So?"

"What will my title be?"

"Senior Vice President of Marketing."

"My last position was Marketing Manager."

"I know. So?"

I sit tall in my chair and twist to face Amon. I can't help but smile as I offer my hand to him, "Deal."

Amon shakes my hand. "How soon can you start?"

Chapter 6

The sky is an unusually bright shade of peach this morning. I don't think I'll ever get used to this view. It's only been a few days, but each morning has been completely different yet uniquely beautiful. My new apartment looks out over the Ventnor fishing pier, practically sitting right on the boardwalk. From my window, I have a bird's eye view that lets me drop in on moments in passerby's lives. But when I'm lying in bed, all I see is ocean. It's like being on a cruise ship. The color of the sky is constantly changing, as is the mood of the waves. It's unpredictable and I'm enjoying that.

The airline never found my bags, and no request for a reimbursement would help—what I lost can't be bought. Perhaps it's for the best. Mom says I don't need chains from my past holding me back.

The sizzle and drip of the coffeemaker breaks the morning quiet. Mom must be awake. She insisted on coming down for the weekend to help me get settled in my new place, even though there's hardly anything to do.

The entire building was updated two years ago with state-of-the-art high-efficiency everything. And my apartment is completely new. No one has even sat on the navy and white striped sofas, walked on the light-toned wood floors, or admired the anchor art hanging on the walls—other than the designer. Living in the desert of Las Vegas, this style never worked for me, but I love it here.

I force myself out of bed, throwing on my bathrobe then linger by the window. It's April, but still brutally cold. Today is freezing but yesterday was sixty-degrees. The boardwalk is empty except for a handful of very determined runners. One's face is bright red and twisted in a pain-filled grimace. The boardwalk has been pretty quiet, but the landlord told me it starts to get busy in April and by June it'll be a zoo. The windows of the building have a mirror tint so that I can see out, but no one can see in.

"Sweetheart," my mom calls from the kitchen. She must've heard me climb out of bed. "Do you want your silver in the drawer to the left or right of the sink?"

"Does it really matter?" I mutter. "Left, I guess," I yell back.

"I think right is better."

"Okay. Whatever."

"The clothes you ordered finally came," Mom says from the door to my bedroom. She's holding a large box. "There're two more boxes by the door. If you grab those, I'll start organizing your closet."

I take my time carrying the two boxes in. As much as I love my mom, it's easier to just let her do things her way.

"When did you start wearing cardigans?" she asks as I set the last box down.

"Casinos are always cold."

"Is this how you've always dressed for work?"

"Yes." I open the second box.

"Wool slacks. You can't really intend to wear these?"

"Yes, I do. That's how people dress in the business world."

She takes a step back and glares at me. "You don't think I know how people dress in business?"

"It's not a photoshoot."

She doesn't respond; just starts unpacking again.

"Flats. All of your shoes are flats."

"I'll be walking a lot."

"That's no excuse."

"You don't know what working a real job is like."

"I've worked and walked miles and miles in heels. A job is never an excuse to be ugly."

"It's not that bad."

"Your performance is a direct result of your appearance. You are one of their top executives. You're not going to dress like some frumpy, forgettable, invisible girl."

"It's all I have."

"Pack all of this junk up and return it. I'll be back."

Mom slams the door on her way out. She's right. What the hell was I thinking? I'm not ready to be the Senior Vice President of Casino Marketing. I haven't worked in so long. My brain—at least the part of it that holds my recent memories—is still wrapped in haze. Worse, I've never worked on the east coast. I don't have relationships with the local press. Local customer behavior is a complete mystery. I don't know anything. Better if I bow out before I fail miserably and bring an entire casino property down with me. I need to start smaller.

I pick up my phone and call my dad.

"Lilith, everything okay?" Dad says, a hint of concern in his tone.

"I'm fine. You?"

"Are you ready to start work tomorrow?"

"That's why I'm calling. I don't think I'm the right person. They need someone with east-coast experience. Someone who has an established relationship with the press. Someone who knows the market. Has a database of east-coast reps."

"What?"

"I mean," I swallow. "I'm happy to help, maybe as a consultant. I just think they need someone with more local experience to be the V.P."

"Lilly, please tell me you're not changing your mind."

"I don't think I can do it."

"You can. Trust me. There's no one else for this job."

"Dad, I don't know anything about Atlantic City." My voice cracks as my composure slips. "They're hiring a completely inexperienced person to run the most important department in the casino and—"

"Lilly, you grew up in a casino. Las Vegas and Atlantic City, at their core, aren't all that different. And . . . you've already signed the contract."

"I can get out of the contract."

"Don't be so sure." My dad pauses and lets out a breath. "Please, Lilly."

"It's not that I don't want to. I just want the casino to be successful and I think there are better . . . or . . . more equipped people for the position."

"Petal." That name again. "I've been in this business for decades and I have absolutely no doubt you're the one for this job." He lets out a long slow breath, static on the line. "I don't want to sound harsh, but you won't get another chance like this. This is it. Just give it a try. Okay?"

I exhale slowly and close my eyes. "Okay."

"That's my girl. I'll talk to you tomorrow."

I collapse back on the bed, hoping my dad is right. Beyond the window, the unending ocean shifts, always in motion, always changing. I feel inconsequential but find a strange comfort in that. If I fail, at this point does it really matter?

When my computer chat rings, I already know it's Tori. I get up and hurry to the dining table, where my computer's set up.

"Hey," I say as I click open the chat.

"Guess what?" Tori smiles.

"What?"

"My professor invited me to co-author a paper with him before I officially begin my program."

"That's amazing!"

"Thanks." Tori squeezes her eyes shut. "I have a minor issue. I don't have a place to stay. Princeton's only about an hour-and-a-half from Atlantic City. When my semester officially starts in August, I'll have on-campus housing. But I was thinking, if you have room, maybe I could stay with you till then?"

"I have an entire extra room and would love that!"

"Really?" She leans closer to the camera.

"Of course." I smile.

"Thank you! Thank you! Thank you!"

There's a click at the front door as a key slides into the lock. Mom is back with bags and bags and bags. She kicks the door closed, then walks by me on her way to my bedroom. She pauses for just a moment.

"Hello, Victoria," she says.

"Hi, Mrs. Umbra," Tori exclaims, waving through the video feed. "I'll let you get back to moving, Lil. I'm so happy. This is gonna be great!" Tori smiles.

"See you soon."

I click out of the chat, then join mom in my bedroom closet.

"I thought you cut ties with her," Mom says, not taking her eyes off the satin shirt she is hanging up.

"We reconnected."

"Oh. And?"

"She got into Princeton's doctoral program."

"That little mouse of a girl is perfect for academia. Maybe you should send her your wardrobe as a congratulatory gift."

"She's going to spend the summer here. I'll give it to her then."

"What?"

"I'll give it to her when she's here."

"She can't come here. She'll be a distraction."

"She'll be busy, too."

"Mmm." With one eyebrow raised, Mom just stares at me for a tense moment. I'm fully prepared to argue my case. Then she smiles. "Help me hang these clothes, then I'll take you out to dinner."

My new wardrobe is beautiful. Silk, velvet, and satin hang in rich gem tones. I shove the boxes filled with my other clothes into a dark corner of the closet.

"Perfect," Mom says as she places a pair of heels on the shoe rack. "Get dressed. I'll open a bottle of wine. Wear something nice. I got us a reservation at Mangia. It's very hard to get into, you have to know someone."

Grabbing whatever my mom has folded at the top—a pair of black velvet jeans and a winter white sweetheart sweater—I dress quickly. Knowing her, she chose this outfit for tonight.

She's waiting for me in the kitchen, with two glasses of deep red wine. Passing me a glass, she holds hers up. "Cheers."

"Cheers," I echo.

"I have a present for you." She smiles and pulls out an antique red leather jewelry box from behind the counter. "It's a good luck charm." She opens the box.

I gasp. "It's beautiful."

"This necklace has been in our family for more than two hundred years. It's a five-carat black diamond set in rhodium. It's *extraordinarily* rare." She places the necklace on me.

The pendant lies just below my collarbone. The deep neckline of my white sweater accentuates the jewel. It's a large teardrop black diamond, set in a braided cage of black metal, and surrounded by smaller blue diamonds.

"It looks like something a queen would wear."

"I know."

"Why haven't I ever seen you wear it?"

"It was always meant for you, but I've worn it plenty."

"I'm afraid I'll lose it," I say, still admiring myself in the mirror.

"Sweetheart, it's practically indestructible. Rhodium is a very strong metal. As strong as your father and I know you are."

"I love it. Thank you."

"It's our family legacy and will bring you great luck."

"Even better." I smile and take another sip of wine.

"Ready?"

I nod and take the last sip of my wine.

My mom winds through the streets of Atlantic City. The sun just sank below the westward horizon and the town's undercurrent is at its strongest. In the short time I've been here, I've learned Atlantic City is a haven of vice. In places like this, the onset of night brings frenzied excitement with it. I can't exactly put my finger on it, but there's a definite current in the atmosphere.

"Mom," I say, and she twists to look at me for a moment. "I understand what you did for me and I appreciate—" My seatbelt suddenly squeezes my body followed by a thump—thump—thump—thud. There's a man lying on the hood of the car. His face is inches from mine, separated by nothing more than glass. His eyes, wide and unblinking, drill into mine. His hair is matted and knotted. A visible layer of grime smears his face. I'm not sure if he's smiling or snarling at me. His eye twitches, and I recognize the madness behind it. My mom sprays windshield washer fluid and flips on the wipers. He's up on his hands and knees so quickly that I'm not sure how he got there. Now that the shock has dislodged from my chest, I'm flooded with tingles of panic. He throws his head back towards the sky and laughs wildly.

"Well, isn't he having fun?" Mom rolls her eyes. "He better not have dented my hood. I swear if he broke off the hood ornament." My mom hits the unlock button. "It would take me forever to find a suitable jaguar. They don't make them anymore." She pushes the door open.

"Mom, stop! Don't get out of the car."

In a swift movement, she spins both legs and steps out. "Shoo! Get off my car. It's a classic!"

The man stops laughing. He looks at her and sinks down like a tiger ready to pounce. Then, slowly, he slides back off of the car, away from my mom. He hides behind the front side for a moment, then pops up and sprints off.

"You shouldn't have gotten out of the car," I say as soon as she sits back down.

"I had to make sure my car was okay. Besides, he was harmless and I'm famished. You must stop being afraid of everything."

"I'm not."

She looks at me flatly.

Maybe I am.

We pull up to an old multi-story house; the date on the side of the building says it was built in 1921. Its brick foundation and white asbestos siding blends in with the neighborhood.

Mom parallel parks her fully restored Jaguar XJ6, worth more than my house was, in a tight street spot. "We're here."

I look around but don't see a restaurant anywhere. "Are you sure about this?"

She just smiles and climbs out of the car, and I follow. I'm either getting used to the cold or the harshness of Spring's leftover winter wind is quietly abating. She slinks into a tiny alley, then down a few steps and through an inconspicuous door in the basement of this random home. If my mom wasn't leading the way, I'd turn around.

Following her into a small room, we jam our winter coats onto a packed coat rack. From the entryway, I peek into the adjoining room. Tucked into a large cellar, buzzing with conversation, is a very busy restaurant. The ceilings are low, and tables litter the space with people stuffed into every chair.

"Naomi," a waiter, dressed in formal whites, calls from the main dining room. "We have you set up back here."

"Thank you, Demetri."

"You must be Lilly. It's an honor to meet you," Demetri says to me.

Honor? "Nice to meet you." I smile and fight the urge to roll my eyes.

"I've heard so much about you. Whenever you need a table, call this number." Demetri hands me a card with nothing but a number embossed in gold and a symbol. I expected to at the least see the word Mangia, but only the cryptic logo is printed—two slightly crooked 'V's, like lightning strikes connected on one side with a 'μ' in the middle, all surrounded by a circle.

"Thanks."

Our table is in a back room and has a noticeable amount of extra space around it. Demetri snaps his fingers, and a teenage boy brings out a large antipasto platter then pours wine into our glasses.

"You're amazing," my mom says to Demetri.

With the slightest bend, he bows to her, then disappears.

"They're a little weird," I whisper to my mom.

"Don't be so uptight. It's part of the fun."

"And what's the deal with this stupid card? Nothing but a symbol?" I hold up the card before tucking it into my purse.

"Sweetheart, I would think you, of all people, could appreciate a clever marketing ploy." She takes a sip of her wine.

"It's a little creepy, this whole place is creepy," I say, picking up a piece of rolled prosciutto.

"Lilith, this is exactly why you had a breakdown," she snaps. The word 'breakdown' knocks off what little confidence I've managed to collect these past couple of weeks. "When anything is outside of your realm of understanding, you can't handle it. A silly gimmick has you all flustered."

I swallow the sting of that statement with a sip of wine. "That's not exactly why I fell apart."

"Yes, it is. Your life didn't go as planned and you were unable to adjust." Mom tosses an oil-soaked olive in her mouth and bites down.

"I lost someone I loved."

"And?"

"*And?*"

"That you loved. Past tense. Move on."

"I couldn't just move on. My whole life was planned with him. Our house, our wedding. It was taken from me, Mom. All of it. Sorry if *my sadness* gets in the way of—"

"Exactly. That's your problem. Life is sad when you're confined by a plan tightly fit within your comfort zone."

"Confined by a plan?"

"Life should be fun! Lived outside of our comfort zone. How many men have you even dated?"

"He is—*was*—the love of my life," I say through a scowl.

"You poor child. I never realized how much you take after your father. Thankfully, he met me, and I was able to open him up."

"Ugh." I blush. "This is so awkward."

"Who decides to marry the first person they go to bed with?" She punctuates her annoyance with a loud tsk. "All I'm saying is there's so much more to life than a plan."

Fire burns my cheeks. "Let's change the subject." I grab another piece of prosciutto. This time I add a slice of cheese, and stuff the whole thing into my mouth. Saltiness tingles my tongue, bringing out the savory umami of the meat. I take a sip of wine. With it, the flavor melts into the alcohol satisfying all five basic tastes. I close my eyes and take another sip, savoring this rare moment of pleasure and distraction.

"All you have to do is enjoy life as much as you enjoyed that bite of food. It's simple once you get the hang of it." She smiles and takes another long sip of wine, then bites an olive in half. The waiter brings over a plate of grilled calamari. He bows to my mom and disappears.

"Why do they act like they worship you here?" I stab my fork into a tentacle dripping with olive oil.

"Your father and I love it here. Look around. Everyone is enjoying themselves."

She's right. Every table appears happy. I see the waiter drop off a platter of dessert to another table and bow. "Do you ever miss Las Vegas?"

"No. I enjoyed our time there, but Atlantic City has so much more to offer."

"More?" I raise my eyebrows. While I may have only been here a couple of weeks, I know this isn't true.

"There's history here."

"Is that a cute way of saying run down?"

"Not even close." She glares at me. "These events in time create energy and leave their mark. It's electric and there's so much of it here."

"I didn't realize you were so into . . ." I pause, trying to find the right word but finally settle on, "history?"

"History, as you put it, becomes a current, an energy, a force. Once you learn to tap into it, you can have anything you want." Mom looks at me for a moment, then picks up her glass of wine. "Cheers to you, Lilly. To the future, to you finding your current, and to a whole new world for you."

As difficult as she can be, it's easy for me to appreciate how my mom views the world. She's always been able to pivot quickly and make the best of any situation. Like a cat, she's always landing on her feet. Not afraid to explore the ledges. And she always walks out on top. At this point, I realize that I need to make some changes. Try to be more like her, I think, and tuck the sadness a few levels deeper.

"Cheers." I raise my glass. "To a new start."

Chapter 7

I can't sleep. The sun hasn't yet risen, but I'm too wired to stay in bed. I grab a cup of coffee and nestle into the sofa that overlooks the ocean. An indigo glow brightens the horizon as soft shades of coral run from the dark waters. A handful of people are already running on the boardwalk. Unlike yesterday, it's warm today. Will be nearly seventy-degrees, apparently normal for the east coast. Nice or not, the early morning air is still cold to my desert blood.

"You're up early," Mom says from the kitchen.

"So are you."

"I have a few morning meetings in New York City. If you get ready, I can drop you off on my way out."

"Okay, thanks." I watch a young mother push a stroller down the boardwalk. She draws nearer, and I realize, she's not pushing a child but a hairless cat. I can't help but stare.

"Lilith." My mom walks over to the window. "What a lovely sphynx," she says, pulling my attention away.

"What?"

"The cat."

"That's weird, right?"

"Lilith." Mom frowns at me. "Who are you to judge?"

Me? I can't breathe without you judging, but I don't reply. Though I can't help but wonder what brings someone to the point they push a hairless cat around in a stroller. My thoughts tumble, and I'm hit by an unexpected memory. He had a picture. Framed. Of a hairless cat that had been tattooed. It hung on his apartment wall. I laughed the first time I saw it in his apartment until he told me it was a real tattooed cat. It was weird and cruel, and I didn't believe him, but he showed me the cat online.

"Lilly," Mom says again, touching my shoulder. The memory swirls into smoke and disappears. "I'm leaving a few bottles of these herbs here for you. Don't forget to add a dropperful to your water a few times a day. Here." She hands me a glass. "Drink this now."

I down the water and hand the glass back.

"Don't forget," she reiterates.

"I'll be ready in twenty minutes," I say and head to my room. When I try to return to the memory, put it into some sort of solid context, I can't. It's a snapshot floating in a pool of confusion. I push those thoughts from my head. I'm in a better place now. Starting over.

The horizon is now lit to a soft shade of tangerine and the sun just crested. I settle on a red velvet blazer and black silk pants, hoping the red makes me appear more confident than I feel.

After brushing my teeth, I look in the mirror. *What did Mom say I needed? A mantra?* I let out a long exhale. I feel stupid talking to myself, but I might as well try. I let out another slow breath. "I am not bound by the confines of my comfort zone and I'm not afraid to fail." I repeat it to myself, but that last part is a lie. "I am not bound by the confines of my comfort zone, and I will not fail. I will not fail.

If something goes wrong, I will fix it. I will not fail." This will be my new mantra.

It doesn't take long to do my makeup and hair. I put on my good-luck necklace, the family heirloom, and look in the mirror one more time. I feel different. "I am not bound by the confines of my comfort zone, and I will not fail." Twice more I say it. Flash myself a smile. Nod at my reflection. I am ready.

Driving down Pacific Avenue, Atlantic City's street corners are quiet. Delivery trucks are out. Nurses are heading into the hospital. A few storefronts are open but that's it. As soon as we turn off Pacific, I'm astounded by how much better Golden Sands looks. Looming over South Carolina Avenue and the boardwalk, The Golden Sands holds court. There's something regal about this old building in fresh clothes. The windows are clean. A bright, new coat of white paint has recently revived the exterior.

"Amon certainly doesn't waste any time," Mom says. "I love how aggressive he is."

"Yeah, it looks great."

My mom pulls into the porte cochère. The doorman starts to walk over, but she waves him off. There are a few nice cars lined up, typical of any casino valet. I must admit, I'm a little surprised by how nice the cars are. There's a Ferrari and a Bentley, but it's the Mercedes that catches my attention. It's a little red convertible and the exact car I've always wanted. If things in Vegas had gone as planned, I would have bought that car. I even test drove it. Not long before I met him.

"You'll do well, Lilith."

"Thanks." I start to get out, but my mom grabs my wrist.

I turn and look at her. "You look beautiful," she says, "and power-ful. Don't worry about being sweet."

I nod once and bite the corner of my lip.

"I mean it," she continues. "In Vegas, everything is nice and new, and people can afford to be sweet there. Everyone is tougher out here."

"Okay." I smile. "I'll be tough."

She looks at me with an eyebrow raised.

"I will," I confirm. She nods her approval, and I climb out of her car.

As I stand in front of the revolving glass door, I can see myself in the mirrored glass. *I am not bound by the confines of my comfort zone. I will not fail.* And I am tough. Though I can't quite get myself to take those first few steps in. Who am I kidding? I'm a nervous wreck. I don't even know where my office is. What the hell was I thinking?

"Ms. Umbra," the doorman calls, walking towards me. His uni-form is a full-length, light wool overcoat and a derby hat. He looks like he stepped out of the roaring 20s. He's sweating slightly, even though it's barely over fifty degrees.

"Yes?" I look at him and smile.

He hands me a set of keys. "That red Mercedes is yours and that's your parking spot. Mr. Asra wanted me to tell you it's a corporate gift. He also asked me to let you know that Charlotte, the front desk manager, will show you to your office. She's waiting for you right inside."

"Wait. That. Red. Mercedes. Is mine?"

"Yes, and your parking spot. Whenever you're here, park right there."

"Really?"

"Yes, and I already let Charlotte know you're here. She's waiting for you right inside." He motions towards the door.

"I think you made a mistake. Amon didn't say anything about a car."

"No, that's definitely your car."

Holding up the keys, I glance back at my mom. She smiles before driving off.

I pause, trying not to blink. "Well . . . thank you." It's the only response I can muster through the shock.

"Thank Mr. Asra," he says.

"I will. Ah, what's your name?"

"Tom."

"Nice to meet you, Tom." I grab his hand to shake it.

"It's a pleasure to meet you, Ms. Umbra." He seems nervous all of a sudden, shifting his head and shoulders to clear space between his neck and the collar of his shirt. "Please, Charlotte's waiting."

"Right." I smile and take one more look at my new car.

The revolving door is heavy and a little hard to get moving. As I'm pushing, I catch a glance of my reflection and feel like I'm looking at someone else. My eyes drift to the necklace. It vibrates. Panic grabs my throat and squeezes. I freeze. The revolving door slows. Then it happens again. It's the mirrored glass shaking from the side door's vibration as it opens and closes when Tom steps in and out. What is wrong with me? *I am not confined by my comfort zone and I am not scared. I am not scared. I will not fail. I'm tough.* These stupid mantras better work. I take a breath. Recollect myself.

And push my way in.

The Golden Sands holds that same sense of wonder from the first time I was here. I can almost feel the current that my mom was so adamant about. Though today, I'm more pragmatic, and have to admit it's a bit dated. At a guess, the lobby décor was added some time in the 1990s. There're red and tan marble floors and lots of heavy, dark wood. It's an easy fix and I already know what my first project is going to be.

"Ms. Umbra."

I spin to my left. A beautiful girl with long blonde hair dressed in a dour, knee-length skirt suit, walks towards me.

Update the uniforms too.

"I'm Charlotte, the front desk manager."

"Nice to meet you. Please, call me Lilly."

Charlotte nods and smiles. "If you're ready, I can show you to your office and walk you through all of your employee codes and logins."

"Perfect, thanks."

"Follow me." Charlotte leads me down a hall past a few empty retail locations that are available for rent. "We could really use a few shops, especially a gift shop. The few people that do stay here are always asking me where they can grab basic things like Tylenol, you know, stuff like that. A coffee shop would be nice, too."

"Noted," I reply.

We take a left turn into a mirrored bank of elevators, and Charlotte pushes the call button. I catch a glimpse of myself, reflected into an endless trail of doppelgangers in the mirror behind and straighten my posture to see myself standing tall to infinity. It reminds me of those mirror mazes you ran through as a kid.

"This is our original, historic tower," Charlotte says. "The executive offices, well, yours and Amon's, are on the eighth floor." She opens the folder and grabs a keycard. The elevator arrives. "This is what you scan to get to your floor." She holds the card up and the elevator light for the eighth floor illuminates automatically.

My stomach drops as the elevator shoots up, an overwhelming feeling of entirely unearned promotion creeping into my skin as I'm hit with a full-blown episode of imposter syndrome. *What have I done to earn this position? Have successful parents?*

When the door opens and we step out, a bit of simple comfort settles me. A dark wood door stands to the right and a glass door to the left. Charlotte points to the right, "That's Amon's personal apartment." Then, she points to the glass door. Inside there's a small reception area and a desk. A basic casino office. Like every other office I've had, it's completely utilitarian and something I'm comfortable with.

"Is that my office?"

"Yes." Charlotte scans the card again before opening the glass door.

After setting my things down on the small desk, I pull the chair out to sit.

"Oh." Charlotte looks at me with her eyebrows knit together. "This is where your assistant works. He comes in at nine. You're much earlier than we expected. Your office is this way."

Fire swirls up my neck and lands in my cheeks. I attempt a cool laugh, but it comes out more like a cough, and I quickly stand.

Charlotte walks me into a short hallway that ends with two more glass doors, both with names etched on the outside. The door on the right reads: Ms. Lilith Umbra, Senior Vice President of Marketing and the door on the left reads Mr. Amon Asra, Managing Partner.

Charlotte opens the door and holds it for me.

"Oh," I gasp, "I wasn't expecting this."

The office looks like it was pulled from the pages of an *Architectural Digest* feature on high-power, Wall Street CEOs. Everything is brand new. There's a floor-to-ceiling black marble backsplash that spills down the rear wall and into a white marble waterfall desk with black wood inlay. If Mary Queen of Scots had been a modern businesswoman, this would be her office. Framing the desk and backsplash are two backlit bookcases decorated with modern sculptures and books. Charmingly, Amon has framed some of the *Las Vegas Magazine* covers with me and placed them on the bookshelf. Which, I admit, makes it look like I do belong here. A matching kitchenette with a small beverage refrigerator and bar area extends along the inside wall. On the opposite side sits a wall of windows looking south over Atlantic City, the ocean, and the bay.

Charlotte pushes a button on the desk. A monitor pops up and a keyboard slides out. "Ms. Umbra, if you'll take a seat, we can get your passwords set up and get you signed into the systems. Are you familiar with Optima? Not that you'll need it often, if at all, that's just what we use—"

"I know Optima." It was the hospitality management software we used at One.

"Perfect." Charlotte pulls the plush, black-leather chair out for me.

"Okay, Ms. Umbra—"

"Please call me Lilly."

Charlotte clears her throat. "My apologies, Lilly. The first screen will be your username and password setup. Whatever password you choose will get you into every system."

A male voice fills the room. "Charlotte, thank you so much. I can take it from here."

As I look up, for a split second, I think he just walked in. Kai. *No, don't even think his name.* This is a new beginning . . . a new beginning. But the man standing in the entrance to my office has those same eyes.

"Ms. Umbra," the man with Kai's eyes continues. "I got here as quickly as I could. I'm very sorry I wasn't here to greet you. I didn't expect you so early."

I clear my throat. He even dresses like he did: perfectly pressed slim fit slacks and a button down. "Um, that's okay."

"Let me properly introduce myself. I'm Jordan. I'll be yours and Mr. Asra's administrative assistant." Jordan flashes a gleaming, toothy smile.

As the surprise settles and I truly look at him, I see he doesn't really look like Kai. Jordan just caught me off guard, that's all. *A new beginning.* "I'm Lilly. Nice to meet you."

Charlotte retreats from her position. "If you need anything else, Ms.—I mean, Lilly, just let me know," she says and hurries out.

"Thank you so much, Charlotte," I call after her. She turns briefly at the door, flashes a meek smile then disappears down the hall.

Jordan pulls a chair over and sits next to me. I inhale a woodsy haze of vetiver tinged with jasmine.

"Are you wearing Penhaligons?" I ask.

"Impressive," Jordan says, "How do you know this scent?"

"My dad wears it. The bottle with the gold goat head, right?"

"Yes," Jordan says. "The Inimitable Mr. Penhaligon. He has good taste. So, how far did you and Charlotte get?"

"Not far, we were just about to set up my password and username."

"Perfect. We actually set up your username yesterday. Go ahead and type it in. It's Lilith4q510."

"Any capitals?"

"Just the first L."

"4q—what?"

"4q510."

"I should write this down."

"Already done." Jordan opens the top right desk drawer. I glance in and see it stocked and organized. He pulls out a leather-bound notebook and flips open the cover to show me the first page.

"That's so helpful, thank you."

"Now hit 'enter,'" he instructs. The screen flashes to a password setup cue. I set my password. It gets rejected.

"I'm sorry, I should've told you to use a combination of letter, number, and special symbol."

I do and it's rejected again.

"I used letters, numbers, and a special symbol. I don't know why it didn't accept it."

"Try again," he tells me.

Rejected.

"Are you comfortable sharing your password with me? I have access to the same systems."

"Okay." I slide over so he can reach my keyboard.

"What would you like your password to be?"

"Umbra, capital U, 1113 and an exclamation mark."

Jordan types in the password. It's accepted and my home screen opens. Jordan stands and returns the chair.

"I wonder why it didn't work for me."

"Mmm." He cocks his head slightly. "The same password will get you into every system we use. Can I get you anything?"

"No, thank you. I think I'll just familiarize myself with the systems."

"If you need anything, call." Jordan takes a few steps then turns back. "Mr. Asra won't be in for at least another hour. Would you like me to arrange a tour of the property? Peter, our Director of Facilities, gives great tours."

"Yes, please."

Jordan nods then quickly disappears. I search for the CMS platform Golden Sands uses and find IGM; luckily, it's a program I've used during my time at multiple casinos. I run a quick drop-and-hold percentage report for the past six months. This will tell me how much money came in through the casino—the drop—versus how much stayed, the hold. The hold percentage for most casinos varies, usually somewhere between five and fifteen percent, depending on the game. For an average sized house like Golden Sands to be mildly successful, the drop each night should be close to a million dollars.

The report comes up and I frown. Golden Sands' drop averaged $55,000 a night for six months? That can't be right. If it is, it's abysmal. The total revenue would be around three thousand dollars, which means the property has been hemorrhaging money.

"Ms. Umbra," a small speaker built into my desk announces, "Peter is on his way up. If you'd like to talk back to me, there is a small button right under the speaker. Push that."

I do. "Thanks, and please call me Lilly. Do you know if the numbers in the CMS platform are accurate?"

"Yes, they are," Jordan replies.

"How is that possible?"

"That's why Amon got this property for such a reasonable price."

I run the same report for the six months prior and it's not nearly as terrible. The drop during that period was sixteen million with a total revenue of just over a million dollars. That's still not good, but nowhere near as bad as the following six months.

I push the speaker's button. "Jordan, did something happen here six months ago? The casino revenue basically died off."

"Not that I'm aware of. I just buzzed Peter up. Is there anything else you'd like me to work on while you're on the tour?"

"Do we have a media contact list?"

"We have a few different lists. I'll go through each one, make sure they're current, and condense them to one master list."

I do a quick Google search of Golden Sands and hit the News filter. As I scroll through, there's not much. A few local press articles about the casino's imminent closure and record-breaking losses, but nothing that hints at the reason for this sudden downturn in revenue. Then I find a post referencing an online news story from six months ago. It looks like the original story has been pulled, but someone posted screenshots.

It initially ran in *The Undertow*, a local, very small online news outlet based in Ventnor. The story claims the entire marketing team at Golden Sands suddenly suffered a mysterious illness and quit. There's no record of this story anywhere online. It's not on *The Undertow*'s site. It's not that unusual for an entire marketing team to leave at once. In the casino business, marketing teams often travel from job to job as one, but it's still worth looking into. I click on the name of the person that posted this story: Jacques de Molay.

"Lilly, Peter is here," Jordan says through the speaker.

"Thank you." I place my keycard in my blazer pocket and make my way to the reception area.

Peter is tall, dressed in khaki pants and a beige button-down shirt that matches his spray of sandy hair—a mix of gray and taupe. He wears the same retractable keychain tether hooked to a belt loop that every Facilities Director I've ever met has worn. Several keys and keycards dangle from it. Peter's posture has dropped a little after years of walking the long corridors. This makes him seem kind, almost like he's trying to come down to my level.

"Hi Peter, I'm Lilly, nice to meet you."

"It's nice to meet you, Lilly, and great to get some fresh life in this place. It sure can use it." He smiles, warm and friendly—the genuine kind that reaches the eyes. "Ready for your tour?"

"I am."

Chapter 8

"I thought we'd start the tour in the new tower and work our way back in time."

"Great," I say as the elevator starts its descent to the ground floor.

"Golden Sands comprises two towers joined by the casino. The Palace Tower was built in 2004 when a small pre-existing tower was torn down. This tower added three-hundred and ninety-three hotel rooms and sixty-six suites. Combined with the Atlantic Tower, we have a total of nine hundred and sixty-nine rooms."

"That's a decent amount. What sort of condition are they in?"

"We are currently two-thirds of the way through our renovation of the Palace Tower rooms. The Atlantic Tower is very nice. Mr. Asra is replacing the linens, adding new flat screen TVs, and new coffee makers. But other than that, they were in great condition."

"Have those replacements been completed?"

"The last floors will be switched out today."

"Do you know if anyone has sent out press releases about the renovations or done any room-reveal tours?"

The elevator bounces to a stop on the ground floor. The doors slide open, and we step out into the mirrored elevator bank. "No, nothing," Peter says.

"Perfect." I pull out my phone to make a note. A sudden gasp catches in my chest as I glimpse someone right behind me.

"Are you okay?" Peter asks.

Just my reflection bouncing between mirrors again. "Yeah, sorry. I'm just sending myself an email with these notes and thought I forgot my new email address, but I have it." The lie leaves heat simmering in my cheeks. Though I really do email myself our tour notes.

Peter watches as I tuck the phone back into my blazer pocket. "Ready?" he asks, and I nod. "This way." He points to a hall up ahead. "We can cut through the casino."

The jingle-jangle of slot machines always makes me smile. I expect to get my first glimpse of the Monday morning senior bus trip crowd—the day-trippers for which Atlantic City is famous. We come to a small set of steps down into the casino, and I stop at the top with a view of the entire floor. There's not a single person in the casino. I follow Peter down onto the house floor. It's completely empty. The entire pit is closed. Not a single dealer is working. The slot machines ding and spin with no one in front of them.

"I've never seen a casino this dead," I say to Peter.

"It's been like this for a few months now."

"Since the marketing team left?"

"Not long after."

"Was there some mysterious illness?"

"How did you hear that?"

"I stumbled on a social media post," I tell him.

"They started the rumor to get out of their contracts. But they were terrible at their jobs anyway and needed to go."

As we walk through the casino, a tingle slithers up my spine as goosebumps prickle my skin. Empty casinos don't feel right.

"The main table-games pit runs down the center of the casino. We have—*had*—Six Deck and Eight Deck Blackjack, Craps, Single Zero and Double Zero Roulette, Three Card and Four Card Poker, Baccarat, Pai Gow Poker, Pai Gow Tiles, Let It Ride, Mississippi Stud, Spanish 21, and occasionally War."

"That's a nice mix. Pretty standard," I say.

"To the right is our second pit, our high-limit table games, which is right by our high-limit slot area."

Decadent gold and marble set this area apart from the main floor. "They look nice," I say, trying to at least find something good as we walk by the empty area.

"Up to our left, is our casino bar, The Dunes. It opens on weekends."

Stale beer makes the entire area smell like a mix of skunk and urine. They must not have cleaned the floors from the weekend yet. Vinyl booths wrap around the exterior while a black bar weaves down the center. Midnight carpet with bright red, blue, and yellow ribbons remind me of New Orleans after Mardi Gras. The awful aroma must be held in the old carpet. Nothing will get that out except new flooring. I add another note to my cell phone.

We follow an aisle as it weaves past the pit and through the slot machines. Casino floors are cleverly designed with passageways that lead you around but not out. The labyrinthine design is no accident, and I'm swept up into the wonder. I stop to study a bank of slots for an idea of what machines they have at Golden Sands. They have their penny slots in a prime location near the bar, right where the dollar slots should be. Another note for my phone. When I look up, Peter is gone. I hurry back to where I was but he's not there either. Dread squeezes my core. I take off down an aisle in the direction we were heading. Still no sign. I've never been in a casino completely alone. Apprehension claws its way up the rungs of my rib cage. This isn't right.

"Peter?"

Nothing. It's quiet, except for the taunting dings and spins of the slot machines.

"Peter!"

Nothing.

"PETER!"

Nothing.

Cold beads of sweat form under my collar as goosepimples prick my neck. I look up at the dozens of strategically placed 'eyes in the sky.' I'm being watched. Casino security cameras are so advanced they can zoom in and read a text on my phone. This should give me comfort but only makes my heart hammer against my ribs. I find the closest aisle, knowing if I head back towards the bar, I should find a path to the hotel lobby. From there, I can get back to my office. My breath comes in short bursts as I speed-walk through the aisles, neck rigid, shoulders hunched. I whip around each corner, faster and faster until—boom. I bounce backwards and land on my butt. White-hot pain shoots up my spine, then settles into a deep throb that matches my racing pulse.

"Lilly! Oh no, are you okay?" Peter asks, looking down at me.

I clear my throat. My cheeks are red hot, and I know my makeup can't cover my embarrassment. "Sorry. I was rushing to catch up to you and when I turned that corner. I didn't see you."

Peter offers me his hand. "Don't rush on my behalf, my schedule is completely open."

"Noted, per my backside." An awkward chuckle escapes me. Did I really just say that? If I could crawl under my desk right now, I would. I try to smile, as I brush myself off. My cheeks are still afire. Why the hell did I panic like that? I have *got* to calm down.

Peter looks at me, his head slightly cocked to the side. "Ready to move on?"

"Yes." I smile and realize I'm holding my breath. The pings of unease remain camped at the base of my gut.

Peter winds his way through a short aisle that leads to a down escalator. "Would you like to see our bus lobby?"

"Sure. How often do you get bus trips in?"

"We haven't had any since the marketing team left."

The escalator is not turned on and I stumble slightly when I take the first step. It's always disorienting to walk on a stopped escalator, so I force myself to focus. The last thing I want is another embarrassing fall. Luckily, the escalator is short. A blur of movement flashes in my peripheral vision. When I look up, an unkempt man lunges toward us—my muscles lock, my throat closes. Blood rushes in my ears like a roar, drowning everything else out. He throws himself down at our feet and when he looks up at me, recognition nearly sweeps my feet out from under me. It's the homeless man we hit in the car last night.

"Queen Lilith," he says, still on his knees as he drops into a deep bow.

The blood drains from my face. "How do you know my name?"

"Are you presuming that because I'm homeless, I can't read?" He feigns an over-dramatized shock and points out my name badge as he stands.

"Buddy," Peter says. "I told you that you can't keep staying here. There're new owners."

"But I like it in here," the homeless man—Buddy—replies.

"It's time to go. Why don't you go over to the soup kitchen or rescue mission?"

"And give up these luxurious digs?" Buddy shakes his head.

"I'm going back up to the casino," I whisper to Peter.

I turn to head back to the escalator and freeze. Buddy is standing right behind my shoulder. So close his hot breath pours down my neck—a rotten mix of stale cigarette smoke and vomit.

"You don't know what's coming for you, do you?" he whispers in my ear.

A breath catches in my throat and seems to solidify, instantly forming a lump. I try to swallow but it's no use. My right foot inches forward, and I slowly turn to face him. But he's not right behind me at all. In fact, he hasn't moved. "What did you say?"

"I said, 'ave a nice day, m'lady," Buddy says in a heavily affected, almost comedic, British accent.

"This is the last time, Buddy," Peter says. "Next time I'm calling the cops. I mean it."

Buddy spins a few times then sings as he ambles off, "Peety Piper picked a peck of pickled peppers and had a flock whose fleece was white as snow. And everywhere that Lilith went, her Peety Piper was sure to go." Buddy cackles, spins a few more times. His layers of jackets flare. He slams the glass lobby doors open and disappears into the concrete bus depot.

"That's the bus terminal and above it is our parking garage." Peter points out. "Sorry about that. He's been staying here, but I'll make sure he's out."

"I . . . I've seen him in other places."

Peter nods. "Everyone knows Buddy. You could say he's kind of like the unofficial president of the homeless population here."

Still shaken, I follow Peter onto the stopped escalator and trip again. It must be stress that's sent my imagination into overdrive. This day is not going as I'd hoped. At least it can only get better. Golden Sands is doing so badly that anything I do will be an improvement. I just need to focus on work. Make a to-do list. I take a few deep breaths to regain my composure. *I will be more like my mom. I will thrive under stress. I will prove that I'm capable. And I will not be bound by the constraints of my comfort zone.*

Weird is good. Weird is interesting. Atlantic City is weird and that's okay, I'll get used to it. *I will not be bound by the constraints of my comfort zone.*

I'm so focused on my mantras that I don't notice when Peter stops, and I walk into the back of him. "Sorry," I say and quickly pull out my phone. "I was thinking about another note. We need to get the bus trips going as soon as possible," I say as I type it into my phone.

"Your head must be spinning," Peter says.

"What?"

"There's so much to do. Your head must be spinning."

"Oh." I smile and let out just a breath of a chuckle. "Yes. I'm trying to decide where to start."

Peter pushes an elevator button and I realize we're at the Palace Tower. "If there's anything that I can do to help, let me know."

The elevator door slides open, and we step in.

"Actually, we need to move some of the slot machines around. I'm going to talk to Amon about it today. So that will probably be the first order of business. I'm also going to recommend renovating the casino bar."

Peter pushes the button for the ninth floor. "The renovation on that bar is starting today." Peter checks his wristwatch. "It should be getting underway as we speak."

"That's one thing to check off the list."

The doors slide open, and I follow Peter to room 936. "This is a newly-renovated, standard king in the Palace Tower," he says and pushes the door open.

Finally, the day is turning around. "It's nice." Crisp clean white linens are neatly folded on the bed. The hardwood dresser is in great condition and the flat screen television is state-of-the-art. I'm so relieved to see this room easily holds up to any on the Strip. This view makes it even better.

"What's that over there?" I point out of the window.

"That's the Brigantine Inlet. Brigantine is the next barrier island to the north. The only way to get there is through Atlantic City."

"It looks nice."

"It is. That's where I live."

"Cool."

"Would you like to see any other rooms?"

"If they're as nice as this, I'm good."

"There are a few floors still being renovated, but they'll be complete within the next couple days."

"Perfect." I add another note to include a room tour in the media day.

"I thought we'd make our way back to the Atlantic Tower underground through the tunnels," Peter says.

"Tunnels?"

"Yeah, they're part of the original structure." Peter opens the door, and I follow him out. "An old building was torn down to make room for the Palace Tower, but the tunnels were preserved. Employees still use them to move between the two towers. We also have a few employee areas down there."

Once we're back on the elevator, Peter holds up a key card, then pushes the button labeled BB. The elevator drops quickly, sending a tickle into my stomach.

"Has anyone told you about the history of this property?" Peter asks.

"I know it was Atlantic City's first casino and part of the property dates back to the 1920s."

"Close. This property has been a hotel since the late 1800s, the Chalfonte-Haddon Hall. The original structures were wood and were eventually torn down. The building that now houses The Atlantic Tower was the Haddon Hall, which, you're right, was built during the 1920s. In my opinion, the most interesting phase of this property's history occurred during the 1940s when it was taken over by the United States military and converted to the Thomas England General Hospital."

"Really?" I ask as the elevator slows to a stop and the doors slide open.

The basement is dark and damp. Yellow light bounces off the drab concrete tunnels. Goosebumps prickle my skin as the chill finds its way through my jacket.

"Yeah, thousands of surgeries were conducted here. It became the largest hospital during that time. It was well-known as a neuro-surgical center, amputation center, and a rehab. These soldiers had suffered catastrophic injuries. They couldn't live the lives they were used to, being in wheelchairs and stuff. So, the military turned this whole place into a recovery center. Mental health, occupational therapy, that kind of thing. I mean, you could write a book on the history of this building. The last soldiers that survived left in 1946."

"Incredible."

"I believe this area was the morgue."

"What?" My goosebumps seem to thicken.

"This is where they stored the bodies."

Down here, the air is a bit thicker. There's a heaviness to the atmosphere, and I'm beginning to understand what my mom was talking about—the leftover energy. It feels different down here. And not in a good way.

"Wow," I say when all else fails me. It's easy to imagine the bodies lined up down here.

"Follow me," Peter says, but my legs don't want to move. I want to get back on the elevator.

A clamor a little farther up catches my attention, followed by a flash of movement and I freeze. *Please don't be a rat or something worse.* Then an employee crawls out of the shadows. I don't want to move, but I also don't want to be too far from Peter down here, so I force my feet to inch towards Peter and the employee. As my eyes adjust to this light, I can see an old mattress stuffed into a dark corner.

Peter's genial demeanor shifts in an instant. "That was supposed to have been removed," he says before turning his attention to the shell-shocked employee. "Next employee that's caught napping down here will be immediately terminated. Do you understand?"

The tired employee nods.

"Make sure everyone knows that!"

The employee quickly runs off.

Peter takes out his phone. "I always forget there's no reception down here. Do you mind if we make a quick pit stop? I want to make sure that mattress is removed."

"Okay."

"It's on the way and I can introduce you to some of our Facilities team."

I force a smile. A wave of dizziness washes over me and I realize that I've been taking small, shallow breaths. The air is stale down here, and I force myself to take a deep inhale. The pungent scent of sour earth sends my stomach into somersaults. A sodium-vapor light flickers up ahead and my heart flutters in response.

"How big is the basement area?" I ask, a weak attempt to dispel the quiet.

"It's very large. The shipping dock unloads to an underground warehouse, so we have some storage areas. Facilities has a few offices down here. Then everything's connected by these tunnels. It's very safe, just don't explore alone 'til you really learn your way around."

"I don't plan on spending much time down here."

"The tunnels can be very confusing. Some lead nowhere. They used to run under the street and connect multiple buildings, but most of those buildings have been torn down and the tunnels closed off."

I have to jog a little to keep up with Peter, he's moving so quickly . . . for which I'm grateful. We take a quick left, followed by a right, and another left—I think.

"Am I going too fast?" Peter yells back to me.

"Nope," I say as my heel catches and I stumble, nearly going down. As I regain my balance, I turn to look for whatever caught my heel. It felt like a trick kids do to each other, but I don't see anything that could have tripped me.

"Sorry," Peter says. "I should've told you to wear your walking shoes."

"I should know better than to wear shoes like this to work." Mom's insistence that heels belong in a workplace hadn't considered a basement tour. The lights flicker then go dark. It's pitch black. "Peter!" I grope at the darkness, searching for something to hang onto. My fingers brush across something soft—Peter's sweater. I grab on. The dark is so absolute that my fingers instinctively tighten into a frenzied clutch, as though this sweater is the only thing that anchors me to the real world. "I'm sorry," I say.

"Did you say something?" His voice is much too far away. Whatever I'm holding onto, it isn't Peter's sweater. Immediately, I let go and swallow as a current of cold, dense air pours down on me. "Peter?"

"Yeah, I'm here," he yells from up ahead.

"Where?" I know someone is right by me and it's not Peter. My scalp tingles like thousands of ants have poured out of the darkness and are working their way through my hair. As I gasp for air, I'm hit with the acrid aroma of old fabric, wet and rotten. Part of me wants to thrash my arms, wildly fighting off whatever is close, but the other part wants to shrink back and hide in the dark.

"Just a little farther up. It's very dark. Hold on."

I freeze. Even my breath becomes shallow. Tears burn.

I'm completely and utterly paralyzed.

Something inches closer.

Chapter 9

The soft glow of a cell phone breaks the darkness. Then the phone's flashlight illuminates the dim walkway. Peter's definitely not close enough to touch. The lights flicker again, then come back on. The tunnel is empty save for Peter and me.

"Old electric. There's a breaker somewhere around here, but I think we're good."

How could he have moved away from me that quickly? But . . . he's not wearing a sweater. I take a deep breath, searching for an explanation. Maybe I somehow grabbed my own jacket. Maybe something soft on the wall. Maybe I was just scared and imagined the whole thing. Nevertheless, the memory of this touch has turned into a horde of tiny spiders digging into my flesh. I try to brush the itchiness off, but it's under the skin.

He takes off again and I stay close. I'm definitely breaking personal space boundaries, but I don't care. We take another left and come to a door. Peter does a quick double-tap, then opens it.

"Hey, Pete. Didn't expect to see you down here today. Everything alright?" A bald, pasty, middle-aged man stands on the other side of the door, looking directly at me before working his way over to the only desk in the space, coffee mug in hand.

"All good, I'm giving our new V.P. of Marketing a full property tour. This is Ms. Umbra—"

"Lilly," I interrupt and smile. There's a large bottle of hand sanitizer resting on a shelf, and I grab a couple of quick pumps.

"Lilly," Peter says, correcting himself. "This is Billy, Joel, and Antonio."

Harsh light illuminates every scratch and nick in the old linoleum and cheap furniture. Joel sits behind a large computer on the fiberboard and Formica desk, while Billy and Antonio lounge at a faded oak table, Billy's feet resting on top of it. Each has a large mug in front of them, filling the office with the bitter aroma of strong coffee. Antonio nudges Billy to get his feet off the table, tosses a nut into the air, catches it in his mouth, and grins playfully at me.

"Billy. Joel." I smile, but they just look at me. "Like the singer," I say, the joke falling flat.

"Who?" Billy asks.

"Never mind. It's nice to meet you," I reply.

"We're kidding. That's a bit of a running joke down here. Welcome to the cave," Joel says. They're all wearing plain, solid blue uniforms. They're also all unnaturally pasty. Even Antonio's Mediterranean skin seems lighter than it should be.

Smiling and making a mental note to be more original in my jokes, a sprinkle of relief dissipates a bit of the pressure that's been steadily building on this tour. Not so much because they're joking around with me, more because I'm around people and light. It's not just me and my imagination.

"We're having some electrical issues down here today, but I replaced the breaker for this area so that should help," Billy says as he tries to smooth his thatch of frizzy blonde hair.

"We also saw the mattress down here," Peter says, "with someone napping. I thought that was supposed to have been taken out."

"I took it out myself last week," Antonio says.

"It's back," Peter tells them.

"We'll get it out today," Joel says.

"Thanks, can you also send out a memo from Facilities to every department that if anyone is seen napping or relaxing on that mattress or any mattress they will be immediately terminated?"

"No problem," Joel says.

Peter smiles at me. "Ready?"

I nod. "It was very nice to meet you all."

"You too, Lilly," Joel says. "If you need anything at all, give us a call. This office is extension 4444. Easy to remember."

"Thank you."

Joel smiles. "How do you like your office? We got it done last week."

I smile. "It's beautiful. Thank you so much. The nicest office I've ever had, or even been in."

"We aim to please. Need anything, you know where to find us," Joel says.

I follow Peter back out. A shiver of cold air prickles my skin as we make our way through the dark hall.

Peter points to a large ramp. "This goes up to street level, it's where our main deliveries come in and out. That's where they brought the bodies out when this was a hospital. There's a picture in storage of bodies lined up right here, waiting to be taken out, draped with American flags."

"Where are photos or other things from that time stored?" I imagine all the bodies lined up, head to foot, blanketed in red, white, and blue. The fear I felt before is still there, but beginning to grow into curiosity. I've never worked at a property with such an important history. I use that curiosity to tamp down my nerves and remind myself there's nothing here that can hurt me.

"I'll point it out to you," Peter says as we take a left turn.

"Is it archived or preserved?"

"No, it's just locked in a closet. Though now you mention it, preservation might be a good idea at some point."

I add another note to my growing list as we come to another bank of elevators. Peter pushes the call button and the door slides open. We step in and Peter pushes the button for the thirteenth floor. As the elevator rises, the heaviness of the basement's atmosphere abates, and a sense of relief pours over me. I take a deep breath; even the air already seems fresher.

"What's our next stop?" I ask.

"This is the last part of our tour. The theater and a few meeting rooms are on the thirteenth floor, then I can point out the storage closest, and then we'll go back to your office."

"So, we're back in the original tower?"

"Yes," Peter says as the doors slide open. "This is the top floor of the Atlantic Tower. This is where the surgeries were done while it was the hospital. Though it hasn't been used for anything in at least five, maybe even ten years."

"Has anyone ever suggested changing it from the thirteenth floor to the fourteenth? Most, not all, but most of the casinos I worked at in Vegas skipped the thirteenth floor."

"No. This is historic. It has always been the thirteenth floor and will remain that. Besides there's no rooms on this floor, so there's not really a need to consider changing it."

"Makes sense. I was just curious."

The elevator bounces to a stop.

I follow Peter onto a floor that looks like all the others I've seen. There's the same marble and tan carpeting that's in the Palace Tower. Though instead of hotel room doors, there's more elaborate cream, wood double-doors that I assume lead to different meeting rooms. Three sets of doors line the south side of the hall, facing a plain wall covered in an art-deco, geometric-patterned cream and gold wallpaper. The east and west sides of the hall are anchored by a single set of double doors.

"Looks nice," I say.

Peter turns towards the eastern set of doors. "This is the theater. It's original. Amon recently restored it and renovated the entire floor. It's my favorite room in this whole place," he says as he turns his key and pushes the door open.

"Wow," I say as we step inside. "It's beautiful."

A heavy red curtain drapes its way across the stage. Intricate pilaster designs dance up the walls and across a framework of columns. The cream walls are gilded with gold accents. I almost expect Josephine Baker to step out from behind the curtains.

Mosaic tiles in black, white, and gold swirl along the floor and pull me towards the stage. Antique, dark-wood folding theater chairs form the rows. Where the aisle meets the stage, the tiling culminates in a design made to look like a sun, formed from the black mosaic tiles. It looks familiar but I can't place it—a simple circle with a pattern of extending geometric rays.

"Is this original?" I ask.

"As far as we can tell. The flooring was in bad shape, so Amon brought in a restoration expert from New York to help us get as close to the original design as possible."

"It's incredible. I hope Amon plans to take advantage of this space."

"I'm sure he does. Would you like to see any of the other spaces on this floor?"

"A quick peek," I say as I follow him out.

Peter pulls the theater door shut behind me. He unlocks the first set of doors along the hall. "Each room is the same size and there is a removable wall to make the space bigger."

"Nice." Fresh floral carpet and newly painted walls tell me the space was recently updated.

I follow Peter to the opposite end of the hall. "Now this one is much more interesting," he says as he opens the door.

The same new carpet and fresh paint extend into this room. Huge windows run along each side of the space, framed by intricate pilaster designs and navy satin curtains that fall from the high ceiling. Tucked up in the vaulted ceiling is a set of catwalks.

"There's a large deck outside," Peter says as he leads me to a door at the opposite end of this room.

The deck looks south over all Atlantic City, the back bays, and the ocean.

"Is there plumbing in here?" I ask.

"Yes, but not for a full kitchen, if that's what you're thinking."

"No, I was thinking more of a pre/post-theater bar or club."

"Then, yes, this space could definitely be turned into a bar."

"I love it."

"So does Mr. Asra. The last area I'd like to show you can only be reached by stairs. Is that okay?"

"Sure."

Peter leads back down the hall towards the theater and to a small door tucked back near the elevator bank. "Make sure you hold on to the railing. This is an old stairwell and lots of people have taken tumbles here."

"Okay," I say, though the stairwell doesn't look old. Its uniform painted concrete has been kept up, and the stairs are an even height.

Halfway down, Peter lurches forward, stumbles, and catches himself on the railing.

"Are you alright?" I ask as I grip the railing even tighter and briefly consider taking these ridiculous heels off. Though, I suppose I should keep up appearances, at least for the first day.

"Fine. Told you, these steps are tricky."

We stop at a door and Peter uses his key card to scan us in. "This is the twelve-and-a-half floor." Peter opens the door and holds it for me to follow.

"What in the world is this?" The floor is small, about half the size of a regular floor. There're six small rooms, a bathroom, and an open area. Each room has a miniature picket fence that extends from the room and encloses a small area of artificial turf. Only one door is closed.

"During the twenties and thirties, when this was a hotel, there were staff that lived here. This was their quarters." Peter walks me to the middle room. The door is open, but the space is empty. There's a small window on the back wall, a small sink, and a tiny closet. "This was Miss Bernie's room. She lived here until she died in the 1970s. I didn't know her, but I've heard some stories."

I can't help but laugh. "This might be the craziest thing I've ever seen at a casino. What are these other rooms used for?"

"The unions use them as supply closets. Electricians have one, carpenters have one. And this room is where all the historic artifacts are stored."

"I'd love to look in there."

"Sorry, I don't have access."

"I have a master key, maybe mine works."

"You should wait for Mr. Asra. He plans on having an expert archive everything and wants to keep it protected till—"

"I'll be careful." I take out my master key and try it in the lock. It unlocks.

"Ms. Umbr–Lilly, please. Don't go in," Peter begs.

"It's fine. I won't break anything." I push open the door.

"Mr. Asra won't be happy."

I hear Peter, though I can't imagine Amon will get mad. My curiosity is riding so high, I almost can't stop myself. I'm drawn to this room, the true story of this property. It's so different from the casinos I'm used to. This story, this history is what sets The Golden Sands apart and it will be essential to our marketing plan moving forward. I have to see what's in here and I cross the threshold.

The room is a mess. Stacks and stacks of papers are piled every-where. I pick up a piece of heavy cream paper from the nearest pile. It's a menu from the Haddon Hall Café dated summer 1927. My mind races with ideas. Maybe we can have Gatsby-themed player parties and recreate some of these historic menus. Casino gamblers love a good, themed party and it doesn't get more authentic than this. I move a little deeper and pick up a brochure from 1929. A picture of ladies walking out of the Haddon Hall in bathing dresses, advertising direct access to the beach under the Boardwalk.

A door slams, and I spin to see the one to this room is shut.

I try the handle. Locked. "Peter!" I yell and try the handle again—definitely locked. "Peter! Can you open the door?"

Nothing. When I try the handle again and again, it won't budge. The cauldron of panic boils in the pit of my stomach.

I force myself to cool it down. My panic has led nowhere, each time evaporating into nothing. I'm in control. I take a deep breath. I'm locked in a closet. That's it. No big deal. What's the worst that could happen?

"Peter?"

There's no response.

Chapter 10

There's no signal here so I tuck my phone back in my pocket.

Peter wouldn't leave me . . . I'm pretty sure. So, I settle in and look around the small room. Papers are piled haphazardly on the shelves. There's so much crammed in here. A metal briefcase catches my eye, and I slide it off the shelf and click it open. Inside is another case made of clear acrylic, and resting in this case is a mottled brown metal weapon. It looks like a knife without a handle or possibly the tip of a spear. It's sharp and pointed at one end then weaves wider, supported by a round cylinder that runs up the center. I guess that's where the knife handle or shaft went. The metal looks aged, old, but the wrapping in the center is brilliant gold.

A loud click sounds from behind me with startling volume, and I close the case, sliding it back onto the shelf. I spin to see the door opening behind me. Amon enters. He looks at me then looks at his watch. "8:15 a.m. and already you're getting locked in closets." He turns around. "Thank you, Peter, I've got it from here."

When I look behind Amon, the color has drained from Peter's face. Though at least twenty years Amon's senior, Peter cowers in his presence. "Thank you, Mr. Asra. It was nice to meet you, Lilly. You know where to find me if you need anything."

"Thank you so much. It was very nice to meet you, and the tour was incredibly helpful," I say to Peter. He flashes an uncomfortable smile then scurries to the stairwell and disappears. As soon as the stairwell door closes, I look at Amon. "I'm sorry. Peter told me not to come in here."

"Don't be silly. Your key gets access for a reason. You can spend as much time here as you please." Amon moves deeper into the room.

"Don't let go of the door, we'll both get locked in here."

Amon smiles and takes a few steps closer to me. The door stays open. "Did you think you were locked in here?"

"I was. Didn't Peter call you to come get me out?"

"No." Amon shakes his head and grins. "I would've liked to have been the person to show you this room first, but it seems your curiosity got you here instead."

The door slams shut, and I jump.

Amon laughs. "This is my favorite room in the entire property. There's treasure in here." He pauses and raises an eyebrow. "Well, I think it's treasure."

I expect Amon to grab the silver case I had been examining, but instead he spins and pulls a piece of paper off the nearest shelf. "This is an actual menu from the 1920s. An actual menu that was printed almost a hundred years ago. They saved it. They saved so much of this stuff."

"It's incredible!" Somehow, all awkwardness drains from the room. We're back to business. "I think we should do a series of Gatsby or Roaring 20s-themed player events. We can recreate some of these menus. And, I saw a few brochures, we can do a social campaign where we recreate some of the original pictures."

"I love that."

"What do you think about incorporating some of the history into our rebranding?"

"That's exactly what I was thinking, and we will get to that, but I should probably tell you about this room before you get locked in again." Amon winks at me.

"What?"

"When I took over, this was basically a forgotten junk room. Everything still needs to be properly archived, but I've stepped up security until we can get to that. There's a camera, not tied into the property's surveillance. A little personal security." Amon points up to a small camera in the corner of the room. "You and I are the only people that have access to this room, and the door does automatically lock and seems to have a tendency to close on its own but let me show you how to unlock it from the inside." Amon slides a stack of files out of the way and reveals a button on the wall. "Push that button." I do and hear the door click. "I like to keep it a little hidden. In case someone wanders in." He opens the door and holds it for me, motioning for me to join him.

"What's in the silver case?" I ask as we walk out.

"An ancient Roman spear tip."

"Was that here when you bought the place?"

"No." Amon smiles. "I'm an art and artifact collector and wanted to keep it safe in here, 'til my apartment was finished."

"Your apartment here, in Golden Sands?"

"Yes."

"Is it finished?"

"It just got finished." Amon holds the door to the stairwell for me. "What did you think of the tour?"

"It was fantasti–" I trip walking up the steps and try to catch myself on the railing but miss. Amon manages to wrap his arms around my waist and keeps me from bruising my knees on the concrete.

"These steps are tricky," he says.

My cheeks feel as if they could singe paper so I don't turn around. "Yes, Peter warned me."

"So?"

"Oh, um, well, what was . . . ?"

"The tour," Amon prompts as he helps steady me on my feet.

We continue. "Oh, right. I was going to say that this is unlike any casino in the world. Its history, I mean. I think we should use that. But, and there's a big but, a lot needs to change."

"I'm not sure I like the sound of that," Amon says as he opens the door to the thirteenth floor.

I lead us out of the stairwell, into the elevator bank, and hit the call button. I catch a reflection of myself in the mirrored hall. For a fleeting moment, it seemed as if the reflection was someone else looking at me, appraising me. I follow its eyes as they shift to the side, but only see Amon.

"Why don't we continue this talk in your office? You can fill me in on the big 'but.'"

I shake off the odd experience, tell myself it was a sort of déjà vu, and face him. "It's not as bad as it sounds. It's actually good news when you think about it. Considering how abysmal the casino has been doing for the past six months."

The elevator arrives and we step in. I scan my card, and the eighth-floor indicator lights up. It's good to have some kind of purpose, a direction to head towards again. Makes it easier to step over those uneasy feelings that have tripped me up. The panic I felt in the casino and basement already seems far away, as if somewhere between the basement tunnels and standing here with Amon, a reset button in my brain was pushed. Maybe my parents were right. Maybe work is what I need.

"I'm confused," Amon says as the elevator drops.

"I'm saying there's a clear reason why the casino is doing so badly. That means we know what we need to fix."

"You think it's that easy?"

"I didn't say easy."

The elevator doors slide open, and we step off. Jordan notices us and presses a button to open the office door. He stands to greet us, picks up a file, and walks out from behind his desk.

"How was the tour?" Jordan asks.

"Very informative," I reply.

"Great. Here is the press file you asked for." Jordan hands me the file.

"Thanks. Have any press releases gone out regarding the new ownership, renovations, anything like that?"

"No," Amon says. "We've made no official announcements."

"We need a press release out today to generate some buzz."

"Would you like me to draft the release?" Jordan asks.

"That would be great," I tell him. "Mention new ownership, new executives, new marketing department, and—do you have a dollar amount in renovations that have been done so far?"

"Close to twenty million," Amon says.

"Definitely include that," I say.

"No problem." Jordan sits back at his desk.

Amon follows me to my office. I still can't believe that this is my office, and a strange thought pops into my mind . . . that ancient spear would look nice on the shelves behind my desk. That wouldn't be possible, though. After all, it belongs to Amon. It isn't part of the hotel's history. I sit at my desk and Amon sits across from me.

"Thank you so much for this office and the car." I pause and smile at Amon.

Amon smiles back. "I told you the first time I met you, you're my secret weapon. Of course, I need to take care of you."

"I will do my absolute best." I smile, a big toothy grin, I can't help it. "But we have a lot to get through." I pull my phone out and find a text message from Tori. I tap it open.

Tori: The university invited me out early to begin my research paper. Is it okay if I come out earlier than planned?

Quickly, I reply: Of course.

Then I open my notes from the tour.

"Everything okay?" Amon asks.

"Yeah." I push the button on my desk to raise the computer monitor. "My friend's coming to live with me this summer."

Amon's eyebrows momentarily knit together then smooth. "Nice. When is he coming?"

My phone vibrates with another message.

Tori: I booked my flight. See you Friday!! Thank you so much!!!!! <3

"She. And Friday."

"Oh."

"Don't worry, she won't be a distraction. She'll be busy working on a research project at Princeton."

"I wasn't worried." Amon smiles. "So?"

"So?" I ask, not sure what else he wants to know about Tori.

"The tour. Where do you want to start?"

"Oh, right, sorry." Tori has already been a distraction I refocus. "First and foremost, Golden Sands needs player development hosts, a new loyalty program, and casino promotions to start as soon as possible."

"The new marketing team starts today," Amon says. "I have a dinner meeting scheduled for you to meet them tomorrow. Does that work?"

"That's perfect. Do you have any information on them? Are they bringing players' lists with them? Where are they from?"

"Yes, hold on one second." Amon moves to the filing cabinet at the side of the room, rummages through a drawer there then returns with a file in hand. "Here are all of their resumes."

"I read that the last marketing team left because they all got some weird illness?"

"That was before I took over, but I heard they wanted out of their contract so they could move to another casino in town. I assume the illness was 'wanting-to-leave-itis'."

I nod. "Next." I look at my list. "The casino bar needs to be renovated, and that carpet needs to go."

"That should be completed by tonight."

"I love a to-do list that's to-done."

"Makes two of us."

"Next, the casino layout needs some tweaking. The penny slots have prime placement; you should have the dollar slots there or at the very least a mix of dollar and quarter-slots. Who is the casino manager?"

"His name is Guy Durand. He's coming in with the new marketing team. The team sent me a proposal for the casino floor plan and new loyalty club." Amon pulls out his phone and opens an email. "They'd like to call it the Atlas Club. The levels are the ocean, the palace, and the sanctuary."

"I like that. It's easy to work with. What about entertainment? On the tour, I thought the thirteenth floor would be perfect for a long-running show and you can turn that large meeting room into a pre/post-show club."

"I have a show coming in this week. Do you really think that room can be turned into a bar or club? I love that idea."

"Definitely, I already checked with Peter. You can't do a full restaurant there, but a bar is no problem."

"Amazing. Done."

"With a bar and theater, I think we should lean into the fact that Golden Sands actually has a thirteenth floor and market a full experience around that."

"That's possibly one of the best ideas. Ever. Love it."

"What show?"

"It's called Li-RV. It's been in New York for a few months. Impossible to get a ticket. I honestly can't believe they agreed to come here."

"Perfect. With those essentials underway, we should consider doing a grand re-opening celebration and plan a media day."

"Yes, definitely. I want to do that as soon as possible." Amon's eyes widen and I can sense his excitement. He's keeping it in check, but it's definitely there.

"How soon?"

"This weekend."

"That's not possible. We don't have media contacts. But even if we did, they need at least a few weeks' notice. We could never get them here that soon."

Amon steeples his fingers, resting his chin on them. Rocks slightly in his chair and lets out a deep exhale through his nose. "Say we could, what do you think a media day should include?"

"I think we should do this as if we're a brand-new casino. We'll invite them to stay overnight. The day will begin with a big press conference followed by a property tour, dinner, and the show."

"Perfect. Let's do it. We'll invite them this weekend."

"I . . . I don't think that's even in the realm of possibility. We're not ready. Have you seen the casino?"

"It'll be done by Thursday, the latest." Amon slaps the desk with his palm, smiles at me and stands. "I'll let you get to work then. I have a club to design."

"I'm not sure we will be able to get many press to commit with such short notice."

"I have faith in you," Amon says over his shoulder.

As he leaves, Jordan comes around the corner and almost bumps Amon before he walks into my office. "Here is the press release. I also put a copy into the drive."

"Thank you." I take the paper, and Jordan takes a seat as I read. "This is fantastic, much better than I could've done. Are you a writer?"

"Actually, I am."

"I can tell. I bet we see this release show up word for word."

Jordan's lips start to turn up at the corners, like he's going to smile but then stands and smooths his starched pants. "Do you need anything else right now?"

"No. I'm going to start reaching out and introducing myself to some of the local press."

"You know where to find me if you need anything."

I upload the press release to the Newswire, our distribution network. I target every journalist in the tristate area—New York, Pennsylvania, and New Jersey, then I added a few more nearby states, Connecticut, Delaware, I keep going . . . there's so many on the East Coast. After a brief geography lesson, I hit send, and the press release instantly hits the inboxes of thousands of media contacts.

The Jura coffee maker on the marble counter in my office catches my eye. Caffeine would be good right now. When I grab the matte-black porcelain mug, I notice the glass dropper with the herbal concoction mom made sitting on a silver tray next to a crystal water pitcher and glass.

"Jordan," I call, barely loud enough for him to hear me.

"Yes?" He pops his head through the door almost instantly.

"Can you show me how to use this coffee maker?"

"Sure." He walks in and pushes a button on top. "This button wakes it up. Then use this button to choose your coffee." He points to another button, and I choose plain coffee, strong. The machine kicks into action.

"Is this water fresh?"

"I just put it out."

"Did you put that dropper there?"

"Yes. Charlotte brought it up while you were on your tour. She said your mother dropped it off for you. She told her to ask me to give it to you along with some water."

"Thank you," I say, sending Jordan back to his post.

The coffee maker steams the last bit of coffee into my mug, and I deeply inhale the warm caramel aroma. While I look forward to the boost of energy this cup will bring, there's something soothing and calming to this ritual.

I open the press file. Jordan has the contacts organized by region. Zeroing in on the local press, the name Charles Sharp bubbles to the surface. After a quick Google search, I know I've found my guy. He has his finger in everything local; everything related to casinos, dining, and entertainment in general. Even has a successful nationwide podcast. I pick up the office phone and dial his number, but it goes to voicemail. Without leaving a message, I hang up and grab my cell phone intending to leave a voicemail from this phone instead and dial the same number.

"This is Sharp."

"Hi Charles, my name—"

"No one calls me Charles. It's Chuck, Chuckie, or Sharp."

"Alright Sharp, my name is Lilith Umbra, call me Lilly. I'm the new Senior V.P. of Marketing at the Golden Sands."

"You have a Vegas number."

"I recently relocated from Las Vegas to Atlantic City."

"I heard the Golden Sands sold, but wasn't sure if that was true. For all I care, the place could burn down. I don't even think Atlantic City would notice."

"That's harsh."

"The place is old and run down."

"Was run down."

"You mean someone actually invested money there?"

"Yes, over twenty-million in renovations have already been completed."

"No shit. Why?"

"It's an incredible property. It's unique. The history is amazing."

"Yeah, it has history alright."

"So you're familiar with the property? How it was built in the 1920s then turned into a hospital during World War II?"

"That's not what I was referring to. How long have you been there?"

"Today is my first day."

"Oh." Sharp goes quiet.

"Reconnecting with the press is my number one priority," I say, standing and moving towards the window. I wait a beat, hoping Sharp replies. When he doesn't, I go on. "That's why I called you personally. I wanted to introduce myself and tell you a little about all of the exciting changes we've made, and wanted to invite you here to see some of them." Through the window, Atlantic City's sprawling beaches and rows of casinos stretch out before me—a view I'm starting to think will never get old.

"I won't set foot in there," Sharp says, pulling me back to our conversation.

While taken aback, I plunge ahead as if this is a normal conversation, steamrolling any hesitation. "If someone offended you in the past, I apologize and want you to know that we have a new owner, new executives, new marketing staff—"

"No, that's not it."

I let a moment of quiet settle on the line. "Whatever the issue is, I will do my best to correct it."

Now there's a pause on the other end of the line. "Uh." Sharp lets out a breath. "I have a few meetings in the city tomorrow. There's a Starbucks in the Hard Rock. I'll be there at ten and have about thirty minutes before my meeting. Can you meet me then?"

"I'd love to."

"See you soon."

"Than–"

Sharp hangs up.

His bio is still up on my computer. I hit 'Images' and at least a thousand pictures open. Charles Sharp is a common name. Scrolling through the search, I click on 'C-Sharp Flat Out—All Things Casino, Food, Music, and Nightlife Podcast.' In the photo, Charles Sharp sits behind a microphone, he's looking off to the side and has a big, crooked grin, like he just said something funny to someone. His sandy-blonde hair sticks out from under a flat cap. I like him. He has one of those smiles you know is authentic. Clicking out of the podcast site, I scroll some more. All the pictures of Charles are candid shots. Nothing staged.

Sharp's blog is packed with posts. Overstuffed, even. After a few minutes of reading, it's easy to see why he has such a following. He has a way of making the reader feel like he's talking to them. Sharp is clever and witty, the vibe of someone you want on your side. A casino in Philadelphia must've done something that made him seriously mad, and he held nothing back. The comments under that particular article are equally scathing.

A quick knock on my door diverts my attention and I notice the sun has gone down.

"Hey," Amon says from my doorway. "I'm leaving, I have a late meeting, off-property. You should go home and get some rest."

"I didn't realize how late it was."

"Jordan's ready to leave too, but he'll wait for you."

"Okay, I'll wrap up what I'm doing."

Amon spins to leave, then turns back. "Are you having dinner with your mom?"

"No. She went back to New York."

"Are you alone tonight?"

"Yeah." I close my computer and gather my things.

"I can cancel my meeting. You want to grab dinner?"

"No, honestly, I'm fine. I'm looking forward to a quiet night." I feign a small yawn.

"You must be exhausted."

"I am."

"Alright, I'll see you tomorrow. Come in a little later though, okay?"

I nod. As soon as he's gone, I quickly leave. Partly because I don't want to hold up Jordan, but more because I want to drive my new car.

I climb into the driver's seat. The smell of new leather and wood is invigorating and I take a nice big breath then hit the ignition. I've always liked to go fast. In control, but fast. The car comes alive beneath me, the power of the engine begging for release. It purrs as I pull out of Golden Sands. A sense of satisfaction stirs in my chest. Not so much because of the car, but more with the realization that this is the first time I've craved excitement since I lost him. I still miss him, but maybe this is a sign I'm ready to get back up to speed again.

Unfortunately, this will have to wait. The speed limit on the island doesn't go over thirty-five and there's a light on practically every block from Golden Sands to my apartment. My shoulders sink a little. The little red Mercedes may be more of a Vegas car, made for highways, though I imagine there must be some fun roads to explore winding through the pine barrens. The urge is too much, and as the light turns green, I stomp on the gas. The car shoots forward. Out of nowhere, Buddy runs into the street. I brake hard, saving him—and me—from an awful collision.

Buddy stares at me for a moment, puts his finger over his lips—shhhh—then sprints into St. Nicholas' Church. My hands shake on the wheel as I sit there for a moment, watching him. The church looks dark; it must be locked. Buddy ducks into the alcove and taps on the door. It cracks open barely enough for him to dip inside. A car horn blares behind me, yanking me back to reality. As I make my way home, I can't stop wondering what Buddy was doing in a locked church at night.

Do churches around here let homeless people sleep inside?

Yesterday's weather was a beautiful tease, only making today's more depressing. Everything seems the same shade of gray. The encroaching chill tells me to stay in bed. I stretch, leg muscles scolding me for all the walking I did yesterday.

I take my time getting ready. Amon said to come in later, so that's exactly what I plan to do. Except for the sound of my coffee steaming, my apartment is silent.

Sipping my coffee as I look out my large bay window at the boardwalk and beach has become my new morning ritual. Few people are on the boardwalk this morning. The young woman and hairless cat are out with the stroller again. She appears to relish the stares and gasps when others notice what she's pushing. She wears skin-tight black leggings and a thermal shirt, strutting and smirking every time she gets a reaction. Weird.

By the time I arrive at work, I only have about forty minutes till my meeting with Sharp. Rather than go up to my office and attempt to conquer the mountain of work I have waiting, I opt to take my time walking next door to the Hard Rock.

With a few moments to spare, I linger in my car and text Tori.

So glad you're coming out this week! Need me to grab anything for you?

Dropping my phone in my purse, I make my way through the valet towards the boardwalk ramp.

A cold wind blows through the porte cochère sending a shiver through me. Tucking my hands into my pockets, a vibration shakes my purse. I dig my phone out. It's a text message from Tori.

> Tori: My plans changed. I'm going to Princeton tomorrow. I will be there for a few days. Can I come to you on Thur?

What's one day? Of course, I text back as I make my way towards the boardwalk, bumping right into someone.

"I'm so sorry," I say, stuffing my phone into my purse. I look up with an apologetic frown. It's Amon.

"Has no one ever told you how dangerous it is to text and walk?" His smile is wide, a little cheeky.

"Bad habit, I know. What are you doing out here?"

"I went for a walk. Where are you headed?"

"I'm running next door to meet a local press guy."

"That was fast. Who?"

"Charles Sharp."

"Oh," Amon says through a tightened brow.

"Do you know him?"

"Not personally. I've just heard he can be difficult, but he is influential."

"We could really use some of that influence."

"Want me to drive you there?"

"I wanted to walk."

"It's cold. Do you have a coat?"

"No. It was so nice the other day, I didn't expect it to be cold."

"Welcome to a Jersey Shore spring. Here, take my scarf." Amon drapes his black cashmere scarf around my neck.

"Thanks." I smile and double the scarf.

"Let me know how it goes."

I climb up the ramp to the boardwalk, mentally skimming through everything that still needs to be done . . . and dig my phone back out and text Amon.

> Me: I forgot to mention that we need to bring in some retail. Empty halls look bad. Charlotte also said that we really need a gift shop with some basic necessities.

He responds immediately.

> Amon: I have a gift shop, women's fashion boutique, and a grab and go coffee shop opening later this week. I have one more retail spot to fill. Any ideas?

> Me: What about a wine and liquor shop? They're pretty standard in casinos.

Done, Amon texts, as I trip on an uneven board.

Also, don't text and walk, he quickly adds and I can't help but chuckle at the impeccable timing of that last message. A thought crosses my mind and I glance back at Golden Sands to see if he's watching me from somewhere, but I don't see him.

While the temperature is in the fifties, the ocean offers the sort of cold that hits hard. There's a density to the chill that gets under your skin. Glad I have this scarf, I pull it up around my chin, inhaling Amon's scent as it weaves into the salt air.

It takes less than five minutes to get to the Hard Rock, right across from Steel Pier. This is the first time I've seen the rides and carnival games during the day. A ping of unease twists around my neck. There's something eerie about empty amusement parks. The pier extends hundreds of feet over the ocean, empty rides standing guard. The view from those rides must be incredible.

As I push my way through the revolving door and into the Hard Rock, I loosen the scarf, so it drapes over my shoulders. Following the signs to Starbucks, I manage to walk in right behind Sharp.

"Hey Sharp," the barista greets him. "The usual?"

"Yes sir."

"Four twenty-five," the barista says.

"It's my treat today," I say from behind.

"You must be Lilly," Sharp says, turning to face me. "That's not necessary."

"I'm happy to. You're the one taking time out to meet with me."

"Well, thank you, then," Sharp says.

"Can you add a Grande house brew, black to that please?"

"Seven ninety-nine," the barista says as he fills my cup.

Sharp grabs his drink and leads me to a table towards the back of the coffee shop.

"Thanks again for meeting, Charl—Sharp," I say as we sit. "It's so nice to meet you."

"Nice to meet you too, though I'm afraid you're not going to like what I have to tell you."

"I'm well aware of some of the past mistakes previous owners have made, but we are changing all of that."

"It's not . . . I . . . I'm not someone that's inclined to believe in these sorts of things. But it's undeniable."

"What?"

"Golden Sands has a very dark past."

"If you're referring to the time it was the surgical hospital during World War Two, that's not dark, that's heroic. It's a very interesting part of Atlantic City's history that's not talked about enough."

Sharp lets out a huff of frustration. "Stop with the positive PR spin. You need to just listen to me. Okay? I'll start from the beginning."

I nod.

"Did you know this hospital came in and out of existence in basically five years, and during that short time it became the largest hospital in the U.S.?"

"I knew that it was a major hospital."

"The hospital housed psychiatric patients in one tower, neurological—including paraplegics, and amputees. Those early years were horrific."

"I can imagine." I sip my coffee, but it's so hot it burns my tongue. My eyes water as I fight the urge to spit the brew back in the cup.

"They tried to boost morale," Sharp continues. "Awarded over nine hundred Purple Hearts there and had staff that was solely focused on improving the living conditions. But imagine the mental state of these men that had been so badly injured storming the beaches of Normandy, their lives changed forever and now stuck in Atlantic City."

"It's sad, but it's a part of history. I toured the property yesterday and I was in the basement morgue."

"Wrong. The morgue was on the twelfth floor. Bodies were stored in the basement because it was cooler until they could be taken out."

"Oh."

"But that's not even what I'm talking about. Bad things happen there. Again and again."

I look down at my coffee, not sure how to respond. I wasn't expecting this. "I'm not sure I follow."

"In September of 1944, the worst hurricane in Atlantic City's history hit the island. The Great Atlantic Hurricane, while the hospital was at its busiest. They had to evacuate whatever patients they could. There was no power. The hotel was flooded. People died."

"I didn't know that."

"It destroyed so much. The hospital had a limbs unit where they built prosthetic limbs that were all ruined."

"Wow. It's amazing the building survived, at all."

"You're missing the point. They also ran a streptomycin experimental program, which I haven't been able to find that much information on, but you can put two and two together."

"Antibiotics are a good thing."

"Testing drugs of any kind on human beings, especially injured vets, is not a good thing."

I stifle a shiver. "I think you're taking too dark of a view. Maybe it saved their lives."

"That's just the beginning. Throughout the years more accidents, deaths, and tragedies have happened there than in any other property in Atlantic City."

"It's a casino. Accidents happen."

"There have been more suicides than—"

I can't help but think about the tour yesterday and my hands begin to itch. I wring them out, forcing myself to power ahead. "It's been open the longest—"

"I adjusted my numbers based on property age. Whether you believe me or not, there's something going on there."

Where is this coming from? "We're improving the structure. We've renovated almost the entire property. I will ensure that safety is a top priority."

Sharp rolls his eyes and drops his head in frustration, then looks directly at me. "You're missing the point. Golden Sands is cursed. I wish I could put it another way, so you'd understand. I know it sounds crazy, but it's true. I've been covering the property for almost two decades. Bad things happen there."

Now it's my turn to drop my head in frustration. "Look, Sharp, I'm not a particularly religious person and I certainly don't believe in hoodoo magic or curses, specially in business. I was hoping to build a good relationship with you as our local press aficionado, but if that's the sort of stuff you lean into, I'm not sure we'll ever see eye to eye," I say, standing. "Thanks for meeting with me. I appreciate your time."

Sharp grabs my arm and pulls me down. "I'm coming off crazy. I know. Believe me, I realize this sounds completely insane. But, like I said, bad things happen there. I've kept track of every one of them. I'll send you the files."

"Please do . . . wait . . . No. . . . No thanks. We are starting over. I can't speak to, control, or change how the property was run before. All I can do, is tell you things are different now."

Sharp lets out a breath then leans in close and whispers, "I signed a confidentiality agreement. I could get in big trouble for telling you this. But the marketing department all got very ill. No one knows what it was. Two of them almost died, and not one of them is anywhere close to back to normal."

"I heard that was a scheme for them to get out of their contracts."

"If that were the case, they'd be working now. None of them are."

"Then why was the story so thoroughly squashed?"

"How did you hear about it?"

"Some cryptic Facebook post from a fake account. Which doesn't lend much credibility to your story. Was that you?"

Sharp shakes his head. The frustration is clear on his face. Genuine. "This conversation is not going in the right direction."

"I'm not sure it's going in any direction. Any sane direction, at least." I stand again, ready to leave, but something besides his hand holds me in place. I need Golden Sands to succeed. Sharp doesn't seem like the crazy type, although everything he's said certainly points to that. He removes his hand and motions for me to sit again. I do.

"How much do you know about the Asras' background?"

I shrug. "My parents have known them for decades. Amon has had a very successful banking career and he's highly educated."

"They have ties to some very dark organizations. Did you know they purchased a castle owned by Nazis and turned it into a school?"

"In Germany? Yes, but I'm not sure what's wrong with taking back and preserving history. They use it to educate future generations so that mistakes from the past aren't repeated. That's an honorable thing."

"The castle was used for occult ceremonies."

"I'm not sure where you're going with this."

"There's a link there, I just haven't found it."

"They're Egyptian. Are you trying to say they're linked to Nazis?"

"No. Forget I said it. I . . . I . . . ." Sharp pauses.

"You realize how this sounds, right?"

"Yes. Yes. I do. Believe me, I do. That's what's so frustrating. I don't believe in ghosts, but I was pushed down a flight of steps. Thrown like a fuc–" He stops himself from swearing. Rubs his temple. "I know without a doubt, the building is cursed or haunted or whatever you want to call it. No one in their right mind would buy it unless they had dark intentions."

"Are you playing a joke on me because I'm the new girl?"

"I swear to you that this is not a joke. You need to know this."

His eyes look haunted, wide, full of fear. Sharp truly believes what he's saying. "Have you ever spoken to someone? A psychiatrist?" I try to keep as sympathetic an expression as I can.

"I'm not crazy. I know how ridiculous this sounds. Listen, I'll make a deal with you."

"What?"

"If you keep this conversation between me and you, just until I put the pieces together, I'll give the Golden Sands a ton of great press."

"Oh." Is it wrong of me to make a deal with someone that is clearly delusional? Then again, he's a creative type; maybe he's prone to conspiracy theories.

"You also have to share any information you come across openly with me, I don't mean business secrets or anything like that, just anything that doesn't seem right."

"I don't know." I turn gaze into my coffee cup. I've never been in a situation even remotely close to this. I've worked with the press for my entire career, and I've dealt with some unique personalities, but this is on a whole other level. "If the Golden Sands is so dangerous, why are you willing to send people there with your good press?"

"Frankly, it's a means to an end. I need to know what's really going on there. I've suspected something is off for a long time."

"What if I prove to you that you're wrong?"

"Then no harm, no foul. You get your good press, and I get my answers. Besides, I'm sure you've looked me up. You know my reach. One interview with a poor, unsuspecting customer that had an awful run in with bed bugs, rude dealers, tight slots, food poisoning. You'd be surprised by what sort of tales come across my desk. That could put the nail in the coffin, so to speak. I can make your job easy or hard, up to you."

I narrow my eyes, the heat of anger simmering in my chest, "Is that a—"

"Threat?" Sharp leans back in his chair. "No, of course not. I have no ill intent towards you. I just want you to keep this between us."

"If it's so easy to ruin the Golden Sands, why don't you do it?" The table next to us looks over with creased brows. "You seem to have it out for the property anyway," I say, lowering my voice.

"There's something more going on and I need to know what that is. It's been eating at me, and this may be the only way I can get any inside info—the kind of thing I need to settle this once and for all."

I lean closer to Sharp. The tables around us are filling up and I don't want to be overheard. "Even if it means there are logical reasons for what you're worried about?"

Sharp nods. "Do we have a deal?"

"All I have to do is keep this conversation between us?"

"And meet with me every once in a while."

I extend my hand. "Fine."

Sharp shakes my hand, then pulls it a little closer to him. "You're my only chance to figure this out. I know something bigger than Golden Sands, bigger than Atlantic City is going on. You seem nice, Lilly. Stay safe."

I pull my hand back and stand. "I have to get back."

"You can expect your first headline tomorrow morning," Sharp says as he stands and disappears down a nearby hall.

As I make my way back through the Hard Rock, passing by Elton John's suede wingtip shoes and Slash's Harley, I tell myself that I'm doing the right thing. I also notice there are people here. The casino isn't packed but there are plenty of customers for a Tuesday morning, which reinforces how bad The Golden Sands is doing.

As I push my way out of the revolving door, a hard gust of cold wind smacks into me. I make my way back along the boardwalk, picking up my pace as I think about Sharp. Am I exploiting him and his obsessions? If he is truly suffering from mental illness, he would have delusions that take place everywhere. Could it be so focused on one place? He's imaginative and I can handle that. I get along with creatives. My brain works like that as well—look at where my mind was during yesterday's tour.

I can work with this.

In fact, how crazy Sharp sounded reminds me that I need to get myself grounded. All things considered, this meeting is a win on multiple levels and if we get a good headline out of it tomorrow, even better. Besides, Sharp has a hugely successful platform. Massive reach. Between his podcast, blog, local, and national press, he's the leading voice in all things casino and entertainment up and down the east coast. Would he be able to maintain that if he were struggling with his mental health? Worst case, I simply distance myself and let today's meeting fade to a bad memory.

I need Golden Sands to succeed. I won't get another chance. Which means, I need Sharp.

Chapter 11

The Golden Sands lobby is disturbingly quiet. Cold marble reflects the icy stillness of the large space. It's completely empty. A chasm of doubt opens beneath me. What if Sharp is right? Fear climbs up from the depths, wrapping cold fingers around my throat and squeezing until nothing remains but pure, paralyzing dread. I play Sharp's claims on repeat. No. They're insane. Beyond ridiculous. I can't let him shake me . . .

Without a doubt, my personal success, getting back on my feet, is completely interlaced with this casino. I need it to do well. I take another breath.

"Lilly!" Amon calls my name as he rounds the corner. "I've been calling you."

"You have?" I pull my cell out of my pocket. Five missed calls. "Oh. You did. I'm sorry, I must not have had service in the Hard Rock."

"No worries."

"What's going on?"

"Phone's been ringing off the hook since the press release went out."

"Really?" I follow Amon to the elevators, taking a few deep breaths to clear out any remaining tingles of fear. I shake my hands out, clearing the icy prickles a little faster.

Metal screeches on metal as the elevator doors slide open and we step in. I don't remember them being so loud this morning.

"Can you remind me to have facilities lubricate those doors?" Amon asks. I nod and add a quick note in my phone. "How was your meeting?"

"Good. I think . . ." I pause, not sure what to say next. "He's an interesting character. But he said there'll be a good headline in the paper and on his blog tomorrow, so we'll see." A pang of guilt taps my shoulder. I don't like keeping things from Amon, but for now I'll play to Sharp's eccentricities. At least until I see where this goes.

"I've heard he's not the easiest to deal with. Apparently, he threatened to give this property in New York bad press if a group of him and his friends weren't comped."

"He didn't ask for anything," I lie. "For free."

"Just be a little wary of him." Amon looks at me.

Maybe I shouldn't play to Sharp's eccentricities.

"Amon, actually—" The grinding screech of the elevator doors sliding open interrupts me and Amon steps out, leading the way to the office.

"What were you saying?" Amon asks as he holds the door for me.

"I see you found her," Jordan says as we enter.

"Yes. Go ahead, Lilly," Amon urges.

"Oh, um, I'm just going to stop in the restroom before we start the calls."

"No problem." Amon smiles. "Let's do the call in your office. Page me whenever you're ready. Jordan, can you order us lunch?"

"Is it lunch time already?" I ask.

"A little past. It's 12:45." Jordan says.

My mind reels. I thought it couldn't be much past eleven.

"Thanks," I say and disappear into my office.

A ray of sunlight reflects off the crystal water pitcher and the glass dropper reminds me I should take some of Mom's herbs. It might help calm me. I set my stuff down on my desk, down a glass of herbal water, then make my way to the bathroom. Taking each step slowly in hopes that I can slow down time or at least catch up.

Flicking on the light in the bathroom, everything shines. Glossy white marble and sleek chrome run from floor to ceiling. I check myself in the mirror. My hair is a little tousled from my walk on the boardwalk, so I smooth it down.

A shadow moves behind me.

My heart hiccups in my chest and the gurgle of water flowing from the faucet becomes so loud it echoes inside my head.

Frozen, I can't take my eyes off the wall as the shade crawls up the marble behind me like a cresting wave of darkness, ready to break and drag me into a suffocating void. A cold gust of air coils around my neck and my breath stops.

The lights flicker and go out.

A wave of nausea punches my gut. My breath returns, loud and rasping, the only companion inside this infinite darkness. A long breath in. A longer, shuddering breath out. The lights flash back on, and I gasp as the pale, limpid face of a girl hovers behind me.

I rush for the door handle, casting a glimpse back as I grip it, only to spot the source of the face. A painting depicting a 1920s' girl hangs on the opposite wall near the door, the bright lighting in the room throwing her reflection onto the gleaming marble. That's all it was: a reflection. Relief drenches me and I laugh out loud, though I don't look in the mirror as I turn off the faucet and leave. Another freezing gust wraps its claws around my wrist, prickling my skin. I brush it off and straighten my jacket. Old buildings are drafty. I'll have to get used to it.

Jordan left a spreadsheet on my desk with the various media outlets interested in the news release story. As I sit at my desk, I'm shocked by the names on this list. It's the biggest publications in the country, like the *New York Times, USA Today, The Wall Street Journal, Time Magazine, Business Week,* and *Forbes.* They rarely cover local gaming stories, maybe the *New York Times* would cover Atlantic City, but this much interest is crazy—good, but crazy.

My desk speaker buzzes. "Lunch is here, can I bring it in?"

"Yes, thank you."

I hear the rattle of glasses on wheels outside my office.

Amon appears pushing a room service cart. "I thought we could have a working lunch."

"Perfect."

He lifts a silver cloche then passes me my salad. A miniature silver gravy boat filled with dressing balances on the side of the platter. The clink of silver and porcelain makes me feel important. When I catch a small reflection of myself in shiny metal, I'm inadvertently smiling. I'm comfortable for the moment, whether that's because I want to be important and needed or because I'm still relieved the face in the bathroom was only a reflection. Either way, I need to keep focused on my work. To anchor down in reality and not let my imagination spook me or Sharp's paranoia infect me.

"Did you look over the media list?" Amon asks as he sits down with his lunch.

"Yeah, are you sure it's accurate?"

"What do you mean?"

"Jordan didn't accidentally pull media requests from another list, did he?"

"Jordan!" Amon yells towards the door. I glance across and think I catch the bathroom door swing open. I watch it for a moment more, but nothing happens.

Jordan peeks into the office doorway. "Yes?"

"Where did you get this media request list?"

"They all called to speak to Lilly. I thought it would be more manageable if I created a spreadsheet. There were quite a few requests."

"Perfect. Thank you. That's all," Amon says and Jordan quickly disappears.

"I . . . I was a little thrown because most of these outlets aren't usually interested in casino stories."

Amon shrugs and takes a perfect bite of food from his chopsticks. "They must realize how interesting this property is."

"This is *a lot* of interest. Do you want to prepare some quotes or wing it?"

"Wing it."

"I would never have encouraged the executives I worked under in the past to wing it, but they weren't you." I flash Amon a half-smile.

"Are you saying that's a bad idea?" He sets his bowl on the cart.

"No, it's whatever you're comfortable with. Most people tend to stutter and lose their train of thought when it's off-the-cuff. But I think you'll be fine."

"It's not my first rodeo." Amon flashes that same half-smile back at me.

"Oh, I know." I grin and stand to place my dish on the cart, but Amon grabs it.

He puts it on the cart and pushes it out to the hall. On his way back he pours us each a glass of water and puts a dropperful of herbal tincture in mine–something that strikes me as unusual, but I don't say anything. Maybe he assumed I wanted the herbs in my water because I keep them close.

"Thank you," I say, deciding to consider it more of a sweet gesture than a strange one.

It's time to make some calls. From the second I pick up my phone and dial, the calls go exceptionally well. The reporters all seem eager to hear from Amon and laugh at his jokes. Every journalist seems to already know about Amon, and they're all amazed by Golden Sands' history. Each outlet promises a headline and jokes that they will be the first to run the story.

I can't help but feel like I'm missing something, though. Like everyone is in on the joke but me. It's not the first time I've felt like this. Growing up, I tended to daydream in school, at lunch, mid-conversation, anywhere, and I learned to fake my way through—even when I was missing huge pieces of information.

"Good luck with everything. It sounds fabulous. I can't wait to meet you in person and see the Golden Sands for myself," Reporter #8 says. I have to check the list to remember who we're talking to.

I answer, "We're looking forward to meeting you as well, Megan. We'll be sending out the invites and weekend itinerary soo—tomorrow actually."

"Perfect. Amon, it was so great to talk to you and you too, Lilly. Talk to you soon. Ta-ta." Megan's voice rises to a painfully high octave on the second 'ta'.

"Bye, Megan," Amon says, his voice so smooth after hers.

I hit the disconnect button on the comm center. "That was the last one," I say, relaxing back into my chair.

"You think that went well?"

"Are you kidding? Every reporter committed to our media day that's wildly soon and promised an article within the next day or two. It couldn't have gone any better. It almost doesn't seem possible, right?"

Amon smiles, then checks his watch. "I wish you had time for a break, but we were supposed to be at the marketing meeting fifteen minutes ago."

"No problem." I smile and pull my clutch out of my desk. "I'm going to touch up my lipstick, then I'm ready." I pull out my compact mirror and catch Amon watching me; he smiles. Applying the buttery, crimson tint, I smush my lips together and make an extra loud smacking sound, then return the smile.

"Ready?" Amon asks, standing from my desk.

"Where is this meeting?"

"The thirteenth floor."

Chapter 12

The thirteenth floor means it's in a meeting room, which according to Sharp was the morgue. After so much time in Las Vegas, seeing a thirteenth floor still feels so strange. I agree with Peter, The Golden Sands should keep it and preserve history. Though, thinking about what this space was used for at the Thomas England General hospital and being up here at night fills my gut with a tornado of butterflies.

I hope it's in one of the small meeting rooms, maybe an intimate dinner with my team. "How many people will be there?"

"I believe the count is fifty-seven."

"Fifty-seven?"

"It's the entire casino marketing department including the special events manager, the entire player development team . . . oh, and I invited the casino operations managers."

"Do I need to—" The ding of the elevator cuts me off. The doors slide open quietly, releasing a rumble of loud chatter from beyond. As we round the corner, I nearly run into a waiter dressed in formal attire holding a silver tray of champagne flutes.

"Champagne?" Amon asks as he grabs two glasses.

"I don't think I should."

"Have it. This is a celebration, don't think of it as business."

"Ummm." Not sure how to respond, I look down.

"You look nervous. Relax."

"I do?"

Amon bites his lip, shrugs, then passes me a glass. Bubbles, flowery with hints of grapefruit, tickle my nose. The champagne stings my throat as the first sip slides down. I quickly take another, then a third.

"Ready?" Amon asks.

I nod.

Instead of walking towards the dinner, he puts his arm around my shoulders and pulls me a little closer. "You'll be fine." Amon clinks my glass.

His warm gesture stuns me. I haven't been hugged since before *it* happened. It's comfortable. Reassuring. I lean into him for a second, then pull away. He looks down and smiles, then walks down the long hall towards the double doors opposite the theater.

As we near, the chatter grows quiet. The door is cracked open but not enough for me to see inside. By the time we reach the door, it's silent.

Eerily silent.

Amon pulls the door open. He doesn't hold it for me but puts his other arm around my shoulders and we step in together. Every eye is glued to us. On my initial scan of the room, I note it's packed with men. Most casino marketing teams lean heavily towards the X chromosome, but that's changing with each passing year. There's a bar set up to the left and a large congregation of suited men. Smaller groups are interspersed around the room. Large, round tables take up the center.

It's almost imperceptible, but everyone in the room bows their head towards Amon. That's a common greeting in the Asian games department and with international hosts, so maybe they've adapted it throughout.

"Team, thank you for being here. I'm honored to introduce you to our new leader, Lilith Umbra."

The room erupts into applause.

Once it quiets, Amon continues. "As you know, we were very lucky to steal Ms. Umbra from the Las Vegas Strip where she brings a wealth of experience. Ms. Umbra, would you like to say anything?"

I smile, stand a little taller and look out at the crowd. "Please call me Lilly. It's such a pleasure to be here and I'm looking forward to meeting each one of you. Like Amon said, we are a team, my office door is always open. I'm so excited to start . . ."

Blood drains from my face. As I'm addressing the room, I see *him*. In a sea of suits, there *he* is, completely casual, in a sweatshirt. Standing there, leaning over a chair in the back, whispering to someone. It's impossible. The room spins and my vision tunnels. All I can hear is the pounding of my own heart. The last time I saw *him* whole was when I kissed him goodnight, then watched him drive off. There was nothing recognizable left of him on the morgue table, except his tattoo. I look at the arm he has resting on the chair. He has the sleeves of his hoodie pulled up and I can make out ink. It's not clear from here, but there's definitely a tattoo. *He's* staring at me, his brow crinkled in confusion. It's *him*, but I know that's impossible. I'm not crazy. My vision tunnels further, there's nothing left in the room but *him*.

Then people start to clap.

Amon squeezes my shoulder. "Cheers to Lilly and to you all. Welcome."

He squeezes again, then lifts his glass to mine. "Cheers." I clink his glass setting off an orchestra of crystal jingles.

"Let's eat," Amon announces, and everyone moves towards their seats. He leans towards me. "Everything okay?"

"Oh yeah, sorry. I was taking everyone in."

"Our table's right there in the middle. I'll grab us a drink and meet you there."

I hear Amon and nod, but don't take my eyes off *him*. He's staring back at me, but the way he does is so very different.

"Lilly . . . Lilly . . . Lilly?" Amon grabs my shoulders and turns me to face him. "Don't you hear me?"

"Sorry." I look at Amon, my brain struggling to justify what's going on. I jam my hands in my pocket and grab my phone. "I have to make a quick call. My phone's been ringing nonstop." Pulling my phone out, I look away from Amon, back towards *him*. He's still there, watching me. "I'll be right back."

The room is packed, groups of people block my view. Weaving my way through the crowd, I keep my gaze down, but I can feel everyone's eyes on me.

"Ms. Umbra." I look up. A tailored Gucci suit steps in front of me. In the suit is a miniature blonde version of Amon. Perfect hair. Perfect grooming. "It's wonderful to meet you. I'm the new Vice President of Player Development, Felix Hoffman, I'm looking forward to working for you. I've heard so many great things."

Taking a moment to center myself, I look up at Felix. I'm not even sure that it was actually *him*. It couldn't have been *him*, I know that.

Though I also know I need to talk to the person I saw, I don't want to appear unhinged in the process. "It's nice to meet you, Felix. Are you sitting at our table?"

"I am."

"Perfect. I will meet you there in two minutes and look forward to continuing our conversation. I have a quick call to make." I smile, but don't wait for a response.

With my eyes down and my phone held up as a shield, I weave quickly through the crowd and make it near to the back of the room. Finally, through the throngs of people, I raise my head. *He's* still there talking to someone and they're watching me. He's pulled his hood up and lowered it to cover his eyes. I have a straight shot to him along the back wall. I don't run, but I want to.

They watch me a little longer, then *he* spins and vanishes out a back door. I'm a hair away from running. The door he left through is locked, and I shake it harder, but it doesn't budge.

"I think that door's locked." Turning, I see the guy that he was talking to standing behind me. Dark circles ring his eyes. "Where are you trying to go?"

"Who were you just talking to?"

"What?" the gray-suited man asks.

Remembering my master key, I dig through my pocket. "Who were you talking to?"

"A new banquet waiter I hired today."

"What was his name?"

I shove the master key card towards the door, and it unlocks. Not waiting for his answer, I run into the hall. It's pitch black. The door slams behind me and the lock clicks loudly as it engages. There's a squelching of footsteps on what sounds like a linoleum floor. Terror freezes every muscle in my body. Then a door clicks, and a sliver of yellow light appears across the large hall.

"Wait!" I run towards the shrinking light.

My hand catches the door just before it crashes shut. I'm prepared to run after him but he's standing there with his back towards me at the top of the stairwell. My heart skips a beat then pounds into a frenzy. Blood surges into my head; I get dizzy. My hands tremble as I reach to touch his shoulder.

"Kai?" As soon as I call his name, he turns to face me. Instinctively, I leap back, crashing into the door behind me. The handle catches my hip, and sends a jolt of pain through my middle that nearly doubles me over. But there's also relief. "Buddy."

"Were you expecting someone else?" Buddy asks.

"Were you just at the marketing banquet talking to someone? Back of the room?"

"Yes," Buddy says but he shakes his head in the negative.

"You're not supposed to be here. Peter said he'll call the cops the next time he sees you."

"What Peety Piper says never goes. I havvey me-self some new clothes. Fore I'm starting me a new job and working amongst me foes."

"I don't understand you," I say and can't keep from staring. He looks nothing like Kai. Wouldn't, even from a distance. How could I have imagined that? *Why* would I? Maybe its guilt—I enjoy being around Amon too much. Makes me imagine things.

"You will." Buddy pauses to cackle. "But now I have to run and so should you." He spins with his arms up then takes off.

"Wait!" I yell after him and he pauses at the top of the stairs. "Pull up your sleeves so I can see your forearms."

Buddy spins back towards me, clicks his heels together, and mimes taking a top hat off and bowing to me. "Doo—do—do . . . doo—do—do," he hums as if he's a magician. He pulls up each sleeve, runs his hands across his chest as if he's doing a magic trick, flips his arms over, then spins again. "Run," he says before he cackles and sprints down the stairs. No tattoos.

Buddy pauses on the first landing and looks up at me. "Run," he says. The mad theatricality of his earlier interaction is replaced with a serious, stern gaze. "Run."

Chapter 13

S haken, I make my way back into the dark hall. The lights suddenly flick on. It's a much larger space than I realized.

Amon is standing in the doorway. "Everything okay?"

"Yeah," I say, heading back towards the banquet door.

Amon meets me in the middle of the hall and places his hands on my shoulders. "I want you to know that in this short amount of time, you've already exceeded my expectations. You're brilliant. Thank you."

"Don't thank me yet," I say and look down at Amon's perfectly shined, black-leather, wingtip boots.

"You don't need to be humble." Amon places his finger beneath my chin and gently lifts my gaze to his. "I know how stressful taking this role is, but you are doing an amazing job."

My shoulders sink again. The weight of dread pressing down on my chest keeps me from taking a full, satisfying breath.

Amon wraps me in his arms, enveloping me in the warm, woodsy scent of his cologne—Penhaligon's is a popular fragrance around here. "You are the single most incredible person I've ever met."

There is something carnal that stirs in the pit of my stomach and sends an electric surge of power through my body's circuitry. Guilt tries to stick a dagger in, but the comfort I feel in Amon's embrace is a powerful shield. I feel like I've known him forever. Yet, it feels out of place; more familial, less business.

Why can't I let a good thing be a good thing? Accept comfort?

My past will not haunt me, I won't let it. *I will not be bound by the confines of my comfort zone.* Leaning into his embrace, "Thank you," I say before repeating my mantra a few more times.

Amon smiles back. Taking my hand, he leads me toward the banquet then pauses. He looks at me one more time, smiles, nods, then opens the door.

The room feels different. Everyone is seated at their table. It's quiet. As I look across the room, all eyes are on me. I force myself to stand a little taller and smile. Our table is in the middle of the room and is the largest. It's also the only round table. The others are set in an alternating pattern of rectangular and square, forming a series of matching zig-zagging lines that extend from ours. I didn't notice it before because everyone was standing, but it's such an interesting event design.

Amon gently directs me to an aisle as he walks down the aisle next to mine. I smile and nod to each person I pass, trying my hardest to acknowledge everyone. The weight of Kai's memory has receded and I'm strangely confident. With each step, I stand a little taller. Walking through the crowd I begin to accept the influence I have here and an almost electric tingle of power stirs in my chest. It feels good. Offers an effective distraction from everything else.

Amon and I reach the table at the same time, and he pulls my chair out for me. The only other person I recognize is Felix Hoffman. Wait, there's an older woman that looks very familiar, but I can't quite place her.

"Lilly this is Felix—"

"Hoffman, V.P. of Player Development," I interrupt and smile. "We met."

"Next to him is Guy Durand, V.P. of Casino Operations; Allison Belmont, Special Events Director; Dustin Litrale, Nightlife Director; Liza Helcom, our Advertising and Casino Marketing Director; and this is the talented Le Madame Morana Quade, Director of the Li-RV show and our new Entertainment Director. She just got in and we're so glad she could join us tonight."

"It's so nice to meet everyone," I say. Glancing around the table, I'm a bit taken back by how attractive each person is. Even Morana, who is in her sixties yet still has such supple, beautiful skin and glossy, dark hair. "Morana, I'm looking forward to seeing the show. When will you begin rehearsals?"

"Tonight."

"Tonight?" Amon asks.

"Yes. Is the theater not ready?" Morana asks.

"The theater is ready, but it's still under union control per the purchase agreement."

"So?" Morana asks.

"They have union guidelines pertaining to hours worked, amount of time for notice—"

"You know we have our own theater crew," Morana interrupts Amon.

"Yes, but like I was saying, we haven't had time to work out an agreement."

"That's not my problem. We are rehearsing tonight," Morana says.

"Fine." A touch of irritation shows in a split-second brow crease then Amon's face goes instantly back to its smooth perfection. "Does that mean we get a sneak peek tonight?"

"Darling, you know that's not possible, but don't worry, you will have plenty of opportunities to see the show very soon," Morana smiles, showing her brilliantly white teeth.

"Morana, did you ever have a show or work in Las Vegas?" I ask. "I feel like I've met you before."

Morana twists to look at me, lifts her shoulder slightly, and smiles wider. "My love, I would remember meeting someone as beautiful as you. You likely recognize me from television or in the press. I've won several Grammys and Emmys. Before becoming a producer and director, I was an entertainer myself."

"I'm sorry, I should've known that," I say, slightly embarrassed.

"Oh, darling, don't apologize. I intentionally keep that side of me quiet. My show name was entirely different." Morana gracefully circles her hands up to frame her face. "Being two people is much more fun."

"I could definitely see that." I smile to Morana then direct my attention to the rest of the table. "How did you all come to work at Golden Sands? Did you come from other Atlantic City casinos?"

Everyone chuckles, then Felix speaks up, "Several people in this room came from other Atlantic City casinos, but not us. We've all worked with Amon for close to ten years."

"In finance?"

"More or less," Felix says.

"So, no one here has worked in a casino before?" I ask.

"We spent the past year learning and training at a few different casinos," Allie says, brushing her fiery-red hair behind her shoulder, "once Amon had his sights on this property," she says and pins her bright green eyes on Amon.

"Allie has been planning our corporate events for years. She's incredibly talented," Amon adds.

"Did you plan this dinner?" I ask her.

Allie focuses her attention on me. "I did."

"I love the table layout. I've never seen an event set up like this."

"Thank you." She smiles. "And I do realize that casino players are a different crowd. I already have several events planned. Starting this weekend." Allie's shoulders rise, and she seems barely able to contain her excitement. "I have our first player party set for this weekend, and Amon told me how you would like to incorporate the history of this property and the 1920s into some of our events, which works perfectly for this party."

"That's soon! Do you have a theme—"

"Other than the 1920s?" Allie cuts in.

"Yeah, casino players love themed parties and love their parties to be over-the-top. Let me think . . . what goes with a 1920s theme—Oh! I know! Psychics were insanely popular in the twenties and casino players love psychics. Oh." My shoulders slump when reality hits. "But this weekend is too soon. That's probably impossible."

"I love that," Amon adds.

"I can pull it off," Allie quickly says.

"Maybe we can get some press to come as well," Liza says.

"Lilly's already got that handled," Amon says, sending an arrow of anxiety right to my gut.

"Oh, perfect." Liza meets Amon's gaze, and her eyes narrow ever so slightly.

Maybe I'm stepping on toes. "Although," I add, "press is great, but will we have customers here? The casino's been empty and press with no customers would be very embarrassing."

"We have a full players' weekend planned," Felix says. "I emailed you some of the mailers and promo flyers that went out. It's called Golden Sands Casino Renascence."

Amon nods to me. "In the future, you will have full control over our promotions, of course, but this was done before you started."

My phone dings and I know that it's the email. The creative is brilliant, an ivory background is framed by art deco gold geometric borders. Emblazoned on top in gold and black block letters, 'The Golden Sands Invites You to Join Us for The Official Renascence Party and Player Appreciation Weekend – All new and old players will receive $500 in free play, $200 in comps, and so much more!'

"The invites are beautiful, but how's the response?"

"Our customer response has been better than good," Liza says. "We had an eighty-percent response rate and from that group, close to a thousand customers have made reservations."

Felix grins, eyes alight. "Our high-end customers' responses have been great as well. We're expecting full occupancy by this weekend."

"That's almost too good to be true," I tell them. "But you are giving away a lot to a lot of people. This weekend will lose money, although I think it's worth it for the buzz it will generate. After all, we're trying to change a lot of people's opinions on the Golden Sands and the only way to do that is to get them in the door. If it's built into the budget, and knowing Amon," I pause for a moment, look at Amon and smile, "it is."

"You already know me well." Amon smiles at me and lifts his glass of red wine. The rest of the table follows, including me. "Now, no more talk of business. That's not what this night is about. Who would like to tell Lilly what the backbone of my business—my life—philosophy is?"

"Conquer life by living it to the full," Guy says, holding his glass a little higher.

"Exactly," Amon says. "So, let's enjoy ourselves tonight."

"Conquer life by living it to the full," Dustin echoes.

"I like that. Cheers," I offer.

"Hear, hear. Conquer life by living it to the full for us and our guests," Morana adds.

We clink as many glasses as we can reach as the first course is brought out.

Foie gras toast triangles with mesclun greens—the one thing I swore I'd never eat again. After seeing videos of geese and ducks with tubes down their throats and a yellow paste oozing out from every orifice, barely alive, their feathers wet and greasy . . . I pledged to boycott foie gras.

When I look around the table, then the room, everyone is wrapped up in the enjoyment of this dish. I tell myself there are a handful of humane purveyors of foie gras, and this may be from them. The dish has already been prepared and served. Plus, I didn't technically buy or order it. I pick up a toast triangle and take a bite. The creaminess of the fat melts into the richness of the liver and I catch myself chewing with my eyes closed. I take another bite, then another. It's delicious. My plate is soon empty.

"Lilly, what do you think of Atlantic City so far?" Allie asks.

"So far, so good. It's a huge change from Las Vegas, but I needed a change."

"Same here," Liza adds. "Don't get me wrong, I love New York but change is good."

"Change *is* good," I confirm.

The conversation is easy. I'm comfortable at this table. The food is delicious and the wine flows freely. By the time the banquet wraps up, I feel good. I like the people I work with. Everyone is beautiful and smart, but surprisingly grounded.

Following the banquet, the player development hosts stay for some team building along with Guy and Felix. Dustin, Allie, and Liza decide to grab another drink and work out some of the logistics regarding turning that space into a nightclub. And Morana is going to go through her theater checklist while she waits for the cast to arrive for rehearsal. Which leaves Amon and me.

"I'll walk you out," Amon says as we get up from the table.

"I was going to go back to the office and do a few more things before I leave."

"They can wait. You accomplished more today than I hoped you would during your entire first week. Get a good night's rest. It's almost nine already," Amon says as he opens the door for me.

"But—"

"I'm serious. I don't want you to burn yourself out before things even get going. You've already been here for more than twelve hours.

Go home. Relax." Amon closes the door behind us, cutting off a roar of laughter from the banquet.

The hall is quiet and empty. "Fine," I say.

"Do you need anything in the office?"

"I have my things with me, but I didn't turn off my computer or lights."

"Don't worry about that, Jordan took care of it."

The door to the theater is open and I look in as we pass by. Most of the lights are off, but a soft glow from the hall fills the space. A shape moves near the stage. It's a little dark and hard to make out but as we near, the shape solidifies into a man dressed as a soldier. Not a modern soldier. I can't place his uniform, but I know that it's from another era. He must be a performer in Li-RV, getting ready to rehearse. A period show might be perfect to fit into our historic theme.

Amon calls the elevator and the door slides open. Now quiet, the screeching gears have been daubed.

"Have you seen the show?" I ask as the doors slide closed.

"I saw an early version in New York when it first opened."

"What period is it about?"

"It's not really a period-specific piece. Why?"

I frown. "Oh. I saw someone in the theater. I assumed a cast member in a historic soldier's costume."

"Mmm," Amon says as the door slides open to the ground floor.

As we walk by the casino floor and into the lobby, still no guests are present, but the casino is a frenzy of action. Dozens of workers are placing slot machines on carts. The dreadful bar that smelled like decades of stale beer has been completely taken apart and is in the process of being put back together.

"I can't wait to see this tomorrow," I say as we make our way by the front desk.

"It will be done by the time you come in tomorrow."

"How is that even possible? You're able to get more done than anyone I've ever worked for."

Amon opens the door for me. "It's because I have great people, like you. Thank you for today."

"Don't thank me, it's my job."

"Well, I'm grateful." Amon waves before heading back inside.

Having a sports car in Atlantic City is a bit like having a stomachache on Thanksgiving. Though tonight, the street is unnaturally quiet and the urge to hit the gas as I pull onto North Carolina Avenue is only quelled by the eeriness of the dead-empty block. As a distraction, I turn the radio on. 'House of the Rising Sun' is playing and I turn it up a little louder.

When I pull into my apartment complex, a car is parked in one of the spots I'd been allotted. Too tired to deal with it tonight, I'll call the property manager tomorrow. Besides, I don't need the extra spot for a few more days. As I grab my things and make my way up to my apartment, I inhale a cold, briny breath of ocean. I stop and take another deep breath. I haven't spent much time near the ocean so it's hard to describe this smell other than it's completely intoxicating. In this quiet, I hear the waves breaking softly just over the dunes. Closing my eyes, listening to the sea and breathing in the ocean, I imagine my feet in the sandy dunes and sink into this moment of calm. I'm going to like living at the beach.

A car door closing in the distance pulls me from reverie and I start up the steps towards my apartment. It's a quiet complex. In fact, I haven't seen a single neighbor since I moved in. That said, most of these condos are owned by shoobies—Jersey slang for summer residents and snowbirds—those that flee to Florida for the winter. It would be nice to have someone else around.

As I make my way up the stairwell, a muffled giggle interrupts the sound of soft ocean waves. I turn toward the source. Nothing. Maybe it was a bird in the distance. Continuing up the steps and into the open-air hall toward my apartment, I take a few deep breaths—

This time it's unmistakable: a little girl is laughing. My pulse quickens. I spin around, but the hall is empty. *Calm down, she's probably in one of the condos.*

I fumble for the keys in my purse and pick up the pace towards my front door. The giggle erupts again.

Loud.

Close.

Wicked.

My fingers tremble. My breath comes up short, as I jam the key at the lock, missing once, twice. Panic drums in my chest, each heartbeat pounding against my ribs.

Then I feel it. A presence. Someone is rushing up behind me.

I spin around and hold my key in my fist so it's sticking out between my fingers, right under my knuckles, ready to jab and stab at whoever might be there.

But there's no one.

Just the empty hallway again, a single moth battering itself against the light overhead. I catch my breath, do my best to steady my heart. If I can make it to my car, I'll go back to Golden Sands. Back to safety.

The hall is still utterly empty. I inch my way down the dark walkway, passing beneath the struggling moth that bounces against the glass in a series of soft, rhythmic pops. Another ten feet and I'm to the stairwell.

With my free hand, I grab my phone and dial 9-1–

Arms wrap around me from behind.

The laughter, loud and hysterical, burns in my ears. A hand covers my mouth, sealing in my scream.

Chapter 14

"Got ya!" Tori says, wrapping her arms around me in an ecstatic embrace.

"What are you doing here?" I ask as my breath escapes me. My pulse slows and my senses return to normal.

"I had to come out early. Dorm mix-up. Long story. But I don't have to stay here. I can get a hotel room," Tori says.

"Don't be silly." I hug her. "I'm happy to see you. But you scared me half-to-death. You haven't gotten me like that since we were ten!" I say with a laugh.

"It's so good to see you. You look amazing and your car, wow!"

"It was a gift. But . . . wait . . . What happened?"

"Can we go in? I've been waiting in my rental car for hours."

"Oh, my gosh, yes. Sorry!"

"I'll grab my things. Be right back."

"Need help?"

"No, I'm good," Tori yells over her shoulder as she hurries back towards her car.

My hand still shakes a little when I open my door. *So much for my weaponized key ring.* I froze when Tori grabbed me—complete mush for the taking.

"Hey," Tori says, from behind me. "I picked up a bottle of wine on my way down. Want a glass?"

"Oh, not tonight. I'm exhausted."

"I haven't seen you in months and you won't have one glass with me?"

"I had a glass at a work dinner, and I have another long day tomorrow."

"It's just one glass, come on."

"Fine," I say. "I'll open it while you put your things in your room. It's the first door on the left and that's your bathroom."

"Yay, this is so amazing. I'm so excited!" Tori disappears into her room.

Kicking off my stilettos, I didn't realize how much my feet hurt till I take my first flat step of bliss. Feeling much more comfortable, I grab two wine glasses from the kitchen and pour the pinot grigio.

"Wow. No way. That's the ocean, right there," Tori says as she stops in front of the living room's large sliding door and bay of windows on her way back. The moon is full and hangs low on the horizon. Its gold light shimmers off the black ocean in jagged crests.

"That *is* the ocean," I say, bringing the wine into the living room and plopping on the couch.

"It's so beautiful." Tori collapses next to me.

"So, what happened?"

"My professor feels terrible. She and another professor both put a last-minute, short-stay dorm request in. So, the room was double-booked. The other student was from India, and since I have you, I gave her the room. You're not mad, are you?"

"No, of course not. I'm glad you're here. I just feel bad that you sat in your car for so long. Why didn't you call?"

"I tried, like a thousand times. I tried texting and got error messages. Even emailed you. See?" Tori pulls out her phone and shows me the sent message. I grab my phone. No missed calls. No texts. No emails, not even in the junk folder.

"Are you sure you used the right email? It's new."

"Yes, I even called The Golden Sands because I wanted to check with you before I came here. The person I spoke to, I don't remember their name, gave me your email and told me that was the best way to reach you."

I check Tori's phone again; the email is right.

"Was it a guy or a girl?"

"A guy, but I didn't get his name."

I check my phone again. There's definitely no email from Tori, but my trash folder has been recently emptied, which I didn't do. "Sorry. I guess reception is pretty bad in there. It's an old building."

"No worries. I'm here and I'm so happy."

"Me too." I smile.

Tori's eyebrows knit together, and she leans in and puts her hand on my knee. "How are you doing? I was so worried about you."

"I'm much better.

"I'm glad you're doing better, but I wish I'd known everything that was going on. It all happened so fast."

"It was a difficult year."

"Year? It was definitely not a full year. Look." Tori pulls out her phone and shows me some pictures of us together at Toro in Las Vegas. "Do you see the date? It was from five months ago."

My mind starts to spiral and I feel slightly lightheaded. "That feels like years ago."

"You weren't seriously dating anyone then."

"I think we'd only gone on a couple dates."

"That was the last time I talked to you. Then I hear you quit your job out of the blue and move. And, when I finally talk to you, you tell me that you were engaged, I was going to be in your wedding, but your fiancé was killed in a car accident."

When she puts it like that . . . "I don't know. I felt like I'd known him forever. I guess we got serious fast."

"Serious? More like consumed."

"I don't want to talk about this. I'm in a better place and finally at a point where I'm trying to move on."

"I'm sorry," Tori says and sets down her wine. "I just want to make sure you're alright. You know, you're healthy . . . mentally?"

"Like I said." I pull my hands away. "Losing someone is hard." A tear breaks free and leaves a damp trail down my cheek, which I quickly wipe away.

"I know. I know. You tend to get so wrapped up in people. With everything you've told me you went through, then having a breakdown and get better in such a short amount of time is unusual. And with your history of mental—"

"Your dad was wrong. I am *not* nor have I *ever been* bi-polar. That's why my parents took me out of school senior year. Because of your dad. He had it out for me."

"Okay. Okay. I'm sorry. I didn't mean to upset you."

"I'm not upset. We worked hard on our friendship to move past this. You dwelling on this bullshit is annoying. I'm going to bed."

Tori grabs my hand. "No, don't. I'm sorry. You're right. My dad's an asshole. A typical know-it-all psychiatrist. He still can't accept that he was wrong, and I let him get into my head. He's the main reason I'm across the country. I haven't had time to shake him off yet. Forgive me?" Tori looks at up at me with her eyes opened as wide as possible and blinks them in a goofy spasm. "And you're right. I won't bring it up again. You love intensely and that's my favorite thing about you. You are a good, loyal friend. Let's finish our wine."

"I'm tired."

"I'm sorry. Please?"

Reluctantly, and a bit overly dramatic, I collapse back onto the couch.

In return, Tori pretends to zip her mouth, turn the key, and throw it away. "So, how is your new job?"

"Good. I really like my new boss and everyone I'm working with. Oh." I pause, my eyes doubling in size. "If you think the car he gave me is nice, you should see my office."

"He gave you that car?"

"Yeah, as a signing bonus."

"I gotta admit, I'm a little jealous and beginning to question my decision to join academia." Tori laughs.

"Whatever, Dr. Alexander," I smile at her. "Tell me more about what you're doing at Princeton."

"I've been accepted into their doctoral of philosophy program with a focus in the anthropology department. My specific area of study will be the anthropological power of counterculture through the archeology of tradition."

"So, like punk rock?"

"Not exactly, the organizations I'm studying are a little darker and deeper-seated."

"Well, it sounds interesting."

Tori smiles. "To me it is."

"How's Las Vegas?"

"It's good to be somewhere different. I needed a change."

"Cheers to that," I say and toast Tori with the last sip of wine. "Do you need anything before I go to bed?"

"No, I'm good and so glad to be here."

"Welcome home," I say before making my way to my room.

My room is quiet and cool, and I turn on the television to break the silence. On my way to the shower, my phone rings. Mom. I consider ignoring the call, but that will only postpone the inevitable. "Hi," I say.

"How's work going?"

"Really well. I like Amon a lot and everyone that I work with seems really nice."

"How'd you do?"

"I think I did well. We're trying to generate some press so that's mainly what I worked on. Then I met the new marketing team."

"What time did you get home?"

"About thirty minutes ago."

"Long day. That's great. I heard Amon was very impressed by you."

"Mom, please tell me you're not checking in."

"No . . . no . . . After my meetings I had dinner with Mara, she told me that Amon couldn't stop talking about how wonderful you are."

"Okay."

"How do you feel? Have you been taking the elixir I left?"

"Good and yes."

There's a knock on my door. "Come in," I say.

"Hey, sorry, do you have a towel I can use?" Tori asks.

"I should've told you. They're in the hall closet right outside of the bathroom."

"I should've checked. Sorry! Good night." Tori pulls my bedroom door closed.

"Who was that?" Mom asks.

"Tori. There was a mix up at Princeton and she had to come a little early."

"Of course, she did. How convenient."

"I'm glad she's here."

"Really? Because you don't sound convincing."

"I'm tired."

"Don't let her be a distraction."

"Of course not."

"Sleep well," Mom says.

"You—" Her phone clicks off. "—too."

I slip into the shower. Steam fills my bathroom, and the hot water feels good as it washes away the day's grit and takes the stress with it. I purposefully try to hang on to the moments that worked. All I need is to find a balance between my creativity and logic. A way to stop imagining ghosts behind every shadow but keep the ideas flowing. Is that possible? It has to be.

The water thrums onto my hair, and I visualize how the day is going to go tomorrow. How it's going to be better. How I'm not going to get scared. Then I remember the cold air that tightened around my throat. My imagination getting the best of me. I don't want to become like Sharp, or even worse like Buddy. Stress. Maybe I'm too tired. With that thought, I turn the shower off then towel myself dry. Digging through my drawer, I find an old pair of boxer short pajamas I managed to sneak in with the new satin nightgowns Mom insisted on and climb into bed.

I'm barely asleep when I sit up in bed, gasping for breath. The sun is up. *Oh no.* I check my phone. Dead. I hit the guide button on the television that's still on. Eight-fifteen. I plug my phone into the charger, jump out of bed, throw on my suit, and some semblance of a makeup job.

Tori is already awake.

"This sunrise is the most beautiful thing I've ever seen," she says without looking at me.

"I don't mean to rush out on you, but I'm late."

"I made coffee, grab a cup to go," she says, still not taking her eyes from the early-morning ocean.

"Thank you. I need it."

"No problem. Have a good day."

"You too," I say as I tighten the lid on my mug.

"I only have one meeting today, then I'm around. Do you need me to do anything?"

"No, just enjoy yourself. Your keys are hanging on the rack by the door."

"I can make dinner for us."

"That'd be great. Thank you,"

I rush out the front door.

Chapter 15

I slip into my parking spot at Golden Sands at five-after-nine, and slide out of the elevator to my office by ten-after.

"Good morning," Jordan says as I fling open the door.

"Perfect timing," Amon says as he steps out of his office.

"I'm sorry, I wanted to get here earlier."

"Are you kidding? Don't get here any earlier than this," Amon says.

Jordan rises from his desk. "I put copies of today's press coverage on your desk. Can I get you anything else?"

"I'm good, thank you," I say, and make my way to my office.

I have to pinch myself again; I still can't believe that this is my office. When I sit down, I flip through the pile of documents, and excitement tickles my spine. Other than being the last one into the office, I could not have visualized my day starting any better. Every article is extremely positive. The press photos make the Golden Sands look iconic. Stories have hit the cover of everything from the *New York Times* to *USA Today*. And then there's Sharp's coverage. His online post already has over two-thousand likes and it's only been live for a few hours.

Amon knocks on my door, then walks in. "How incredible is that?"

"We couldn't have asked for better coverage, but let's not get too excited until we see if it converts."

"Did you look into the casino when you came in?"

"No, I was in such a rush, I didn't. Is it finished?"

"Follow me, we're taking a walk."

I follow him out of our office and into an elevator. He wears a smirk.

"Are you showing me the new bar?" I ask, one eyebrow raised.

He smiles. "That and more."

The elevator doors slide open and as I step out, I almost walk into someone—a dealer making his way to the table games pit. Then I see more people as we follow him to the casino floor. "There's people here."

"Yeah, but most are employees," Amon says as they weave through a bank of slot machines.

"They're not employees." I point out an older couple perusing the slot machines before moving ahead of Amon. "Good morning." I greet this couple. "Do you mind if I ask you what brought you in today?"

"We follow Sharp's podcast and blog." He shrugs. "Wanted to see what all the hoopla's about," the man replies.

"Welcome, I'm Lilly Umbra, the V.P. of marketing, if you have any thoughts while you're here the hotel operator can connect you to me. Call me anytime. Enjoy your trip."

"It's beautiful," the woman adds, "and we're locals so we plan to come back often."

"That's wonderful. Thank you so much," I say as we move on.

I see Guy walking through the table games pit and he waves to us, obviously happy.

"Changing one-hundred," a black-jack dealer says as we walk by.

The customers aren't just checking things out, they're actually playing. It's far from packed, but it's also no longer deserted. The bar is closed, but Amon grabs my hand and leads me under the ropes and up the short flight of steps into the renovated space. It's unrecognizable from the mess it was yesterday. Black marble and gold metal have transformed this area into a sophisticated, sleek bar that I imagine even F. Scott Fitzgerald would've loved.

From the bar, Amon and I have a clear vantage of the entire casino floor.

"Do you feel that?" Amon asks.

"Excitement?"

"Close. Energy. It's almost like it's alive."

"Yeah, I do." It's true. It feels like a completely different casino today.

"What do you think of the bar?"

"It's beautiful and so different. It even smells good. What is that?" I take another deep inhale. The aroma coming from behind the bar is a warm mix of citrus and vanilla.

"That is a bit of Dustin's magic—"

"Did someone say my name?" Dustin steps out from a door behind the bar.

"We're just admiring your work and Lilly asked what smells so good," Amon says.

"Oh, that's just a little touch. I like to add to the atmosphere," Dustin says. "We make our own simple syrups that smell amazing. So, I always have something steeping."

"It turned out amazing."

"Thank you. The sign's up." Dustin motions above the bar. "The inspector's coming at ten, then we can open for business."

"Nightrise Bar . . . it's perfect," Amon says to Dustin.

Dustin grins. "Thought you'd like it."

"What do you think Lilly?" Amon asks.

"It's cool." The sign is gold metal and shaped into a semi-circle with the words Nightrise Bar and geometric lines that look almost like a jagged sun. Sitting below the sign is an array of antique, colored-glass liquor bottles that look more like art.

"How did you find liquor in these bottles?" I ask.

"We just display our rare top-shelf liquor," Dustin says.

"I can't believe you did this in a day."

Amon smiles at me. "You've spent too much time around average people. We're capable of incredible things, especially now with you."

I try to smile, and hope I can live up to Amon's expectations, but I'd be lying if I said I wasn't intimidated.

"The inspector's here," Dustin says.

Amon nods. "We'll leave you to it."

"It's beautiful. I can't wait to see what you do with the thirteenth floor," I say, and follow Amon out.

As we quickly make our way back to our office, a crowd of guests streams towards the casino. They all seem to stare at Amon.

"Where did they come from?" I ask, knowing that customers brought in by media coverage don't move in groups.

"Felix's junket rep sent two buses down from New York," Amon says.

"Really? I didn't know that buses were coming in today. All I knew about was our free play promotions that start tomorrow."

"I'm sorry, Lilly. This was planned as a way to bring bodies into the building, more to help with training than anything else."

"If I'm going to be the V.P. of Casino Marketing, I should know about everything that is going on in the casino, and before it happens."

"You're absolutely right."

"And how did all the customers know who you were?"

"I think they put together some sort of information packet with a few coupons or something and a letter from me welcoming them here; it probably had my picture."

"What sort of coupons? Were any casino offers included? We need to have a calendar that keeps track of every casino offer, giveaway, or planned event for—"

"That's a fantastic idea," Amon cuts in, "but tell Jordan. He's the perfect person to put it together and maintain it."

The doors slide open and I see Morana waiting inside. Amon pulls the glass door open and holds it for me.

"We need—" Morana starts, but Amon holds his hand up to quiet her.

"One moment, Morana, it's lovely to see you, by the way." He turns to our assistant. "Jordan, Lilly has a job for you. She would like a calendar of every . . ." his voice trails off as he holds his hands up and squints at me.

"We need a color-coded master calendar that has every casino event, give-away, offer, and promotion listed by date. I would also like to know what bus trips or other junkets we have coming in." I glance at Morana. "As well as any entertainment that's booked. It should be in a shared file that's accessible by every department."

"No problem," Jordan says with a smile.

Amon adds, "Can you also make sure the marketing team emails Lilly every promotion or event they have coming up or planned? I want everything approved by Lilly, even creative."

"Of course," Jordan says.

"Thanks," I say and swallow a lump in my throat. I may have overreacted to not knowing about a bus trip; I didn't necessarily want final approval on everything. My cheeks warm.

"Any particular colors for the calendar?" Jordan asks me.

"No, just so that it's coded by department and it's easy to see what's happening throughout the property."

Amon turns to Morana. "Now, that we have that taken care of. Morana, to what do we owe the pleasure?"

"Pleasure?" she snaps through a gritted jaw.

"We will fix whatever you're having an issue with." Amon smiles.

"The union stage crew has locked my people out of the theater. They are insisting on doing the set installation, which is not possible."

"We—"

"And," Morana interrupts, "they said they are going to fine you for allowing us to rehearse last night."

"We'll go talk to them right now," Amon says.

"We? I am going nowhere near them," Morana spits.

"No, no, of course not. Lilly and I will go," Amon says.

"Me?"

"Actually, why don't you go alone first and let me know if they aren't agreeable?"

"Ummm . . ." I can't think of a better response.

"Let me know as soon as it's handled. We need to begin our installation immediately." Morana lets out a huff, spins, and leaves the office.

"What am I trying to get them to agree to?" I ask. This doesn't seem like a task I should be doing, but after Amon clearly gave me full control of all events, including creatives, I almost feel like he's punishing me for over-inserting myself. *No.* I can't think like that. He's just bringing me into the fold.

"See what it will take for them to agree to give us control of the thirteenth-floor theater."

"Okay, and where are they at?"

It's Jordan who answers. "Their offices are backstage at the Grand Theater, around the corner from Flame."

"Thanks."

"Take care of that now," Amon says. "Jordan will have the calendar ready when you get back, along with any requested approvals for any upcoming items."

"Great." I make my way to the elevator.

This is not great. As I wait for the elevator, I don't want to go negotiate, but this is an opportunity to prove my worth . . . as long as it goes well. *I will not be bound by the constraints of my comfort zone,* I remind myself, and step into the elevator.

As I'm heading down to the Grand Theater, I get a text alert on my cell. It's from Sharp, 'Story went live. Check it out. Talk soon.'

I roll my eyes even though there's no one here to see. *Talk soon.* What kind of information does he think he's going to get from me? Does he really want to hear about how much I like Amon, how great he's been, and how well I get along with his team?

The elevator doors to the second-floor slide open with a loud screech. The sound of metal grinding on metal sends a sharp chill from the back of my neck to the base of my spine and I lift my shoulders to my ears, hoping to squeeze the discomfort out. I cover my ears to brace for the closing of the elevator behind me, which seems to save my eardrums from the most brutal of it.

As I shake off the painful squeal of metal, I'm equally surprised by how quiet it is. There's not a sound. The restaurants are closed. If there's another living soul on this floor, they aren't within earshot. The silence makes each click of my heels on marble sound like an explosion. Suddenly, ragtime blasts from overhead speakers and I flinch so awkwardly that I trip over my own feet and bang my knee on the hard marble. With a gasp, I pick myself back up, attempting to soothe my throbbing knee. Initially, I'm grateful there's no one around to see, until I catch a glance of the cameras as I brush myself off. I flash a sheepish smile to the on the eye-in-the-sky and give the camera a quick thumbs-up to go with my vaudeville routine to let the watcher know I'm alright. *Get a grip.* I grab my phone and text Peter.

Me: Can you meet me at the second-floor elevator bank?
The elevator is still screeching, and the background mu-

sic needs to be adjusted up here.

Peter: I can be there in 20. Does that work?

Me: Perfect. Thanks.

The music still blares from the speakers, but there's something odd about it. The syncopation is slightly slowed as if it's being played on an old record player that can't get up to speed. A strange wobble to the tune makes me uneasy. As I pick up my pace, I text Amon.

Me: You need to shut off the background music ASAP. Sounds bad.

Amon: ???

Me: Someone is playing out of tune music on the over-head speakers. It sounds terrible.

Amon: Got it. I will have Jordan look into it now. Thanks.

When I pull open the door to the theater, the empty hall is pitch black.
"Hello?"
Silence.
"Hello?" I call a little louder.
Nothing.

"HELLO?" I yell as loud as I can without screaming.

Bright, fluorescent lights kick on. The theater is big, much larger than the thirteenth-floor space. There're no theater seats. The floor level has long tables set up with table clothes and chairs. There are three stepped rows with round booths, each about a foot or so higher than the row in front. The top row, where I'm standing, is another section of long tables. It's a traditional casino theater and reminds me of seeing shows when I was younger. I'd always order Shirley Temples from the cocktail servers.

"Can I help you?" A gruff voice yells from the stage.

"Hi," I say, making my way down towards the stage.

"The theater is closed. You shouldn't be in here," he barks.

"I'm Lilly Umbra, the new V.P. of Casino Marketing."

"So? The theater is still closed."

As I get closer, the theater tech fully steps out from behind the stage curtains. He's older than me but could be anywhere in his forties or fifties. His stringy black hair is greased to his scalp.

"I need to talk to you about the Li-RV and the thirteenth-floor theater."

"The thirteenth floor is unsafe. No one should be up there."

"Do you have an office we can talk in?"

He lets out an overly dramatic huff. "Fine. Follow me."

"I'm Lilly. It's nice to meet you." I extend my hand, but he just looks at me.

"Ted." He turns and walks backstage.

It's dark except for a few hanging lightbulbs with pull-string switches. Everything from the walls to the floor to the curtains are black. There's a catwalk above and pullies and cords that dangle from everywhere.

We make our way down a short hallway and into a nearby office, which holds mis-matched furniture. There's a desk with a computer and a mix of lounge chairs and couches, each a different color.

"You can sit."

"Thanks." I sink into the closest lounge chair.

"Why are you here?"

"Where are the rest of the stagehands?"

"I need to call them. They're in the light booth, but I want to tell them why you're here."

"Li-RV is a highly specialized show. They have their own crew, and they need to work on their own schedule."

Ted rolls his eyes, then picks up the phone. "Yeah, the new V.P.'s here. She wants to talk about that show." Ted hangs up the phone. "They'll be right down. You know we're union. You can't come in and start demanding things. Our schedules need to be approved a month in advance."

"They have their own crew. You can keep your schedule."

"There are other powers at work here. This is an old building; you can't disrupt it."

"No one is disrupting anything. You, your pay, your schedules, won't be affected."

Ted shakes his head, like I'm missing his point. "We're a union. We have laws that protect us."

The door opens and three members of the stage crew enter.

"Hello, new V.P. I'm Julien, stage-crew manager. You met Ted, this is Ed, they're both in stage design. And, this is Ned, he's lights." Julien is very tall and has a shock of frizzy red curls.

"Ted, Ed, and Ned. Anyone ever call you Red?" I instantly regret my decision to try to lighten the mood.

"No, why?" Julien asks, his face completely serious.

"Oh, ah, never mind. It's—"

"I'm joking," Julien says, without even the slightest hint of a smile. "We're known as the 'eds' and yes, everyone calls me Red. We've worked together here for twenty years."

I laugh. Awkwardly. "Oh."

"Ted hasn't been filling your head with any of his stories, has he?" Julien asks as he, Ed, and Ned sit down.

"Of course not," Ted snaps.

"We started talking about our new show Li-RV," I say. "I realize that you're union and have certain requirements, which is fine. However, as I was explaining to Ted, Li-RV is a highly specialized show. They have their own crew and would like to use them."

"I'd love to tell you that's okay," Julien says. "But we have union laws in place. If those are broken, I'd hate to strike and create all of that turmoil, bad press, and distraction around the property when you're trying to build it back up."

"If you'd give them access to the thirteenth-floor theater, this wouldn't be an issue."

"Like I said," Ted pipes in, "there's other powers at work here. You don't want to disturb those."

"Ted's right. This is an old building. There's a lot that needs to be taken into consideration," Julien says.

I take a harder line. "There are ways around the union and ways to get a union out. I've done it before, and I can do it again if I need. I'd hate to see anything happen to your positions at Golden Sands after twenty years." It's a lie. I've never actually had to get a union out, but I had read of it.

"I'll tell you what," Julien says. "We'll meet with Li-RV and Morana today. We'll figure out a schedule and should be able to get it open by mid-June."

"That's not going to work."

"That's the best we can do. Ed, can you alert the union that we may have to bring some strikers in? We'll set up on the Boardwalk and Pacific Ave., so we may need a couple hundred volunteers."

"Your threats don't scare me. Li-RV is going to have full access to the theater," I say, and stand.

"We'll see about that. Ted, show our new boss out. We wouldn't want her to get lost back here." Julien smiles.

Ted jumps up and follows me out.

"Wrong way," he says as I try to walk ahead of him.

I spin around without saying a word.

"Listen," Ted leans in and whispers, "it's not what you think. This is an old building; it has to be handled with care."

"Mr. Asra owns this building, of course he's not going to do anything to damage it."

"You don't understand. This building is old. It has a history."

"I know, and we plan to capitalize on that and honor that tradition. That's what separates us."

"You're still not getting it. There're entities that inhabit the building. If you get them mad, they do things."

I can't believe this tactic. "Are you trying to say it's haunted?"

"More than just haunted."

"That's ridiculous and possibly the worst attempt at negotiations I've ever heard."

"I'm serious. I was almost killed by a sandbag one of these things tried to throw at me."

Shrugging, I lift my hands. "By throw, do you mean it came loose and dropped?"

"I tied it up there myself. There was no way it could've come loose." Ted picks up the pace and I stay close behind.

"You can't seriously expect me to believe this."

"Other things have happened too. They've reprogrammed lights. Moved lights. Pushed people down stairs. Made people sick."

I stop walking. "What do you mean, they made people sick?"

"The last marketing department all got sick, and no one knew what they had or what caused it."

"They all wanted out of their contracts. If you ask me, it was a brilliant, though completely immoral, scheme. Their non-compete clause was forgiven and they're all happily working elsewhere."

"How do you even know about that?"

I sigh, tired of the rumor mill gone amok. "Listen, Li-RV is taking control of the thirteenth-floor theater whether you like it or not."

"We'll see. The IATSE is powerful and very connected here. They'll not only strike, but make sure another headliner never sets foot inside this property."

"The IA . . . what?"

"International Association of Theatrical Stage Employees Local 719, our union."

"Right." I roll my eyes and make my way off stage.

Boom!

I jump and spin to see a cloud of dust rise from the stage from a sandbag that just crashed to the stage.

"See? You're making them mad already."

"Very clever," I say and look back at Ted. "I can see you holding the rope."

Chapter 16

At least the creepy music has been turned off, though it's nowhere near as quiet. Restaurant workers have begun to get the restaurants set up for the day and a few curious guests have made their way up here.

My phone vibrates with a text from Peter. 'Be there in 5'.

Instead of putting my phone away, I dial Amon.

"How'd it go?" he asks.

"Terrible. They refuse to let Li-RV in. They said they'll handle the stage work, but the show can't open until mid-June. They also said they'd strike on the boardwalk and Pacific Ave., if we didn't give in to their demands. Oh, and then one of them tried to tell me the building's haunted and only they can do the stage work. They're insane."

"What assholes. I'll talk to them."

"Sorry."

"It's not your fault. I appreciate that you even tried." Amon hangs up as Peter steps out from an unmarked door that leads into the back of the house maze.

"Hey, sorry I'm late. Mr. Asra asked me to check on the overhead music."

"It's actually perfect timing. What was going on with that?"

"Nothing. No music was playing. They're upgrading the system as we speak, but it's been disconnected since yesterday. They'll have it working by tomorrow morning."

"They must've crossed some wires today. It sounded terrible."

"Yeah, so what elevator was it? We hit them all yesterday."

"I was in the first elevator on the left side."

Peter unlocks a nearby elevator control panel and calls that elevator. The doors slide open perfectly smooth and quiet. "Are you sure it was this elevator?"

"Yes, and it was so loud I could barely stand it."

"There might have been a clump of lubricant that didn't spread evenly at first."

Peter pushes the button to close and open the doors. They're quiet. Not a single moan of metal. "Well, sounds good now. I'll check the rest of them out, just to make sure."

"Okay, thanks. That's so weird."

"Happens on occasion. Here, you can take this elevator. Do you need anything else?"

I shake my head.

As the elevator door slides shut, I check the time—it's only ten a.m., and I already feel defeated. I open my phone and click on the link that Sharp attached in his text. The blog post already has ten-thousand views and over two-thousand comments. Before I even read the article, I scan through the comments . . .

'So happy to hear this.'
'Awesome.'
'Know where I'll be this weekend.'

'Glad someone's doing something with that place.'

'Let old dogs lie.'

'My parents got married there. So glad to hear this.'

'Don't stay in room 646 it's haunted. Check out my review on Trip Advisor.'

'Cool.'

'Be there soon.'

'Hope their comps are better.'

'On my way.'

'It's a dump.'

'Love the history.'

'Can't wait.'

The reaction is overwhelmingly positive. When I read the article, I see why. Sharp took the history, the Asra family background, and the casino and twisted it all together into a tale of resurrection. I can see why so many people follow him; he can spin a great story. Reading it even makes me excited. So much so, I didn't notice the elevator doors opened on the office floor until they closed too fast for me to stick my hand in and stop them. The elevator starts to drop. I try to push the eighth-floor button but it doesn't light up. So, I try another floor. Nothing. The elevator comes to a stop on the sixth floor but just stays there. I try to push the eighth-floor button again. Still nothing.

I pull out my phone to call Peter; he must still be messing with the controls. No signal. Can't even get bars. My phone suddenly flashes and shows full reception. I dial Peter, but nothing happens. An ice-cold breeze swirls around the elevator, bringing with it a chill I feel in my bones. I dial Peter again. Nothing. My phone won't connect and the bars vanish. *Should I hit the elevator alarm? Or would that bring unwanted attention?* I close my eyes for a moment and take a few slow, deep breaths. When I open them again, my phone has bars. I quickly hit call. It connects.

"Hello," Peter answers on the first ring.

"Hey, Peter, I'm stuck in the elevator. Are you still at the controls?"

"No. Something came up and I had to run right after you left. I can get back there in fifteen minutes."

"Fifteen minutes?" The elevator bounces. "Wait. I think it's moving."

The elevator drops and comes to a stop on the second floor. The doors slide open, and Amon is there.

"Don't take this elevator," I say as I step out. "I almost got stuck in it."

"Really?" Amon asks.

I nod then get back to my call. "Peter, will you check it out?"

"I just realized what happened. When I saw you get off, I shut down access to the elevator and called it back to the second floor. Got a call from Antonio and had to run, so I canceled my call. When I did this, the controls inside the cab were disabled until someone externally called it. Did you not get off on the eighth floor?"

"Nope, that makes sense. All good then." I hang up, and stick the phone back in my pocket.

"What happened?"

"Nothing, I was reading an article and didn't get out in time on the eighth floor. Then Peter overrode the controls. Anyway, did you already meet with the stage crew?"

Amon sticks his hand in the elevator and stops it before it closes. He steps on and I follow. It works perfectly. My stomach drops as the elevator rises, and I catch my reflection in the polished gold metal of the elevator door. The brass slightly distorts our reflections, giving us a wavy appearance, but there's something else that's wrong.

"Yes," Amon says. "They send their apologies for being so rude and disrespectful to you, and they've all agreed and signed off on Morana's crew."

"And they're not going to strike?" I ask, still staring at our reflections.

"Of course not. That was such a ridiculous threat."

"What did you say to them?" A shadow moves behind me and I spin. Nothing's there except an extra-heavy glint of dust that hangs in the air.

"I can be very convincing when needed."

"I'm sorry they wouldn't work with me," I say.

Amon smiles at me and the entire elevator seems to light up. Being near him makes me feel better and I realize I'm falling under his spell. Returning the smile, I spin back towards the door, my cheeks warming.

Amon puts his arms around my shoulders. "Are you kidding? I'm the one that should apologize to you. I should've put them in their place from the beginning."

Amon still has his arm around my shoulders as we walk into our office. "Jordan, can you order us breakfast?"

"Of course. What would you like?"

"I'm okay," I say. All I really want is to get to the coffeemaker in my office.

"You have to eat. Jordan, order her some fresh berries and yogurt or maybe a couple poached eggs?"

"Berries and yogurt, please," I say and start towards my office.

"Wait," Jordan calls. "I was just going to put these in your office. This folder is some of the press that we've started to receive. I'll keep it filed, but thought you'd like to go through it first." Jordan hands me a manilla envelope.

"Perfect. Thank you." I take the envelope and turn towards my office.

"Wait, I have one more file for you. These are the upcoming promotions and their creative for you to sign off on. If you approve, initial it. If you want to make changes, you can write your changes directly on the promotion's creative." Jordan heaves a massive folder into my hands.

"Paper?"

"We're going to do this online soon, but we had a software glitch and are in the process of switching programs."

"Oh, okay, thanks."

I drop both folders on my desk, grab a cup of coffee, and collapse into my chair. The press file will be much easier to conquer, so I grab that first.

Sharp's post is on top, printed out along with the first fifty comments. I flip past. Next is a *NY Post* story, 'New York's Most Eligible Bachelor is Ready to Play' and then there's a picture of Amon standing in front of Golden Sands.

Son of international hotelier and New York's recently chosen 'Most Eligible Bachelor' has taken a gamble and

is ready to play with you. After launching three of the
Nation's top performing PE funds, Amon Asra is fo-
cusing on Atlantic City and plans to turn around the
town's worst-performing casino. Asra's funds were so
successful thanks to his uncanny ability to find unap-
preciated companies and repackage them into successful funds. Can Asra work this same magic at the Jersey
Shore? Something tells me he can, and we can all go
along for the ride. Combined with the success of his
father's international bank, Asra's making a solid bet.
The Egyptian-born banker has a unique understanding
of finance that has garnered him international acclaim.
Amon seems to be filling his father's shoes remarkably
well. Our money's on the Asras.

After reading this article, I'm a little intimidated. I had no idea
Amon was so well-known. His chiseled features photograph incredibly well.

"Here's your breakfast," Amon says, walking into my office.

I quickly flip to the next story, making an awkwardly loud paper
rustle. "Oh, thanks." A light sweat breaks out just below my collar.

"Have you looked through the press?"

"That's just what I was doing."

"I'm embarrassed."

"What could New York's most eligible bachelor possibly be embarrassed about?" I smile.

"You read it."

"I did and I have to say, it would make me want to check out Golden Sands."

"Oh, really? Why's that?" Amon grins and I feel my cheeks go from warm to fire as sweat dampens my blouse.

"Umm, well, let's just say they sell the whole package very well."

"It's still embarrassing."

"Whatever."

Amon sets my fruit and yogurt bowl on my desk. "Okay, *Girl on fire.*" Amon winks before leaving my office.

Before I know it, the day is over. Between approving creative, reading through the flood of good press, and looking at the upcoming promotions, time seems to move in hyper-speed.

By the time I get home, I'm exhausted. Happy but exhausted. I'm looking forward to a quiet dinner at home with Tori. Things were a little awkward and I want to smooth them over but the apartment is quiet. The only thing out of place is a yellow sticky note on the kitchen counter. 'Sorry! Had to go to Princeton. Will be here for the night. I'll cook dinner tomorrow. Promise! Tried to call. Couldn't get through. XOXO, Tor'

I try to call her. No answer. I text. No response. Too tired to think about dinner, I collapse in my bed. Just before falling to sleep, my mind races running through all the things that could've happened to her. She's never not replied and always has her phone glued to her hand. Even if she can't talk, she'll send a quick text. *Did she get in a car accident driving back? Could she have been mugged or kidnapped on her way to Princeton? Is she mad at me?* It's not like her.

Chapter 17

I get to work earlier today, but still not before Jordan. Over the past twenty-four hours, I must've gone through ten thousand promotional pages. I signed off on everything, but five promotions and the changes I made were minor. *How is it Thursday already?* This first week flew by. I've barely seen Tori. Still haven't heard from her and it's bothering me. I know something happened.

A knock on my office door pulls me from my thoughts; it's Amon. "Hey, Morana called and said they finished the theater load-in last night. The morning run-throughs have gone incredibly well, and they'd like to do a full-dress performance for us tonight. I thought we could have dinner here, then see the show."

"Oh, I'd love to," I pause, remembering my plans with Tori, and let out a huff. "My friend wanted to cook dinner for us tonight. I'll cancel with her."

"Why don't you invite her here?"

"Really?"

"Definitely."

"Thanks."

"Of course," Amon says, leaving as quick as he arrived.

I grab my phone and text Tori.

Me: Hey, are you alive?

Tori: I'm sorry! I meant to call you but didn't leave the library till after midnight and didn't want to wake you.

Me: Want to come to the casino for dinner and then see a preview of the show that's going to open soon?

Tori: Wait. What?!? I already grabbed everything for dinner.

Me: Can you save it for tomorrow?

Tori: I guess. But I thought we could have some time to ourselves to catch up.

Me: I know, but this work thing came up. Sorry.

Tori: No. It's fine. I get it. I'll see you tonight.

Me: Thank you! <3

"Hey," Jordan calls from the door to my office. "I have another file of creative for you to sign off on."

"Great." I shake out my sore hand. "I thought this was it." I close the file I was working on and hand it to Jordan.

"This is the last of it, they just came in. Then you're totally caught up. Need anything?" Jordan drops a light file on my desk.

"I'm good. Thank you."

I crack my fingers then open the next file. By the time I look up again, it's getting dark, the sky above the ocean is a murky navy. *How is it already a quarter-to-six?* I need to freshen up, and although I know this is ridiculous, I'm dreading the bathroom. I've been avoiding it by taking periodic walks through the casino, justifying the avoidance with my curiosity to check the action on the casino floor. Tori will be here any minute and the last thing I want is for her to see me afraid of my own bathroom.

Reaching my hand in first, I flick on the light. It's fine, completely fine. As I close the door, I glance at the painting and swear the girl's eyes move, like she glanced away. My heart pounds, but I force myself to laugh at this clever Mona Lisa trick. *I'm fine. I'm fine. I'm fine. I will not be bound by the constraints of my comfort zone.* As I reapply my red lipstick, the lights flicker. *I will not be bound by the constraints of my comfort zone.* The lights blink again. Then again and again. *I live in reality, not my imagination. Old electricity.* In the strobe of the lights, I see a face behind me. An icy hand coils around my neck. I want to scream but can't. Can't breathe. My heart flips and stops, then races. The throb of blood pulses so fast and hard that I feel it in my fingers. *No . . . No . . . No . . .* "NO!" I'm finally able to scream as the lights flicker once more and come on.

"Lilly?" There's a knock on the door. "You okay?"

I take a few deep breaths. It's just old electric and my imagination. *I* know that. A few more deep breaths. When I look at the girl in the painting, she's smirking at me.

"Lilly?"

One more slow, deep breath, and I open the door and step back into my office.

"Hey." I smile at Tori.

"Are you okay?"

"Yeah, why?"

"I heard you scream."

"Oh, I dropped my lipstick and thought I got it on my shirt, but I didn't." I force a smile.

Tori laughs. "Yeah, you'd never get that red out."

"Did you find your way up here alright?"

Tori nods and her eyes widen. "Your office, by the way, is the nicest I've ever been in. And your assistant . . ." Tori mouths the words, 'is so hot.' She fans her face.

I laugh and roll my eyes when Amon knocks and walks in. Tori's mouth drops before she collects herself, though her eyes stay wide.

"Amon, this is my friend Tori, from Las Vegas. She was recently accepted to Princeton's doctoral program and just moved to New Jersey. Tori, this is my boss and the new owner, Amon."

"It's so nice to meet you," Tori says, stepping around me.

"You as well, Tori. Princeton is an impressive university. What are you studying?"

"Anthropology."

"Really?" Amon's eyebrows raise as Tori nods and smiles. "I've always had a deep interest in anthropology. If I wasn't relocated to this life, I would've gone into the same field, though I do manage to feed my interest as a collector."

"Amon has this incredible spear from the Greek—"

"Early Roman period," Amon corrects.

"I'd love to see it," Tori says, inching closer to Amon.

"I'm still getting my collection situated after moving here, but I will give you both a tour soon." Amon steps around Tori and places his arm around my shoulders. "Lilly is my secret weapon here. She's incredible."

"She knows the industry," Tori agrees.

I grab my purse and the files from my desk. "Let me give these to Jordan."

"Did you go through those entire files?" Amon asks.

"I did."

"Told you—my secret weapon. You must be ready for a glass of wine. Shall we?"

"I'm starving," Tori says. "This is so nice. Thank you for inviting me."

Tori follows Amon and I bring up the rear, my arms loaded with the files and my purse. I happily drop the pounds of paper on Jordan's desk before making our way to the elevator.

The sun is setting behind us as we walk into 'il Sotto', Golden Sand's Italian fine-dining restaurant.

"Did you redo this restaurant?" I lean into Amon.

"No, it was really well maintained."

"It's beautiful," Tori says.

"This is one of the oldest restaurants in Atlantic City. I was told it was modeled after the Villa—"

"Carlotta?" I interrupt.

"In Italy, you've been?"

"It's my favorite museum in Lake Como. It's so beautiful there." I say.

The walls are painted a soft cream with elegant pilaster filigree and pastel murals depicting lovely young girls dancing around a calm body of water surrounded by lush greenery. Their dresses flow in the soft garden breeze. Arched doors with floor-to-ceiling windows overlook a deck that sits above the ocean. Delicate Italian glass chandeliers sway from the ceiling seeming to reach for the sea.

A maître d, dressed in a formal black suit, shows us to our table. Amon pulls out a chair for Tori.

"Thanks." She looks back and smiles.

I take the seat next to Tori and Amon sits across from me.

"Tori, is this your first time to New Jersey?" Amon asks.

Tori nods. "It's my first time on the east coast." She pauses and leans in a little. "And, to be honest, I'm a little surprised it's so beautiful. Not at all, how I imagined the armpit of America."

"Wait till the summer. You'll think you're in another world," Amon says.

Felix walks up behind us. "Wait till you see the beach club we have planned for Golden Sands. You'll feel like you're at Scorpios in Mykonos."

"Thanks," Amon adds, "to Golden Sands' age and history, we are the only property in Atlantic City with riparian rights that allow us to operate a structure on the beach. It'll be one-of-a-kind, like you." Amon's eyes meet mine before flicking to the group. "The building's already there. It used to be a restaurant. We are just redoing it. The restaurant will be open all year, but in the summer, it will open onto the beach where we'll have Riptide Beach Club."

"Really?" I ask.

Amon nods. "Dustin sent me the finalized renderings." He pulls out his phone and hands it to me.

I show Tori, then pass the phone back. "It's beautiful," I say.

"I know where I'll be this summer," Tori adds.

"Oh, Felix, I'm sorry. This is my friend, Tori, from Las Vegas. She's living with me this summer until she officially starts her doctoral program at Princeton."

Felix smiles. "Princeton, nice. It's lovely to meet you, Tori."

"Felix, can you join us?" Amon asks.

Felix checks his watch, and I notice his platinum Rolex Daytona. My mother gave my father the exact, extremely expensive watch. I'd never seen another Rolex like it. Its onyx face had a gunmetal symbol of a circle with a snake wrapped around it. She told him this watch was exceptionally rare.

"Yes, I'm free 'till eight. I'm going to a preview of Morana's show."

"So are we," I say.

"Perfect, sit," Amon says.

"That's a beautiful watch. My father has the same exact one."

"I know," Felix tells me. "Thanks. It was a gift."

"You know my father?"

Amon's eyebrows momentarily knit together as he and Felix exchange a brief glance. "Oh," Felix pauses. "Amon, it *was* Mr. Umbra that we met with in New York when you first thought about purchasing the Golden Sands, right?"

"That's right, I almost forgot about that. My father set up a meeting with your dad and my team because your dad's consulting on another property here."

"Rise," I say and Amon nods.

"We both were wearing our watches. That's why I remembered," Felix says.

"Is that a symbol on it?" Tori asks.

"It is. It's an ancient Egyptian symbol that means prosperity—"

"Through chaos," I finish.

"I find symbols so interesting and powerful," Tori says. "They'll be a main focus of my studies. May I?" She holds her hands across the table towards Felix. He places his hand in hers and she pulls it a little closer. "Stunning," she says, looking at Felix, then releases his hand. When she does this, I realize she looks different, prettier. Her hair is blonder, her lips a little fuller and redder. She's wearing shoes with heels and clothes that show off rather than hide her ample curves. I can't help but think my mother would approve.

Felix smiles back at her, his eyebrow raising slightly. "Symbols can be powerful. What's your area of focus?"

"I'm in anthropology, but my focus is the psychology and power behind symbols and rituals in history's most powerful cults."

"Cults?" Amon asks.

"Yes, beginning with the Greco-Roman cults, including the Eleusinian Mysteries, and moving through to modern or nearly modern times."

"How do you differentiate between a cult and a religion?" Amon asks.

"That's a great question and that line can be extremely thin with some religions we have today, but I won't name names." Tori winks. "Though I classify religions as working within a wider culture and cults as mainly being counterculture."

"Mmm, counterculture?" Amon says. "Haven't most religions originated from counterculture movements?"

"That's a valid point and you're right, but that's also what differentiates a religion from a cult. Once a movement—" I notice Tori's back stiffen slightly; she's readying herself.

"Cult," Amon interjects.

"Not yet. It's neither a cult nor a religion. That changes. When a movement is widely accepted by a people, it supports the culture, and those people practice and document the rituals and traditions—then the movement becomes a religion. On the flip side, if the movement is kept secret, it remains counterculture, and is never accepted by a bulk of the population—the movement becomes a cult."

"So, it boils down to control?" Amon asks.

"What do you mean?" Tori asks.

Amon drums his fingers on the table. "Religion is really just a tool to control through fear. Is that what you mean by supporting the wider culture that it's in?"

"Define control through fear," Tori says.

Felix chimes in. "If you break the ten commandments, you answer to the devil in hell."

Tori shakes her head. "Those commandments give order to society and help it function. That's not control. That's support."

"That's debatable," Felix says with a smile.

"Are you religious, Tori?" Amon asks.

"I was raised Catholic."

"Christianity," Amon starts slowly, "would have fit very nicely into your definition of a cult for over three-hundred years after Jesus was crucified."

"There's no timetable of the origin of a religion," Tori says.

Amon tilts his head and says, "So, what you may consider a cult in your research today may turn into a religion tomorrow. Then what would happen to all your research?"

"It would still apply." Tori smiles. "Change is inevitable. It's not the end result that gives us the answers, but the process . . . the movement."

Amon chuckles. "That, I can agree with you on."

"Tori, can I ask you a question?" Felix says. "Do you go to church every Sunday?"

"No, I think the last time I attended was Christmas."

"Then you're breaking a commandment and you know what that means." Felix smirks at Tori and she smiles back.

"That's just the definition I use to differentiate for the sake of my research."

"So, you're more of a researcher, less of a practitioner?" Amon asks.

"I practice in my own way and really just enjoy the history and tradition of it," Tori says.

"Yes, it does have a fascinating history," Amon says. "I'd love to talk to you more about this, but have learned religion and politics are best left out of dinner conversations."

"Are you religious, Amon?" Tori asks.

Amon gives her a grin. "I've studied every religion and have my own set of beliefs."

"Well, Lilly doesn't believe in anything." Tori looks at me with a playful smile.

"That's not true." I laugh. "Tori's still mad at me because I told her Christmas was exploited by retailers to get people to buy ridiculous amounts of gifts and I refused to buy her a Christmas present one time when we were like fourteen."

"Yeah, well, I bought you a gift," Tori mutters, a smile pulling at her lips.

"So, what do you believe, Lilly?" Felix asks.

"I don't know. I guess I believe there's *something,* but that none of us has any idea what that is. I think humans created religion, and as such, it's flawed. And it's definitely been used to do some terrible things."

"And it's been used to do some wonderful things," Tori adds.

"Yes, definitely," I say.

As if sensing the softening of our conversation, our waiter brings over an antipasto tray and bottle of wine.

Amon puts up his hand to stop the waiter from filling our glasses. "Anyone in the mood for a martini first?"

"Make mine extra dirty, Beefeater, two olives," Felix says.

"Same," Tori says.

"Extra dirty, but Grey Goose," Amon says.

"I might stick with wine," I say with a shrug. "I am still trying to remain a little professional."

Felix gives me a wink. "Our corporate climate is as much about having fun as it is working. You'll figure that out soon."

"Yeah," Tori says. "Come on, if I'm here, you're not totally working and it's my first official night here."

"We are celebrating," Amon says.

"Martinis go right to my head," I say.

"You'll be fine," Tori says.

"Are you always so uptight in work-mode?" Felix asks.

"Felix," Amon snaps.

"What?"

"Don't be rude. Lilly is the reason Golden Sands has so many people here today."

"I know, I just don't want her to burn out. Lilly, we're cool right?"

"Grey Goose, dirty, for me please," I tell the waiter. He smiles and nods, placing the open bottle of Opus One on the table, then disappearing.

"So, do you know anything about the show we're seeing tonight?" Felix asks Tori and me.

I shake my head. "No, Amon told me it was a very popular show from New York, but that's it."

"Very popular is an understatement. Immersive theater has been big in the city for a while, you know, with *Sleep No More* and *Bottom of the Ocean*."

"What are they?" Tori asks.

"It's a more involved theater experience. At *Sleep No More*, everyone wears these masks and you wander through an old hotel where each room has been transformed into a different sort of stage and the actors play out the scenes in those spaces. And *Bottom of the Ocean* is performed for like five audience members at a time; it's supposed to be about rituals and ceremony."

"That sounds cool," Tori says.

"Yeah, they're fun," Felix says, "but according to early reviews they can't compare to Li-RV, which critics say is, I quote, 'life-changing.'"

"That sounds amazing," Tori says.

"Yeah," I say. "I can only imagine how successful it's going to be. I mean, the Cirque shows changed Las Vegas, so if this is anything close to that—it will be huge for us."

"That's exactly what I thought," Amon says, smiling at me.

Before I know it, I've downed a martini and two glasses of wine, feasted on ragu alla Bolognese and chicken cacciatore, topped off with panna cotta. My cheeks are sore from laughing.

Felix checks his watch. "Amon, the show is supposed to start in five minutes."

"Already?"

"Yeah."

"We should go," Amon says.

"Though I was enjoying myself here," Felix says as he slides his chair out, looking at Tori with a tight-lipped grin.

Tori is lost in his gaze, and Felix steps around the table and pulls her chair out for her, offering his hand as she stands. Before Amon can do the same for me, I quickly slide my chair out and try to stand, but in my haste, the floor seems to wobble and I flop back down. Amon offers his hand, and I accept.

"I told you, right to my head." I smile.

"You're fine." He tucks my hand into the crook of his elbow.

I do feel fine, a little better than fine. Amon looks down at me and smiles. His green eyes are speckled with gold; from this close, they seem to glow. Squeezing his arm a little tighter, I can feel his muscles and he pulls me in closer. The warm musk of his cologne unleashes a dam of emotions and desires I haven't felt in a very long time. Heat surges from my chest, crawls up my neck, and blooms across my cheeks like fever. Knowing I shouldn't feel this, I immediately look down at my feet.

Amon places a finger under my chin, pulling my gaze back to his. "Ready?" he asks softly.

I can't help but smile back. A feeling of protection wraps a comforting blanket around me.

Chapter 18

A s the doors slide open to the thirteenth floor, warm candlelight creeps into our car. The entire floor has been transformed, taken back to another time. Gold candelabras in every height are the only source of light. Red satin curtains hang from the ceiling and spill down the walls through the hall, obscuring any hint of modernity.

A performer wearing a long black cape, face hidden by a low-slung hood, steps into the elevator lobby and stands facing us, holding only a gas-lit lantern. He stands for a moment too long, then slowly spins counterclockwise and walks towards the theater.

"This is so cool," Tori whispers.

It is cool, but with this much open flame and drapery, there's no way this show will pass code.

"Amon," I whisper, pulling him closer, "this looks incredible, but I'm worried it won't pass code."

"It already has. It passed earlier today."

"Really? How?"

"I'm not sure. All I know is that the show, the set, and the full experience were approved earlier today."

"But with all this open flame and material—"

"Lilly, *relax*. Enjoy it. You don't have to worry about every detail." Amon stops, turns towards me, and holds both of my hands. "I appreciate that you do, but tonight I want you to have fun."

"I'm sorry."

"Don't be sorry." Amon tucks my arm back in his and we catch up to our guide. "I love that you care. But I want you to have fun, too."

Our guide pauses in front of a wall of curtains, pivots towards us, lifts both arms, and says, "Per ostium hoc, industriam vocamus Li-RV."

"Latin," Amon whispers.

"Do you speak Latin?"

"Speak, no. Understand, yes."

"What did he say?"

"Something like 'through this door, we invoke the energy Li-RV.'"

"What?"

Amon shrugs and swirls his pointer finger next to his temple—the universal sign for crazy. I erupt in a brief but loud laugh and draw a sharp glare from Tori and Felix, who are clearly caught up in the mood of the show.

'Sorry,' I mouth. As I'm trying to stifle any more outbursts, something sends an icy shiver sliding down my spine. I'm not entirely sure why, but it's enough to stir the swirl of unease in my stomach into a sense of dread.

Our guide abruptly lowers his arms at the exact time the curtains rise. "Intra!"

Black and red curtains sway from the ceiling. At the center of the billowy drapery hangs a massive chandelier made from all sorts of antlers and animal horns.

"Tenebrae ad liberandum nos!" Our guide yells and the light is swallowed by darkness, thick and absolute, robbing me of even the outlines of those standing beside me.

I can't see my hand when I hold it directly in front of my eyes. A blanket of silence comes with the darkness. Everything is still. I squeeze Amon's arm a little tighter and draw a sharp breath. He leans over and whispers, "I'm pretty sure that meant something like 'darkness delivers us.'"

A strobe fires a pulse of bright light into the center of the curtained space, illuminating silhouettes in black hoods. They began chanting some sort of strange song. Then two candle flames materialize beside us, held aloft by robed figures who emerge from shadow like apparitions. More candles ignite in sequence, a constellation of flickering stars, forming a glowing pathway.

All the seats have been removed, at least from what I can see. The candlelight leads us to a single church pew, and we take our seats. I'm trying to stay in the moment, but it's hard to imagine how this sort of show will translate to a casino attraction. Casinos don't have the artistic luxury of presenting shows to only five audience members at a time, and I can't see how the same scene could be presented to an audience of hundreds.

As soon as we sit, the theater goes dark again. Tori reaches over and squeezes my hand. "This is so cool," she whispers.

She's right, I think, *I need to relax.* I remind myself that *I am not bound by the confines of my comfort zone. I am not bound by the confines of my comfort zone. I am not bound by the confines of my comfort zone.*

A single violin whines a low, slow song. Candles on the floor swirl to life, speeding a trail to the black mosaic design on the floor, encircling the round geometric sun in flame. A sole dancer emerges from the darkness and steps into the circle. She's completely covered in a skintight, red bodysuit. Even her face is obscured by the crimson material. A thick black ponytail spills out from the top of the suit, surrounded by a spiked crown forged from gunmetal. The room goes dark and silent for a moment. Then the violin plays again, but much faster and higher. Flames explode from the candles surrounding the dancer, then simmer back to a flicker. A red spotlight shines down on her as her body writhes in unnatural angles. She seems to be in agony as her back curves towards us and every vertebrae in her spine shows through the tight bodysuit. She suddenly slams to the ground. The lights go dark, and silence envelops us once again.

"Aquerragoite," a deep male voice calls out from behind us, from what I guess is the back corner of the theater.

"Aquerraveite," another male voice calls from somewhere in front of us.

"Aquerragoite," a high-pitch female voice calls from the left of us.

"Aquerraveite," the deep male voice whispers directly behind me. Caught completely by surprise, my spine goes rigid.

"Ahhhh," I scream, and everyone laughs. Amon squeezes my hand, letting me know that I'm safe, and I join in the laughter.

A bell chimes three times, and a wall of fire erupts around the circle. As the flames die down, there's another person in the circle. Behind the girl in red stands a male dancer wearing form fitting black pants with no shirt. The red spotlight descends over his chiseled body, invoking a dance of shadows in every bulge of muscle. The top of his face is covered by a black leather mask with long curved horns and pointed ears.

The whine of the violin is joined by the low, deep cry of a cello. The male dancer pulls the girl in red up by just her arm and wraps his body around hers. He spins her and throws her. He lifts her leg above her head then pushes her to the ground, barely catching her before she smashes to the floor. Their movements are powerful, but seemingly effortless. As this pas de deux of the damned gracefully twists away, a trail of fire catches on the surrounding floor, tracing out the shape of a star.

The music slows, and the dance finishes with the girl sitting in the middle of the flames, the man standing behind her. The fire has died and all that's left is the soft flicker of the circle of candles.

The soft, lyrical overtone of the violin is soon joined with the deep timbre of the cello. Together, they play a dirge while the dancers remain frozen. Then I feel the single beat of a powerful drum in my chest. The male dancer throws his arms into the air and the girl in red slowly floats upward. She dangles above his head in a lotus position. At first, I have no idea how this is being done. Then I notice the cable braided into her ponytail. The music remains slow, and the drum beats twice more before holding in a fermata.

The drum accelerates into an angry rudiment—a call to war. The riff is soon answered by the powerful bow-cry of the violin and cello. The girl in red flies over our heads, her body contorting into impossible positions. It's hard to watch, but impossible to take my eyes off of her. My heartbeat matches the staccato rhythm of the drum, and my scalp tingles with every spin and drop. The dancer whirls wildly, then lowers to her partner. She wraps her body around his. He lifts his arms into a menacing arc. A single spotlight freezes on them, turning the pair into a dark sculpture. The music slows to just the plaintive cry of the violin. Then the theater goes dark. Silent.

Completely still.

I listen for even the slightest hint of movement. A clue for what's coming, though I sense absolutely nothing. In the complete and utter darkness, I'm lost.

A row of candles flicker to life, just feet from our seats. They seem to float, and rise until they illuminate the wild faces of the performers holding them. Wicked smiles peel across their faces. They're wearing red, yellow, and blue jester costumes—backwards—and brightly colored patchwork hats with long floppy ears that remind me of a donkey. They giggle like they know something we don't. The one on the left hits the jester in the middle, who elbows the entertainer on the right. The jester on the right—closest to me—stumbles forward, grabs my arm and pulls me up. Then they wave to Amon, Felix, and Tori to stand. I grab Amon's hand, pull him to his feet, and the jesters erupt in unhinged giggles.

They urge us to follow. We do. They giggle frenziedly and pat each other on the backs, which, according to their twisted costumes, is their fronts. The rest of the theater is a pool of complete blackness. The darkness swallows our seat. The only light in the entire theater hangs just around the backwards-jesters.

They continue to walk, and we continue to follow so we're not consumed by the dark. They continue to giggle wildly and whisper to each other in gibberish. We must be moving in nonsense circles because the theater isn't that big, but the abyssal darkness is so disorienting that it's impossible to know. Then the jester on the left farts, and the middle one bonks him on the head while the jester on the right howls with laughter.

This fart-bonk-laugh riposte continues until it becomes so awkward that we're all laughing just to temper the unease. The jesters suddenly stop. Their candles go dark and we're left standing in a sea of black. I reach for Amon and he pulls me close. It feels like we're floating in space.

Suddenly, a spotlight ignites. It lights a doorway in front of us that resembles the vaulted door to a Roman basilica, but flipped upside down, the pointed archway digging into the ground. Even plants hanging from the sky seem to grow upside down. Stained glass with images of saints and angels appear to be falling down . . . down . . . down. A chill stirs at the base of my nape and runs down my spine, setting off a rumble in my gut. I breathe deep, but before I have time to settle my unease, a jester grabs my hand and pulls me through the door.

I don't have time to get my bearings before the darkness seizes me. I'm separated from the group. It's completely silent. Black. My heart races. "Amon," I call in a loud whisper.

"I'm here."

"This is crazy. It's so cool," Tori adds with a giggle.

We're near each other, yet we're all separated. Candles flicker near our feet, and light crawls from the ground until the entire space is lit. The area is set up like a church, though in place of the pews are pillows, cushions, and low beds that sit on a floor of grass.

We're all placed in a different part of the dark chapel. Amon makes his way to me, grabs my hand, and leads me to the front. The cushions are so soft that it's impossible to remain rigid, and gravity pulls us together. Tori and Felix take the row across the aisle from us.

The violin begins once more and I recognize the iconic song, 'O Fortuna.' A bit cliché. But the music changes to Mozart's 'Magic Flute,' which I saw with my parents. The Queen of the Night, dressed in a long black gown, her head covered in a tight leather cap with a crown made of bones, floats in front of us. Black wings sweep from her back. She sings "oh" repeatedly in notes that are so high and haunting, I can't fathom how a human can create such a sound. Then she starts the lyrics, only she sings them in English. I've only ever heard the German version of this aria.

"The vengeance of Hell boils in my heart,

"Death and despair flame about me!

"If he does not through you feel the pain of birth,

"Then you will be my daughter nevermore.

"Disowned may you be forever,

"Abandoned may you be forever,

"Destroyed be forever,

"All the bonds of nature,

"If not through you,

"He becomes pale!

"Hear the gods below pledge of revenge,

"Hear a mother's oath!"

Her voice is so incredible that tears well in my eyes. This has been one of my favorite opera songs since I was a child, and my favorite part of Mozart's 'Magic Flute.' Though I always knew the song was dark, I had no idea it was *this* dark.

As she finishes her song, she floats to the ground. The music changes and I can't place it. The drumbeat quickens, though the cello and violin no longer seem as sad. The Queen of the Night cackles and lifts her arms. Flames erupt. She floats back into the air as the curtains on the stage lift to reveal a huge, life-size altar with multiple levels. This enormous frame fills the stage, like a conglomerate of picture frames held upright and stacked nearly three-stories high—three at the base, three in the middle and three at the top.

Every frame has a scene behind it, like fine-art paintings come to life.

Instead of holding sculpted or painted figures of Christ, saints, and the blessed virgin, there are performers posing in their place. The performers remain so still that I wonder if they are, in fact, statues.

The bottom center position holds an altar with a large black chalice. The top row, above the main panel, displays figures dressed as royalty in billowy gowns and capes—a king and queen of sorts, dressed in royal red with spiky black crowns. In the frame next to them stands someone pious, like a bishop or pope with a tall hat, but dressed in all black. A naked man and woman stand on the far outside upper row. The woman is on the right, her very long hair cascades down like a curtain. The man dangles an apple conveniently in front of his penis. As I look closer, there's a snake wrapped around the naked woman's leg. *Adam and Eve.*

In the arched box on the middle left stand a group of female performers dressed in black bondage costumes. They hold whips and chains while they appear to read from a large black book. On the right, a guitarist and bassist of a heavy metal band, dressed in torn black clothes and top hats, pose with their instruments.

The bottom row of the stage piece has two more boxes on each side of the empty center box. The performers in those boxes are a wild mix of characters—witches, jesters, and some performers that appear to be wearing nothing but rope wrapped around them.

The Queen of the Night laughs as she descends from the air once more to the top of the set. The flames settle and she comes to rest on a perch above the black bishop. Her legs dangle over the box. Resting her hands on her hips, she looks around, laughing more before she quiets. The entire theater becomes impossibly still and silent.

The Queen of the Night slowly and gracefully swirls her hands, then in one swift movement, punches them up. Right in time, the heavy metal band burst into a heart-pounding rock ballad. Performers dive out from behind the massive altar and drop down, stopping themselves mere inches before they crash to the ground. Dressed in bondage costumes that consist of nothing more than a few cleverly placed black straps, they leap to catch hold of dangling silk ropes. The performers swing wildly from rope to rope as more drop from the ceiling. Aerialists, performing on black silks.

The performers from the bottom row pour from their boxes. Twice as many dancers emerge than I originally thought. Men, dressed in nothing but ropes, lift and throw their female partners, who are dressed in torn black rags that cling to their fit bodies, their faces covered with black veils. A group of dancers dressed in the bondage costumes crawl across the stage so quickly and inhumanly that my heart skips a beat. The performers climb the ropes as quickly as they spin down. Some seem to kiss and make love before flipping to the ground. The music is fast and heavy.

There's so much going on that, at first, I miss the procession of performers entering from behind us. The lights brighten a touch, and we're sitting among trees and flowers. I'm blown away by how they pulled this off.

These new performers are dressed as anthropomorphic characters—humanoid animals. Leading the procession is a satyr that walks on his hands while his hooves dangle over his horned head. A centaur walks backwards with a bird-girl doing handstands and backbends on his hind legs. It's the most incredible costume I've ever seen. They're followed by a group of rabbit-girls that cartwheel and tumble. A man and his bride walk backwards, arm in arm—the male performer in black pants and a horned mask, while the female dancer is in all white with the face of a lamb and a gold crown between her petite pink ears.

As the two groups converge on the altar, the music slows and is joined by the soft song of the violin and cello. The Queen of the Night sings a rock opera in a language I don't understand—soft but powerful.

There's so much going on. I don't know where to look. The ballerinas leap before collapsing in a perfectly choreographed dance that's so precise, not a single arabesque is out of place or time. The aerialists rise and fall above them, while the Queen of the Night hits impossible notes. At the center of it all, the male performer in black horns dances a pas de deux with his lamb. She holds her body in the most beautiful lifts and spins. They make the impossible look easy. He lays her on the altar beside the challis and climbs on top of her but she spins, placing him beneath her. He wraps her in his muscular arms for a moment, before letting her go. She gracefully swirls her arms in the air and holds her position.

The man takes out a knife and stabs the lamb through her heart.

Blood fountains from her chest, and she smiles wickedly as the crimson fluid fills the chalice next to them. The performers' dance becomes dark and chaotic. Strobe lights come on. The music is now heavy and fast.

It's too much.

The room spins. I'm dizzy. Blood drains from my head and pools in the building, nausea in my gut. I start to sweat and shiver. My mouth waters as my entire core seizes in one massive, painful cramp. I stagger to my feet but don't know which direction to run. The strobe lights are disorienting. I'm completely turned around and moments from vomiting all over this intricate set. Hand over my mouth, I race out of the chapel door and find Morana standing there. My stomach spasms in its first attempt to erupt. Morana grabs my arm and quickly guides me out of the theater and to the bathroom.

She touches my cheek, soft pity on her face.

I remember where I've seen her before.

Chapter 19

Acid burns in the back of my throat. I barely make it to the toilet when the hot, sour contents of my stomach pour into the cold porcelain bowl. My gut heaves violently. Over and over. The bitter remnants of bile sting my throat. Slowly, the spasms ease. I spit as much as I can, then flush the toilet and rest my forehead against the cold metal of the stall partition.

My mind races as I desperately search what few memories I have from that first night coming home to my parents. All of which is wrapped in a thick veil of Xanax-induced fog. But I have one clear memory–the doctor. The same dewy skin. The same face.

Morana.

That's impossible. Right? I flip between the two images in my mind. Maybe it's not the same face. In my memory, their hair is different. I was so out of my mind then. The image of her, the doctor, is so clear. Could I have superimposed a clear memory on a broken one? *Why am I so bothered by this?*

A tap turns on, pulling me from my thoughts. When I peek through the thin crack in the stall, I can't see anyone. I look under the door. No one is in here. The metal screech of an antique faucet cuts the silence and a second sink turns on. I stand to leave, but the lights go dark and terror wraps its chains around me. My breath becomes shallow, though my heart pounds so hard I worry it will give me away to whoever is in here.

I quietly close the toilet seat and crawl on top. The click of a hard-soled shoe echoes off the tile floor near the door, moving towards me. Something like a cane or crutch scratches the floor as it nears. I hug my legs into my chest and try to stay as quiet as possible. Barely breathing, my head swims. I tuck deeper into my legs and gulp for air as quietly as possible. The grating stops directly in front of my stall. My eyes shoot open, but it's too dark to see anything.

The air pressure changes. A painful heaviness fills my eardrums as the most horrid sound spills into my stall. A pain-filled, high-pitched keening claws at my ears. I cover them with my hands, nails digging into my scalp.

Something bangs on my stall door.

"Lil?"

I gasp and open my eyes. The lights are back on. The air pressure has returned to normal.

Another knock on my stall door. "Lil, are you okay?" Tori's familiar voice calls through the stall.

I clear my throat. "I . . . I think so."

"Oh, thank God. I panicked when I came in. The lights were off and I thought you'd passed out or something. Did you not turn the lights on when you came in?"

"They were on when I came in and then turned off on their own."

"Someone must not have realized you were in here and turned them off. What happened to you? Did you get sick?"

"Yeah." I uncurl from on top of the toilet and rest my feet on the ground, rest my elbows on my knees and my chin in my hands.

"How do you feel now?"

"I'm . . . I . . . I don't know what happened."

"What do you mean? Do you still feel sick?"

There's a knock on the exterior bathroom door and then I hear it push open.

"Lilly, are you okay? Can I come in?" Amon asks.

I sit up taller, straighter, take a few deep breaths. *Could I have really imagined that—that feeling—that sound—all because someone accidentally turned off the lights?* I wring my hands and stand up.

"Okay," I say, and open the bathroom stall.

"Here," Amon says, and passes me a glass of coke. "I got you a coke. How do you feel?"

"Better." I take a sip.

Amon takes a shuddering breath. "I will never try to talk you into drinking a martini again."

With a shrug, I sip the coke, and walk over to the sink. "I didn't feel drunk enough to get sick," I say, looking at my reflection in the mirror.

"The good news is," Tori starts, "you won't have a hangover tomorrow like I will. Speaking of, I'm ready for another drink, are we heading . . ." Her voice trails off.

"How do you feel now?" Amon asks.

"Okay. Not sick anymore."

"Dustin is holding a soft opening of this club for the performers. He would love us to check it out."

"Really?" I let out a breath. "I don't know."

"It's opening tomorrow, so it's really our only chance to check it out."

I take a long draw of coke. "Alright, we'll meet you in the hall. I just want to freshen up." I grab Tori's hand, so she stays.

"Do you want me to get you anything else?" Amon asks as he makes his way out.

"No, thanks. I'm fine."

"Yay," Tori says. "This is so fun! It's like we're back in college. What was that saying puke and—"

"No, it's not like that." I pull her to look at me. "I didn't drink enough to get sick."

"Maybe you got motion sick from the lights, combined with a few drinks?"

"Something weird happened in here. Something was in here with me. It . . . It—"

Tori grabs both of my arms and turns me towards her. "Lilly, we just saw the craziest, most imaginative, insanely intense show ever. Then you get sick and someone turns the lights off on you, so, of course, your imagination is going to play tricks on you."

Could that be it? "I guess."

"Lilly, look at me," Tori says. "Good. Now take a deep breath." I do. "You have worked so incredibly hard and have so much on your plate. This place is amazing. That dinner was delicious. I don't even have words for how unbelievable that show was. And when I came in, the casino was packed. It's okay for you to enjoy the seeds of your hard work."

I nod. "You're right. I just feel like there's still so much to do and these weird things keep happening."

"Ah, yeah, that's called stress."

Stress. "You have a point," I force myself to say. I want to go home and crawl into the security of my bed, but more than that, I want to prove that I'm better now, that I can be successful. I toss a piece of gum in my mouth, grab my lipstick. While I apply it, I stare into the mirror . . . *I am not bound by the confines of my comfort zone. I am the guardian of my mind. I am in control. I am not bound by the confines of my comfort zone. I am not bound by the confines of my comfort zone.*

We join Amon and Felix in the hall. Now that I'm not trying to keep vomit in, I notice how complete the transformation of this entire space is. The nightclub sits opposite the theater on the thirteenth floor and is divided by a long, wide hallway. The last time I was up here, there were meeting rooms and other doors that lined the hall, though those are covered by scarlet, velvet drapes that swoop and sway from the ceiling. Simple, circular, wrought-iron chandeliers that appear to be lit by candlelight hold the drapes in place. Ornate brass candelabras line the hall, their candles creating a dance of shadows in the folds of the luxurious material.

Above the doorway is a gunmetal sign, styled in an Old English font, and lit from behind with mercury-blue neon lights: 'Surrender' hangs heavy over the ingress. Music meanders from the space. The deep—boom—boom—boom—bass bounces off the walls, down the hall to where we stand, beckoning us in before the brisk staccato rat-a-tat-tat comes in louder and faster, urging your body to move.

"Ready?" Amon asks as the performers pour from the theater.

We step back to let them go ahead. While they no longer wear their costumes, their physique and grace give them away. They float rather than walk, every movement so controlled, every muscle visible. It's almost like they're another breed.

Felix files in behind the performers. Tori follows and grabs my hand. It's like we're nineteen again, on summer break from college with our first fake IDs.

Inside, laser lights dance around the room, catching on the gleam of the new dance floor at the center of the club. The DJ booth sits at the back, presiding over the floor. The headphoned jockey's arms slide across his table, his body bouncing to the downbeat. At the crescendo, he lifts both arms into the air, and fire shoots out of platforms surrounding the dance floor. As the fire settles, go-go dancers appear on the platforms.

The dance floor remains empty as the performers swarm the bars that flank the open space.

"What do you think?" Dustin asks, startling me from behind.

"How did you pull this off in a matter of days?" I yell over the music.

"Easy. The space and lighting frames were here. We had everything else we needed in our other clubs. All we had to do was the load-in."

"Amazing job, Dustin," Amon says.

"It was Lilly's idea. I just brought the space together. Roped off a booth for you in our VIP section or where it will be," Dustin says, leading us deeper into the club.

We step up onto a platform that overlooks the dance floor, giving us a complete view of the entire club and DJ.

As the coda slows and the intense beat lightens, the DJ comes on the mic. "What's happening party people? Got word the lady of the hour is here . . . She thought this space needed a nightclub and I'd say she was right! We're here because of you Lilith . . . CHEEEER-RRRRS!"

Sparklers behind the DJ stage erupt and spell out 'Lilith' in cursive.

Then a group of girls all carrying sparklers and glowing bottles of Dom Perignon parade to our table. I grew up in Las Vegas where extravagance in nightclubs is the norm but this is over-the-top even for Vegas. As glasses of champagne are passed around the room, two massive birdcages lower from the darkness that shrouds the ceiling to hang just above the bars. Inside each cage a large hoop holds two aerialists that wind, swing, hang, and climb.

A silver bucket of ice with four crystal glasses and a magnum bottle of Dom Perignon are placed on our table. At the precise moment the servers fill our glasses and pass them to us the music hits a womp—womp—womp and the DJ comes back on the mic, "Let's lift our glasses to Lilith. This one's for you. Cheeeers parrrrrttyyy peeeeopllle!"

Flames erupt again and the entire club is lifting their glasses to me. I want to crawl under the table but Tori grabs my elbow, leans over and whispers, "Stand up."

Without thinking, I do. My brain has given up and crawled into a corner and is watching my body go through the motions as I stand and lift my glass to the crowd now gathered below on the dance floor. From some distant part of my brain, I see the crowd scream and cheers, then Tori bellows, "To Lilly!"

Amon and Felix lift their glasses and clink Tori's then mine. Everyone sips their champagne and when I do, they erupt in cheering again.

When I sit back down, Amon puts his arm around me, leans in, and whispers, "I'm sorry. I had no idea Dustin was planning this."

Then Tori leans over. "Lilly, you're like famous. This is so cool!"

I didn't want to drink. Just planned to stop in, check it out, and go home. But that plan is clearly out-the-door. I'm so uncomfortable. Not knowing what to say, I take another sip of my champagne.

Dustin returns and sits beside Felix. "Lilly, I hope you didn't mind our little show of appreciation," he yells over the table.

"Little?" I say and scratch my forehead.

"I have to come clean," he says. "My staff needed to rehearse our VIP bottle service routine in this new location, so I thought this would be perfect. We get practice in *and* let you know we appreciate you."

"That actually makes me feel a little better," I say.

Amon leans in so close, his breath tickles my neck. "We really do appreciate you."

I turn to tell Amon thanks, but his face is still so close that my lips brush his cheek and he doesn't pull back. He leans a little closer. My brain is screaming at me to stop this, it's completely unprofessional, and a bad idea, but I don't move. Don't *want* to move. I take a deep inhale as the musk of his cologne mixes with the sweetness of champagne on his breath. Every part of me wants to lean closer and forget that anyone else is here, but I don't. Instead, I say, "Thank you, I really love working here."

"Good, I think incredible things are in store for you and me as a team," Amon says with his deep eyes searching mine.

"Let's dance!" Tori yells, grabbing my hand and pulling me out of the booth.

"No," I say, trying to sit back down.

"Don't be so boring. Come ooonn," Tori says, her words beginning to drag.

"Go ahead, Lilly. Have fun. This is your night," Felix says.

"Fine." I begrudgingly slide out of the booth.

"Yay," Tori says, laughing wildly.

She grabs my hand, stumbling slightly, then drags me down the aisle of the VIP section. As we make our way down, the dance floor is now packed with the performers from the show. It's as if the music flows into their bodies, and out of their limbs. So graceful, so on beat, so perfect with bodies that make dancing look as easy as breathing.

I spot a dark, empty corner of the dance floor and turn, pulling Tori with me. Though when we step on the dance floor, the throng of dancers separate.

"Lilith."

I spin, but don't know who called my name. Then again, a different voice, male, from somewhere else.

"Lilith." I whip around, but don't know who said my name.

"Lilith." A girl steps in front of me. A grin slowly peels across her face. She still has white makeup around her eyes—the lamb that danced the pas de deux.

"Come. Dance with us," she continues, stepping backwards so gracefully I can't help but watch her. She swirls her arm up and holds her hand out to me so elegantly, I have to take it.

Her body seems to float with each ethereal step back towards the center of the dance floor. I follow, unable to take my eyes from her. Dancers are gifted with the talent to captivate an audience just by the movement of their bodies, and now I understand how powerful that ability is. She sways in mesmerizing arcs that brush against other dancers.

Soon, my body starts to move. My hips sway to the beat. Tori closes her eyes, arms in the air. The electronic music has us under its spell and it feels good to surrender to it. Performers brush up against me, our bodies momentarily moving together, then spinning onto the next. I let go of everything and simply move.

Tori pulls me towards her, and when she does, I see *him* off in a dark corner. Him. Just standing there. His hood pulled low and face in shadow. Without a doubt, it's him. It's Kai.

Freedom vanishes in a heartbeat, hollow panic rushing in to fill the void. I freeze mid-dance, limbs suddenly heavy. His lips curl at the edges and he turns away.

"I'll be right back. Stay here," I tell Tori.

"Where are you going?"

"To get a breath of air."

Tori nods, but I don't take my eyes off Kai. As I push my way through the dancing crowd, he grabs a beer. Right before I break free, he turns. A few more feet and I'll be able to grab him. I want him back so badly. It's been so hard to go on without him. Every time I think I might climb out of the deep hole his loss left me in, he's there—haunting me. If I can just reach him. He takes a sudden left and slips out a door to the balcony. It's barely had time to close when I yank it back open.

A brutal gust of cold air pushes me back and throws my hair in my face. I quickly regain my footing and brush my hair away from my face. He's gone. The balcony is empty. There are no other doors. There's nowhere he could've gone. I rush to the edge and look down at the street below. Nothing. That's impossible. Could he have been a . . . a . . . it's hard for me to even think the word . . . *hallucination?*

No. Not a hallucination. I miss him so much I'm imagining him in dark corners, on other's faces.

My mind rewinds back to the moment I saw him. I was dancing. Relaxed. Happy. Lots of lights and lasers. Lots of people. Before that I . . . I wanted to kiss Amon. I shouldn't have wanted that. I loved Kai. I loved *Kai*. Could I have imagined his face on another? In a dark club with lasers and lights, that seems realistic. I feel guilty for wanting Amon, and this is the result. What is wrong with me?

The chill in the air is sobering, anchoring, as I absorb the stillness of the night. I continue to look down at the street and realize how different this street—like my life—is now.

From up here, I can't see any signs of the late-night madness I've grown accustomed to in gambling towns. No drunks stumbling down the street. No addicts collapsed in empty doorways. No prostitutes moving out to the street corners after they've been kicked out of the casinos and bars.

The neon lights of the city cast an unnatural bright light on the streets, strangely accentuating shadows as well. I've never really taken in the view of Atlantic City at night. The casinos are lit so bright, but stand against the complete darkness of the midnight ocean. All that cuts into the unending darkness is the pull of the breaking waves at the shore. From here, the waves look like strands of cotton wrapped in shadows, being pulled out along the shore. Beyond that, the moon is hidden behind a thick layer of gray clouds making the Atlantic an unending pool as black and thick as oil. I can't help but wonder what sort of monsters lurk below the surface.

Chapter 20

From behind me, a hand clamps my shoulder. I gasp, my breath comes up short, heart pounds so violently, I feel dizzy.

"Sorry," Buddy says. "I didn't mean to scare you."

"No, enough Buddy. You're always just . . . just . . . appearing. What are you doing here?"

"Listen to me. It's not safe for you here. I'm trying to help you. You need to get away. Don't tell anyone where you've gone. Change your name. Run. He's here."

"What are you talking about?" I throw my arms up in frustration.

Catching a flash of movement as the balcony door is sliding open.

"Bud," Dustin says, walking out to the balcony. "What are you doing out here?"

Buddy looks at me, his eyes completely focused and clear. He mouths, 'shush'. Then his eyes seem to cloud and he spins to face Dustin. "Buddy see Ms. Lilly out here so . . . Baa Baa Buddy, have you any booze? Yes ma'am, yes ma'am. What do you choose?" he sings and finishes with a spin and bow.

"Bud." Dustin pulls a small cup from his pocket. "I found this in the office. Remember, we have a deal: if you want a job, you have to take your meds."

Buddy's face crumples into a grimace and he pounds his legs. "Buddy forget." He pulls up his sleeve to look at his bare wrist. "Buddy supposed to take at half-past-a-freckle, but now it's a-quarter-to-an-ass."

"Buddy, come on, man," Dustin says. "Work with me here."

"Buddy will." He takes the small cup from Dustin. "This is the way we take our meds, take our meds, take our meds," Buddy sings and does a few spins. "This is the way we take our meds, take our meds, take our meds." Buddy tosses the pills in his mouth, swallows exaggeratedly, then opens his mouth and sticks out his tongue. "So late in the evening." He bows.

Buddy looks completely different than he did a few minutes ago, before Dustin came out. His posture is hunched, his gaze focused somewhere in the distance, his face expressionless. I suppose that's mental illness for some, with moments of sanity interspersed with child-like madness. I can't help but see the similarity in Buddy's abrupt flip and what's happening to me. Tori pulled me from a fit of absolute terror to calm in seconds. *Is that normal? Could that be just my imagination?* I want to believe that but a small black hole of dread takes shape in the pit of my stomach.

"Thanks, Buddy. Lilly, isn't he doing a great job?" Dustin asks, pulling me from my thoughts. I nod in agreement. "You can go back to work," Dustin says.

"Drink for the lady?" Buddy asks with his head completely tilted to the side.

"No, thanks."

Buddy bows to me, does another spin, and scurries off. Why is he always there when I see Kai? Does something about him remind me of Kai? Or is it seeing commonality in my own mental state? I shiver, shaking that thought from my mind. Turning back to the city, I close my eyes for a moment trying to see Kai, but I can't form a clear picture. He's already fading. I open my eyes and stare out over the city.

Dustin steps closer to me. "Was Buddy bothering you? Did he say anything to scare you?"

"Buddy? No. I think it's great you're trying to help him."

"Thanks. We're hoping that we can build this into a program that helps the city's homeless population regain their footing."

"That's really nice. Let me know if I can help."

"It's a bit selfish, less homeless is better for business."

"That's not selfish, it's better all around."

Dustin leans over the ledge and looks straight down, then twists back to look at me. "So, what'd you think of the show and the club?"

"They're both better than anything Vegas has."

"That's exactly what we were going for." He hesitates, then asks, "Are you okay?"

"Yeah, why?"

"You're out here . . . alone."

"I needed a breath of air for a minute. It was a long, busy day and that show was intense."

"I definitely get it. Are you ready to come back in? I'll walk you to your table and we can stop by the DJ booth, if you'd like?"

"Sure."

Dustin holds the door for me. I didn't realize how cold I was until the warmth of the club squeezes in on me. Right inside, Dustin sneaks behind one of the heavy red curtains and pauses barely long

enough for me to duck in after him. There's a tunnel back here, soft
LED lights along the floor provide just enough light to see where
you're walking, but not much else.

Dustin suddenly stops and I bump into his back.

"Sorry."

"No worries. Are you okay climbing a ladder?"

"Sure."

"We get off at the first stop so it's only about fifteen feet high."

"What's above that?"

"Not much, just the catwalks for the dancers and aerialists. We also
have some access to the lighting."

Dustin starts up first. He pauses for a moment, then disappears.
I begin climbing, loath to admit it's a little scarier than I thought it
would be. Fifteen feet looks a lot higher than it sounds. My foot slips
and my heel catches on the rung. These stupid shoes my mom has
me wearing. The shiny red leather on my Louboutin's might as well
be ice. I can't get a grip. About a third of the way up, I'm shaking so
badly that I kick my shoes off.

I finally make it up. Dustin is waiting and holding the curtain
for me. He takes my hand and helps me in. His skin is so soft, I'm
immediately insecure about my dry, unmanicured hands. He doesn't
seem to notice. Instead, Dustin subconsciously bites his lip as he
reaches around my waist and pulls me towards him and into the DJ
booth. I pull away, pretending to want to check out the booth, only
to realize that he was reaching behind me to pull a small gate closed.

The DJ, his back to us, stands on an elevated platform with his
synthesizers and computers spread in front of him. Black baggy pants
balloon out from his legs, topped with a black tee, black knit cap, and

black headphones. Hidden from public view behind the DJ's stage is a small living room setup with two smooth, black-leather couches and a clear acrylic table with the typical bottle service setup. Buckets of ice, bottles of water, Red Bull, and a bottle of vodka, which catches my eye. It's a clear bottle with a silver and black crystal skull. I've never heard of the brand, Iodanov, but it looks expensive.

"Hello, ladies," I hear Dustin say and look back to see him open the gate and hold his hand out.

Ladies? The three girls who step into the booth barely look eighteen and barely look real. Long, glossy hair hits at their tiny waists, accentuated by skin-tight, black leather minidresses that show off their long, lean legs.

"We found these, they must be yours," one of the girls says holding my shoes out to me.

"I kept slipping on the ladder, so I kicked them off," I say, trying to pull my toes into my pants legs.

"Oh." She laughs. "Louboutin's are slippery." She holds her hand out over the edge of the platform without taking her eyes off me, drops the shoes, and smirks at me.

"Drink?" she asks.

"No thanks, I'm good."

"Dusty?" She bites her plump, red lip.

"No thanks, doll. I'm giving Lilly a tour."

"The *Lilith*?" she asks and Dustin nods.

"Cheers to you," she says to me. "We love this club. Such a great idea."

"Thanks, but Dustin gets the credit," I say, but she's already turned to the table where the other two girls are standing. She bends over at her hips, sticking her perfectly round backside out and makes four Red Bull and vodkas.

"Lilly this is Erebus, our resident DJ," Dustin says.

I twist, not realizing that I had been staring at the girls as Erebus comes down from his stage. I see why he has a harem of girls, he's as beautiful as they are.

"The lady of the hour," Erebus says in a proper English accent. "It's lovely to meet you. I saw you dancing."

"I was having fun," I say, glad that it's dark because my cheeks are on fire.

"I hope to see you more but have to get back up there. This club was a dynamite idea," Erebus says as one of the girls hands him a drink.

"Thanks, but—"

"To Lilith," Erebus says, cutting me off, and holding his glass up towards the girls.

"To Lilith," they echo.

"Bye, ladies," Dustin says.

"See you soon, Dusty," they say in unison so perfectly, they sound like they're in stereo.

Dustin opens the gate for me, and I climb onto the ladder, careful not to look down.

"Bye, Lilith," the girls call.

"Bye," I mumble as I begin to descend.

I gather my shoes and quickly put them on, as Dustin makes it down.

"I'll take you to your table the back way," Dustin says.

I nod, grateful that I don't have to go back through the club. Exhaustion is crashing down on me and filling my limbs with concrete. I'm done.

The tunnel weaves back, and I have no idea what direction we're moving in or where we are. I don't care; I just want to be home in my bed.

We finally come to a ramp. At the top, Dustin pulls the curtain and holds it for me. When I step through, I'm back in the VIP section right by our table. I turn to thank Dustin, but he's already gone.

Tori is in front of our booth, dancing three beats behind the song, her whole torso drapes dangerously forward and I expect her to lose her balance at any moment. Felix and Amon are talking. No one notices me as I linger. It's the first time I've felt invisible all night and I relish it. Then Amon spots me and waves. Tori happens to see Amon wave, swings her head towards me, and stumbles back. Felix manages to grab her and corral her on his lap. I need to get her home.

"Where'd you go?" Amon asks.

"I was grabbing a breath of air on the balcony and saw Dustin. Then he took me up to the DJ booth."

"Yooou went to the DJ-Jaay booth without me, bitch," Tori spits and laughs.

"How was it?" Amon asks.

"Really cool, but I am exhausted and need to get—" I motion with my thumb towards Tori, "—home."

Amon nods. "Yes, of course. I'm tired too. We'll walk you out. Do you need a car?"

"No, I'm fine."

Amon stands and puts his arm around me. "I'm so grateful you took this position."

"Me too."

"Come on, lovely. It's time to get you home," I hear Felix tell Tori.

"Noooo, I don't want to goooo," she says.

"Tor, it's time to go," I snap.

"Noooo."

"We'll come back tomorrow and the day after. This is just the start," Felix tells her.

"Fiiin-eh," Tori says and tries to stand.

Felix wraps her arm around his shoulder and grabs her waist.

"Are you going to be able to get her in? Do you want to stay here?" Amon asks.

"No, I'm fine."

"Do you want to leave her here?"

I laugh. "I can handle her, but thanks."

Walking out, I'm surprised by how many people are still in the casino at one-in-the-morning on a Thursday.

We make it to my car. Felix pours Tori into the passenger seat and hands her a bottle of water.

Amon leans close. "Don't rush in tomorrow. Get some sleep."

"I'll try, but there's so much to do."

"Rest is important. Here." Amon hands me a bottle of water.

In the overhead light, I notice a slight amber tint and hold it up to get a better look. "Is there something in it?"

"I put a dropperful of your mom's vitamins in it for you," Amon adds.

"Oh . . . you did?" My hand lingers for a moment, wanting to give the water back.

"Yeah, why? When she gave the drops to Jordan, she gave me a bottle too. You know our parents are very close. Your mom said the drops would help with the stress of raising a casino from the dead." Amon laughs then holds up his bottle of water with the same amber tint. "It might be psychosomatic, but I think they're working."

"That's my mom." I climb into my car. If I weren't exhausted, I'd be irritated by her suffocating control; instead, I release a deep breath and down some of the water before pulling onto North Carolina Avenue.

"That was sooooo fun," Tori says, taking a drink of her water.

"Yeah."

"What's wrong?"

"Nothing, I'm just tired."

"Lillll, I might be a little—" She holds out her thumb and pointer finger and squints through the tiny opening. "—Lil' drunk, but I can tell something's bothering you."

"I keep thinking I see Kai," I blurt out.

"Fuck Kai, he's dead."

"Tori!"

"Whaaat?" Tori spills a little water on her shirt trying to drink it.

"I loved him."

"You dated him for like two days or whaaattevveerr. Get over it."

"We were going to get married."

"Blah, blaaahhh, blaahhh, just go fuck Amon and move on."

What? "I . . . I can't."

"No shit. Your whole life is going to flip upside down and you won't fucking understand what's happening, 'cause you're so hung up about what you think your life is. You don't know what's fucking coming for you."

"What?"

When Tori doesn't answer, I glance over. With her eyes shut and head bouncing off the window with every bump and pothole, she mumbles something completely incoherent. *Did she really say I don't know what's coming for me?*

Chapter 21

The blare of my alarm pulls me from my thoughts of everything that needs to get done today. I toss my comforter off and drag myself out of bed. My mind is wide awake, but my body doesn't want to move. I manage to shower and dress quickly, using the promise of a warm cup of coffee to speed up my exhausted, heavy limbs.

The Jura coffeemaker grinds to life. The smell of freshly-ground coffee fills the kitchen. I hope it doesn't wake Tori. Not because I care about her sleep, but I don't want to deal with a drunk morning of regrets.

There's a lot of people on the boardwalk this morning, it must be a little warmer today. A text chime pulls me from my daze.

Mom: Don't forget to take a dropperful of your herbal tincture. Best on an empty stomach. The tincture has nootropics that prevent mental exhaustion.

Me: K thx

Mom: K thx? When did you start texting in that ridiculous code? Typing complete sentences is not difficult.

Me: I'm trying to get to work.

Mom: Your father and I are coming down this weekend, but not till tomorrow morning.

Me: Great.

Mom: Did you take your tincture?

Me: Yes. I text then grab a glass of water and put a dropperful in. Mom has stashed vials all over the place.

As I grab my cup to leave, Tori stumbles out, last night's makeup smeared all over her face. She looks like a sad clown from an Emmett Kelly Weary Willie painting.

"Hey," she croaks.

"I'm late."

"Wait, I'm sorry. Was I that out of hand last night . . . did I embarrass you?" she asks through her even sadder clown eyes.

"No, you were fine."

"Then why are you mad at me?"

"I'm not. I'm in a rush." I try to walk past her, but she grabs my elbow.

"I'm sorry," Tori says and pulls me to face her.

"It's fine. I have to go."

"No, listen. I'm sorry I wasn't gentler in my choice of words, but I'm so proud of you. The casino is incredible. You are doing such a great job. And Amon is literally the perfect guy."

"I—"

"Just listen. I know it was traumatic and sad and a lot to process, but you deserve to be happy again. You're my best friend. I love you."

"Okay," I say, my guard softening.

"Are you still mad?"

"No. You have a point. But it's hard . . . and messing with my mind."

"You need to rip that bandage off to get back in the right head space."

"I wish this was what you'd said last night."

Tori scrunches up her nose and closes her eyes, then opens them wide. "I'm sorry. Can we go out to dinner tonight? Just us?"

"I'm going to have to work late, but maybe I can sneak out for a quick bite."

"I heard there's this secret restaurant."

"Yeah, I know it. If I can get out of the casino, I'll make us a reservation."

"Yay . . . Ouch . . . Do you have any Advil?"

"Above the fridge."

"Thanks."

"Go back to bed," I say over my shoulder as I walk out the door.

It's much warmer than I expected, as if the weather gods flipped a switch. It has to be at least ten degrees warmer than yesterday. It feels like a beautiful spring day.

I'm still not used to this fickle weather, and it seems to influence my mood. In Vegas, nice weather is an almost daily expectation so, I suppose, I lost a bit of the appreciation I now feel for the sun's warmth. The day has barely started and I'm already in a better mood.

It's not just me; I see it in the crowds walking to the boardwalk. People are smiling at me, saying good morning.

"It's a beautiful day," a stranger says as he walks by and smiles.

"It is," I say as I duck into the parking lot behind my building. I never thought I'd be one of those people to comment on the weather, but here I am . . . a true New Jerseyan.

It takes me longer to get to work today because there are so many people out. They also seem anxious to walk across the street, forcing me to stop at every other crosswalk and miss just about every green light. I don't mind. It's still early, not even eight yet, my windows are down, and my music is up.

When I pull into the Golden Sands, I run smack into a traffic jam. How can there be so many people already and this early in the morning? I expected this weekend to be better, but this is insane. Casinos don't go from ghost town to Times Square in such a short amount of time. It doesn't seem possible. And it's not normal traffic—judging by the luxury cars, it's traffic with money to spend. Though, I suppose Amon and his team did a lot before I started, the property is practically brand new, and the tourism season is only starting to pick up. I'm not complaining. Never look a gift horse in the mouth. That's something my mother taught me from a very young age. Things always seemed to go her way. Maybe some of her luck is finally becoming mine.

A valet sees me and clears traffic so I can pull into my spot now flanked by a Rolls Royce Cullinan and a Porsche Panamera, both with New York plates. As I get out, I notice the Cullinan has a small black symbol in the back window that looks vaguely familiar—two slightly crocked 'V's that look like lightning strikes connected on one side, with a 'μ' in the middle, and all surrounded by a circle. I'm sure I've seen it somewhere.

A car slams on its brakes barely screeching to a stop before it runs me over. If I'd stepped out a split second later, I wouldn't be standing right now. "Sorry," I say and wave to the driver. I feel so stupid.

"No, no, I'm so sorry," he says through the rolled down window of his BMW. "Are you okay?"

"I'm fine, I should've looked. It's my fault."

"No, I shouldn't be in such a rush. I saw an opening and tried to speed to the front. I can't apologize enough."

"It's fine. I'm fine." The man is even more shaken than me. He looks like a Wallstreet guy. Young, rich, handsome, dressed well, driving a nice car, though the confidence you'd expect of this sort is severely lacking.

"No, everyone saw what I did."

"It's okay." I look around; the entire madness of the busy entrance has frozen, and everyone is staring at us. "I'm fine," I yell to all then look directly at the driver. "Thank you. I wasn't paying attention."

"No, this is not good. This is not good." The driver glances around the covered driveway in an almost panic.

"Bro, she's fine. It's fine," the passenger—and basic clone of the driver—says , though he appears equally shaken.

"If I would've hurt Lilith—"

"You know who I am?"

The driver nods.

"How?" I ask and the passenger passes him a magazine. The driver holds it up. *Business Week*. On the cover is a photo of me, silhouetted, and the same of Amon pasted in front of a sprawling shot of Atlantic

City centered on The Golden Sands. The headline reads, 'Dynamic Duo Gives AC the Upper Hand: Could this finally be the rebirth this struggling shore town's been waiting for?'

"I'm so—"

I raise my hand to stop him from apologizing again. "Please, it's not a big deal. It sounded worse than it was. Enjoy your weekend. Can I have this?"

"Of course," he says.

"Thanks." I continue through the porte cochère more carefully. As I do, I hear the normal chatter of the busy area slowly return to normal. Though, I can't shake the feeling everyone is still staring at me. I hurry through the doors.

The lobby is busy but lacks the madness outside. There's a calmness carried on the aroma of morning coffees. The check-in line is moving well. Charlotte has the front desk fully staffed and the lobby decorated with fresh flowers. To evade attention, I duck into my shoulders and look down, making a beeline towards the hall.

"Lilly."

Ugh, I turn towards the voice. Relieved to see it's someone I know. "Charlotte, the lobby looks beautiful, and you have the flow down. Great job."

"Thanks, things are going really well. I'm glad I caught you. We had to reset the access cards last night. Here's your new card." Charlotte hands it over. "I'll take your old one so they don't get mixed up and we can recycle it."

"Oh." I hand Charlotte my old access card and put the new one in its place. "Did something happen?"

"Nothing to worry about. A possible security breach. This is just a precaution."

"What sort of security breach?"

"I'm not exactly sure. Maybe someone lost a card. All I know, I was told to make sure you received the new card when you came in, which wasn't supposed to be for another few hours. I'm glad I happened to be out front and not in my office."

I nod and turn down the 'Hall of Mirrors' as I've started to call it. Every morning I'm forced to look at the unending reflections of myself on my way to the elevators. The mirrors on every wall and column reflect the elegant light marble and make the tight hall feel more open in a dizzying sort of way. It works from a design stance, although it forces me to notice how tired I look today over and over.

There's a small crowd gathered in the elevator lobby, suitcases in tow. When the elevator dings, the closest shove their way on till it's full. The door begins to close as more customers file into the elevator bank and I consider taking the stairs. Then a hand sticks out through the crack of the closing elevator doors, and they open back up.

"We have room for one more," says a voice directed at me.

I quickly look up. "Thank you."

"You're welcome, dear," an older woman with lots of makeup, a swirl of bright red hair, and piles of costume jewelry says.

"You're back," I say instantly recognizing her.

"Oh yes, this is our favorite casino, and we were invited to the party tomorrow. Do I know you?"

"Not officially, we've just crossed paths around town." I scan my card, so the eighth-floor call button lights up.

"We do love Atlantic City," the woman says as the elevator begins to rise.

I nod and force a fake smile in hopes that will avoid any more conversation.

"Oh, now I remember you." She winks at me.

Instead of forcing another smile, I opt for a sip of coffee as the elevator arrives to the fourth floor.

"Oops, this is our floor. Come on," she barks to her husband behind her.

I hold the door open as they drag their luggage off the elevator. "Enjoy your stay."

When the doors close, I keep my eyes down to avoid any more conversations. After two more stops, the elevator finally gets to the eighth floor. I slip out quickly and quietly. I've never seen a casino so busy so early on a Friday morning.

The office is completely dark. Every light is off, and every shade has been drawn. When I hold my key card to the access, I notice that there's a new lock on the door. *Did someone try to break in?*

I immediately flick on the lights. Check the time on my phone. 8:07. Jordan should be here in an hour or so. I'm fine. I've never been comfortable alone, but *I am not bound by the confines of my comfort zone. I am not bound by the confines of my comfort zone. I am not bound by the confines of my comfort zone.* I take a deep breath. Stand a little taller. Close the door behind me and walk to my office, flicking on every single light on my way.

This isn't so bad. I push the remote to open the heavy curtains that block out every ounce of sunlight. As daylight pours into my office, I feel better. Though I already need another cup of coffee.

Finally, at my desk and ready to work, I grab the *Newsweek Magazine* and read the article. It paints me as an efficacious Vegas gaming executive perfectly paired with one of New York's most successful finance players. The article goes on to describe 'The Golden Sands as the oldest new casino on the block. An incomparable merger of historic elegance and modern intimacy. You simply cannot build a property like this. Such places have to be cultivated over decades, almost a century, to earn the sort of magic it now holds. By a stroke of luck, this historic building is home to a winning casino. There is simply nothing else like Golden Sands nor will there be, at least not for the next hundred years. Book now, because word will travel fast. Win or lose, this is one roll of the dice you won't want to miss.'

I chuckle. It feels good when your ideas are well received. Golden Sands could easily have been called the oldest dump on the block with a little lipstick on a pig. Instead, we called it historic, magic, unique and now everyone wants to come here. I suppose when everything else is trending newer and bigger, people want 'historic' and 'intimate.'

Banging from somewhere out in the hall pulls me from my thoughts.

"Hello?"

Nothing.

"Jordan?"

Nothing.

It goes quiet, but now there's a heaviness in the silence.

A presence.

Maybe it was just someone walking around upstairs.

Where was I? My to-do list. The players' party tomorrow. I dial Alli's extension, hoping she'll be in this early.

"This is Alli."

"Hi. It's Lilly. I'm glad you're in."

"There's so much to do, I wanted to get an early start."

"That's why I'm calling. How is the party planning going?"

"Great. I'm meeting Liza at 10:30 to finalize everything. Would you like to join us?"

"Sure. How are you feeling about it?"

"Incredible. Your idea for our first party is brilliant. The 1920s' theme fits perfectly with our history and it's beautiful from a design standpoint. Oh, and it ties in with the psychics—which are all confirmed by the way."

"Perfect. Oh, I wanted to tell you that I found some actual menus from the 1920s that are archived. I thought it'd . . ."

I hear the scratching again. It sounds like someone is walking or dragging their feet across the carpet right outside my office.

"Hello?"

"Yes, sorry. I . . . What was I saying?"

"The menus."

"Right, I thought it would be cool to incorporate the actual menus into the party."

"I absolutely love that idea!"

"I'll bring them to the meeting. Where is it?"

"The Grand Ballroom."

"Awesome. Thanks."

"No, thank you, Lilly."

I hang up the phone and listen. The scratching grows louder.

"HELLO?"

No response.

My gut goes hollow. A chill snakes its way from deep within my core down my legs out to my arms and up around my neck leaving a trail of pins and needles in its wake. My throat tightens like a closing fist.

"Jordan?" I call as I tiptoe my way towards the hall and the sound.

The sound is coming from Amon's office but the door is closed. I stand in the hall between his and my office and listen. Someone is definitely walking around in his office.

"Amon?"

Nothing.

"AMON?"

Someone or something bangs against the door—hard enough to make the wood shudder in its frame. Panic floods my veins, turning my legs to water as I stumble back. The door rattles again, more insistent this time. I run, pulse hammering in my ears. When I make it to the elevator lobby, reality hits me: I'm trapped. My access card lies forgotten in my office, along with my phone and everything else. There's nowhere for me to go except Amon's apartment.

I pound on his door , hoping it will drown out the beating of my heart. I dig my heels into the carpet and brace myself. My ribcage, like a damn about to break, tries to contain the thundering in my chest as I turn to look through the glass door of the executive offices expecting to see a maniac run towards me at any second.

I spin back, fists raised, to hammer on the door with all my strength and tumble in as it opens.

Amon catches me. "What's going on? Are you okay?"

I push the door closed behind me. "Someone's in your office," I say in jagged exhales as I try to catch my breath.

"That's impossible."

"No, I heard them walking around in your office. They even banged on your door."

"Okay. I'll call security."

Amon's only wearing satin pajama bottoms.

"I'm sorry. I shouldn't have come here."

"Don't be ridiculous. Sit down. Let me get you some water."

As Amon gets water from the kitchen, I hear him call security. I calm a little and look around. It's part apartment, part museum, and the nicest home I've ever been in. I sit on the elegant, black-leather couch as he brushes by me to set the water on the white-marble coffee table.

"Your door is locked, right?"

"Yes, bolted and it has a steel core that's impenetrable."

"Really?"

"Yes, I'm a collector but I don't want to keep things stored in a vault, I want to enjoy them. So, I have extra security."

"You live in a vault?"

"That's one way to put it."

Looking around, I spot a Picasso, Van Gogh, Dali, and Ruben hanging on the walls. I've only seen such in museums. I'm no expert, but I know enough from art history classes in college to recognize the masters.

"Your apartment is beautiful," I say as I scan the walls.

"Thanks." He sits next to me, setting his phone on the table.

The ancient Roman spear catches my eye. It's been moved. No longer in its case, it sits with some other relics on a contrasting set of black lacquer shelves. The other vestiges appear to be ancient bowls and figures, I assume they're Roman as well but really have no idea.

Amon's phone dings and I see a text message from Peter. 'Security is on their way.' Then I notice Amon, is looking at me and knows I'm reading his text.

I awkwardly look away. Embarrassment has fully set in. Then I see a pair of high heels haphazardly resting by the door on the perfectly patterned black chevron hardwood floor. The only thing out of place in this otherwise impeccable space. *Oh no, I'm such an idiot.*

"I'm so sorry," I say jumping up. "I'll wait outside."

"What are you talking about?"

"I shouldn't have bothered you. I didn't know you had someone here. I can wait for security in the hall."

"What?"

I point to the shoes.

"Oh." Amon laughs. "Those are my mom's." He grabs my hand and pulls me back down then puts his muscular arm around me and pulls me close. "You're welcome here anytime."

I want to lay my head on his shoulder and lean into this moment, but instead I twist to face him. "Do you think that whoever tried to break in last night, got in?"

"Oh, that. Security thought someone stole an access card and got into our office. After I went through the footage, I realized it was Tori, but they'd already changed the lock."

"Tori?"

"Yeah, while we were at dinner, she went to the bathroom then came here. You didn't give her your card?"

"No, she must've just grabbed it."

"Let me get dressed and we'll figure out who is in my office. Make yourself comfortable."

My curiosity pulls me back to the black shelves and I head over for a better look. The spear is rather drab looking, tarnished metal wrapped with a soft gold decoration and braided metal wrappings. I wouldn't call it beautiful, but there's something extraordinary about it. I'm overwhelmed with an urge to touch it. To pick it up and hold it. I don't think I've ever actually held something that's thousands of years old. I brush my finger lightly along the metal wrapping and swear I feel a gentle electricity pulse from it. I reach my finger out to touch the tip.

Chapter 22

"Ready?"

I jump, pull my hand back and nod.

Amon is dressed casually in black, pressed cotton joggers and a cashmere pullover. I've never seen him in something so relaxed.

Peter is in the elevator lobby as a group of security officers, some in black suits and others in uniform mill about the office.

"We've isolated and detained the culprit," Peter says as soon as he sees us.

"Really?" Amon asks, concern flitting across his brow.

"Follow me," Peter says.

"Is it safe?" I ask.

"Ms. Umbra we have the threat fully contained," Peter says and leads us into the offices. As we walk through, I hear soft snickers in our wake.

We pause in the reception area as a tall guard exits Amon's office, muscles tear at the seams of his black suit. "Here he comes," he announces, a hint of a grin pulling at the side of his mouth. Before I have time to wrap my head around what's happening, a uniformed guard walks out carrying a robot vacuum cleaner and the room erupts in laughter.

I cover my face with both my hands as the heat of embarrassment boils my cheeks. Even Amon is laughing.

"Ms. Umbra, my staff couldn't have asked for a better way to start this busy weekend," the muscular security officer says as he walks by. He pats my shoulder and adds, "Don't be embarrassed or feel bad, you reacted exactly how you should. It's an honest mistake."

I try to smile, but I don't feel it.

"I'm sorry," Amon adds. "Jordan should've warned you."

"What is going on?" Jordan asks from the door, pushing his way in as the security detail files out.

"You didn't warn Lilly about the vacuum, and she thought someone had broken into my office."

"I didn't expect Lilly until ten. I would've already put away," Jordan says, putting his things down.

"And," Amon adds, "she was under the impression that someone had tried to break into the office last night."

"I'm sorry," I say to Amon. "I shouldn't have overreacted."

"You didn't overreact, you did exactly what you should've. Jordan, can you order us breakfast?"

"I'm okay, I have a meeting at ten-thirty," I say.

"Jordan, ask them to rush it, I'll be right back."

As I make my way to my office, I stop to peek into Amon's. The Robovac left what looks like claw marks on the carpet near the door and scratches along the baseboard. There're even a few scratches that appear to climb up the wall. How could a stupid little vacuum do that? I shake off a chill and continue to my office. *I have got to get out of this conspiracy mode. Focus on business . . . The menus.* I'd promised to show Allie the menus at the meeting.

Grabbing my phone and access card, I exit the office.

"Where are you going?" Jordan calls after me.

"To grab something from the storage closet upstairs. I'll be right back."

I opt to climb the roughly four flights of stairs. I hope a little movement will burn off the excess anxiety that's settled in the base of my spine. Taking two steps at a time, and holding the handrail, I make it up in no time, feeling a little better with each step.

It takes me a minute, but I eventually stumble upon the door to the twelfth-and-a-half floor . . . just as Buddy is walking out. He looks at me and freezes.

"You didn't see me. Do you understand?"

"It's fine, Buddy. You work here."

"No," Buddy says, eyes clear, "I'm not supposed to be here. Do not tell anyone that you saw me."

"I won't."

"Swear."

"Yes, I swear."

Without saying another word, Buddy rushes by me at full speed. I never fully know what to make of him. There are so many Buddies. My favorite version is the rhyming, happy, slightly unhinged Buddy. It's a terrible thing to say, but the other Buddies scare me. I'm not sure why. He's never threatening. Maybe it's the vein of sanity that runs through them. Maybe it reminds me how easily that vein can break. Or, maybe it's something else entirely. I push these thoughts from my mind and walk in.

This floor is completely empty and quiet. I dig my access card out of my pocket and hold it up—the door unlocks.

The room is pitch black, and I fumble along the wall for the light switch. Strange. I thought there'd been a window in here, but I must have misremembered. Using my foot to hold the door open, I feel along the wall till I hit the lock release button. The light switch is right next to it.

When the lights come on, the window is now boarded up. Strange again. I rifle through the files and boxes on the shelves and stumble upon an old, leather-bound book. Its red cover is beautiful, and I pull it out. Embossed in black lettering outlined with gold is the title, *The Order of μ* with the same symbol I saw on the car outside this morning, two slightly crocked 'V's that look like lightning strikes connected on one side, with a 'μ' in the middle, and all surrounded by a circle. The date on the spine reads 1919.

When I open the book, a breeze kicks up, maybe from a vent, and blows a couple pieces of paper off a shelf. I pick them up, they're copies of the menus I came here to find.

An emergency alarm blares from my phone and slices through the silence like a bolt of electricity that causes every muscle in my body to convulse. I jump and drop everything. Grabbing my phone, it's an Amber Alert. Harper Walcoff, age 9. Blonde hair, blue eyes. Last seen walking to the bus stop near Leeds Point Road in Galloway Township wearing blue leggings and a white Nike tee shirt. Believed to be in danger. Suspect unknown. If observed, please call 911.' *Sad.* I set my phone down so I can gather everything I dropped.

I rest the menus on top of the book and check their date. Printed at the top of the cream-colored, heavy parchment paper in elegant gold script is the date, 'May 6, 1927', exactly ninety-seven years from tomorrow. Tingles trickle through my scalp and raise the hairs at the back of my neck. The lights flicker then go black.

The air pressure plummets, my eardrums bulging inward with sudden, excruciating pain. A blast of arctic air crashes down, pinning me like an invisible weight. Panic transforms into raw terror, stealing my breath. I collapse to the floor, tucking the book and menus under my legs as I curl into myself, knees against chest. I clamp my hands over my ears, desperate to relieve the crushing pressure. It starts as a low hum, vibrating from inside my skull, before growing into that awful sucking sound from last night. The noise builds into a horrific screech—lungs desperately fighting for air through a closed throat—filling every corner of the room. The cold intensifies, as if a glacier has settled on my shoulders. From somewhere deep and primal, I scream, "Nooooo!"

The lights flicker back on. My ears pop as the pressure normalizes. I grab my things, hit the unlock button, and race for the stairs. Taking them two at a time, I clutch the book and menu in one hand, gripping the railing with the other. Halfway down the last flight, something shoves me from behind. I pitch forward but manage to catch the handrail, slowing my fall. My left foot hits first, ankle twisting on impact. Pain shoots from bone to skin. Nausea rolls through me as I steady myself at the bottom. I look back frantically: nothing. The stairwell stands empty, light steady, air normal.

The pain quiets to a throbbing ache. I don't see any bones sticking out and I didn't feel anything snap so I don't think it's broken, but I haven't tried to put weight on it yet. With a slow, deep breath, I try to roll my ankle. I can. It's sore, but I can move it. Taking a few more breaths, I take a tentative step. A jolt of pain shoots up my leg, but

I'm able to limp. Hobbling over to the door, I pick up the book and menus, and limp to my office, grateful I don't have far to go.

As I pull open the door to the eighth-floor elevator bank, Amon is talking to Jordan beyond the glass door. I clench my jaw and try to walk normally.

Amon opens the door for me. "Are you limping? What happened?"

"I'm fine. I just missed a step and—" My heel catches the threshold and my ankle wobbles. I cry out and stumble, dropping the book and menus.

"You're not okay," Amon says, grabbing my elbow to steady me.

Jordan starts to bring over a chair, but I wave him off. "I'm fine. It's a twisted ankle, that's all." I bend to pick up my stuff, but Amon beats me to it then offers me his elbow.

"I think you should go to the doctor," Amon says as he walks me to my office.

"It's fine, really, I just wish I had some better shoes."

"Sit down." Amon pulls another chair over. "Put your foot here. I'll get you an ice pack and some Advil." He slips my stiletto off then disappears.

I leave the menus. The meeting is not for another forty-five minutes, so I have some time. The book's cover is smooth and substantial. An underlying mustiness of aged leather mixes with faint hint of vanilla. I flip it open. An upside-down pentagram and a goat's head are inscribed on the first page. It's surrounded by a circle. Below the circle is that familiar symbol. The long fingernails of irritation begin incessantly tapping my shoulder. Why can't I remember how I know this symbol. It's everywhere. The tapping fingernails dig in, letting the stab of fear get under my skin. Could I have blocked something out? Lost it in the last few months?

"What are you looking at?" Amon asks, startling me. He walks around my desk and lays an icepack on my ankle then hands me a bottle of Advil.

"This weird book I found in the storage room. The Order of μ. I've seen this symbol lately. I think it may be a devil worship book or something. It's creepy."

"Can I see?" Amon takes the book from me and laughs. "I could see why you'd think that. You don't know what the Order of Mu is?"

"No."

"It's a secret, invite only, very prestigious social club."

"Like the Skull and Bones?"

Amon's eyes practically cross when he looks at me. "No. They're a bunch of craven, preppy, elitist that need a club to feel tough."

I hold both hands up in surrender. "It was just a question." I turn my wrist inward so my arms go into a questioning gesture. "So, like the Chaine des Rotisseurs?"

"Sort of, if the Chaine actually valued history, tradition, and the true art of gastronomy. The Order does have these big dinners but they're extremely exclusive. I mean you're not going to find a website where you can sign up." Amon adjusts the ice pack back onto my ankle.

"Thanks."

"Have you ever been to Mangia?" he asks.

"Oh my gosh." I grab my purse and pull out the card from Mangia, the exclusive, in-the-basement restaurant where Mom had treated me. It's the same symbol. "I'm an idiot." I show him the card before tucking it back into my purse.

"They're a bit antiquated. But they've been around for hundreds of years and are highly regarded on the fine-dining front. The symbols they use predate any of the negative organizations you assumed, though of course people love to spread rumors about them, particularly if they can't get in."

"That's a pretty intense social club. Don't tell me you're a member."

Amon narrows his eyes. "What are those menus?"

"This is so weird." I hand the menus to Amon. "I thought it would be cool to recreate some of the historic menus for the party, so I went up to the storage area. Out of nowhere these two menus blow off the shelf. When I looked at them, they were dated for the exact same day, but ninety-seven years ago."

"Fate." Amon winks at me, then looks at his phone. "I'll be right back." He sets the book down on the far end of my desk as he leaves.

My phone dings. It's Tori.

Tori: Can we meet for dinner? The Advil did the trick. I'm feeling so much better.

Me: I'll let you know asap.

Me: I heard that weird sound again, like last night. And the air pressure got all weird.

Tori: Have you ever had allergic tinnitus? Sounds like that. Google it. You're not in the desert anymore.

I check a health site I know is legitimate. 'If you've got allergies, you're at risk of developing tinnitus—a condition commonly called "ringing in the ears." This pitch of this ringing can be high or low, or loud or soft. You might also hear a totally different sound, such as clicking, buzzing, roaring, or even hissing.'

A wave of relief washes over me and I feel like I can take a full breath. The symptoms fit and give me a diagnosis that's easy to deal with.

Me: You're right. Sounds like tinnitus.

Tori: Now can we please go to dinner tonight?

"See if these fit," Amon says as he returns carrying a pair of Gucci platform loafers with the unmistakable horse bit detail.

"No way, how in the world did you get those?" I ask, setting down my phone.

"I'm sorry, did I interrupt you?"

"Oh no, Tori just wants to go to dinner. No big deal."

"You should go. Why don't you take her to Mangia."

"Really?"

"Definitely."

"We'll go early, then I'll come back here to make sure there're no issues heading into the weekend."

"Perfect." Amon gets down on one knee.

I take the ice pack off. The throbbing has settled to an uncomfortable ache. "Did you borrow those from someone?" I ask as he settles my foot on his knee.

"What?" He crinkles his brow and purses his lips. He has the most perfect pout, and I forget what I just asked. "No! They're brand new and now they're yours," Amon says and slips the shoe on my left foot. It fits perfectly.

I put the other shoe on and Amon offers me his hand to stand.

I take a few steps around my office. "Oh." I let out a breath. "It feels so much better. But, seriously, how did you get them?"

"The new retail store coming in is opening today, they had them."

"Thank you," I say, holding Amon's gaze.

"Breakfast," Jordan announces from the door as he carries a tray in and sets it down on my desk before leaving.

Amon sits at my desk and starts on his breakfast.

I check the time on my phone. I have twenty minutes, so I peruse the menus while I eat my parfait. Some items I easily recognize . . . oysters on the half shell, oyster cocktail, fried oysters, baked halibut—I get it, this is a beach town. There're also typical meats like roast chicken, roast tenderloin of beef, roast ribs of beef, boiled leg of lamb. Boiled? Sounds a little gross. Boiled onions—gross again. Or maybe chefs just use a fancier word now, like braised. Then I see some menu items that are less familiar, like toasted corn flakes, green turtle soup, tongue, and rejuvenation—or blood—soup.

"You're deep in thought," Amon says.

"Oh, I was trying to picture what blood soup is."

"It's actually delicious."

"You've had it?"

"Schwarzsauer."

"What?"

Amon laughs. "Schwarzsauer. It's German blood soup I grew up eating."

"Oh, okay, showoff. What about tongue?"

"Of course, it's delicious braised in a red wine sauce."

I visibly shake off a chill. "Couldn't do it. Nope. No blood or tongue for me."

"You'd be surprised. Here." Amon hands me a spoon. "Can I see those menus before you take them."

"Sure." I pass them over.

"Incredible," Amon says, reading over them. "I can't believe you found these."

"They sort of found me," I add between bites.

Amon pours us each a glass of water. He adds a dropperful of herbs to each. He catches me watching him.

"My mind feels so much clearer since I started your mom's herbal tincture. Adaptogen elixirs are very popular now. Your mother is on to something. She should go into business." Amon hands me the glass.

"She's been making these as long as I can remember," I say, setting it down and noticing the time. "I've got to run." A sharp but tolerable pain shoots through my ankle when I stand. "Well, maybe not run." I slip past Amon towards the door.

"Hey, I made you and Tori a reservation at Mangia for tonight at 5:30."

"Thank you."

"Stop thanking me."

"Never," I say from the threshold of my office.

"Bye," he calls after me; I can hear a smile in his tone and grin. I'm lucky to work for someone like Amon.

I catch my reflection on my way to the elevator and notice an obvious limp. This week has taken its toll, and I'm overcome with insecurity. I adjust my gait to make it a little less noticeable but return to limping when my ankle screams in pain. It's more than the physical pain that's bothering me. It's a reminder—a confirmation, or exclamation point—to the fact that I'm not as perfect or whole as the rest of Amon's team.

The elevator doors slide open, and the noisy chatter from the packed car turns to dead silence. The only sound is the nondescript electric muzak that plays in the background. Everyone in this elevator knows I don't belong here and that's why they're staring at me.

When I finally step off the elevator, their whispers pick back up. *Are they really talking to me or about me?* They're all staring at me as the doors slide shut, and appear to be chanting something in unison. *Are they pointing at me?* But the doors close before I get too close a look. I squeeze my eyes closed for a moment. *Stop.* I need to pull it together.

When I open them, I see myself in the wall of mirrors that line the bank of elevators. A mix of disgust and despair settles over me. I look so tired, disheveled, and broken. As this realization sinks in, I watch myself slump even lower. Then I meet my gaze. *No. Lilith Layne Umbra. No.* I stand up taller. Smooth out my clothes. *I am not bound by the confines of my comfort zone or my insecurities.*

A high-pitch scream shatters the quiet, bouncing off the marble floors from the nearby restaurant gallery.

Chapter 23

I rush towards the scream, ignoring the pain in my ankle. Two women stop to stare at me. I skid to a stop. The women, already with drinks in hand, are hugging and screaming with excitement. *What a fool, I am.* I stare at the ground and stride past.

Their conversation resumes so loudly it reverberates through the walkway. Although, their thick accents make it difficult to understand. From what I gather, it's been a long time since they've been 'Down the Shore to Lannik Ciddy and they love being near the wodder'. I've been here long enough to know that means they're happy to be in Atlantic City.

Red passes me on his way to the theater and waves. A stunning gold and diamond Rolex decorates his wrist. *Amon's negotiating tools.*

"Nice watch." I smile and wave.

"Thanks," Red says before disappearing into the theater.

Allie and Liza are in the ballroom when I arrive. They're so beautiful. So perfect in their curve-hugging pencil skirts and stilettos. They don't even notice me limp in. Together, they conduct an orchestra of workers as they set up the large ballroom. Up and down, left and right, mere flicks of their fingers send teams of men scrambling with heavy tables and chairs.

"Hi," I call, but they don't hear me.

I move a little closer. "Hi." Still, they don't hear me.

"Hi!"

They finally twist to see me.

"What happened?" Allie asks, eyeing me as I limp forward.

"I missed a step and twisted my ankle. I'm fine."

"Oh good. Are those the menus?" Allie asks.

"They are, these menus were actually served exactly ninety-seven years ago, tomorrow."

"That's brilliant. May I see?"

"Sure." I hand them over.

"Allie and I were going over the flow and structure. We have several tiers of players coming, so it's a bit complicated," Liza says.

Allie nods. "I was thinking that the highest tier would have a full sit-down dinner in the Cove Ballroom. In here, I think we should have the bulk of our players and psychics and maybe heavy passed hors d'oeuvres and several small buffet stations."

"We can't decide if we should have all of the players start in here with the psychics and pull the high rollers for the dinner or have the two completely separate?"

"Ideally," I say. "We'd separate. But how are you working the psychics?"

"We have close to fifty psychics," Allie says, and points to the center of the ballroom. "I'm having tables set up there to allow the players to move around as they like."

"I did bring up the point that some of our VIPs may not be open to mingling in line," Liza adds.

"We always try to make everyone feel like they're important with gifts and parties, but the whales get our full attention. That's why it's best to separate the two, you can spoil the whales while keeping everyone else feeling special."

Allie frowns. "When you say 'whale' . . . ?"

"Oh, sorry, a whale is just a high-roller, you know our highest-tier players."

"You didn't know that?" Liza squints at Allie.

"Anyway," Allie says directly to me, "in that case, we could rotate a few of our psychics into the VIP dinner. We have plenty. How does that sound?"

"Perfect," I tell her. "How many VIPs do you have for the sit-down?"

"Fifty-two."

Liza adds, "and, right after the dinner, the VIPs are going to see a special presentation of the show, so we can send the psychics back to the main ballroom then."

"Even better," I reply.

Liza continues, "Following the main party, we have some free play we're giving out to customers as they make their way to the casino. We've programmed it to hit their player's cards as soon as the party is over."

"Great idea."

"These menus are incredible," Allie interrupts.

"Can I see?" Liza asks and Allie passes them over then pulls out her phone.

"Chef is on his way up. I want to duplicate this menu exactly, at least for the VIP dinner," Allie says.

"Not totally identical, right?" I ask.

Allie tilts her head. "We could probably leave off the toasted corn flakes, but why not be fully authentic?"

"You don't think blood soup and tongue may scare away our customers?" I ask.

"Are you kidding?" Liza asks.

"The weirder the better," Allie agrees.

"Trust us," Liza adds.

My phone dings with a text. Sharp: 'We need to talk.' I tuck my phone back into my blazer pocket.

"Really, you don't think psychics, blood soup, and tongue is too over the top?"

"Here," Allie says, pushing her phone to me. "This is an article about some of New York's top restaurants."

As I scan through the article, I have to admit this menu doesn't seem as weird as I thought. These restaurants include Black Ant, a Mexican eatery that serves insects in dishes like ant guacamole and grasshopper-crusted shrimp. Then there's Camaje Bistro that serves dinners to blindfolded patrons, and Sik Gaek that serves live, squirming octopus. A shiver breaks free when I imagine taking a bite of a live octopus.

"The octopus?" Allie asks.

"That's awful, that poor animal."

"I wonder if the tentacle is still squirming when you eat it?" Allie asks.

"It is," Liza says.

My phone dings again and I hand Allie back hers, not wanting to read about any more of New York's strange restaurants.

Sharp: I need to talk to you now.

Me: In a meeting. Call you later.

"Everything okay?" Liza asks.

"Yeah, just a needy journalist."

"Speaking of journalists," Liza says. "We have quite a few coming this weekend."

With a nod, I say, "That was my next question. I was going to see if we received confirmation from them. Our invite went out so last minute."

"Actually, they're already checked in."

"Amazing. That should give us some good press going into the summer. They'll be at the party, I assume, and is the tour set?"

Liza nods. "Yes, and yes."

My phone dings again.

Sharp: Can you meet?

Me: Today's not good.

I type before returning my phone to my pocket.

"Do you think this party will be full?" I ask.

"We know it will," Liza says. "We've had to turn away some of our lower-level players."

My phone dings again.

"The layout will be finished today," Allie says. "The décor load-in will start early tomorrow morning."

"Awesome. If you need me, call anytime. I'm going to see what Sharp needs."

"Sharp, the journalist?" Liza asks.

I nod.

"You should invite him for this weekend."

"I will," I say as I start to walk out.

"One more thing," Liza says, and I stop walking and pivot back to face her. "Can you or ideally you and Amon meet the press group at four for a glass of champagne before I give them a tour?"

"I definitely can and I'll ask Amon as soon as I get back to my office. Can you email me a list of the press here this weekend?"

"Of course," Liza says.

"Thank you." I make my way out of the ballroom, dodging convention workers carrying tables and chairs on my way.

As I clear the doors my phone dings again and I already know it's Sharp.

Sharp: I need to talk to you. NOW.

Me: Fine. I'm going back to my office. I'll call you in five.

Sharp: No. You can't call. Come outside. I'm waiting in my car on South Carolina. Cut through the lot. You'll see me in a red Kia Soul.

Me: Seriously?!?

Sharp: This is life or death.

Me: Fine.

I step onto the escalator to the ground floor. The pain in my ankle reminds me I shouldn't be walking, stoking my irritation into a full-blown fiery annoyance and pinning the target on Sharp. I sneak out a side door and cut through the still-slammed valet area, carefully avoiding cars as I go.

My phone dings and I expect it to be Sharp, but it's Amon.

Amon: Where are you? I ran down to check on the party and saw Allie and Liza. They said you were on your way back to the office.

Me: Sorry. Sharp texted me that he's in the area so I'm going to say hi. I'm inviting him to the party tomorrow. I won't be long.

Amon: Sounds good.

I rush—or hobble—through the parking lot and spot Sharp parked near the ramp to the boardwalk. He seems nervous, but what's new? He is focused on his phone. He doesn't notice me so I walk around the back of the car and up to the passenger door. When I gently tap, he jerks and drops his phone. He unlocks the car, then locks it again as soon as I'm in.

"I figured it out," Sharp whispers in a loud hoarse burst. "And it's so much worse than I thought."

"Are you alright?"

"None of us are alright."

"Sharp, pull it together. You sound insane." I wince when I tell him this and quietly add, "We both need to."

"I'm not crazy and neither are you."

"What is going on?" I let out a slow breath, unable to decide if it's dread or annoyance that's eating away at me.

"I told you the Asras were tied to a dark organization, but I had no idea why they showed up in Atlantic City." Sharp narrows his eyes, like I should know what he's talking about.

"Go on," I snap.

"Remember how I told you the building is haunted?"

"Yeah," I say with a heavy roll of my eyes.

"I know you've had experiences."

"No, I haven't. I'm stressed and I have tinnitus from allergies."

"What?" It's Sharp's turn to look irritated.

"Never mind."

"I know why the building is haunted."

"Because it was an old hospital during World War Two, right?" I drag out the sentence to make sure Sharp knows I'm not buying what he's selling.

"Not just that, it goes back further. The original owners were reportedly Quakers, but then a management company took over the property in the early 1900s that was owned by the Ledes family."

"So?"

"You haven't heard of them?"

"No."

"There're roads named after them. They used to control everything."

"Get to the point."

"Supposedly, one of them was a witch and gave birth to a devil. You've heard of the Jersey Devil, right?"

"Um, no."

"It's a famous urban legend here. Do you know anything about this area?"

"I *know* that's completely ridiculous."

"Yeah, but crazy stories usually have origins grounded in fact."

"Get to the point."

"Maybe there was no devil or witch, per se, but the Ledes family was evil."

I motion for Sharp to speed it up.

"They were part of a satanic cult that did horrible things inside of what's now the Golden Sands."

"A cult? You have lost your mind," I say.

"No, and I think it's the same organization that the Asras are part of."

"This is ridiculous."

"You don't understand. They would have these ceremonies, or feasts, and they would sacrifice—"

"So, you're trying to tell me this prominent family went around murdering and sacrificing people for a satanic cult and now roads are named after them and they never got caught?"

"Exactly."

"That's stupid."

"No, it's not. They didn't get caught because the entire town was in on it. If people wanted a sweet beach vacation, they'd go to Cape May. People came to Atlantic City for darker reasons. It was a city of vice and now it's come full circle and they're planning something big."

"Sharp, man, you need help."

"Have you heard anything about The Order of μ?"

"It's an exclusive dining club. Amon was just telling me about it."

Sharp looks at me with his eyes so wide they look like they might fall out of his head.

"Yeah, they wear these funny necklaces, and they get knighted," I add.

"No, that's Chaine des Rôtisseurs."

"Well, The Order of μ is like that. If it was an evil cult, he wouldn't be telling me all about it. Have you been to Mangia? They're part of it"

"Yeah. I mean no, you're wrong. It's—"

A sudden tap on the window interrupts Sharp and we both jump. It's Amon.

Chapter 24

S harp waves, turns off the car, then leans in like he's unbuckling his seatbelt and whispers, "Do not say anything or we're both dead."

"Mr. Asra," Sharp says, climbing out of the car. "I've been looking forward to meeting you. You've got amazing things going on." Sharp smiles and extends his hand.

A smile creeps across Amon's face, it almost looks wicked for a moment before warming up as he shakes Sharp's hand. "I was on my way to the Hard Rock to catch you, luckily I happened to see you out here."

"I had a little extra time and thought I'd save Lilly the walk."

"Nice." Amon looks at me as I walk around the car to join them. "I wanted to personally thank you for the story. Our property is packed this weekend, thanks in large part to you."

"That's what Lilly was just telling me. I'm happy it helped."

"Did she invite you to our events this weekend?" Amon asks.

"I was just about to," I say.

"I thought the grand opening events were in a couple weeks?" Sharp asks.

"The public events are, but we're having our first player event party, VIP weekend, and show opening this weekend and we are inviting just a few of our favorite members of the press, which of course includes you."

I force a smile. Part of me wants to tell Amon how crazy Sharp is, but another part buried deep thinks I should keep quiet. I need to get back to my office and read more of that book.

"Details, please," Sharp says.

"We'd like to invite you to our VIP party tomorrow," I say. "Which will be a celebration of the property's history. We're serving the same menu that was served in 1927 and will have a bunch of psychics doing readings. Then you're invited to see Li-RV."

"Players love their psychics, don't they?" Sharp laughs.

"So, I take it we'll see you there?" Amon asks.

"As long as I can get someone to cover the Dierks Bentley show tomorrow, I'll be there."

"Sounds good," Amon says.

"Thanks, Sharp," I say. "We could use an article from you leading up to summer and our grand opening."

"You got it." Sharp looks directly at me before he climbs back into his car.

Amon waves to Sharp, then puts his arm around me as and we head back.

"That was a strange place to meet," Amon says.

"He didn't have time to come inside. I didn't have time to go to the Hard Rock. Our valet is so busy, I told him to pull up a street down."

"Why didn't you just call him?"

"You don't think that's what I tried to do? Sharp insists on meeting in person."

"I don't like him."

"He is definitely weird. Did Liza and Allie ask you if you can meet their press tour at four for champagne?"

"No."

"Oh, I thought you said you stopped by the ballroom."

Amon looks at me for a moment, his eyes narrow. "Yeah."

"Oh . . . ah . . . They're giving a press tour this evening and they'd like us to meet them before their tour for a champagne toast at four. Are you free?"

"I will be. Can you have them meet in Rapture?"

I pull out my phone and text Allie and Liza.

They quickly reply with two thumbs up.

"Done," I say.

"Great. Let's walk through the casino. Can your ankle handle it?"

"Yeah."

"Are you sure?"

"Walking is helping," I lie.

"Good." Amon offers me his elbow. "Did you notice how busy the valet is?"

"Oh, I noticed."

"My secret weapon."

I know Amon means that as a compliment, but it floods every cell in my body with a bone-crushing sense of dread. The machine was in motion before I stepped on board. When I think about what I've really done since being here, it's nothing beyond what a decent marketing manager would do. And yet the results have happened so quickly.

"I don't think I had much to do with this," I say.

"Are you kidding me? The club was your idea. All the press we've received. The party. The casino layout. That's all you."

"Those were just small details."

"Details that worked incredibly well. Look," Amon says as we cross the street into the porte cochère where a line of cars still snakes from the street through the valet. "This is because of you."

Because of me? That's just not possible. My heart races with each step closer to the Golden Sands entrance. The unease flooding my body suddenly roars into stabbing pins and needles. My hands dampen with an ice-cold sweat. I want to run . . . but I don't. I want to tell Amon how wrong this feels . . . but I don't. Instead, I blurt out, "Sharp told me this building is haunted."

Amon looks at me, his eyebrows slightly crease, his head tilts just a little. I can't tell if he's mad or convinced I'm insane. Then his eyebrows lift. "Really?"

"Yes. That's why he won't meet in here."

"This guy never ceases to amaze me. Do you believe him?"

"What?"

"Do you think this building's haunted?"

"Huh? Ah, I don't—"

"I'm joking. People in America think that any building older than fifty years is haunted. It's ridiculous." A sly grin peels across Amon's face. "Sharp's crazy, but he's in the story business and people do love a good ghost story. Maybe we can use that to our advantage."

"What do you mean, like promote Golden Sands as haunted?"

Amon shrugs. "Maybe."

"I don't know, definitely not now. Maybe in the fall."

"Yeah, just keep it in mind." The valets hold traffic for us to cross through the porte cochère.

The bellman holds the door and my heart flipflops in my chest as we walk through the main entrance. Everyone is staring at me. I look up at Amon, he nods slightly acknowledging the attention of the lobby crowd.

I pull on his arm, whisper, "What is going on?"

"Liza had copies made of the various articles and placed them around the property, so everyone recognizes us. Smile," he says looking directly at me. "You're famous."

I smile and try to imitate Amon as he works the room. I search out kind faces to make eye contact with and can't find any. Instead, all I see is mad excitement plastered on face after face—an intensity pinned on me in a pool of dark eyes. My heart races, and I stare at the ground—again.

Amon's fingers find my chin, tilting my face upward until I'm trapped in his gaze. His eyes lock onto mine, unyielding, permitting no escape. "Lilly, head up. This is your moment. Ready to walk through the casino?"

Unable to form words, I nod.

Casino players are a different breed. Being a player is a lifestyle, regardless of whether it's for a weekend or a mid-week bus trip. Players are loyal to their chosen casino. Above all else, they develop an affinity for the president, C.E.O., owner, or whatever you want to call 'the boss'. Some of the most successful promotions I ran in Vegas were things like 'Meet the President' or 'Coffee with the C.E.O.'. I never fully understood a player's need to put a face to their 'competition' when they know full-well they'll never have the edge—that always goes to the house.

The one thing I do know is that I don't like being 'the face'. I don't like being recognized.

The crowd parts as we move through the lobby, and I start to hear a buzz or a low hum. At first, it sounds like everyone is whispering the same thing just beneath my range of hearing. But not everyone in the vast sea of faces appears to be speaking. Those that are, seem to be locked in different conversations. My gaze drifts down to the floor and I try to focus on the whisper, I try to make out words, but all I hear is a deep "Om".

"Do you hear that?" I ask Amon, stopping just before we cross from the lobby into the casino.

"What?"

"I think they're whispering about me."

"Who?"

"Them." I motion behind us with my head.

"They probably are, you're a celebrity."

"No, like they're all saying the same thing at the same time." I wipe the beads of sweat from my forehead.

"That you're beautiful?"

"Amon, please."

I rub my temples and look down, fighting back the sting of tears. Amon lifts my chin, again. "Lilith, I know how uncomfortable this attention can feel at first, but you'll get used to it. Eventually, you'll love it."

I drop my head again and he wraps both hands around my cheeks, gently pulling my gaze to his. "I'll let you in on a little secret. I'm."

ROLL THEM BONES   289

Amon's eyes look up to the left then back to me. "I hate using this word, but I'm kind of famous in a few circles. That's why people are staring. It's me not you." He ribs me with his elbow.

"Oh, that's right, I forgot I'm with New York's most eligible bachelor."

"Exactly and I'm in Page Six way more than I'd like to admit."

"As long as they're staring at you and not me, it does make me feel a little better." My turn to rib him.

As I try to tune out the lingering hum of whispers, I close my eyes and am suddenly hit with a cacophony of casino sounds. The ding of the slot machines, the flipping of cards, the music, the cheering. I take a deep breath, steady myself, and slowly release it. These are sounds I'm used to.

No one is staring at me and the whispers are gone. I feel like myself again. It's barely noon on a Friday and the casino is busy. Players are at the tables and slot machines. This level of success is what I dreamt of. It's been my goal for as long as I can remember. *Why can't I just enjoy it?*

"Hey, it's Leaving Las Vegas."

"Excuse me?" I spin to see an older man walking out from a bank of slot machines.

"You don't recognize me, do you? I mean, I can't blame you—"

"Lilly, is everything okay?" Amon interrupts.

"Yes," I tell him, then return my attention to the man. "I know . . . I know you, I just can't remember how."

"Did you ever find your baggage?"

Bingo! "Tony! How could I forget."

"How could you remember is a better question." A warm smile blooms from cheek to cheek.

"What are you doing here?"

"I come to AC almost every weekend."

"That's right. You know, at that time, I would've told you you're crazy if you told me I'd end up in Atlantic City."

"I mean, who could blame you. You're from Vegas."

"Honestly, this is a nice change."

"It suits you." Tony pats my shoulder.

"Is this where you always come?"

"No, normally I go to Harrah's but I follow Sharp's blog and listen to his podcast. He's talked a lot about the new Golden Sands and I wanted to check it out. Thought I'd switch it up this weekend."

"I'm glad you did. Welcome."

"Thanks," Tony says.

"Will you be in the casino later? I'll look for you and we can catch up."

"I will. I really hope to see you," Tony says before walking back into the maze of slot machines. I remember him telling me how much he loves gaming and how positive he was, and I could use a dose of that mentality.

"I'll find you," I yell to him, and he throws me a smile before disappearing around a corner.

"Are you really going to meet him?" Amon asks as we continue through the casino.

"Yeah, why?"

"Who is he?"

"He was the limo driver that picked me up from the airport and took me to my parents."

"You're meeting up with a limo driver?"

"Yeah. I could use his perspective."

"Okay," Amon says, and scans his key card at the bank of elevators.

As the elevator slides open, a security guard holds the crowd so that Amon and I can ride alone. Admittedly, I'm grateful, I need a respite from the crowd of strangers. It might have been part of the reason I was so glad to see Tony. I'm craving familiarity, even if it's from someone I only spent a few hours with.

When I do a quick appearance-check in the mirrored doors of the elevator, there's someone in a hooded robe standing behind me and I gasp. When I spin, it's Amon looking at his phone. I hope he didn't notice and chance another look at my reflection. For a chilling moment, I don't recognize the eyes staring back at me. They seem darker.

"What's wrong?" Amon asks.

"Nothing."

Amon grabs my shoulders and spins me towards him. "Don't believe anything Sharp says."

"What?"

"He gets to you. Every time you meet with him, you come back . . ." Amon pauses, appearing to carefully contemplate his next word, " . . . uneasy."

"No, I don't."

"He's in the business of stories. He's a journalist. He spins tales. That's what he does."

"I know," I say. I step off the elevator as soon as the doors slide open.

"Should I order lunch?" Jordan asks as soon as we walk into the office suite.

"I'm fine," I brush by him. I'm eager to check out the book and hurry to my desk.

The book is gone.

Chapter 25

"Where's the book?" I ask, tearing into the reception area where Amon is still talking to Jordan.

"What book?" Jordan asks.

"The book I found with the menus. The Order of μ."

"I'm sorry, Lilly, I haven't seen it." Jordan stands from his desk and files a folder in a nearby cabinet. "When did you have it?"

"This morning."

"I saw it," Amon says. "In your office. Didn't you take it to the meeting?"

"No," I snap.

"Are you sure? I think you grabbed it with the menus before you rushed out," Amon says.

"No." *Did I?* "I don't think I did."

"Why don't you text Allie?" Amon suggests.

"I'll text her," Jordan says.

Moments later, Jordan adds. "She said you didn't give her a book, just menus. But she remembers you carrying a few things into the meeting. Do you want her to look in the ballroom for it?"

"No, that's okay. I'll go."

Amon says, "I'll go with you. Jordan, can you get Peter to take an elevator out of service?"

"You don't have to come," I tell Amon.

"I don't mind."

"He's sending elevator four now," Jordan says. "Text him when you want him to open it and send it back up here."

"Thanks," Amon says then opens the office door for me as the elevator doors slide open.

"Wait, I need my phone." I duck back into my office. Grabbing my phone, I flip through my desk one last time, but still don't see the book anywhere.

In the elevator, I try to retrace my steps. I was eating breakfast and reading the menus. Started to check out the book, then handed it to Amon.

"You were looking at the book," I say, breaking the silence.

"Yeah?"

"Then you set it down."

"Yeah?"

"I remember I couldn't reach it, so we started talking about the menus."

"Okay, then you handed me the menus too."

"Yeah, but the book was out of my reach, why would I have grabbed it to go to a meeting when I intended to read it after the meeting?"

"Maybe I set the menus down on top of the book and you grabbed everything in a rush. Why are you so consumed with this book?"

"I just want to know where it is. It could come in handy for future events if we intend to use the history of this property."

"I told you it's just a stupid dining club," Amon snaps, his jaw tightening as irritation flits across his features.

"I found it and I want to read it."

"That's why I'm helping you find it," Amon says, smoothing away the tension that briefly creased his face.

"Sharp said the Order of μ is something else," I blurt out.

Amon rubs his temples "I can only imagine, do tell."

I regret bringing Sharp into the conversation. The man sounds crazy and the last thing I want is to sound crazy too. "He didn't go into specifics, all he said is that's it's not a dining club, it's something darker."

"Darker? Ohhh, sounds spooky. What a whack job." Amon says, his patience growing shorter along with his.

"Yeah, but I still want to read it."

"I don't blame you. Sharp knows how to sell a story. Why do you let him get you so riled up?"

"He doesn't."

"He totally manipulates you."

"No, he doesn't."

"You don't think he's working an angle?"

"No," I say as the elevator doors slide open.

There's a group of people waiting, and they're surprised when the elevator opens without the call light turning on.

"Sorry," Amon says, blocking the door as we step off. "This car is out of service."

Another elevator arrives and the group clamors towards it.

"Really?" Amon resumes our conversation as we make our way towards the Grand Ballroom. "You really don't think he's working an angle?"

"What angle?" The women from earlier are sitting at the recently opened bar, still drinking and still talking very loudly. Their voices grate like nails on a chalkboard. I want to tell them to shut up, to stop talking so obnoxiously loud.

"He's trying to build a story that he can sell," Amon says. "Trust me. He's baiting you. All he needs are a few ghost stories, he'll do a blog post or two. Then write a book on haunted hotels in Atlantic City based on 'true stories'." Amon makes air quotes around true stories. "And make millions off of it and the movie rights."

"That's a stretch."

"Not for him."

"He seems to believe what he's saying."

"You're a sweet, trusting person. The perfect target. I'm sorry, but I'm just trying to protect you from someone trying to profit from your inadvertent assistance. Trust me, my family has endured these types before."

"He didn't say one thing about writing a book."

"Of course, he didn't. Look around," Amon says. "Look at this hand-carved coffered ceiling."

Gold leaf, hand-painted vines swirl along the dark wood arched ceiling held up by pilaster columns which frame Flame Steak and the Pearl Bar and Grill along restaurant row.

"It's beautiful." I shrug.

"It *is* stunning, but it's antique and could have been taken right from an old, haunted mansion in some Hollywood movie, right?"

"Yeah," I admit.

"Have you seen this plaque?" Amon points to the wall just past restaurant row towards the Ballrooms.

"Yes. The Thomas England General Surgical Hospital commemoration."

"Exactly. The Golden Sands has a story unlike any other casino in the world and Sharp wants to be the one to profit from it. He's using you."

Amon has a point. Sharp is always asking for information. Still . . . "I don't know. He already has a huge audience. I don't even think a story like this would translate to his audience." I pick up my pace to the ballroom.

"A. Historic. Haunted. Casino. Are you kidding? They'd eat it up." Amon opens the door to the ballroom for me.

It's a hive of activity inside. Large, round tables are being rolled into place. Smaller tables form two circles at the center of the room. A large, dark-brass and black-glass art deco chandelier has been hung. Dozens of workers dress the tables with black and gold linens.

"Wow," Amon says. "This looks brilliant. Lilly, the 1920s' theme is perfect."

My eyes scan the tables. "The book's not here."

"Excuse me." Amon taps a ballroom worker on the shoulder and the man stops smoothing a table linen to face us. "Is there a supervisor here?"

"Me. What can I do for you?" He checks the diagram printout in his hand and motions to a group of guys rolling a large table in.

"Did you pick up or see a book with . . ." Amon pauses and looks at me.

"A red leather cover. It's antique," I add.

"In here?" he asks, and I nod. "No, sorry."

"Are you sure?" Amon asks.

"Positive." The man spins back towards the room. "Whoa, whoa, whoa," he yells to a group of guys pushing a cart of rectangular tables in, and makes his way to them. "Where are you taking those?"

"It's gone," I say.

"Seems so," Amon admits.

Irritation makes my skin itch from the inside out. *I can't believe I lost the book.* I just wish I could know without a doubt that Sharp is crazy and I had hoped this book could've given me the bit of clarity I crave. Though, Amon has made a good point about Sharp's motives. *Ugh!* My hands begin to cramp and I notice I've balled them into fists. The book is gone. That's that.

I take a deep breath and shake my hands out. "Can you text Peter? I need to get back to the office," I ask, rushing by him towards the elevator bank.

Amon hangs a few steps back, texting, as we make our way through the busy corridor. The elevator door slides open as soon as we step in front of it, then promptly closes before anyone else can step in.

I watch the numbers light as we slide past each floor.

"What do you have planned for this afternoon?" Amon asks.

"I'd like to run a few casino reports and prepare for the press tour."

"At four o'clock, right?"

"Yes. Thirteenth floor."

The elevator door opens. Jordan is already there holding it wide.

"Thanks," I say as I breeze by.

"Ready for lunch?" Jordan calls.

"No thanks," I answer not even turning.

"Amon?" Jordan asks.

"Let's go out. Invite the team. Lilly?" Amon calls as I turn down the hallway to my office.

I pause, take a step back and look around the corner. "Yes?"

"Jordan and I are going out to lunch with the whole team. Would you like to join us?"

"Is it work related?"

"No, not at all. The opposite."

"I'm having an early dinner. I was going to skip lunch."

"Lilly, come with us." Amon's eyes widen. "Conquer life by living it to the full."

"I really want to get some work done before meeting Tori for an early dinner. If I eat now, I'll never be hungry and it's Mangia."

"I get it. We'll miss you." Amon bites the corner of his lip, and I almost change my mind.

"Call me if you need anything," Jordan says.

"Thanks." I stare at Amon before retreating to my office. The whole team will be there, except me. Is that a mistake? A sickening prickle digs into my gut and I realize, I'm jealous that Amon will be with Allie and Liza. I swallow attempting to bury that emotion and head to my desk.

With the bathroom door now closed and the office blinds wide open, I click on my computer. I should run casino reports but instead type 'The Order of mu' in the search engine. Nothing related to any satanic cults—or any cults for that matter—comes up. Unless you consider fraternities and sororities cults. If I manage to dig up anything with substance, I'll ask Tori but at this point she'll just think I'm crazy.

I fall down a rabbit hole about the mythical lost continent of Mu. Augustus Le Plongeon studied the Mayan civilization and proposed the idea of Mu, and I can't tell if it's just another name for Atlantis or a different lost land. What catches my attention is the archeologist's claim that Queen Moo, a survivor of the catastrophe that destroyed Mu, founded ancient Egypt while other survivors went on to establish the Maya civilizations.

As I tumble deeper, deeper, finding articles from clairvoyants and occultists alike, prophesizing lost continents and elite races of humans. All from around the same time—the late-1800s to the early-1900s—

A knock sounds. It seems to be coming from the front office. Reluctantly, I pull myself away from the computer. Pain surges in my ankle with the first few limps towards the door, then settles. My bathroom door rattles as I pass. "Not now," I mutter, more to remind myself that it's just the air coming on and Sharp's claims sparking my imagination.

More knocking. Louder now. It's joined by some rattling, and I freeze just outside the threshold to my office, taking a few deep breaths. *I am not bound by the constraints of my comfort zone or my imagination.* Then strain my neck to peer around the corner. It's Buddy. Relief washes over me. I don't know what he's doing, but don't feel like taking the time to find out.

Back at my computer, I click through pages devoted to lost continents. Apparently, there's several. One page catches my attention, Vril for a New World Order. There's something vaguely familiar about it. *Vril* . . . I don't know . . .

Fully aware that I'm getting sucked into the world of crazed con-spiracy theorists, the pull of its gravity drags me into hidden worlds beneath the earth's surface.

Vril found its origin in a science-fiction book about a supreme race living beneath the earth's surface who control the power of Vril—a sort of mysterious life-force energy. Great idea for sci-fi, but how or why it became anything more, I can't figure out. As I read on, a vein of resentment towards my mother sprouts and feels strangely like indigestion. I consider taking a sip of water from the leftover glass on my desk but it has her stupid drops so instead I stretch up and rub my diaphragm. Does she realize how ridiculous she sounds when she talks about an energy force?

With growing annoyance, I click on a link and read about Admiral Byrd, Operation Highjump, and his lost diary. Supposedly, well I guess factually, Admiral Byrd took a large fleet of sea and aircraft to Antarctica between 1946 and 1947. The 'supposedly' part surfaced years later when claims came to light that Byrd made contact with a race of superior beings that inhabited inner-earth. Why am I reading about this? This is why I hate the black hole known as the Internet. It's nothing but a distraction. But . . . maybe my overworked mind needs a distraction, a momentary recess from reality.

My phone rings—Mother. I consider not answering.

"Hi, Mom."

"Darling, we're here. When can we see you?"

"I have a meeting then I'm going to dinner with Tori."

"She's still around?"

I hold the phone away from my ear and consider 'accidentally' disconnecting, but let out a breath instead. "You know she's staying with me for the summer."

"You're leaving work early to have dinner with Tori on one of the most important nights yet?"

"It's just for a quick early dinner, then I'll be back."

"I can only imagine how that makes you look to the other executives."

"Amon made the reservation for us," I snap.

"Just because he offered, doesn't—"

"Mom, why did you call?"

"Your father and I want to see you."

"I'll be working late tonight."

"Perfect, we will be at the casino so we will see you then."

She hangs up before I can object.

I swallow down my irritation and chase it with more internet scrolling, 'The Nazi Occult Order of the Vril Society.' *Nope.* It has conspiratorial fiction written all over it. Trying to dig my way back to factually supported information, I hit a link for Operation Paperclip, top-secret U.S. program that brought Nazi scientists to America. Nearly 1,600 German scientists were forgiven for any war crimes and brought to the States with their families in exchange for their knowledge. One of the most notable scientists was Wernher von Braun, perhaps the most instrumental rocket developers at NASA. Again, I find myself losing track of my search. How did Operation Highjump bring me to Operation Paperclip?

What does any of this have to do with a cult? Then I stumble upon a buried link to Jack Parson, rocket engineer and occultist. This seems to be more in the right direction. Parsons has been dubbed the father of modern rocketry. One of the founders of NASA's Jet Propulsion Laboratory (JPL). Though, he was also a member of a satanic cult, which included actors, opera singers, scientists, and German expatriates. Parsons was known to practice rituals using satanic symbols and sex—attempting to conjure demons and other beings. *Can this really be true?*

Nothing else comes up other than general mentions of occult practices. Though, I do come across a picture of the castle Sharp claimed Amon grew up in. There's a copy of an old picture of Nazis conducting some sort of ritual or ceremony, several dressed in hoods, gathered in a strange circular room with the same geometric circular mosaic that's in the thirteenth-floor theater. At the center is Heimlich Himmler, dressed in his formal SS uniform talking to a man dressed in a black suit that looks eerily like Amon. The quote under the photo reads, 'He who does not carry demonic seeds within him will never give birth to a new world.'

I close out of this page and search the castle's history. Following World War II, it was seized and fell into disrepair. Decades later, a private foundation purchased, restored, and re-opened it as a museum and school. The school's slogan brings me up short. 'Conquer life by living it to the full.' Felix and the team toasted that. At the top of the page is a tribute to a founding member, Francois Durand—Aleister Asra's partner. I search the name. Durand, his wife and young baby were murdered by another suspected cult, The Temple of the Solar Knights. The leader of this cult claimed the baby was the Antichrist and stabbed the child repeatedly with a wooden stake. Not long after, the Knights of the Solar Temple committed a series of murder-suicides, taking out fifty-three of their own members—a supposed nod to the fifty-four Knights Templar that were burned at the stake, namely Jacques de Molay, the last Grand Master of the Knights Templar.

I know this name. That Facebook post about the previous marketing team was made by Jacques de Molay, but there'd been nothing else on his profile. One quick click confirms FB is a dead end.

My phone rings: it's 3:30 in the afternoon and I've wasted all that time chasing my own tail. I dug up just enough weird history to realize that we do a good job at hiding some dark secrets, while not enough to prove any of Sharp's claims. *I'm such an idiot, wasting my day on a hamster wheel.*

I answer my phone. "Hey Tori," I say, dragging out my words.

"What's wrong?"

"Nothing."

"Are you still good for dinner?"

"Yeah."

"Then what's wrong?"

"You'll think I'm crazy."

"Or, I'll make you feel better. Try me," Tori says.

"It's stupid."

"Did you have another episode? Do you want me to grab some allergy meds on my way?"

"No."

"Then what?"

"This stays between you and me, okay?"

"Of course."

"You study religions and cults, have you ever heard of The Order of μ?"

She hesitates. "Why?"

"I found an old book about them. Amon said they're just a silly social or dining club, but Sharp claims they're a full-blown cult. Keep in mind that Sharp also claims The Golden Sands is haunted."

"Where's the book?"

There's excitement in her tone, but she missed my point. "Did you hear what I said? This place is haunted."

"I heard, but where's the book?"

"I don't know. I lost it before I could read it."

"How?"

"I went to a meeting and when I came back to my office it was gone. Maybe I accidentally brought it to the meeting and set it down somewhere. I don't know."

"You have to find it."

"Why?"

"I've heard rumors about this order and have been trying to find information on them *forever*. They're supposedly a satanic cult that wants to resurrect the Antichrist. Apparently, some notable people have been members, like celebrities, scientists, you know, rich people, but there's no information on them anywhere."

"You mean Sharp's right?"

"Who's Sharp?"

"A journalist. He said they're a powerful cult, but he's crazy."

"If the rumors are true, they're extremely influential."

"Who are they? This sounds like a conspiracy theory."

"Most people claim they're a fictional cult teetering on the border of a conspiracy theory, but I think they're real and I want to prove it. If I could find actual information on them, I'd make that my doctoral thesis. We need that book."

"There's no way they're real. There're no such thing as powerful Satanic cults. What are you going to tell me next, *these are the celebrities that drink blood to stay young?*"

"No, I don't think they're an actual Satanic cult, but my thesis proposes they are the most powerful secret organization in the world, like the Freemasons or the Illuminati, but that's actually stayed secret, and I need that book. You have to find it."

"It's gone."

"I bet Jordan took it. I don't like him. You need to check his desk."

"Why would he take it?"

"He's trying to hide something. Where are you?"

"In my office?"

"Can you look through his desk? Just tell him you need something."

"He's not here."

"Then go check his desk now."

"Wait a minute. Have you heard of the Temple of Solar Knights?"

"Do you mean the Templar Knights?"

"No, but there was something about the Templar Knights. The Temple of Solar Knights is another cult."

"If they're associated with the Templar Knights, they're not a cult."

"No, they're officially a documented cult, according to authorities. I just don't know about The Order of μ."

"I haven't heard of solar knights, I'll do some research. But, right now you need to look for that book."

"He didn't take it."

"Then prove me wrong."

I let out a sigh, but can't find a response.

"Are we still good for 5:30?"

"Yes."

"Are you going to check Jordan's desk?"

"Yes," I say, and hang up.

Could Jordan have taken the book? I'm almost certain I left it in my office, but why would he take it? Jordan and Amon are still out; I'll take a quick look around *just to prove Tori wrong*. What would it hurt?

Chapter 26

I jet into the reception area. It's quiet, but an overwhelming sense of being watched freezes me. Forcing myself to sit at Jordan's desk, I open the top drawer. Just pens and pencils. A camera had caught Tori coming into the office, and I may be being watched. *That's fine. I'm just looking for something, whiteout maybe or a highlighter.* I reopen the top drawer and pull out a highlighter. Amon will be back soon because we're meeting the press tour in about a half-hour. I have to hurry. I open the next set of drawers. Files. Two more drawers. Files. I scoot the chair back, pausing only to check the elevator bank for lights or movement. If an elevator is on its way, the light will come on. All dark. All quiet.

Studying the desk, I've searched every drawer and nothing. When I look under the desk, I notice a small bump out. I slide his chair back a touch, and spot a keyhole. I crawl under his desk. It's another drawer, but it's locked. I peek over the desk. No lights. I pull on the drawer again, harder, and then as hard as I can. It doesn't budge. He must have a key somewhere. Maybe he carries it, but his inclination towards very tight-fitting slacks makes me think he hid it.

Another quick glance towards the elevator lobby; I'm safe for the moment. I search each drawer for a key, but find nothing. *Think. Think. Maybe . . .* I don't know if I've watched too much TV, but

I open the top drawer, tapping around the edges, moving pens and pencils along the way. *This is stupid.* Ridiculous even. *Who do I think I am? Sherlock Holmes? Why am I even questioning Jordan? What is wrong—*

A hollow thump. I tap again. Definitely hollow. No lights above the elevator, so I toss the pens out of the tray and try to push on the bottom. Nothing. But when I pull out, the bottom piece slides. The key.

It fits the drawer lock. Damnit. It's just papers, but . . . the book is underneath. Quickly grabbing it with one hand, I shove the papers back in place, close the drawer, and lock it when I hear a soft ding. The arrow above an elevator lights up. Panic roars. My hands tremble. I drop the key in its hidden compartment and try to get the cover back on, but I'm shaking too badly. Using both hands, I wriggle it back into place. I toss the pens and pencils back over the compartment and practically dive back into the hall. I hear the elevator door slide open as I sprint to my office. Seconds later, the glass door opens, and I hear Amon and Jordan. I toss the book in my handbag and bury it under everything else, then tuck it back under my desk.

My heart is pounding. I feel the blood pulse in my neck. I clear my search history and open my email. 4:15 . . . Shit. What was I supposed to have done? The press list. There's a cool dampness around my neck and underarms, I catch a hint of the sulfurous odor of stress-sweat. Opening the email from Liza and Allie, I hit print. I'm going to look and smell like such an awful idiot if I don't know who we're about to toast.

"Almost ready?" Amon asks.

"Give me like five minutes. I just want to freshen up really quick."

"Are you alright?"

"Yeah, why?"

"You look a little—"

"Just nervous. I always get nervous before meeting a press junket for the first time. I'll be fine. Just give me a couple minutes, okay?"

"Sure," Amon says and disappears.

I skim over the press list, trying to familiarize myself with the attending journalists, but my mind is racing and nothing registers. What just happened? Why would Tori suspect Jordan and be right? Why did I listen to her? More importantly, why *was* she right? Why would Jordon steal the book and lie to me? I bite my lip hard. *Keep moving forward.* I grab perfume from my handbag, douse myself, throw on some lipstick, and do my best to pull myself together.

I secure my handbag over my shoulder, grab a notebook, and tuck the press list into it. Take a few deep breaths and I down a glass of water with the herbal tincture. Psychosomatic or not, I need to calm myself, and my mom's concoction is all I have.

"Ready," I say, two seconds before I round the corner from my office to the reception area. I'm going to give myself away. *Calm the fuck down. I will not be bound by the confines of my comfort zone. What does that even mean? I'm an idiot.*

"That was fast," Amon says.

"We only have five minutes to get there."

"Relax we can be a few minutes late."

"Oh, I thought you were ready."

"I am. I just wanted to give you some time to calm down."

"I'm calm."

Amon nods. "You're bringing your handbag?"

"What?"

"Your purse. You're bringing it to the meeting?"

"Yeah, yes." I clear my throat. "I'm meeting Tori right after this junket so I can get back quicker."

"Okay." Amon holds the door for me. "Is Peter sending the elevator?"

Jordan points as the light above the elevator flashes on.

What was I thinking? Jordan's going to realize I took the book and call Amon while I'm stuck on the thirteenth floor. This was such a terrible idea. But does Amon even know that he took it? If he doesn't know, maybe he won't call and rat me out.

Every muscle from my neck down my back reflexively tightens as the elevator doors slide open unleashing that awful grating screech of metal on metal.

"Didn't Peter fix that?" I ask.

"What?"

"The elevator screeching."

"I didn't notice," Amon says, not looking up from his cell phone.

I pull out the press list to get a handle on this meeting, and my mouth drops open. It's not a list of journalists, it's a list of the country's most successful media icons—celebrities in their own right. Dame Beatrix Beuford, editor-in-chief of *Icon Fashion Magazine*. Russel Muldone, owner of the largest news corporation in the world. Ellen Winifred, a former television host and now media mogul. Ted Williams, owner of the largest cable network and media conglomerate in the world; and Andy Hopper, currently the most successful news anchor on television.

In shock, I look up to tell Amon who we're meeting with and freeze—a dark, shadowy figure looms behind me in the reflection. I gasp, choking on my own breath and erupting into a violent coughing fit. "Are you okay?" Amon asks.

I nod but can't get a word out. When I turn around, no one is there, of course. I continue to cough, facing away from Amon.

From the corner of my eye, I see him hit stop on the elevator panel.

I finally get a few gasps in to calm the coughing. When I look back at the reflection, the figure is gone. Part of me wants to believe it was just a shadow in the reflection, but another part is beginning to understand that it's not. That Sharp may be telling the truth.

"What happened?" he asks.

I take a shuddering breath.

"Should we go back to the office?" he asks.

I shake my head and take a few more deep breaths.

"I'm fine," I croak out. "Accidentally inhaled wrong."

"Take your time," Amon says.

"I'm good." I clear my throat one more time and my voice returns. "Much better."

"Ready?"

"Wait. Actually, you need to tell *me* what's going on? This isn't a press tour we're toasting. These are the biggest media moguls in the world. They don't come to events like this."

"You're on to me," Amon says, looking down at his feet.

"What do you mean?"

"When I first meet people, I don't like them to know my full story and where I come from."

"What's that have to do with your press tour including some of the most influential people in the world?"

"I'm getting there. They're close family friends as well as business acquaintances. My parents own a large international bank in Germany. They've done business with my father and became friends."

"I obviously realized you grew up wealthy and that your dad's in banking. You don't exactly hide it well."

"I'm not trying to hide anything. I just want my professional goals to be taken seriously."

"So, you invite some of the most powerful people in the world that would never in a million years actually come to a casino in Atlantic City?"

"My parents invited them. They think it's adorable when Amon has a cute, new little toy to play with. That's why I want them to meet you."

"Why?"

"You're professional. You're an expert. You can talk casino with them and they'll see I'm serious."

"I wouldn't even know how to talk to them."

"I'll lead. I just want you to fill them in on the casino side of things. Talk about the casino floor layout and other casino stuff. They'll be here for the whole weekend."

"These are your family friends. You go talk to them. You don't need me."

"Friends is a lose term. My father manages their money, and if they suspect even a penny of their money is somehow mismanaged . . ." Amon's voice trails off and he looks at his feet again, then back to me. "They need to see you. They need to know this is a serious endeavor."

"Fine," I say as my phone vibrates uncomfortable loudly.

"Do you want to get that?"

"No, I'm sure it's Tori." I chew my lip. "Let's get this over with."

Amon nods, flips the elevator call button, then rests his arm on my shoulder. He leans close to me. "You'll be fine."

I close my eyes and take a breath.

Amon takes my hand and when the elevator door opens, leads me down the hall towards the club. Shadows dance on the draped walls like unhindered flames. Rather than doubt my sanity, I look at the ground. I've seen these drapes before. Know the shadows in this hall. This is all part of the show, but I'm ready for intermission.

When Amon opens the door, Allie, Liza, Dustin, and Felix are waiting just inside. Two on each side of the door. A sudden bright flash momentarily blinds me.

"Perfect. One more."

Trying to clear the glowing orbs from my vision, I look up at Amon.

"Brilliant. Love it."

"Let me introduce our dream team, Ms. Lilith Layne Umbra and Mr. Amon Asra," Liza announces.

As my sight returns, I notice the team of photographers.

"I wish I could take some credit." Amon smiles at the crowd. His teeth sparkle with a burst of camera fire. "But it's Lilly calling all the shots."

"Humility doesn't suit you, Amon." I elbow him and grin to the group. "You bring a lot to the table."

As if perfectly cued, the group cackles with laughter. While I realize this is happening, it feels as though I'm watching it on close-circuit television.

"We are quite the team, aren't we?" Amon looks down at me.

"Indeed we are," I say, looking up at him . . . *Indeed we are . . . where are these words coming from?* A pit of disgust blooms in my abdomen and spreads tendrils of repulsion up my core to crawl through my flesh, making me uncomfortable in my own skin—or at least that of the person I'm pretending to be.

From the corner of my eye, near the bar, I see him. Kai. *No. No. No.* I had a handle on this. Another flash blinds me and when my vision returns, he's gone. I scan the room, the same room I always see him in. *I imagined him. I imagined him. I imagined him.* It was someone else. It had to be.

"Since taking over," Allie announces from the side, "Lilly has initiated a series of casino-focused modifications that have tripled our drop—that's casino-speak for the amount of money the casino takes in—and taken our hotel occupancy from eight-percent to one-hundred. And, I trust you all are very happy with your accommodations." A soft, stoic, two-finger applause momentarily growls through the group.

"That's not quite the full story," I hear myself add. "Amon and his team are capable of moving mountains in a very short amount of time."

Their eyes seemed pinned on me with a sort of hunger I can't place. Am I meant to perform for them? Amon's own little dancing monkey? The 'cute, new little toy' he referred to instead of the Golden Sands?

"We are grateful to have *you* to tell us what mountains to move," Amon says. "How about we toast?"

On cue, a team of waiters carry around silver trays with glasses of Dom Perignon.

Amon lifts his glass to me. "To Lilith."

I lift my glass to him. "To Amon and his team."

"To The Golden Sands," Allie adds, lifting her glass to the crowd.

The icy bubbles tickle my nose and burn my throat, but I need the calm this glass brings.

"Lilly and I will now leave you to enjoy your tour. We hope to see you this evening in the casino."

"It was a pleasure to meet you," I stupidly add. I didn't actually meet anyone.

"The pleasure is all ours, dear," a man from the crowd says, but a final flash of cameras blocks my view of him.

I smile. Drain my glass. Follow Amon out. I gasp as someone steps out from behind the door.

"Buddy. What the fuck are you doing here?" Amon yells.

Buddy stumbles back. Hugs his arms and tucks his chin deep into his chest.

"Amon!"

Amon lets out a breath and smooths his shirt. "I'm sorry, Bud, you just startled me. You shouldn't be up here."

"He works here," I counter.

"He's not working this event."

"Up and down the Golden Sands, in and out the casino, that's the way the Buddy goes . . ." Buddy sings in his rhyming fashion. Does a full spin. "Pop goes the bubbly!"

"I can't believe they scheduled you up here," Amon says. "Do not say a single word to anyone in that group. Do you understand?"

Buddy vigorously nods.

As we walk away, I can hear him sing, "Amon and Lilly go down below to fetch a glass of bubbly. Amon fell down and lost his crown and Lilith came tumbling after . . . Buddy be nimble. Buddy be quick. Buddy gonna light that candlestick."

I glance back at Buddy just before we turn the corner to the elevator lobby. When he sees me, he does a quick spin, winks at me, and takes a jester's bow with one leg outstretched. I notice Amon's jaw clench. "We shouldn't have tried to hire him."

"He's harmless."

Our elevator is waiting. Amon takes my hand, pulls me inside and into him. Then kisses me. I'm startled, but in an instant his warm and tender lips leave me leaning into his embrace.

"You are incredible." He brushes my hair away from my cheek. "You were perfect in there."

"I . . . I . . ."

Amon places a finger on my lips. "Lilly, I'm crazy about you."

"I'm serious about my job."

"I know. That's why you're so incredible. You're the first girl I've ever met that hasn't tried to pursue me for what I have."

Without a doubt, he's telling the truth, and it makes me a little sad. From a professional standpoint, a strong part of me realizes how wrong this is, but there's a bigger weakness in me that wants Amon. Against my better judgement, I stretch my neck up and kiss him back. This time longer. A subtle surge of static electricity tingles my lips. I just pull away when my phone vibrates way too loudly.

"Tori?" he asks.

"I'm sure." I grab my purse and push it behind me, hoping Tori doesn't text me again.

Amon reaches towards my handbag but instead grabs my hand. "Then we'll continue this." He kisses me again. "After your dinner."

I bite my lip and hit the lobby button on the elevator.

Chapter 27

S afely in my car, my bag on the passenger seat, I grab my phone then quickly pull out of the porte cochère. A car horn blares followed by a sudden screech of brakes. *Shit!* When I glance in my rearview mirror, I see the red face and middle finger of the angry old man I just cut off. I wave and smile, then hear an engine rev and the angry guy's Cadillac zooms past me.

Once I pull on to Pacific Avenue, I check my phone and notice seven text messages and three missed calls—all from Tori. The city is too busy to check each text, so I call her.

"Did you find it?" Tori asks before the phone even rings.

"Yeah."

"You have it with you?"

"Yes!"

"Where are you?"

"In my car, two minutes away."

"Perfect. I just got here."

A dark shape darts out from an alley and I slam on my brakes, barely missing it. A mangy black cat with a wispy pink tail hanging out of its mouth stops and looks at me, then meanders off.

The few blocks I have to drive take forever. The city's unusually busy. My knuckles have turned white; driving in Atlantic City grates your nerves more than most commutes. Especially with the jitneys, green and white shuttles that run along Pacific, fighting for riders. They cut in and out of traffic, and Pacific's just a four-lane, thirty-five mile-per-hour road. A barista recently told me about a girl that was standing too close to the road when a jitney raced by and the mirror hit her so hard, it nearly decapitated her. Her head stayed attached, but the bone was completely severed, so her cranium flipped down below her shoulder and landed on her chest when her body collapsed. The driver didn't even stop.

I finally make it to Mangia. It's tucked into one of the rare, quiet blocks between Pacific and the boardwalk that doesn't have a casino. I don't remember the street being so dark, but then again, my mom was driving. There's no street parking, but I find a small lot hidden at the end of the block and pull in. I don't see Tori anywhere, but notice a group huddled in the darkest corner of the lot.

A sudden tap on my window startles me.

"Sorry," a young man yells through my window. "Are you having dinner?"

"Yes."

"Put this ticket on your dash. There's no charge, but I'll keep an eye on your car for you."

"Thanks," I say and pull a five-dollar bill out of my purse.

"Thank you," he says, handing me the ticket and sticking the money in his pocket.

I hurry past him towards the basement entrance.

"Hey," I hear Tori call from up ahead. "Where is this place?"

"Right here."

"In a house?"

"Yeah." We walk down the tight alley towards the basement door.

"Are you sure?"

"Yes!" I pull open the small door and hold it for Tori.

"Ms. Umbra, welcome back. Your table's right over here."

"Thanks, Demetri."

Our table is tight in the middle of the main dining room. It's only five-thirty, but the restaurant is already busy. When I look around the room, a pool of eyes dart away from mine. I take a small step away from the table.

"Is this okay?" he asks.

"Do you have anything in a quieter area?"

"The only table not taken at the moment is in a back corner and I didn't want to stick our—" he leans in and whispers, "most important customer in the corner."

"We prefer a quiet corner, right?" I look at Tori and she nods.

"Your wish is our command," Demetri says, then whistles, points to our table where a bottle of wine waits. He swirls his finger in the air, then points towards the back room.

A team of servers rushes out and moves everything. By the time we get to our new table, it's already set. A server hands Demetri the bottle of wine and he opens it as we sit.

"Thank you," I say as he pours.

"Of course, my dear. Your charcuterie will be out momentarily," he says and promptly disappears.

"You look pretty," I tell Tori.

"Thanks."

"I love that necklace."

It's a delicate gold medallion about the size of a quarter that sits perfectly below her suprasternal notch. There's a double-cross stamped into the soft gold with flowery swirls around it.

"Thanks. You have the book, right?"

"Yeah. Is it new?"

"What?"

"The necklace?"

"Yeah."

"Where'd you get it?"

"My parents gave it to me before I came here."

"Was it a gift for getting into Princeton?"

"Lilly, the book."

"Shush, wait." I motion towards the doorway where a server is heading our way.

Tori just shrugs. "Yes, the necklace was a gift for getting into Princeton. It's the Cross of Lorraine."

I smile awkwardly as the waiter sets a platter on our table. When he leaves, I reach into my purse and pull out Mangia's card. "This is Mangia's card for people they know to call and make reservations. It's impossible to get into if you don't know someone."

I show Tori the card, and her eyes grow wide.

"Do you recognize this symbol?" I ask.

"It looks vaguely familiar, but I'm not sure," she says, looking up and away from me.

"The same symbol is on the cover of the book, which makes me think Amon was telling the truth about it being a social club."

"Or—"

"Let's just be quiet about this, okay?"

Tori nods. Before I pass the book over, I tuck it onto my lap and peek through the pages. I flip to an image of a man with a goat's head; long, thick black horns curl up, and he appears to be standing behind a girl on her hands and knees on some sort of stone altar. Only she's not quite a girl, she has the head of a lamb. His naked body is pushed against hers. In one hand, he holds a long dagger to her neck and in the other, he holds up the bloody, decapitated head of a cherubic child.

A waiter sets bread down on our table and tops off our wine. "Everything okay?" he asks.

"We're great, thank you," Tori says and waits for him to leave before leaning in. "Let me see it."

I pass the book to Tori, not wanting to look at it anymore. It's just a drawing, but makes me nauseous. My hands feel like they're covered in rot and grime.

"This is bad," Tori whispers, looking up from the book.

"Why would Amon—"

"Sweetheart, how unexpected. What a lovely surprise!"

I spin to see my mom walking in.

"Victoria, I'm so glad you're here," Mom says. "Let me introduce you to our dear friend. This is Dr. Alexander Bennet, the director of admissions at Princeton." My mom grins at Tori, and I know she's about to pounce.

"Nice to meet you," I say.

Tori squirms in her chair, but remains quiet.

Demetri shows them to the table beside ours. My dad pats my shoulder when he walks by, but says nothing. Mom grabs an olive from our platter and bites it in half before sitting down.

"Wonderful to meet you, Lilith," Dr. Bennet says. "I've heard so much about you."

Demetri opens a bottle of wine and fills their glasses with the deep-crimson liquid.

"Victoria, you must know Dr. Bennet, no?"

Tori doesn't respond initially, then looks at my mom, then Dr. Bennet. "Actually, no, we have not had the pleasure of meeting yet."

"That's strange, isn't it?" Mom says.

"Stop." I look pleadingly at my dad, urging him to intercede. He just looks down at his hands resting in his lap.

"Do you know what's even stranger?" Mom looks directly at me, an eyebrow lifted in triumph. "Ms. Victoria is not a student at Princeton, she's not in any doctoral program. Never even applied."

"She's starting this fall," I correct.

"No, sweetheart, she's not."

"Tori?" I look at her, but her eyes are downcast.

"Go ahead, Victoria, please enlighten us," Mom says, not hiding the sneer in her tone.

Tori looks at me. "I missed you. I wanted to get out of Las Vegas, and I was too embarrassed to admit I'm a failure."

My mom erupts in laughter. "Oh darling, that's good."

I ignore my mom. "Why would you be embarrassed? It's not like I was exactly in a good place myself."

"I didn't want this trip to be about me, I wanted it to be like old times."

Another cackle from Mom. "Oh, God, now that's a stretch. Victoria, you can do better!"

"You didn't need to lie," I say. "You shouldn't have."

"It's not a complete lie. That's what I want to do someday. I'm even going to sign up for some classes there this fall, just not matriculated."

"I get it, it's okay." I grab Tori's hand across the table. "I just want you to know that you never have to lie to me."

Mom sighs. "I can't listen to this anymore. Lilith, she's a weak, lazy, mouse of a girl. She's jealous of you and wants what you have. She always has. She's using you. Can you now be done with her once and for all?"

Tori's face reddens. "I don't have to take this from you. You're nothing but a rotten old bitch." Tori stands and rushes out.

I consider chasing after her, but don't. I'll give her space and talk more tonight.

"Old?" Mom scoffs. "She's ugly and that can't be fixed."

"Why did you do that?"

"Do what?"

"Make a show of it."

"It's more fun that way." Mom lifts her glass of wine to me, then tosses an olive in her mouth and bites down. As usual, my dad just sits there, letting my mother say and do whatever she wants, regardless of how awful it is. "Besides, I'm your mother. It's my job to do what's best for you."

"No, not like that. Tori's right, you can be such a . . . a . . . bitch."

My dad looks up at me for a split second. I think he might say something, but looks instead at my mom, waiting for her reaction. When a thin grin cracks the corners of her mouth, his attention returns to the antipasto platter on their table.

"Doesn't that feel good, darling?" she says.

"I'm leaving." As I get up, I notice the book is gone. Tori must've taken it.

"Won't you join us for dinner?"

"No."

"It's like a bandage, darling, it will just sting for a second. You'll forget all about her by tomorrow, I promise. Now join us."

Dr. Bennet chimes in. "I've heard so much about you. I would love the chance to talk."

I look at Dr. Bennet in disbelief. "I'm sorry, but I can't."

Without looking back, I rush through the crowded restaurant and to my car, hoping to catch Tori but she's gone. Her phone goes right to voicemail, and she doesn't respond to any of my texts. I consider running home or trying to find her, but why should I be the one to do that? She lied to me. Was she using me for a free vacation—No, I don't think so. Though, I'd be lying if I said it didn't bother me at all.

My phone dings, pulling me from my thoughts. I expect it to be Tori, but it's Amon.

Amon: Coming back soon?

Me: Yes. Leaving now. Is something wrong?

Amon: Come right to the office. It's important. We're missing something.

Chapter 28

My sports car is finally coming in handy as I race jitneys to get back to Golden Sands. Worry gnaws a hole in the pit of my stomach. Security has set up gates on North Carolina Avenue and traffic is backed almost all the way to Pacific. I do a quick scan for police cars, ambulances, and fire trucks. While I love my car, it sits low and I can't see much beyond the wall of SUVs. Everything inside my car glows red from the sea of brake lights. All that's keeping the pit of worry from exploding into a flame of panic is the steady drum of my fingers on the steering wheel.

A security guard in a suit recognizes my car and waves me over. Of course he recognizes me, he cleared the Robovac out of Amon's office this morning. As I break from the stream of traffic, I see a fire truck parked towards the back of the porte cochère.

"What happened?" I ask.

"Nothing, ma'am. We're just trying to keep traffic moving. Orders are to send guests to self-parking, so our valet stays clear for our VIPs."

"Why's the fire truck here?"

"Oh, there was just a small issue with a sensor in the sprinkler system, but it's been fixed and we're all good to go." The guard holds his finger to his ear. "Copy. I'll send her through now." He releases his hand and places both on my open window frame. "Ms. Umbra, would you mind moving through to your spot. They're going to stop traffic to get the fire department out and they'd like to get you in first."

I nod and pull through the space in the blockade. A few cars pull in behind me, but the traffic through the valet is nowhere near as crazy as it was earlier.

Peter is waiting for me, which can't be a good sign.

"Is everything okay?" I ask as Peter holds the door for me.

"Yes, a sensor in the fire sprinkler system went off. An electrical short, nothing major, it's fixed. I'll walk you up. I have an elevator held."

"An electrical short? How did that happen?"

"Not sure, probably just a glitch. It's common in a building this old."

"Oh, okay." I say, what else can I say. *Tell me what's really going on? Am I a dead man walking? Why else would Peter escort me?*

A group of customers crowds behind us in the elevator bank as they wait to be carried up to their rooms. Before they can protest, Peter announces, "Sorry folks, we should have this elevator back in service shortly. We're just doing one more test run to ensure it's fixed and we'll send it right back down."

Not a single guest complains or tries to jump on. I'm surprised. There's typically at least one bull of a customer that insists on shoving their way in.

My stomach drops when the elevator rises, calling my mind back to reality. Amon's going to confront me about the book. What else could be missing? What will I even say? Maybe I should've gone to find Tori instead of coming here. Peter suddenly steps close behind me, leans down, burying his nose in my hair, and takes a long slow inhale. His long, cold fingers twist my hair in the nape of my neck.

Panic freezes me, as if my brain thinks stillness can make me invisible. When fight or flight kicks in and my mind registers that I have no place to run or hide, I quickly step forward and spin to face him. But he's not there. Peter is leaning against the back of the elevator, texting. Before I can say anything, the elevator dings and the doors slide open.

"Everything okay?" Peter asks.

As my mind desperately searches for any bit of logic that can explain what just happened, I glance through the open door and see Amon and Jordan waiting. Every drawer in his desk is open, and my heart sinks even lower. I'm about to get fired for . . . stealing back something stolen from me? That shouldn't be right, but it doesn't matter—I'm about to be canned. My parents are coming here. This night couldn't go any worse. A shiver tightens my spine. I try to shake it off along with the feeling of those cold fingers in my hair, and step off the elevator.

Jordan and Amon both look up. I just stand there as the elevator doors close behind me and any hope of getting out of this situation goes down with it. Amon opens the door for me and I walk in.

"So?" he asks.

"So?" I respond, throwing my hands up.

"You took something from Jordan's desk."

"He took something from me first. Or you did."

Amon lets out a breath and seems to deflate. His head drops and posture sinks. He takes my hand and says, "Lilly, I should've been honest with you from the beginning."

I pull my hand away and take a few steps back. "What do you mean?"

"The book . . ." Amon's voice trails off.

"So, it's true." I take a few more steps away from him and bump against the glass door.

"What? No—"

"Yes, it is." I press myself against the unyielding glass.

"Lilith, you don't understand," Jordan says from behind his desk. "Amon tell her."

Amon takes a few steps back and sinks into a chair.

"I saw what's in the book," I say. "It's . . . it's . . . it's not right."

"I know," Amon says, resting his forehead in his hands. "That book is dangerous."

I'm done. I want to get out of here. When I turn to pull open the door, it's locked.

"Lilly, calm down," Jordan says.

"It's not what you think," Amon says. "You know how I was born here but moved to Germany. The reason we moved is that I was bullied so badly that I attempted . . ." Amon's voice trails off.

I look at Jordan, my hand still on the door handle. "What's he talking about?"

"Amon was so badly bullied that he attempted to end his life when he was very young. It was relentless and cruel," Jordan says.

"I'm sorry, but what's that have to do with a satanic cult?" I try to pull the door again.

"The Order of μ is not a satanic cult," Jordan says.

Amon nods. "It's not. It's exactly what I told you it is, an exclusive social club."

"Not according to that book. Not according to Sharp. And, not according to Tori."

"What's Tori possibly know about the Order?"

"She." I pause to replay my conversation with Tori over, then over again. "She said she heard." I pause and bite my lip before admitting. "Rumors that it was a Satanic cult but hasn't been able to find anything out at all. That's why she wanted this book."

"Rumors, Lilly, rumors. Do you know how many crazy conspiracies there are about rich celebrities? Have you heard the one about what rich actors drink to stay young?"

"Yeah." I admit and look down at my hands. I don't have a response to that. "If it makes you feel any better, she doesn't think it's actually a cult."

"It's not. My parents were—are—very wealthy, even by New York standards. I went to a private school and lived in a very exclusive area where most of the other kids had dads that were also in finance. My dad was managing a ton of money and everyone wanted a piece of it. And they wanted in to the Order. They thought that would give them access to this pool of money. When they were rejected, the other kids at school began saying things to me."

"I still don't understand what this has to do with anything."

"I'm getting there," Amon says, lifting his eyes to mine. "It started slowly at first. Just repeating things they heard from their jealous parents, like that my family was greedy, my dad hoards everyone else's money, and that he made up a fake organization because he was too much of a loser to get into the Skull and Bones and Freemasons, like their fathers were."

I've watched a late-night documentary or two on those organizations. Elitist and secret societies, some with charitable arms, like the Freemasons. Ironically, Skull and Bones had started at Yale by disgruntled students who, themselves, couldn't get into existing groups at that time. "And?"

"And, then we inherited the castle in Germany. My mom had very distant family ties to it way before Heimrich Himmler took it over. It was abandoned and falling into disrepair, so the government approached us with a proposition to retake ownership under the agreement we'd be responsible for the repairs and upkeep."

"Okay?"

"When the kids at school found out, it got really bad. They called us Nazis and because of what Himmler did in the castle, they said that we were in a satanic cult. The final straw was when they made that fake book."

"*Kids* made that book?"

"Kids or their parents. Several families in the school were into antiques, my parents thought one of them had found that book and changed the cover. It's an authentic book, just with a fake cover."

I frowned, uncertain how to respond. Kids, and their parents, could be cruel. But that twisted, seems like a stretch. Where is this going? I look at Amon, scan him. He looks small, crouched in his chair. I cross my arms and wait for him to continue.

"When someone at school put that book in my backpack, I believed it too. I was only twelve. It scared me. They told me the only way to save myself was to commit suicide so that God could save me from my parents and . . . and I tried."

"That's terrible," I say, take a step towards Amon. I can see the gloss of tears threatening the corners of his eyes. "I'm sorry." It's hard to see Amon as a hurting child. Now, people practically throw themselves at his feet. Could an outcast kid grow into this?

"The kids at school told me to take every pill I could find in my parent's medicine cabinet, chase it down with vodka, and go to sleep forever. And that's what I did. Luckily, they didn't have anything stronger than Tylenol. They found me and had my stomach pumped. After a few days in the hospital, I was fine."

"I'm sorry you had to go through that." He does look broken, with a vulnerability I've never seen before, sitting in the corner of his assistant's office. But someone is lying. Is it Amon? Or did Sharp somehow dig up old rumors? I mean, I could see Sharp spending time in those conspiracy group chats. And, Tori? Is she so desperate to get into Princeton, that she's reaching at crazy rumors to uncover the next secret organization?

"After that." Amon pauses for a moment, seeming to wait for my attention to drift back to him. "We moved to Germany. Turned the castle into a school and that's where I grew up and met Jordan, Felix, and Dustin. So, it worked out, wasn't easy, but I've kept that book as a reminder of how hard I worked to be here and to make sure no one else ever has to read it."

"You should've told me that from the beginning." I reach out and take his hand.

"I don't like to talk about it." Amon squeezes my hand.

He seems so small and hurt. *And, genuine* . . . "I'm sorry."

"It's my fault," Amon says. "I should've been more careful with it. Do you have it?"

I put my hand over my mouth, then pull it away and shake my head. "No, Tori does, but I'll get it back from her. I was just so freaked out by what Sharp said, and then the book was missing. She convinced me to search Jordan's desk and when I did, I was sure something was going on."

"I understand why you'd think that," Amon says.

"I'll get the book back from her. Don't worry."

"Where is Tori?"

"I'm not sure. She's not answering my calls. My mom made a scene at dinner, and she took off."

"What?"

"It's a long story. Tori lied to me about being enrolled in Princeton, my mom found out and—"

"Wait, Tori lied about going to Princeton. We had full conversations about what she's studying."

"I know."

"That's weird."

"I know. She wasn't fully lying. She's going to take some classes nonmatriculated." I throw my hands up.

"And now she's missing?" Amon asks, momentarily glancing at Jordan.

"She's not missing. She's just not answering my calls or texts."

Amon looks puzzled. "I'm sure she'll turn up, but she definitely lied to you. There's a huge difference between attending Princeton and touring the campus. Was she using you to get a free vacation?"

"Have you been talking to my mom?"

"What?" Amon asks, his expression one of confusion.

"She said the same thing, but no. It's not like that. She . . . needs space. She was humiliated for trying to do something to improve her life. I feel bad for her."

"Do you always see the good in people?" He waits for me to respond, but I just shrug. "I think we both know how difficult it is to find true friends, I know you'll make up and get the book back, before she really gets the rumor mill going."

"I'm sorry, this is like a tragedy of fools. If only you told me—"

"If only Romeo told Juliet," Amon interrupts. "Enough talk of tragedies this is more a comedy of errors, anyway." Amon clears his throat then grins. "Have you seen how busy the property is?"

"And," Jordan adds, "I think you'll want to see this. I ran a few reports. I don't fully understand the system, but I ran the same reports you had, only with today's date. We've already set a casino drop record, and I ran this report at six pm."

Amon points to me. "I told you. She's our secret weapon."

"Definitely," Jordan agrees.

"I don't deserve the credit," I say.

"Oh, but you do," Jordan says, "in ways you can't possibly know."

Chapter 29

My focus darts to Jordan. Was that a sneer in his tone. *Ways I couldn't possibly know* . . . "What do you mean?" I ask, my lip lifting at the corner.

"Jordan just sees how lost we are behind the scenes. My team is obviously very capable, but we needed your direction."

"Exactly." Jordan slides his chair into his desk. "I think I'll go home, if you don't need anything else."

Amon waves Jordan away. He grabs his shoulder bag and disappears into the stairwell.

"I'm going to walk the floor. Want to come?" I ask Amon.

"Sure." He pauses to text someone. "Peter is sending the elevator." He tucks his cell phone into his jacket pocket. "Just to clarify, what do you mean by 'walk the floor'?"

"Check on the action. Make sure everything is going well, there're no issues."

"You make that sound easy," Amon says, opening the office door as the elevator arrives.

"With you there, it may be a little more of a scene. Customers love to see the *big boss* in the casino."

"I mean, it's going to be a huge scene with the really *big boss*." Amon elbows me.

I roll my eyes as the elevator begins its descent. While I'm trying to lighten the mood, I still feel bad about the misunderstanding and wonder where Tori went. As Amon scans his phone, I can't help but watch him. He's a beautiful distraction and there's a part of me that craves this. A part that's quickly rising to the surface.

Before the doors even open, I can hear the raucous noise from the casino, an unruly mix of boisterous crowds, background music, and the ding of fake coins pouring from the slots. Real coins haven't been used in slot machines for close to twenty years, I mean give or take the outlier that keeps coins around for nostalgia.

When I see the crowd streaming towards the casino, a switch in my brain flips. I'm seeing things from an operational standpoint. What's working, where the flow carries gamblers deeper and deeper into the casino, and where the ebbs seem to spit potential players free. It feels good to not dwell on my own stress or parents or Tori.

"Hey," Guy says from behind us. "Pretty impressive, right?"

"Yeah, it's busy, but looks like everything is going well," Amon says.

"It's running incredibly smoothly," Guy says.

I nod. "I didn't expect this many people. Tomorrow, we should switch some of our ten-dollar limit tables for higher-limit tables."

"Definitely, I was going to ask you about that. Our drop had been so low leading up to today, I thought we'd need more low-limit tables. But if you'd like, I can change that first thing tomorrow."

"Off-hand, I'm estimating that, what, thirty percent of our tables are ten-dollar limits?"

Guy nods.

"I don't see an open seat at any table," I say. "Keep one ten-dollar minimum in each game, two in blackjack, and raise the rest. Try that anyway."

"Will do. Let me know if you need anything else," Guys says as a pit boss waves him over.

"Thanks, Guy," Amon says.

"You know," I lean into Amon, "this is just going to make your job harder. From here on out, you're going to have to maintain this level of fervor."

"Look at these faces. Something tells me they'll be back."

I've spent much of my life in casinos, but I've never seen a crowd like this. Makes me feel a bit like Alice when she wandered into the tea party. Everyone is having fun, which strikes me as strange. In a typical casino, a large portion of gamblers treat it like it's their job, while others have decided to make a career of complaining. But it's different here. Everyone is very obviously having a good time. If this is what the Atlantic City crowd is like, I should've come here years ago.

A loud burst of cheering draws my attention to a craps table across the aisle.

"Roll them bones," the dealer says.

The driver of the Porsche I stepped in front of throws the dice. They tumble down the green felt and bounce off the side wall before both settle on six.

"Boxcars," the dealer yells over the group. "Craps . . . whoa . . . whoa . . . whoa . . . we have a winner. The lady in black."

My eyes search the group for the lady in black. She's about to get a thirty-to-one pay-out. *Morana*. The corners of her mouth twist into a knowing grin. Anxiety's fingers coil around me and squeeze, stirring unease deep within the pit of my stomach.

"Slow down. Where're you running off to?" Amon calls from behind as I quickly move on from the pit.

"Nowhere. Morana just won a big bet."

"She's always been lucky."

"Tell her to take her luck to another casino. It's not appropriate for her to play here."

"It's fine. Besides, no one tells Morana anything," Amon says, seeming insecure for a fleeting moment—a look I've never seen on him.

We weave through the main aisle that separates the table games pit from the slot machines. We're quiet as we take in the boisterous excitement swarming around us.

"There she is!" I hear Tony's distinct voice drift from the maze of winding slot machine aisles and spin to see him walking towards us.

"Hey, Tony, how's it going?"

"I've been on a lucky streak since I walked through these doors, and I'm never lucky."

"I'm happy for you." I pause for a moment and look at Amon. "Tony, I'd like to introduce you to Golden Sand's owner, Amon Asra."

"Nice to meet you, Tony," Amon says, holding out his hand.

Tony's eyes widen as he excitedly shakes Amon's hand. "All my years at a casino, I've never met an owner. I met a C.E.O. once. He was a great guy. They don't make them like him anymore. Now, they're all corporate guys that hide in their office, wherever that is. I can't believe I'm meeting an *owner*. I'm babbling, aren't I? I know it. I know I'm babbling, but I feel like a VIP."

Amon chuckles. "You are a VIP, Tony. Lilly's told me all about you."

"Yes, you are," I say. "I wanted to see if you'd like to join us for a drink in the casino lounge, The Dunes."

"Me?"

"Yes, of course," Amon says. "I think you can give us a unique perspective."

Tony beams. "Yeah, okay. Thanks."

We cut through a side alley, wind past the nickel machines, up a few steps, and straight to the lounge. The Dunes is packed. The song, *Bad Habit* carries over the sound system at a level that's just soft enough to talk over and just loud enough to dance to. There's a bachelorette party decked out in plastic crowns and sashes, taking up the entire dance floor and flirting with the DJ.

Two booths that line the wall overlooking the casino floor are reserved, but other than that, every seat is taken. Amon puts his hand at the small of my back and guides me to the closest reserved booth. The second we slide in, a long-legged, big-breasted cocktail waitress is there.

"Can I get you a drink, Mr. Asra?" she asks.

"Tony, what do you drink?" Amon asks.

"Do you have Campari?" Tony asks and the waitress nods. "I'll take a Campari and soda."

"Make that two," Amon says.

"Three," I say.

The cocktail waitress nods and strides away.

"So, Tony, Lilly says you're a fan of gambling?"

"After I lost my wife, as corny as this sounds, casinos helped me find a reason to hope again and something to keep me busy."

"What do you mean?" Amon asks.

"Every time you place a bet, you get that moment of hope. That little bit helped keep me going when she died."

"I'm sorry, Tony," I say.

"Nothing to be sorry about, you know," Tony says, and I purse my lips together in solemn agreement.

"Did your wife like to gamble?" Amon asks.

"We'd only been to Vegas once and barely gambled. I didn't start coming to Atlantic City until after she died, and only because I was so lonely at home."

"Do you have any kids?" I ask.

"No, we never had any kids, and we were both only children, so we never had much family."

"What about friends?" Amon asks.

"All our friends are busy with grandkids and family. Besides, spending time with them only makes me miss her."

"Do you come to Atlantic City often?" Amon asks.

"Almost every weekend. I've made friends here and my host always checks on me, even when I'm home."

"Who's your host?" Amon asks.

"Angie, she's been with Harrah's for almost twenty years."

"Does Angie know you're here?" Amon asks.

Tony smiles sheepishly, then shakes his head. "I wanted to try something different this weekend, but didn't have the heart to tell her."

"I won't tell her, but I don't think she'd mind," I say.

"Do you have a host here, yet?" Amon asks.

"No."

Amon suggests, "Let's get you one, not that we expect you to change from Harrah's, but just so you have an option. What do you like to play?" He asks as he taps something into his phone.

"A little bit of everything, but blackjack's my favorite."

"What do you think of our casino?" Amon asks.

"Oh, I love it. It's really beautiful."

"Do you have any suggestions?" I ask.

"If I'm being completely nitpicky, just because you're asking, the tables are packed, maybe a few more higher-limit tables."

"Ah, we have a high roller here, my kind of guy." Amon smiles.

"I wouldn't go that far, but, you know, the . . ." He leans into the table and lowers his voice. "Ten-dollar tables get packed with every yahoo that wants to play a hand. You get one dumbo that hits on a fifteen when the dealers showing a two and the whole tables blown."

"Oh, I see and didn't even think of that, but Lilly's already made that suggestion, anyway."

"Of course she has." Tony smiles at me.

"Earlier this week, the casino was dead," Amon says. "So, we set the limits on the low side. Thanks to Lilly, it's . . . well . . . you can see."

The waitress brings over our drinks, leans in a little extra close to set Amon's down first, then Tony's, and finally mine. There's something so familiar about her, but I can't quite place where I've seen her before. As she walks away, her very high, black heels seem familiar too. Then it hits me. She's the young girl who pushes her hairless cat on the boardwalk. A bitter hint of disgust singes the back of my throat. She doesn't take her eyes off Amon, like she's waiting for him to notice her. He doesn't. The corners of her mouth turn down, and she eventually shuffles off.

Amon raises his glass. "I haven't had a Campari and soda since summering on the Amalfi Coast when I was younger."

"That's why I drink it. My wife and I drank them on a cruise we took to Italy."

"Here she is," Amon says. "Tony, this is your new host, Helena."

When I see her, I wonder why she's in a casino and not on a movie set in Milan. She's the spitting image of a young Sophia Loren.

"Tony, it's a pleasure to meet you. I have a player's card loaded with your free play and a couple of meal comps, and this is my card. Call me if you need anything. I've also added you to the list for our player's party tomorrow." Helena passes Tony the cards, showing off her crimson-manicured nails filed to perfect points.

"Wow, thank you so much," Tony says, taking the cards and tucking them into his worn leather wallet.

"Thanks, Helena," Amon says.

"No problem. Let me know if you need anything else. Tony, I'll check in on you later and if you'd like, I'd love to take you to dinner." Helena leaves as quickly as she arrived.

A huge childlike smile has cemented itself on Tony's face

The ice rattles in Amon's glass as he takes the last sip of his Campari and soda and sets it down. "I'm going to do a lap around the casino floor. I'll grab you on my way back," Amon says, standing. I nod and look up at him, all traces of that broken little boy are gone but I wonder if that's what's given him a soft spot for the underdog, the loners of the world. "Tony, it's great to meet you. Thanks for giving Golden Sands a chance."

"It's an honor to meet you, Mr. Asra. I can't thank youse enough."

"Please, it's Amon, and no thanks needed. I'll catch you later." Amon places his hand on my shoulder, then walks out of the lounge. As he leaves, Amon keeps his eyes glued to Tony, even glancing over his shoulder at him.

Chapter 30

Tony takes a long pull on his cocktail. Still smiling, he says, "I'm happy to see you doing great. I don't know you well, but you didn't seem okay when I picked you up from the airport. It made me sad to see such a beautiful young girl in such a dark place."

"I wasn't in a good place. Like you, I'd lost someone I loved."

"I didn't know that. I assumed the Vegas lifestyle had gotten to you."

"No." I sip my cocktail.

"I'm sorry," Tony says.

"Like you said, nothing to be sorry about, but I do have a question. How are you so positive and happy?"

"Why wouldn't I be? I mean, of course I miss my Franny, but life is meant to be enjoyed."

"Cheers to that." I hold my glass up and Tony clinks it. I think of Amon's group toasting to 'Conquer life by living it to the full' and wonder if this is what they mean.

"Cheers," he says. "This is my happy place. I know that sounds stupid. But stepping up to the blackjack table is exciting. It's fun. I meet people from all walks of life. I've made friends, sometimes I even win. It gives me something to look forward to."

"Can I ask you how you got past the grief? I'm haunted by it." I lean across the table and lower my voice. "Literally. I think I see *him* and I imagine things."

"Grief is brutal. It plays tricks on you. You have to find something else that makes you happy and force yourself to move on. Otherwise, you'll drive yourself crazy."

"I think I'm getting there."

"Going crazy?"

I laugh. "No, you know what I mean."

"I'm kidding. I can tell. You look and *smell* way better."

I roll my eyes and laugh. There's something comforting about Tony's straightforward honesty. "I'm glad I ran into you."

"Well, I'm even more glad I ran into you. Youse got a good thing going here."

"Thanks, Tony. Don't spend too much money here, just enjoy the comps."

"I'm careful. I never spend more than I can afford. Besides, I have no one to leave my money to so I might as well enjoy it."

"And you should." I notice Amon wave to me from the bottom of the steps that lead from the bar to the casino floor. "I'm going home for the night. I'll see you tomorrow?"

"I'll be here," Tony says.

I give him a hug before climbing up from the booth. "Thanks for everything, Tony."

"Are you kidding me? Thank you! I think I might take Helena up on her dinner offer after I hit up the blackjack tables."

"You definitely should." I wave bye and join Amon on the casino floor.

He puts his arm around me as we stroll along the outside aisle, back towards the elevators. "I think our work is done for the night. Things couldn't be going any better."

I inhale his leather-and-musk cologne and notice a sensation I haven't felt in a while—fluttering in my stomach, clammy palms.

"Yeah." I can't think of anything else to say.

"Want to grab dinner? Oh, wait, you already ate."

"Actually, I didn't."

"Sorry, I forgot. Have you heard from Tori yet?"

"Nope."

"How about we grab takeout and go to your house? I don't think I've left this property in weeks."

"Sure, that sounds great. But . . ."

"What?"

"If Tori's home, you won't be mad at her. Will you?"

"No way. I'd love to explain things face to face." Amon squeezes me. "We'll take your car. Do you have your keys?"

I nod.

"Then let's sneak out." Amon pulls me into a hallway that cuts through the back of the house. It's a stark change from the casino floor. Bright fluorescent light glares off the cream linoleum tiles. Scuffed white walls display motivational posters left over from the 1990s. Dated graphics on yellowing paper remind employees to be a friendly addition to the team. Though their heated interactions back here sound anything but friendly.

Tucked just out from the public's access is the bar that funnels drinks to the casino players. Busy cocktail servers yell out their orders as the bar staff rushes to serve them. Unlike a public bar, this one has no liquor on display. Black rubber mats ensure no one will slip and the floor can be hosed down at the end of a shift. Ugly or not, this is arguably the most important bar in the casino. Gambler's drink for free while they're playing, at least in Las Vegas and Atlantic City, and it's the cocktail server's job to keep the drinks flowing.

"They must be happy," Amon says.

"What?"

"Look at the tip bank."

A clear plexiglass box is nearly filled with bills that range from dollars to hundreds and a colorful mix of casino chips.

"Want to bet that it's never been even half-full before this?" Amon asks.

"I'll take that bet. I'm sure at some point it's been at least half-full."

Amon shakes my hand, sealing the bet. "Who's worked here the longest?" he yells above the noise.

Everyone at the bustling bar spins at once to look at Amon, then in near-perfect unison they point to one of the bartenders.

"I have, Mr. Asra," he says.

Amon reads his gold name tag. "How long have you worked here, Mike?"

"Seventeen years, sir."

"Wow, impressive. In those seventeen years, has the tip bank ever been this full?"

"Not even close, sir."

"What's the most, other than this?"

"When I first started, the casino did really well. I can't remember what show we had, but the casino was packed and we got it a good third of the way full."

Amon briefly raises his eyebrows at me, then directs his attention back to the bar. "We want you all to know how much we appreciate your hard work, so at the end of the shift tonight, whatever the tips end up being, we'll double it."

The bar erupts in cheers.

"Thank you, sir," the head bartender yells.

"You should thank Ms. Umbra. It's her idea."

"Thank you," he yells.

As we continue down the hall, it quickly becomes quiet. To be honest, I'm completely lost. I realize I've barely set foot in the employee areas and make a mental note to learn my way around, maybe even eat in the cafeteria.

"So." Amon stops walking and leans against an empty wall. "I believe you lost a bet."

"Yeah, and?"

"You have to pay up."

"We didn't bet anything."

"Yes, we did. You said if you lost, you'd kiss me." Amon pulls me into him.

"Oh, really?" I glance up and down the deserted hallway, my pulse already quickening. "Okay."

I slide my hands around his neck and draw him to me with ravenous hunger. Our lips meet—electric, fervent. When I pull away, desire tugs like breath after an exhale. He leans in again, and this time the kiss deepens, our lips fitting together as if designed for each other alone.

Then—icy fingers creep into the base of my neck. Amon's arms encircle my waist, so it can't be him. I try to banish the sensation, but it persists, ghostly fingers threading deeper into my hair. Yet Amon's lips remain warm, inviting. I press myself against him, surrendering to the heat between us, our kiss growing more desperate.

Until someone coughs at the bend in the hall.

I pull away from Amon's embrace, "Sorry," I say looking down the hall.

It's the cocktail waitress from The Dunes. "I didn't mean to interrupt," she says, "but I need to use the restroom."

"No worries, you didn't," Amon says, not taking his eyes off of mine, his arms still around me. I look back towards the waitress, briefly meeting her gaze as it tightens on me, a snarl twisting the corners of her mouth, before looking back to Amon.

The cocktail server lets out a distinctly irritated huff as she clobbers past us, her high heels clacking on the linoleum.

"Let's go," I say, my cheeks must be glowing under this harsh fluorescent lighting.

Amon grabs my hand. The icy fingers finally slip away.

We wind behind the VIP check-in and exit the front door. Security is everywhere, and have set up more blockades, so the valet area only has a trickle of cars waiting. Yet the street in and the rest of the parking area is jammed. This can't be from our promotions.

"I'm glad we're getting out of here for the night," Amon says, waving to the bellmen.

"What's going on? I mean, really. Why is it so crazy out here?" I stop Amon, cornering him before he climbs into my car.

"Someone leaked names of a few of the celebrities arriving for the weekend."

"Celebrities?"

"Yes. Technically, they're just friends but—"

"Such as?"

"David Guardian—"

"As in Batman?"

"Yes. Adam Sanchez, Ricky Nevill, Wynonna Coleman, Beatrix Lynn—"

"They're. All. Here?"

"On their way. You'll meet them tomorrow."

"You say 'someone leaked' . . . as in someone on your staff?"

He shrugs, a small smile playing at his lips.

"You should've given me a heads up."

"And, ruin the surprise?"

I could be upset that I wasn't in the loop about this marketing ploy, but one look in those eyes, I melt. "There's so much I don't know about you." I climb into my car.

"You'll learn," Amon says as security clears a path, and I pull through.

Chapter 31

"She's gone," I tell Amon.

All of Tori's things have been packed up. She's left nothing behind. Not even a note.

"What about the book?" Amon asks.

"I don't know."

"I should have destroyed it years ago." Amon drops onto my couch, sinking into the cushions.

"I'm sorry." I sit next to him and take his hand. "This is my fault."

"It's not, Lilly. I should've been honest with you, but I was embarrassed."

"I can't believe she would just pack up and leave like this."

Grabbing my phone from the coffee table, I quickly text Tori.

Me: Please call. I need to talk to you. There's been a misunderstanding.

When I look back at Amon, his downcast eyes glisten in the low light. A wrecking ball of guilt slams into me, and I lay my head on his shoulder. "I'm sorry."

"No, Lilly, I'm sorry. Sorry I wasn't straightforward with you from the beginning. You deserve better. I never meant to cause a rift between you and Tori."

"That's because of my mom, not you. It's just that, she was my best friend, my only friend. I've known her since I was five."

"I know how it feels to have no one. But now you have us." Amon brushes my hair behind my ear.

My phone dings and I grab it. 'Error. Message cannot be delivered.' I dial her number. Not in service.

"She disconnected her phone." I drop my phone on the table.

"That's a little extreme, don't you think?" Amon shifts on the couch to face me.

"Yeah, I mean, I know she's embarrassed, but to just completely take off like this . . ." I collapse back into the cushions.

"I think she's been using you. Now that you've figured her out, she's erased all ties."

"Using me for what?"

"Do you really want me to list everything?"

I nod.

"To climb the social ladder, to get a break from her boring existence, a free vacation, friends that she's incapable of making on her own—"

"Alright, alright. But how can you just cut someone from your life like that?"

"She was completely pretending to be someone else. Only sociopaths do that. Which means, Tori doesn't feel emotions. Doesn't form personal connections. That's why she needed you. Now you figured her out, you're just a stain on her ego, so she erased you."

"I don't know. She wasn't completely pretending to be someone else. I think she wanted to make some changes and was trying till my mom so callously ripped her back down." Tears pool in my eyes.

"Don't cry," Amon says, and leans in to kiss my forehead. "You're probably right. I have to remind myself that not everyone grows up with the monsters that I did."

A tear boils over. Amon wipes it with his thumb, then kisses my cheek.

"I'm here. I'll always be here, and I promise you'll never feel like this again." Amon gently lifts my chin so that I look into his eyes. From this close, pools of amber sit behind an almost auburn ring of brown, which make his golden eyes seem to glow.

"I've fallen for you, Lilith Layne Umbra. It kills me to see you sad."

"It's not your fault," I say as another tear breaks free. Instead of wiping it away, Amon kisses my cheek where the tear trails down.

"Still, I wish I could fix it." He stares into my eyes. "I love you."

Amon doesn't give me a chance to respond. His lips capture mine, and I'm grateful for the reprieve from words I'm not ready to say. This magnetic pull between us overwhelms me—comfort and danger intertwined. It makes me feel more alive than I've felt in so long, maybe ever. Before I can think, I'm straddling him, fingers tangled in his thick, glossy hair, drowning in sensation. The world beyond this room dissolves. Tori, the casino, my fears—all vanish beneath cresting waves of desire that silence every racing thought.

I break away, breathless, my eyes never leaving his. Our fingers intertwine as I rise, leading him to my bedroom in silent invitation. The moment we cross the threshold, he turns me in one fluid motion, lifting me as if I weigh nothing. Suspended between his strength and gravity, his lips claim mine again as he carries me to the bed.

He kneels between my legs as I reach for his shirt.

"Are you sure about this?" he asks, brushing stray hairs from my face, his lips ghosting across mine.

"Don't make me think right now," I whisper, pulling him back to me.

Amon peels away my clothing, his body pressing against mine with delicious weight. He's perfect—strength contained within careful restraint. Every muscle defined but not imposing. I unbutton his pants, and then he's there, inside me, filling the emptiness with warmth that pulses through my veins like liquid electricity. My body arches toward him, surrendering to waves of pleasure I can neither control nor resist.

Amon's lips trace my neck, his breath hot against my skin. "You're mine."

I gaze into his face, falling deeper with each movement, and nod, unable to deny what feels like truth in this moment. His kiss consumes me before his release, and my body melts beneath him, tension dissolving into pure bliss. He pulls me against him, tucked perfectly into the curve of his arm.

"You're incredible." His lips brush the crown of my head.

"No, you are," I murmur as he kisses me again. "I don't want to move."

"Don't." He draws the comforter over us, holding me tighter, as if afraid I might slip away.

I must have drifted off, because the next thing I know, I'm trying to quiet a ringing phone in my dreams.

"This is Amon."

I force my eyes open, blinking to clear the blurriness. It's still dark.

"What? . . . Who? . . . Who found him? . . . Does anyone know? . . . I'll be in soon."

Amon sets his phone on the nightstand, then leans over and kisses me. My eyes have drifted shut again. "Hey, how'd you sleep?"

"Better than ever," I say without opening my eyes.

"I've got to get into the casino. I'll send a car for you later." Amon lightly rubs my back.

"Wait. What? Why? What's going on?"

"There appears to have been a suicide," he says.

"What?" I force my eyes open and sit up to face him.

"Yeah, security got a report of running water in one of the hotel rooms. They went up and when there was no answer, they did a wellness check and found a body."

"Do they know who it was?"

Amon looks down at hands as he twists the dial on his watch.

"Amon, who was it?"

Amon looks at me and shakes his head.

"Not Tony," I say.

"I'm sorry." Amon pulls me back into his arms.

"No," I say, pushing back. "That's impossible. He was excited about the party today."

Amon tries to pull me in again and this time I give in. He wraps his arms around me. "He left a note. It wasn't long but said that he was tired of being alone and wanted to be with his wife again."

"No, this has to be a mistake. He was so positive and happy. It can't be him."

"I'm really sorry, Lilly. You didn't really know him that well, did you?"

Lifting my head off Amon's chest, my gaze meets his. Pity pools in the furrows of his brow. "It's still shocking and—"

"Sad. I know. I didn't mean it like that. I only meant that maybe he came off as positive but was truly deeply depressed."

"He *was* alone but not lonely. And he said he had no one, I mean no family, to leave his money to. That's why he liked casinos so much." I hold my hand to my mouth as our conversation replays in my mind. "Was he trying to tell me last night and I missed it? I should've done something. I feel so bad."

"Don't. There was nothing you could've done. He probably had this planned for a while."

"I don't know. I thought he seemed so happy."

"You just never know. I've got to get dressed and go in. Mind if I shower here?"

"Of course not."

"I'll get ready too, I should go in with you."

"You don't have to."

"I want to. I feel like I should."

"Okay. Jordan dropped off a bag for me." Amon climbs out of bed, and I feel a sudden surge of desire . . . and loss . . . as he slips from me, exquisite in nothing but his boxer briefs. He hesitates, leans over the bed and kisses me. I wish it could last forever. Even the visions of Tony disappear in that moment. "I'm going to grab it and make coffee. Want a cup?"

"Please."

I don't waste any time getting from bed to a hot shower. Prolonging this moment can only be painful. I'm finishing up sliding the Egyptian cotton towel over my back to dry myself, when Amon walks in with a tray holding two steaming coffees and two small glasses of water tinted by my mom's elixir.

I wrap myself in the towel. "Thank you," I say as Amon hands me the glass of water.

"I love your mom's drops. I hope you don't mind."

"Not at all." I take the empty glass from him, and he gives me a quick peck before jumping into the shower.

The aroma of freshly brewed coffee carries on the steam in the bathroom and I breathe it in before taking my first sip. The mirror tells me I look exhausted. So, I dab on an extra layer of eye cream before taking another sip of coffee.

"I really like your place," Amon says.

"Thanks."

I catch a glance of Amon's perfect silhouette as he rinses the shampoo out of his hair.

His eyes catch me in mid-appreciation, and he pretends not to see. Embarrassed, I divert my own stare. "I'm really glad that I came back with you last night," he says.

"Me too." My cheeks flush under my newly applied makeup.

Hurrying to finish my makeup, I brush my teeth before getting dressed. I slip into my Max Mara high waist palazzo pants my mom acquired for me, and starched white shirt, leaving it open just enough to tease. Not like me at all. The fabric clings to my body in a way that's both restrictive and flattering. Despite the discomfort, I can't help but admit that I look good when I see myself in the mirror, ready to face whatever the day throws at me—*even if its suicide?*

When I struggle to slip on a pair of Jimmy Choos my mom got me, my ankle explodes in pain and I swallow a cry, opting to stay barefoot for now.

"Ready?" Amon calls from my bedroom.

"Yeah," I say walking out of my closet.

"You look stunning."

"So do you." I instantly regret my choice of words as they tumble out of my mouth. But he does, he *really* does, as he stands there in his impeccably tailored Brioni suit. Effortless. And yes, stunning.

"Thanks," he says, meeting me near my dresser and leaning down to kiss me again. "This is an heirloom, isn't it? It's beautiful." He lifts the necklace my mom gave me off the jewelry stand.

"Yeah, it's been in my family for over a hundred years."

"You should wear it."

I hold my hair up and Amon clips the jewel in place, letting it slide into that empty spot at my throat. I press the cold metal against my chest, and he kisses my neck. Hot. Electric. Demanding. I stifle a sigh.

"Can I drive?" he asks, walking to my front door.

"Sure."

Amon rests his strong hand on my leg then wraps his fingers in mine. There's no traffic. It's early, and the city is still sleeping. Looking down at my hand interlaced with his, I realize I'm happily falling for him. That is, until we turn off Pacific. The moment Golden Sands comes into view an inexplicable tsunami of dread pounds me with such force, it leaves me feeling seasick. I don't want to be here.

The blockade is still in place, though it's quiet. Security quickly moves a cone and we pull through to my spot.

"Here we go," Amon says.

"I wish we were still in bed."

"As soon as we get this situation under control, we can take a nap at my place. It's going to be a big day later with a lot to celebrate."

Chapter 32

The doorman rushes over and opens my door for me. "Thanks," I say, reluctantly climbing out.

Just inside the glass lobby doors, I notice Peter talking to a couple of cops and a priest. They appear casual and relaxed. *How weird.* As Peter spots us, he leaves the small group and meets us just outside the glass doors.

"I'm sorry they called you in," Peter says. "Captain Everette is in your office with Jordan. Everything's been taken care of; he just wants a statement from you to close the file."

"Of course," Amon says.

My focus drifts away from the conversation and back to the officers just inside the lobby. *Do priests regularly join the police in situations like this?* He looks so young. The priest catches me staring and my eyes dart to the ground . . . to the black combat boots he wears with his clerical collar and black garb. When I look back up, the priest is still watching me. He looks away and follows the officers out the glass door and past us without as much as a glance in our direction.

"Do you think anyone noticed the commotion?" Amon asks as I tune back into the conversation.

"No, definitely not. We used the loading bay. If anyone finds out about this, it's because a cop or fireman leaked it."

"Thanks, Peter," Amon says as we follow him to the elevator bank where he has an elevator held.

"Of course," Peter says. "Call me if you need anything else."

"I'm glad I went to your house last night," Amon says as the elevator rises.

"Me too."

"But I'm starving. We never ate dinner."

"Sorry, I should've asked you if you wanted something."

"Eating was the last thing on my mind. I'll have Jordan order food as soon as I get this taken care of."

I nod.

"Are you alright?" Amon asks as the elevator comes to a stop.

"Yeah, it's sad but—" the elevator doors slide open.

The cops are sitting around the office, casual and relaxed, laughing with Jordan. Not what I expect cops investigating a death to look like. A uniformed officer notices us step off the elevator and opens the door for us.

"Mr. Asra, I'm sorry they called you in so early. I told them it wasn't necessary. This is a straight-forward case, and we have it wrapped up already." Captain Everette stands and reaches to shake Amon's hand.

Amon shakes Everette's hand. "Thank you, Captain. I've been looking forward to meeting you. I wish it were under better circumstances. I appreciate you handling this in such an efficient and delicate manner."

"Of course. Our casinos are very important to this city, so it's in all of our best interest. Your property, of course, is even more important."

"Why?" I ask and the whole room stares at me.

"My apologies, Captain," Amon says. "This is Ms. Lilith Umbra, our Senior V.P. of Marketing."

"It's a pleasure, Ms. Umbra." Captain Everette says, looking directly at me. "Why what?"

"Why is The Golden Sands more important than other casinos?"

"The other properties weren't on the verge of bankruptcy and closing," Amon interjects.

"Oh, right." Captain Everette adds, "If one casino closes, it's bad for the whole town."

"Captain," Amon says, "thank you for personally seeing to this, but we don't want to take up too much of your morning. What can I do for you?"

"This won't take long at all, but if I can get a quick statement from you, I'll close this case."

"Of course, come to my office." Amon begins to lead Everette away.

"Wait, are you one-hundred-percent sure that it's a suicide? How were you able to do a full investigation this quickly?" I dig my heels into the carpet, ready to demand they give Tony his time and the investigation he deserves.

"Oh yeah, this is as straight-forward as they come," the captain says. "To start, our guy left a note. It was typed so he'd been planning this."

"How did he do it?" I ask as Captain Everette and Amon try to leave once more.

"Better to spare you the details, my dear," Everette says. "But he was clean about it and considerate."

My dear? "I'm a vice president, if this is leaked or employees ask questions, I need to have all of the information in order to talk around this situation."

"Come with us, Lilly," Amon says.

I follow them into Amon's office. My gaze is drawn to the scratches on the wall again. Amon sits at his desk while Everette and I take the seats opposite.

The captain, glancing at his notes, begins, "Mr. Anthony Vitale checked in yesterday at approximately one fifty-four p.m. He spent about an hour and a half in his room, then went to the casino. He started on the nickel slots, then played a few hands of blackjack until having a drink with you at the casino lounge. Since you're here, Ms. Umbra, I should ask what your relationship with Mr. Vitale is?"

"He was a limo driver and picked me up from the airport. He's a nice, sorry, was a very nice person, so Amon and I had a drink with him."

"Okay. Well, after your drink, he went back to the blackjack tables. After a few hours, a host on the property took him to dinner at the coffee shop. He went back to the tables till one a.m. then headed to his room. At three a.m. facilities got a call reporting running water. Security did a wellness check and found him. He was in the bathtub, unresponsive. He had two-inch slits on each wrist. There were no signs of intrusion. No physical evidence of a fight. There was a simple note that said, I quote, "I want to be with my wife." The scene was almost immaculately clean. By the time the body was found, the running water had washed all the blood down the drain. Our investigation is finished. The room has already been returned. If you can sign this document, it's case closed."

"Of course." Amon reaches for the document and quickly adds his signature, then passes it back. "Thank you so much."

"Wait," I interject. It all seems so cold. Efficient. Wrong. "How did water wash all of the blood down the drain without it overflowing with the rest of the water?"

"Good question," the captain says. "There was no leak, it was a handheld shower. He propped himself up against the back of the tub, cut his wrists, then rested them both directly under the flow of water."

"Who reported running water if there wasn't a leak?" I ask.

"The room next door complained about the noise. Any more questions?"

I shake my head.

"Thank you for your time. Case closed."

Captain Everette stands, and we follow, "No, please. I can show myself out. One of your security officers is on his way up to take us out the back way."

Amon retakes his seat, and gestures for me to sit too. "Thank you, Captain. Anytime you want to have dinner or see a show, let Jordan know."

"He's already set me up." Captain Everette does some sort of short, awkward wave that's part salute and part goodbye.

"What do you want for breakfast?" Amon asks me.

"I'm not hungry." When I stand, a wave of dizziness hits, and I grab the chair for balance.

"You need to eat. I'll have Jordan order you a fruit and yogurt parfait and a few soft-boiled eggs."

"Thanks," I say as I turn to leave.

I go straight to my coffee maker. As I'm waiting for my coffee to brew, my phone dings. *Please be Tori.* But it's Sharp, 'I heard there was a "suicide" CALL ME!! We need to talk.'

My jaw drops. Already the word is out? 'Who told you? This is confidential.'

'Not important. Are you alone? Can you talk?'

'In my office. Just me. But this was a clear-cut case. It's already been closed.'

Coffee fills the cup. My phone rings. I know it is Sharp. "What?"

"This was not a suicide," Sharp insists. "The cult is planning something big."

"It's not a cult," I whisper, "the book situation was a misunderstanding. Amon was bullied as a kid and some classmates made it up."

"That's bullshit. That *suicide* was a sacrifice and there's more coming."

"Do you realize how insane you sound? I honestly think you need help."

"The body had no blood when it was found and there was no blood at the scene. Anywhere. Which is impossible."

He even knows the details? "No, it's not. He set it up so that the blood would be washed down the drain."

"Are you kidding me? You can't seriously believe that?"

"It's possible."

"Okay, well, his eyes had also turned completely white, and his face was frozen into an expression of pure terror, his mouth was wide open at an unnatural angle."

"That sounds like ridiculous gossip."

"It's not. It came from a completely reliable source. He said the scene was weird. Real hush hush. And the captain showed up, which is completely unheard of. He thinks the officer he was with got sent accidentally—all the other cops seemed prepared to make the suicide call right off. Keep it under wraps."

I sigh. "It's a political situation. They don't want this to get out because it would be bad for the whole town."

"Is that what they told you?"

"I really think you should talk to someone, you need help. You have to stop this and stop calling me."

"Really? You find this situation completely normal?"

I sigh. "I was with the guy last night and would've never thought he was suicidal. And the police captain being here, yeah, it's weird, but these situations are always weird." My tone inadvertently rises as if I'm asking a question.

Sharp hesitates. "Go to his room, six-forty-six. Prove me wrong. If you don't find anything out of the ordinary, I'll stop bothering you."

"He was in room six-forty-six? How do you know?" The hairs on my nape bristle.

"Yeah, he was. My source specifically told me. Why?"

"No reason." I've read a few reviews that specifically mention room 646 and claim it's haunted. Not that I believed them, but I don't want to admit the coincidence to Sharp.

"Oh, I thought you were referring to the online reviews that claim it's haunted. You aren't scared to go, are you?"

"No."

"Great. Call me after."

"Fine, but I'm only going to make sure the investigation was actually done well. You know, for Tony." I hang up, a combination of angry, frustrated, and uncertain.

Am I really going to play into Sharp's crazy theories? Yes, I am. For nothing else than to prove him wrong and end this and to pay my respects to Tony. Before I go, I open the hotel reservation system, just to confirm Tony was actually in room 646. According to hotel records, Tony checked into room 1127 in the Palace Tower but had to change rooms a little before ten p.m. due to an electrical issue.

Chapter 33

I rush by Amon's office so that he doesn't have time to ask where I'm going. Then past reception. "I'll be right back," I tell Jordan without stopping then duck into the stairwell.

Taking the stairs is one thing I hate in this building, but it's only two flights and I don't have time to wait for an elevator. Holding tight to the handrail, I move quickly but carefully, favoring my healthy ankle.

I stop at the threshold of room 646. Sharp's right. I'm scared. No. More than scared. I'm terrified, but I can't let him get to me. My hand trembles as I scan my master key card. The lighted lock flashes yellow then goes back to red. I try again, holding my card longer this time. Again. It flashes yellow then turns red. One more time. Yellow then red. Relief prickles my scalp. I shake the door, confirming I gave it a go. It's locked—this excursion wasn't meant to be. Rattling the door handle one more time for good measure, the lock clicks and the door opens a crack. *No, no, no, I should run.* My breath catches in my throat, and I slowly push the door open.

"Hello?"

No response.

I'm doing this for Tony. The room is nearly pitch black. For Tony. I step inside and quickly turn on the lights before closing the door behind me. For Tony. The room looks completely untouched. The comforter doesn't have a single indentation or show even the slightest sign of pressure like being sat on. I'm hit with the overwhelming sensation that I'm not alone. *It's just my imagination. Let's get this over with so Sharp will leave me alone.*

A cold gust rips through my low-buttoned white blouse and prickles my skin with goosebumps. I follow it towards the bathroom, stopping briefly to check the nightstands. Both are empty, except for a gold employee name badge that belonged to a Ralph. He probably took it off while he was cleaning the room and forgot to put it back on, or maybe it fell off when he was making the bed and someone stuck it in there.

Standing outside the bathroom, I rub my hands together trying to muster my courage. No light shines beneath the door but all I need to do is push it open enough to reach in and flip on the lights. *Nope.* I back up. My heartbeat roars. The small hotel room starts to close in on me. I tear open the curtains and flood the room with as much sunlight as possible. *Much better.*

With my bravery bolstered by the light, I inch toward the bathroom door when I think the sink turns on. Panic floods my brain, scrambling every coherent thought. I shove the door open and flip on the lights, then tangle in my own feet as I try to both charge forward and retreat at once. My legs buckle and I land hard on my backside. I blink up at a completely empty bathroom. The sink is off now, but there's a steady drip . . . drip . . . drip echoing against the porcelain basin.

Okay. Sharp is getting to me and I'm imagining things. I push to my feet, take a few steps closer to the bathroom. I don't want to see any blood so I stop just outside of the door to gather myself. I take a deep breath then step inside.

When my foot passes the threshold, I collapse in pain. The air pressure in the room changes. Shooting pain spikes through my ears to the deepest part of my brain. Crippling. My vision momentarily goes black, and I hear that same dreadful sucking sound I've suffered from before. This time it sounds like the building itself is trying to suck life into its lungs.

As quickly as it came, the pain subsides. I open my eyes. The light burns and I squeeze them closed again. It's freezing cold and I tuck my arms into my legs to keep from shivering. Squinting now, I manage to open my eyes carefully.

My vision is too blurry to make out much of anything. I crawl to my knees and rub my eyes. Goosebumps prickle my skin. Breath forms halos around my head. My vision fades into focus. This isn't the bathroom.

The scene in front of me looks like a charnel house. Panic constricts my chest and my breath comes short. My heart races again as I scooch back toward where the entrance used to be, trying to escape the large, skinless animal carcasses that dangle from meat hooks around me. Blood drips onto the white tiled floor. Drip-drip-drip. I want to flee, but there is nowhere to run. The door that was there isn't anymore.

Tony steps out from behind one of the carcasses. He seems like a hologram, a projection or something worse. He doesn't talk, but he gestures for me to be quiet.

From another room, music plays. Grows louder. I'm sure it's from the 1920s. A record player, turning slightly slower than it's meant to. Just like what I heard in the elevator.

He motions me. And I sneak through the maze of butcher's meat. A waiter walks in, followed by a chef. They don't seem to be able to see me. They argue, but I can't make out their words. Like I'm listening from outside the room. The chef pulls a knife from his belt and slices the waiter's throat. A crimson line forms at his Adam's apple then slowly grows. The chef yells something, and three guys dressed in white rush in. They grab the poor soul, whose eyes are glued open in shock. No noise comes from his open mouth. They wrap rope around his ankles then hang him on a meat hook. The men place a large bowl underneath where the blood falls in a thick crimson column.

Am I dead? Is this Hell? I drop to my knees. Tears swell in my eyes and I can't suppress a sob. Tony shushes me again but I can't stop. He hurtles towards me, mouthing something I don't understand. When he gets close. It is clear: RUN.

I leap to my feet. The chef's angry visage snaps toward me. He lumbers forward, knife first, and I run. My shoes slip on the small tiles. My knee collides with the floor and it feels like I split my skin, smashed my knee cap. No time to think. I regain my footing, twist to see the chef gaining on me. I cut through the carcasses, nearly crashing into the pink flesh of a large pig. It's split down its abdomen, emptied of all innards. Snout pulled back, it smiles a taunting death grin at me.

Tony appears near a door and waves for me to follow. I plunge past the hanging pig. I choke back an urge to vomit as I pass the bodies of two children—a boy and a girl. They are severed at the waist, blood draining into another large black bowl. I can't suppress a scream as tears blur my vision.

But I don't stop running towards Tony. I can't stop.

Before I reach him, he steps aside and thrusts open the door. I keep running, I have no choice. I'm in the Grand Ballroom at The Golden Sands. My mind reels. There's a party going on and for a second, I think I must be late. Until I realize that everything is different, if only in small measures. The room looks new, fresh. The women wear flapper dresses. Someone looks vaguely familiar . . . it's Mr. Ledes. Everyone is gathered around a black-marble statue of a man with a goat's head, posed as if pissing. Then the chef appears, staff in tow. He's no longer trying to butcher me. They're wheeling out the black bowl that was placed under the children.

The crowd cheers and Mr. Ledes steps up to the statue holding a crystal glass beneath the carving's penis. The chef tilts the bowl into place behind the statue and soon the statue excretes what I can only assume is blood from his genitals. Mr. Ledes smiles wickedly, takes a long gulp of the ruby liquid. The other partygoers excitedly gather behind him, impatiently waiting their turn at the grotesque fountain.

I scream.

Tony rushes towards me with his finger over his lips, but it's too late. The entire party spins to me. I recognize two men dressed in three-piece suits. One bares a striking resemblance to a young version of Aleister, and the other is my maternal grandfather but young—so young. It's impossible. They rush towards me, arms out. I want to run, but my body won't move. Try to scream again but can't. In seconds, they close-in on me. Their hands wrap around my throat.

I can't breathe.

My world goes dark.

"Lilly! . . . Lilly! . . . Lilly! Wake up!"

As my vision slowly comes into focus, Amon is standing above me; I'm on a bed. "Where am I?"

"You're in room six-forty-six. Tony's room. You fell asleep. What were you doing here?"

As my mind clears, memories flood back. I panic and sit up, pushing myself all the way to the head of the bed. "They're going to kill me," I cry. "They're going to drain my blood and drink it like they did to those poor little kids."

"No, Lilly, calm down. You're exhausted. You fell asleep and had a nightmare."

"No, I didn't. Sharp is right. There's something wrong with this place."

Amon wraps his arms around me. "Come on, let's get you out of here. Let's go to my apartment, so you can calm down."

"No! I want to go home. I can't work here anymore."

"Okay, that's fine. You don't have to. But you must calm down first. Come on." Amon pulls me up.

"I want to go home." Tears soak my cheeks.

"Listen, Lilly, you've been under a lot of stress and exhausted yourself. If this job is too much, I completely understand. But before you leave, you need to calm down."

Amon helps me up from the bed and guides me out of room 646. As he does, I notice something blue sticking out from under the bed.

Pushing Amon off, I rush to the bed, and grab it. Blue leggings and a white Nike shirt are twisted together. They're small, a child's outfit.

"What's that?" Amon asks.

"They were under the bed."

"Oh shit, looks like Tony may have had some dark secrets. We should get rid of those." Amon takes the clothes from me before I have time to object.

"No." I shake my head, unable to move.

"Come on." Amon puts his arms around me and leads me out. "You need to get out of here."

Jordan waits at an elevator and takes us directly to the eighth floor.

Amon escorts me to his apartment. "Sit down, Lilly. I'll make you some tea."

"I don't want tea. I want to go home."

"Lilly." Amon sits beside me. "It was just a dream."

"No. It's . . . it's . . . it's this building. I can't be here anymore."

"Okay, that's fine. But you need to calm down first." Amon goes to his kitchen.

Several things in Amon's apartment have been moved. The spear has been moved, replaced by a new piece of art. The picture looks familiar. A white lamb with a gold crown stands on an altar. Bright red blood gushes from the lamb's heart and fills a chalice. This isn't a coincidence. Sharp's right. Something is very wrong here.

Amon returns from the kitchen with a silver tray holding my breakfast and a cup of tea.

"What's that painting?" I ask before he has a chance to sit.

"Which one?"

"The one where the Roman spear used to be. Why is it there?"

"The Ghent Altarpiece?"

"The painting where the lamb's blood is filling the cup to drink."

"Yeah, that's the Ghent Altarpiece. Well, a very expensive copy, you're not familiar with it? It's one of the most famous works of art in the world."

"No . . . Maybe."

"I'm sure you are. Why?"

"I saw people here, drinking blood. Like in the painting, but it was the blood from children, and I saw—"

"Lilly, that was just a dream. You saw this painting the last time you were here."

"No, it was—"

"As a matter of fact, this painting was a gift from Morana. Li-RV is an interpretation of this exact work of art. You saw similar imagery in the show too."

"No, I don't think . . . No—"

"It's a powerful piece, it's not surprising it would have this effect on you. The Ghent Altarpiece is considered one of the most important works ever created. It's been stolen and found, then re-stolen and re-found. People gave their life to protect it. There're still two panels in the full work that were stolen and haven't been—"

"Stop talking about the painting. You're just trying to distract me."

"No, I'm not. You were sound asleep when I finally found you. Nightmares are just your brain's way of dealing with stress. It makes perfect sense that you'd pull on the imagery you've been exposed to lately."

"I didn't fall to sleep. I was in the bathroom. And, then I was somewhere else. Sharp's right, he—"

"Stop listening to him. He's either completely insane or he has an agenda and he's using you to get it."

"I . . . I don't know."

"Here. Drink some tea."

Right as Amon hands me the mug, there's a knock on his door, and he goes to answer.

"Mr. and Mrs. Umbra, what a pleasant surprise. What brings you here?"

"Lilly wasn't answering her phone, so we came up to say hi and Jordan told us you were here. Are we interrupting something?"

"No, not at all. Please come in. Lilly has had a difficult morning and I'm trying to calm her down. Maybe you can help."

"Lilly, sweetheart, what's going on?" my mom asks as she sits down.

"I . . . I don't think I can work here anymore. Something is going on here. This place is not right."

"Amon, can you give us a moment?" Dad asks, sitting on the other side of me.

"Of course, I'll go to the office for a bit."

"Thank you." Mom waits for the door to close, then turns to me. "You need to pull it together. You are not quitting. You need this job. We need you to *have* this job. Tell her."

"Lilly, we made a large investment in Golden Sands," my dad says.

"No, not just a large investment. We invested everything. Tell her the rest," my mom orders.

Dad looks down at his hands. "If you quit before the property becomes profitable, we lose everything."

"I told your father not to do it. You don't have the mental composition to handle the stress of working."

He looks up, almost pleading. "I know how smart and talented you are, and I know you can do this."

"This is different," I say. "There's something bad happening here."

"Pull it together," Mom says, rolling her eyes. "The only bad thing happening is in your imagination."

Irritation prickles my spine, and I sit a little taller. "You haven't been here. You don't know."

"You have a pattern," my mom says.

"Naomi, enough." My dad looks at me. "Lilly, whatever you want to do is fine."

Mom looks furious at his statement but says nothing. I take a breath, my eyes searching both their faces. It means the world to hear Dad say that and solidifies my decision. I take a breath. "No, I'm fine. I . . . I just needed a minute."

"Lilly, you don't have to," Dad says, patting my leg. "Really. I'll drive you home."

My mom stands, opens her mouth to say something but Dad interrupts, "Naomi, sit down."

Mom's eyes double in size. It looks like she's about to lunge at my dad, but then she stomps off down Amon's hall.

"Come on, I'll drive you," Dad says, standing and offering me his hand.

"No," I say but let him pull me up. "I can't prove her right."

"We heard about Tony, I'm sorry. He was our favorite driver." Dad pats my shoulder.

I nod. As sad as it is, I can't think about it right now. "Tori's gone," I say. "She took off last night and disconnected her phone."

"Good," my mom says, reemerging from the hall.

Ignoring her, I find a mirror hanging on the wall between works of art only to have my irritation replaced with complete and utter embarrassment. My eyes are swollen, and red. Mascara has somehow melted and covers a third of my face. I snatch a tissue and clean myself up. Leaving no makeup on and a puffy face, I look as bad as I feel.

"I'll see you later," I say, and leave before she has time to say anything else.

Amon and Jordan are laughing about something until they see me and quickly become somber. Amon opens the door, and both look at me like some ornament that might break at any moment. I don't blame them.

"Lilly . . ." Amon says. "Are you better?"

"Yeah, I just need a minute," I say, refusing to look at either of them as I pass.

As soon as I sit at my desk, I grab my phone. No texts. No missed calls. I type in Sharp's name. Nothing. Someone got into my phone. I Google his name. Nothing. His card. He gave me his card. Where did I put it? I rifle through my desk drawer. Nothing. Check my purse. My makeup bag . . . where is it? It's in my bathroom.

I flip on the light and open the door as wide as it will allow. My makeup bag is on the far side of the bathroom counter. Careful not to look in the mirror, I rush in. A cold gust washes over me. The lights flicker. I snatch my makeup bag. A shadow climbs the wall.

And the door begins to close.

Shit. I dive through the opening, my heart a hammering pinion, my breath held tight. I skid onto the threshold and trip, slamming into the carpet in my office and splaying out on my stomach.

Without so much as a look, I kick the door shut.

Sharp's card is in there.

Me: Need to talk. NOW. You free?

My phone rings in response but I silence it immediately.

Me: Can't talk. Text me.

Sharp: Been trying to get ahold of you for hours. You okay?

Me: Yeah. I think. I don't know. Something weird happened. But I'm exhausted and it might've been a dream. I don't know.

Sharp: Were you in room 646?

Me: Yeah.

Sharp: Get out of there now. I'm in the area. I'll pick you up in front of The Irish Pub.

Me: Wait for me. I need a bit to get out.

Sharp: I won't leave until you're here.

I reapply my makeup as best I can with my limited time—not for vanity but camouflage. I listen for a second. Amon and Jordan are still talking. I consider waiting, but . . . *if not now, never.*

"Are you going somewhere?" Amon asks as soon as I cross into the reception area.

"Yeah, I need to take a walk. I thought I'd check out the two ballrooms for the party tonight. All the décor should be finished or close to it."

A look of concern creases his brow. "Do you feel up to that now?"

"Yes. Getting back to work is exactly what I need."

"Perfect. I'll go with you."

"No." I clear my throat. "I could use a little time to clear my head, if you don't mind."

"Not at all. I completely understand. You're amazing." Amon's eyes widen as he says that and for a moment I want to run into his arms. There's a genuine sadness there. *Am I losing my mind? Is Sharp using me?* I don't know, but I decide to stick to this plan. At least for now, hear Sharp out. If Amon's right, then I'll simply come back.

"Thank you." I briefly squeeze Amon's hand as I walk by and out to the elevator lobby.

As I wait for an elevator, I glance back at Amon. He's on his phone but looks up and catches me watching him. A warm smile fills his face and a bit of my armor melts. Luckily, the elevator doors slide open before I have a chance to change my mind.

I get off on the second floor but have no intention of checking out the ballroom. There's a bridge just past the Grand Ballroom and theater that connects to The Yacht Club, the casino next door. This area's been forgotten. Old wallpaper peels at the corners. Stains and tears dot the carpets. Leading to the crossover, signs in every size direct customers back to The Golden Sands. But I keep going.

The hallway eventually leads to the bridge, but right before that is a stairwell to the boardwalk. I quickly look over each shoulder then duck into the stairwell. It's a short, single story down and I can already see the door. From a dark corner in the stairwell, an arm reaches out and grabs the rail as someone steps in front of the door and blocks my escape.

The symbol. The forearm tattoo. The wavy clump of arrows. I try to stop but my momentum hammers my weight down on my ankle and I crumble. My thoughts, like a tornado, whip around my mind sending a brutal downpour of anxiety into the pit of my stomach.

It's not possible.

Chapter 34

"Kai?" I pick myself up and start towards him, but a snarl in his expression sends me reeling backwards.

"Yes?" He cocks his head at an unnatural angle.

"You're dead. I identified your body."

"Cor-rection. You *thought* you identified my body."

"What do you mean? What's going on?"

"I have been waiting sooo long to do this," he says, slowly walking towards me with both arms behind his back.

I scramble backwards but hit the steps.

A smile peels across his face then he's spraying something in my face. My head immediately becomes heavy, my vision swimming with patches of black. I fight to stay upright, but everything is so heavy. There's a pinch in my arm, I think, but a coating of numbness makes it hard to tell. With every ounce of strength I can muster, I try to push past Kai, but I stumble to the side, and my vision closes in around me.

I . . . I . . .

Somewhere in the darkness, I hear him call to me. "Lilith."

It's like his voice is everywhere, and when I open my eyes to find him, it's completely black.

"Lilith." I hear all around me.

Is his voice coming from somewhere outside of me? Icy fingers crawl up the base of my neck. Slither into my hair and keep coming until they consume me—thousands of frigid fingers clawing at me. They crawl over me, covering my head, my face, my neck, my body. They're cold. So cold. They begin to constrict, crushing me, filling my mouth and scratching at my eyes. I can't breathe. I can't scream. I can't move.

"Lilith!"

I gasp for air.

"Lilith!"

I gasp again. Nothing. No air. My lungs burn like fire.

"Lilith."

Pain burns in my left cheek and I gasp. This time, air rushes in and I gulp at it.

"Open your eyes!"

I try, but they don't want to budge. Overwhelming exhaustion takes me and I start to give up, relax, let it take me. A burst of pain erupts in my cheek again and I open my eyes.

Mom's hand is raised. "There you are," she says putting her arm back down.

She just slapped me. I open my mouth to protest, but my eyes begin to flutter under the weight of enervation.

"Lilly, wake up. It's your big day and we don't have much time to get you ready."

"Whaaattt?" I croak out.

"Kai, get the salts again."

I manage to open my eyes. Kai waves a small tube under my nose. The acrid smell of ammonia clears the wooziness enough for me to sit up.

"What...what...how?" I still can't organize my swirling thoughts into a proper question, so I stare blankly at both of them.

"Yes, I know there's a great deal to tell you, but we have to hurry right now," my mom says, a gentleness now to her voice.

I shake my head until the word, "no," tumbles out.

"Hold still. Everyone is waiting."

"For what?" The words roll over my tongue that feels larger than it should.

My mom grabs my chin, oddly gentle again. "Hold still. You've already made things so much harder than they needed to be. Thanks to that fucking Sharp, we had to move everything up."

I try to pull away, but my head is still heavy and falls back to rest on the pillow. That bit of exertion leaves me exhausted and my eyes begin to flutter.

My mom shakes me, and I think it's Kai who clears his throat, making the shaking stop.

Mom yanks me into a sitting position and pulls a brush through my hair. She never brushed my hair like this, not even as a child. My hair is messy and it's wearing on her patience. She begins yanking it, unraveling the knots strand by strand. Each painful jerk of the brush helps the fog clear little by little, I realize that we're in a suite.

"That's where I came into the picture," Kai's voice pulls me to glance at him—my fiancé and dead lover.

"Kai did an amazing job of getting you out here," Mom says. "I couldn't offer you to our dark lord, you had to come on your own accord. He had to choose you, you couldn't . . . never mind it's . . ." She leans over and kisses Kai passionately. "All that matters is you're here and it's happening."

Kai licks his lips when she pulls away. "I had to program you, plant some memories, it was actually quite complicated. I mean the formulation, not you. You are a bit dull, smart, but so dull. Sorry, Naomi," he says, and Kai and my mom break into a fit of laughter.

My mom seems to catch herself, clearing her throat to calm her amusement. "She's not dull Kai, *regal*."

"You're right. My apologies." Kai mocks a bow towards me.

A shudder of rage sends adrenalin tearing through me, clearing the remnants of whatever drugs were in my system. A spray of hot, acidic vomit erupts from me.

My Mom and Kai lunge back, barely missing my puke.

"Disgusting," Kai says.

"Kai, how much did you give her?"

"I followed the instructions. She's just has a weak constitution."

Tears sting my eyes. "I loved you. I identified your dead body."

"Really?" Kai grins.

"Oh, darling, I know that seemed traumatic, but it was nothing. We, Kai, is actually quite talented. Kai planted—"

"Programmed," Kai corrects.

"*Programmed* those memories, with a specialized cocktail of drugs, he learned from the best. But the whole process only took about a week. After that, you wanted to come here and start over . . . *on your own accord*."

Kai wraps his arms around my mom and grinds against her.

"Stop! Where's Dad?"

"Celebrating, but he'll be at the ceremony. Don't worry. He has a very important role."

"What ceremony?"

"Ugh, we must get out of this room, it smells. Kai, move her to the living room."

Kai yanks me off the side of the bed. "What about her clothes?"

"Leave them in here."

"You can't do this," I scream.

"Really?" Kai grabs a knife and I freeze. He drags the cold blade along my neck, leaning in to whisper in my ear. "Don't worry, I won't hurt you." Then twists the knife to slice my shirt off. Before he can get to my pants, I unbutton them, and he pulls them off.

"Sharp's expecting me. He'll call the police when I don't show up." I look directly at Kai, daring him with my glare.

"Oh, she didn't hear," my mom clucks her tongue.

"Sadly," Kai says, bowing his head in mock deference, "our friend Charles Sharp suffered a massive heart attack walking into the Irish Pub for lunch. He didn't make it." Kai laughs, then marches me into the suite's living room.

"What are you going to do to me?" Tears stream down my face.

"Darling, this is a wonderful honor." My mom pulls a gown over my head. "Don't you see? You're going to be Lord Lucifer's queen. You will be offered to him tonight. He will come to you on the altar and plant his seed in you. Once you are joined, your body will be sacrificed to him. His child will grow in your corpse and you join him in hell. When the child is born, the beast from the abyss—a man of sin, will join Hell and Earth and flesh will reign."

"No! I won't do it!"

"You're not thinking clearly and you don't really have a choice. You were here—*on your own accord.*" My mom momentarily joins Kai as they both say this.

"He chose you," Kai continues, "It's *his* choice." He pulls me into a seat at a small, round table.

My mom sits across from me and sets a box of makeup on the table, before rubbing her hand along the seat of his pants.

"Where's Amon?" I cry.

"I'm here," Amon yells from another room as he stumbles in with the cocktail waitress from The Dunes, and I realize where I first saw those tall, black heels.

"Amon?" A flood of tears burns my eyes. He looks so different. His usually perfect hair is messy, his shirt unbuttoned, and a half-drunk bottle of Rip Van Winkle dangles from his hand.

"There she is. Our girl. I don't know why Kai said you were so dull. I found you to be brilliant and had a blast last night. Maybe Kai's the dull one." Amon takes a long pull on his bottle.

"Fuck you," Kai snaps.

Long nails dig into my chin as my mom pulls my head to face her. "Stop crying," she hisses, "This is an honor and you're ruining your makeup."

Something in me snaps, turning every ounce of sadness back to anger, and I spit in my mom's face.

"Gag her," she says wiping a wad of saliva from her cheek. Before I can process what's happening, Kai jams a knotted handkerchief in my mouth and cinches it tight behind my neck. She reaches for a black velvet box on the table near her. "Just till we get this done, darling. I'm so proud of you. I know you don't get it right now, but you will."

"Wait, the necklace," Kai says and passes it to my mom, "she was wearing it—"

"My idea," Amon interrupts. "I put it on her after we . . ." He thrusts his groin and bites his lip, "all night."

"Yeah, *great idea*. It fell off when I grabbed her, and we almost lost it."

My mom admires the necklace in her palm before placing it back in the velvet box. She grabs a tissue and tries to clean my face, but I swat her hands away. "Kai," Mom says, nodding at me. He snatches my hands, pulls them behind the chair, and wrenches a zip tie around them.

"Much better." Mom lets out a huff then begins to dry my tear-soaked face before brushing makeup on. "If I take the gag off, will you behave?"

I nod, desperate to swallow the saliva slowly drowning me. Kai loosens it just enough to drape around my neck, reminding me it can be put right back on.

"I can't believe how perfectly this week went," Amon slurs. "We've had it planned for so long and she fell for everything." Amon breaks into a fit of hysterical laughter. "Lilith." He coughs out between laughs. "Robovac."

Kai and my mom join in the laughter.

"I can't believe she bought it," Kai spits out.

"What you two don't realize is that this week took a lifetime of preparation." Mom purrs as she manages to quiet her laughter. "Lilith had to be raised from the time she was born to not trust her judgement. She was so headstrong and smart, this was not easy. Though, I must admit. I still thought there was no way Robovac would work." A brief cackle breaks free. "Did you not see the claw marks on the walls?" She stares at me, and I glare daggers back. "Darling," she says, looking down, "you have no idea how hard it was to make you think you were losing your mind. You can just feel his presence here. Yet you convinced yourself it was in your head."

"What was it?" I demand.

"Morana brought a shadow entity through to—"

"I don't believe you."

She opens her mouth to say something, but Amon's phone chimes and he announces, "It's time."

My mom squeals with an excitement I've never seen. She takes the necklace out of the box and holds it up so that the deep black stone catches the light. It reflects hints of crimson and amber. "Beautiful, isn't it?" She looks at me as if I would or could reply. "Our lord Lucifer shed a single tear as he was cast down from Heaven. That tear grew into a tree and then a piece of fruit. Can you guess what that fruit became?"

She pauses, closes her eyes, and drags her crimson-tipped fingers down her lips in a moment of ecstasy. "I know you know, darling. At least you're smart. It became the forbidden fruit. Original sin that cast Eve from Eden and now binds you to our dark lord allowing him to place his seed in your womb." She drapes the necklace around my neck. "You have no idea how long I have waited for this day. I never wanted to be a mother. But after you were born, I knew you were special." A brief look of disgust flits across her face. "If we fully untie you, you're not going to try anything, are you?" I just glower at her.

"If not, we will have the entire ceremony with you tied and gagged even tighter."

I nod.

Kai starts towards me.

"Wait," Amon says, handing my mom a large, maroon, leather box with a gold clasp. "Let me." As Amon steps behind me he lowers his head, takes a deep inhale into my nape, trails his lips along my neck. The moistness of his touch sends a jerk of revulsion through me. From this close, I'm forced to inhale the rot of bourbon seeping from his pores. I try to pull away from him. "Hey, hey, hey. You couldn't get enough of me last night," he whispers.

"Really?" the cocktail waitress says as she stomps off to the bathroom.

"If only we had more time," Amon says, then cuts the zip tie. As blood rushes back to my fingers, pins and needles surge then turn into a stinging pain. Amon jerks my head back and kisses me. When he releases my chin, I spit the taste of him from me.

"Water," I croak. My mom nods to Kai and he brings over a crystal glass of water. I take a sip and notice the tint of her herbal tincture. I hold the glass and look at my mom. An urge to throw the water in her face overcomes me.

"Don't even think about it," my mom growls, "Darling, you are about to become more powerful than a god. Enjoy this. Don't make me restrain you again."

With pins and needles still prickling my fingers, I let out a slow breath, pour the water out on the floor, then set the glass down. "Plain water," I demand.

My mom sits a little taller, her smile tainted with triumph, and nods to Kai. He brings me a bottle of clear water.

"Is this how you made me think I was going crazy?" I ask, motioning to the glass.

"The tincture? No, of course not. It's herbs. Apple blossom for knowledge, feverfew, bloody dock, cornflower, dandelion, and a touch of snake blood and poppy but not enough for any narcotic effects. And, a micro . . . *microdose* of psilocybin. Not enough to do anything, just to help open your—"

I laugh as loud and obnoxiously as possible, spraying spittle in her face. "That explains everything. Do you fancy yourself some half-baked, two-bit witch doctor?"

My scalp screams in pain. "Enough," Kai says, pulling my hair from behind the chair.

Amon slaps his hand away from my hair. "She's about to be your queen."

"Then explain it," I tell her with as much force as I can muster.

"What?"

"In Amon's office, in the bathroom, the basement, the elevator, the archive room? It was all a hallucination, wasn't it?"

"No, not at all. You didn't imagine anything. Darling, this building is alive . . . in a dead sort of way." A wicked smile peels across her face. "You'll understand very soon, don't you worry."

"Why have you tortured me?" I cry out. "Why didn't you just do the ceremony when I passed out at your house? I remember Morana being there. You should've gotten it over then!"

Mom lets out a huff, her patience growing thin. "We would've but it has to be done here, and he needed to . . . oh, how should I put this?" Mom looks at Kai. "He needed to get your scent so that he could find you during the ceremony. Like when you give a dog a piece of clothing to track a fugitive. His presence hasn't fully been here for ages, you are his guide, his beacon." Her face becomes hard and angry. "You had to come here of your own accord. It's an honor—"

"Enough questions," Kai snaps, interrupting her.

"Kai's right." Mom closes her eyes and takes a deep breath. When she opens them, her face is smooth again. "We have to hurry. Just know that your entire life has been carefully crafted for this moment. This is your purpose. You think I wanted to have a child?" she sneers. "No, but I did it for Father. You belong to him." Delicately, she unclasps the red leather box and pulls out a large gold halo crown. Impossibly long slender gold spikes burst from it. She holds it up for a moment before placing it on my head.

As she's securing the crown, she tells me, "Soon, you will be his for eternity, though no longer of flesh, you will rule over it."

"She looks perfect," Kai says.

Mom holds a mirror up. I don't recognize the girl staring back. Heavy makeup lightens my skin, the gold halo tops my crown, and my dark hair is pulled back in a tight bun. A white lace gown drapes my body in vintage ivory from my neck to my ankles. Everything suddenly becomes clear—I am the lamb.

I look away from the mirror.

"Make her look," Mom orders, and Kai obeys, jerking my chin to face the mirror. "Our high priestess was right. All those years of shame, when I doubted your potential. You were so good, the perfect child. At one point, I didn't think I could endure being a mother for another second. You were so good, I was questioning Father and my own faith. I wanted to give it all away for you. But, Morana assured me that you would fulfil your role. She was right." My mom swells with pride as she stands. "Look at you, you were made for this."

"And I tasted her first. Maybe Vegas was worth it." Kai pulls out my chair.

"I thought all of those memories were just programed." I spit each word with as much venom as possible.

"Not all of them." Kai winks.

"Yeah, well, I tasted her best." A sneer creeps across Amon's face.

"On your feet," Kai orders.

"No."

"Have it your way," my mom says and nods.

Like a lion to prey, Kai and Amon descend on me without hesitation. Each grabs an arm and yanks me up with such force I cry in pain. My bare feet slide along the carpet as they pull me towards the door.

"Okay! Okay!"

They lighten their grip but not their hold and drag me out of the suite and into the stairwell. As soon as we cross into the concrete vestibule, I'm overcome by a strange scent. Shards of terror prickle my skin. Initially, I think it's some sort of earthy herbal oil or candle, but then I'm hit with the distinct, slightly sweet, and pungent smell of lovers tainted with a markedly metallic undertone—blood. I dig my heels into the base of the first step and refuse to walk any further. Kai hits the back of my knee, loosening my footing, and forcing me to walk.

We take one flight of stairs up and come out onto the thirteenth floor. Morana, Aleister, Mara, and my dad are waiting. Each wears a black, hooded robe and hold another except for Morana—her robe is red. She holds a black robe and hands it to the cocktail waitress with an almost imperceptible sigh of disgust.

"Thank you, Morana," the waitress says.

Aleister and Mara hand Amon and Kai each a robe.

"Mother. Father," they greet in unison, and I realize they're brothers, both sons of the Asras.

My dad doesn't look at me as he places a robe on my mom.

He still doesn't look at me but places his hand on my shoulder and gently squeezes.

Morana stands taller. "The moment we have been patiently waiting for has finally arrived." She holds her arms out towards us. "Shall we? You," she singles out the cocktail waitress, "walk behind us and take a seat in the back."

"No. I'm staying with Amon."

"That's not possible," Morana snaps. "Amon. Tell . . ." She looks at him. ". . . What's her name?"

Amon shrugs, and the waitress' face reddens.

"You were just moaning my name an hour ago."

"Sorry, doll, you're a bit forgettable."

Morana rolls her eyes and nods to Kai. He lets go of my arm, spins towards the waitress, knife in hand, and slices her throat before she can move. Exactly like my dream. The waitress claws at her neck and tries to scream but the only sound that emerges is a sick, wet gurgle. Her blood comes out so fast and thick it looks like a ruby choker. It bubbles as she gasps for air before collapsing in a crumbled heap. Kai wipes his knife off on her robe before tucking it away.

"Thanks, bro," Amon says.

Morana snaps her fingers and two very large men in black suits appear and drag the girl's remains towards the club. Morana spins to the theater and begins her slow procession. She is followed by Aleister and Mara, then Amon, myself, and Kai, while my parents trail behind us.

The entire hall is lit by candles, exactly like it was for Li-RV. We pause just outside of the doors to the theater before they open.

Chapter 35

An ocean of black robes ebb and flow in rhythm to a guttural chanting. My eyes dart across the room. In the candlelight, it's hard to see, but the room seems to be much like it was when I ran from the show. The grass on the ground has expanded and there're pillows everywhere. The black robes obscure most of the faces. On the few faces I can make out, they don skeletal animal masks with horns. Others have their heads obscured by hoods pulled low and shadows. There're sporadic groups that grind together, dotted by flashes of bare flesh, and I quickly look away. The stage is the same life-sized, twisted version of the Ghent Altarpiece and the same performers from Li-RV are in their positions. But a large pentagram formed by candles sits in front of the set, and an over-sized mirror now hangs above the stage so the altar is visible to the entire crowd. In the middle of the pentagram is the gold altar almost identical to the one painted in the Ghent Altarpiece. All it's missing is its lamb.

Kai and Amon spin me so that I'm facing backwards. The chanting intensifies, the crowd becomes frenzied, and we begin our procession.

Amon and Kai don't bother to let me gain my footing; they just drag me. From this position, I'm forced to look at the crowd. They remind me of the rats in New York City that swarm Central Park when the sun goes down. Disgusting. Vicious. Ravenous. A pasty leg rests on the pillow in front, and the robed figure next to him elbows him before they both jump to their feet. Recognizing the pallor of these basement vermin, a wave of nausea rolls over me. It's Billy, Joel, and Antonio—the facilities crew. In the front row, I spot the old lady from the elevator at Rise and the first dinner at Golden Sands. She's wearing nothing but the gold pendant symbol and animal horns. Her wrinkled, flabby rolls of flesh make her look like a walnut resting on two frail legs. That necklace—I'm so stupid. Everything was so choreographed, and I fell right into the boiling pot of water. My stomach lurches in a painful heave but nothing comes up.

"Hello, Auntie," Amon says, blowing her a kiss and she does that stupid shoulder shake that quivers down her old body.

At the base of the stage, I try to twist my body and dig my feet in but don't stand a chance. Amon and Kai carry me up the steps and onto the stage. My ivory dress billows behind me. Morana moves into position at the front of the stage as Amon and Kai carry me to the altar.

Morana raises her arms, voice filling the hall, "Friends, brothers, and sisters. This is the moment we have been waiting for. The moment our dark lord returns. The moment a new world order is established, and flesh will once again rule. THIS. IS. OUR. TIME!"

The crowd erupts, cheering.

A strange, unexpected sense of calm settles over me as Amon and Kai force me to lay upon the altar. I hear Tony's voice inside my head, "Run," he tells me.

If only.

Then I hear him again. "When the time is right—run," he says, and I catch a glimpse of him in the mirror where he stands between two soldiers. They disappear so quickly that I wonder if I imagined them.

Morana begins to speak in a tongue I don't understand. Then, the air pressure changes, and I hear that sucking sound. Frantic, I look around, but no one seems to notice it. Then Amon and Kai each grab one of my arms, holding me tight against the table. My mom, Dad, Mara, and Aleister assume positions around the altar. Morana stands by my head.

A gust of wintery air rushes past and a horrible, crushing pressure slides over me.

He's here.

I can't see him but in the mirror, there are almost imperceptible waves, like heat rising off of asphalt. The chanting grows louder. Aleister caresses Morana, then Mara reaches her hands into my dad's pants. They stop and roll their heads.

Those same ice-cold fingers claw at my ankles, creep up to my knees. The chanting intensifies. I strain my neck to peer into the crowd. Everyone is standing. Chanting. Rolling their heads. For a moment, I think they may be under some sort of spell, and I might be able to run. Then, I feel him enter me. A burning cold rips through me.

Instead of feeling filled, there's this awful sucking sensation. Like my entire self is being sucked into a black hole concentrated inside my womb. The pain is excruciating. I'm dizzy; on the verge of passing out. Nausea slams through me and I manage to turn my head just enough to vomit. Between the gut-wrenching heaves, I gasp for air.

Morana moans, and the crowd follows in a wave of voracious ecstasy.

"It's killing me! Make it stop!" I cry.

My mom looks down at me and laughs joyously.

"It hurts so bad! Please! Make it stop!"

"Darling, enjoy this. Pain is good for the soul," Mom croons, her eyes blown wide with lust, "It will be over soon, my beautiful girl."

A jolt of pain cleaves through me, like I'm being turned inside out. My head spins. I'm either passing out or dying.

Then it's over. The pain subsides. And I collapse back onto the altar.

"It is done," Morana announces.

The crowd sighs as if in a singular orgasmic wave.

"Now, the same spear that stabbed Jesus and took his life will take Lilith's and set her on a path to walk besides our Lord Lucifer for eternity." Morana nods towards Amon.

"Oh shit, did I forget the spear?" Amon says with a heavy tongue. He pats his robe and takes a stumbling step back as he pauses to watch me for a moment. Kai takes a step towards Amon with his arms raised, ready. "Nope. Nope." Amon takes another step back. "I got it." He pulls the spear free, holds it high, and the crowd murmurs in a new frenetic excitement.

Amon passes the blade to my father.

"Dad?" I cry as he lifts the spear over his head, preparing to bring it down and into my heart. "Dad, no, don't do it, please!"

"You will make our daughter a Queen for eternity," Mom says. "Do it. Doooo it!"

My dad closes his eyes and raises the blade a little higher.

A series of bangs and crashes sound just outside the theater followed by what has to be gunshots. Everyone spins towards the sound as the theater door slams open.

Tori steps in. One of Morana's security officers rushes her; she doesn't hesitate, and fires. Two more rush her and she shoots them as well.

My dad, still holding the spear over my heart, looks down at me, meets my gaze, and yells, "Run, Petal, run!" His eyes go wild.

He twists, sinking the spear deep into Morana's chest. I scramble off the altar and pause at the edge of the stage. Dad pulls the spear out and has just enough time to sink it into Aleister's chest.

"No!" Mom screams. "Stop him, you idiots!"

Without hesitation Kai and Amon lunge at him before he has time to pull the spear out of Aleister's chest. His eyes quickly dart around the theater and settle on mine, 'run!' he mouths. With bone-crunching power, Amon jams his knee into my dad's ribs, dropping him.

"What the fuck did you do?" Kai screams as he pulls the ancient weapon out of his father's corpse and lifts it above his head.

More gunfire.

I leap off the stage, and pain splinters my ankle, but I don't stop making my way to Tori.

"You stupid bitch!" Mom screams at Tori as I run from the stage. "It's done!" She's on the brink of hysteria. "You can't run from this. You worthless pieces of shit, stop her." But the onlookers remain frozen.

When I glance back, Mom is wild with fury. "Give me that," she orders Kai. "Hold him up." Kai and Amon haul my dad to his feet, and Mom stabs the spear into his sternum, pulling down and opening him up from chest to pelvis. I turn away, though the theater has gone so quiet I hear the slosh of something hitting the stage carried on the acoustics.

Tori fires another shot. "No. One. Move!"

My entire life has been completely upended and finally makes sense. As I sprint towards Tori, energy courses through my veins though making my legs feel so powerful and light they seem disconnected from my body. I can hear the quiet breath of those I run by. Every sound seems louder, my senses are tuned in like never before but I feel more like I'm in a dream than reality. When I finally reach Tori, I grab onto her as she waves me behind. With her gun still sweeping the crowd, we back out of the theater together then sprint down the hall towards the nightclub. Tori takes several shots over her shoulder and manages to hold back everyone in the theater.

There are a series of tunnels and catwalks I hope can buy us some time, and motion her toward Rapture's door. Tori unloads the spent magazine as she runs. "These damn limited-capacity mags were all I could get here," she says.

"What?"

"Never mind."

The club is dark and empty. I grab Tori's hand and lead her towards the curtain tunnels. We duck behind a wall of fabric. Tori loads a new magazine as the nightclub door opens.

"Come out, come out wherever you are," Kai yells, upending chairs and tables. "You can't escape. The building won't let you."

Glass shatters nearby.

"Ever wonder why here of all places?" Kai yells.

I pull Tori back towards the solid wall, away from the curtain. While I can barely see her in this dim light, I press my finger to my mouth for silence then close my eyes and listen. I need to get a feel for where Kai is before we move on.

He's completely silent. Then there's a small rattle from the back corner of the club.

"Ha!" Kai throws a chair that splinters against the wall. "I'll tell you, Sharp was right."

Holding Tori's hand, we hug the wall and continue around the back of the club.

"Oh, Lilith, Lilith, Lilith, you weren't going crazy. This building is very active. You see, thanks to our dear Brother Ledes at the helm, it's been cultivated. Crafted. For a millennia. Like your vision, which was impressively accurate, he had parties and drank blood. Preferably children's which, if you've never had the pleasure, is simply orgasmic. Keeps you young."

I hear a series of small bangs followed by glass smashing; Kai is throwing glasses at the curtain and walls.

"Brother Ledes worshiped Father and laid the groundwork for our order."

A glass smashes just feet from where we are. Tori and I freeze. Holding our breath, we wait for Kai to bust through any moment.

"The property's changed hands several times but could never shake the ghosts left by Ledes."

We inch away.

"When this building was turned into a hospital, it flavored these walls with so much death, it couldn't have been more perfect. Then add casinos, a string of greedy owners, and tragedy just seems to repeat itself here. That energy. Mmm. Perfect."

Kai quiets, and we stop again. His sudden grunt of exertion pierces the silence, followed by a violent thud against the wall ahead—the impact rippling through the curtain in unsettling waves. We hurry towards the crash, hoping Kai won't strike the same location twice.

"We were left with a once-in-a-lifetime opportunity to open a gate between Earth and hell, just enough for our dark lord to pay our dear, sweet Lilith that special visit."

Tori stops and pulls me towards her. "Is that true?" she whispers, and I hold my pointer finger to my lips to quiet her.

We freeze, listening for Kai. Did he hear us? I pull her hand.

Kai laughs. "That's right, it's too late. *You're* too late, Tori. We won. I could kill Lilith now, but we have a party planned and people are waiting. The Order deserves to see the moment our Antichrist enters this world and meek little Lilly joins our dark savior for eternity. Her death is a celebration."

A chair crashes into the wall just feet behind Tori.

"I'll admit, Tori, you surprised us. Same with Lilly's dad. What the fuck was that? Ugh, but squeezing the life out of him felt so good," Kai yells, "You can't hide in here forever, your mom called for backup and they'll be up here with their guns any minute." Kai knocks over another table before he unleashes a cackle of manic laughter. "I mean, it really doesn't matter. Father's seed is *already* in Lilith. I just get to have a fun little hunt to start the party."

When Tori hears this, she collapses to her knees behind me. *Is she praying?* I try to pull her up, but she won't budge. Soon, her words drift to me. "Grand Master Molay, give me the strength to do what

I must to temper the evil that claws at the foundation of our great Catholic faith."

Kai crashes through the curtain right behind her. She shoots; hits him, and he stumbles back and out of the tunnel. She scrambles to her feet, blindly fires a few more times. We flee to the sounds of Kai's desperate, angry gasps for breath.

Chapter 36

I lead us to the ladder that takes us up to the catwalk. At least from up there, we'll be able to see what's coming and can cut across the club to the back hallway and the stairwell. As this plan materializes in my mind—thirteen floors to the exit and an army of sociopaths suddenly seems like an insurmountable obstacle.

I find the DJ booth and ladder, and spin back to Tori. "Why'd you come back for me? How did you know this was going to happen?"

"It's all in the book."

"I'm so stupid. I can't believe you came back for me."

"I had to."

"Thank you."

"Let's get out of here first, then you can thank me."

"Hope you're not still afraid of heights."

"Just go."

Once I get high enough, I scan the club for Kai or ideally his body, but he's gone. I keep climbing till I reach the catwalk. It high and there's barely anything to hold onto.

I pick up the pace on the catwalk and reach the door to the back hall. It's tight and dark, more like a tunnel than a hall. There's glowing tape on the ground: 'WARNING. SUDDEN DROP. USE

LADDER.' One more ladder and a back corridor is all that separates us from the stairwell down to our way out.

Moving as fast as I can, I spin to climb down, when I feel a hand wrap around my leg and yank.

"You stupid bitch," Kai growls.

He pulls again. Hard. Both legs slip off the rung. Tori lunges and grabs my arms, her gun tumbling to the ground. I kick as hard as I can, but Kai has an iron grip.

A gunshot rings out. I look up at Tori and she's as confused as I am. Then Kai's grip loosens, and I hear him fall. His skull cracks open on the floor below.

"Lilly, it's me, Buddy," a voice yells from below. "Hurry up, we have to get out of here now. I won't hurt you."

"Come on," I tell Tori, before starting my descent. I finally reach solid ground, Tori right behind me.

Buddy attempts to pass the gun to me but I point him to Tori and she takes her gun back. "Follow me. We have to hurry, there's going to be a fire."

"Buddy," I grab his arm to slow him. "What's going on?"

"We don't have time. I'll explain later."

As Buddy turns to head through the corridor, I hold his arm. "Did you take your meds?"

"Yeah, I don't need meds." Buddy looks at Kai's body, its legs twisted in unnatural angles. "You're welcome, by the way."

I've only heard this coherent, confident side of him a few times in the past and when I did, it scared me. "Buddy, what the hell is going on?"

"If you would've left when I told you, this would've been so much easier. It's a long story, but we have to move. Seriously." he clutches my arm and pulls me down the corridor.

I tug on his arm as we head for the stairwell. "*Please* tell me what's going on."

"I will but you have to run." He drags me along, and pulls open the door to the stairwell, shoves us in then yanks it shut.

An explosion shakes the building with such force each brick vibrates in a shudder that tumbles down from roof to ground. A hallow boom follows close behind and my ears pop before everything becomes perfectly quiet and still.

"What was that?" I ask.

"Keep moving," he says. We sprint down several flights of stairs.

Out of breath and shaking, I stop on the ninth-floor landing. "Buddy, please."

Buddy pauses and lets out a breath. "I've been following these sons of bitches for years, The Order of Mu, they call themselves. Ever since, they took my baby sister."

"Your sister? I'm sorry, Buddy." I rest a hand on his shoulder. "Did you get—"

Buddy looks down. "No, and I swore that eventually, I'd burn this whole operation to the ground." Buddy holds his arms up emphasizing his current operation. "Snuck right in under their noses with the crazy old Buddy act." Buddy does a signature spin and bow. "My real name's Xander, by the way."

"Are you with an organization?" Tori asks.

"No, but I've had help. Been following them and planning this for years. That's what I've been working on every time you bumped into me. They're arrogant, thought they were so big and untouchable, they almost made this easy."

"You should've gone to the cops," I say.

"Oh, like the captain of the police? You didn't notice him in the ceremony? We can talk about this as much as you want later, but now we need to keep moving."

"What about the innocent people?"

"Don't be mistaken, this is war. There may be collateral damage. But I did everything in my power to save as many as I can."

"What about the sprinkler system?"

"Disabled."

"The fire department and police were called as soon as you set off the first alarms."

"Nope, disconnected the alarms from the call stations. The call is going to look like it was triggered." Buddy looks at his watch. "In about three minutes. While the entire cult was waiting for Kai to bring you back, they didn't realize I was locking them in."

"Come on," Tori says and rushes past us to take the lead. "Will this take us all the way out?"

"Almost," Buddy says. "It takes us to the second floor then there are several ways out from there."

We hurry down a few more flights.

Tori pivots and fires her gun. I search for someone rushing up behind us, but it's only when Buddy collapses, a spray of blood and brains plastered to the wall beside him, that I realize Tori shot him.

"What did you *do*?"

"I'm sorry," Tori said. "But I have a sworn duty as a knight of the Solar Temple to protect our people, our Catholic faith, and our world against dark forces by any means necessary."

"But he was trying to help us!"

"Yes, I know, and he'll be welcomed into Heaven with open arms and sit—"

"What is *wrong* with you?"

"I've taken an oath." Tori raises the gun and points it at me.

"Whoa, what are you doing?"

"I've trained my whole life for this moment."

"You're one of them too!"

"No, we've been following the Order for generations. My parents, my grandparents, we are knights of the Solar Temple. It's our sworn duty to protect the Holy Catholic faith and stop any evil that may try to harm it. It's—"

"I don't know who the *fuck* the Solar Temple is or what you're talking about, but we are on the same side! So was Buddy!"

"Buddy served his own personal agenda. We can't have some vigilante getting in our way. Yes, he helped us, but he would never have allowed me to do what I have to do now." Tori's jaw clenches in resolution but sadness sits heavy in her eyes. "You can't be allowed to bring the seed of Satan into the world," Tori says, her gun still trained on me.

"You don't get it," I yell. "If you kill me, *you* will be responsible for bringing Satan's seed into the world. As long as I'm alive, it can't grow in my womb!"

"Bullshit. Satan is inside you, trying even now to protect his progeny. I can't trust anything you say." Tori begins moving towards me quicker and I back away, scrambling up the steps. Her gun-hand trembles.

"You have to trust me," I plead.

"He's part of you now. I'm sorry," Tori says.

Her hand no longer trembles, and her finger tenses on the trigger. I drop back onto the steps, levering myself. "Please," I beg one last time then kick out at her with everything I have. The gun fires as she stumbles back, losing the battle to keep herself upright. As gravity pulls, she drops the gun and grabs for the railing. Slips. She tumbles back, frantically grabbing at the handrail and manages to stop her fall, but the gun continues to tumble past her.

I clamber past her, eyes trained on the gun as it clatters to a stop on the fifth-floor landing, right beside Buddy's corpse.

As I rush down the flight of steps, my left leg is jerked back, and I come to a screeching halt. A pulse of energy moves over me, almost like the aftershock of an explosion, and I'm thrown to the ground. My ribs collide with the corner of a concrete step, blowing the air out of me and. I hear a crack and a sharp pain rips through me. I clutch at my side as my vision begins to collapse. Then the pain explodes around my entire chest. I look back, thinking Tori tripped me, but she's holding her head. Out of the corner of my eye, a shadow climbs the wall. It wasn't Tori who tripped me. From farther up the stairwell a roar flows out of the shadow like a sonic wave. The fire is moving fast, yet I don't feel heat or smell smoke.

I force myself to my feet, but the pain is nearly too much. I'm doubled over, clutching my guts. I glance back at Tori. She locks eyes with me then the gun and jumps to her feet.

Run! I race down the stairwell, taking two steps at a time. She's gaining on me. I take a second to glance over my shoulder and she leaps off the steps. I throw my body into hers, driving her into the ground. I grab the gun.

Don't look back. I just run, one hand gripping the handrail and the other, the gun.

"STOP!" Tori roars.

Yeah, right. I pass the fourth-floor landing, and my lungs burn and cry out for rest, my side and ankle send spears of jarring pain up and down my body. I ignore them. Passing the third-floor landing, my adrenalin expires, and pain overwhelms me.

"I said STOP!" Tori screams.

Like she thinks I'll listen. My ankle begs me to obey her, my ribs too, but I can't, not if I want to live.

Just steps from the second-floor landing, something heavy slams into the back of my head, sending an explosion of pain searing through my skull. The stairwell spins, and I stumble down the last few steps. *The gun. The gun. Hold on to the gun.* My legs can't support my weight, and I collapse to my knees. I take deep breaths, willing the room to stop spinning. *Got to go.*

I struggle to my feet, but Tori slams into me.

I won't go out like this. All the pent-up anger, humiliation at being the quiet one. The compliant one rages through me. I flip awkwardly to my back, Tori on top of me and I jam the muzzle of the gun into her gut.

"Okay . . . okay," Tori says backing off me, her hands up.

With the gun still aimed at her, I struggle to my feet. She lunges. I fire. Miss. Fire again. This time, the bullet grazes her shoulder. Not deep enough to kill but deep enough for her to feel it.

She grunts. Falls back, grabs her shoulder. Blood soaks her shirt.

"Take another step and I'll kill you." I scramble to my feet, careful to keep the gun aimed.

Tori stares at me for a moment. "Fine." Surrender pokes a hole in her confidence, and she deflates.

"You don't fucking get it," I tell her. "We both want the same thing."

"If you're going to kill me, do it now before I can witness Satan's rise."

"Are you fucking stupid?"

Tori takes a step towards me, and I fire one last warning shot.

"He is part of you."

"His child can only be born to a corpse. *My* corpse. I have to stay alive until I can find a way to undo this."

"You're lying!"

"Why do you think the Order is trying to kill me? That was the final part of the ceremony, the part you stopped!"

Tori's eyes widen. "Shit, shit, shit. No. They told me that was symbolic. And, they told me that if I got to you before the ceremony, I could save you. That's when his seed would be implanted."

"I can*not* die."

"But . . . that's not what the Temple said."

"You saw the book. You saw the Order try to kill me. You know the *truth*, Tori."

"It doesn't make sense." Tori rubs her forehead. "Unless the Temple didn't think they were going to kill you right away and that's why they sent me. Fuck me. They thought your parents were going to protect you. Crown you queen. Then the Order would have Satan's seed right here under their control."

"They underestimated my mom."

"Clearly." She gnaws at her bottom lip. "But what if I'm wrong? What if you're lying? What if the Temple was confused? Maybe they didn't realize that you had to be sacrificed. How can I trust you?"

"Don't trust me. Trust yourself and what you've seen."

Tori shakes her head. "What would they want me to do?"

"I don't know who the hell *they* are that you're talking about. All I know is the rules are clear: if I die, the world ends."

"But why would they want that? Unless . . . unless . . ."

"What?" I demand.

"Nothing." Tori's head drops.

"Tell me."

"Either they thought they could stop this or think they can win."

"Win what?"

"You don't want—"

A series of pops reverberate from the upper floors.

"We don't have time for this," I say, "but I need to know what you know. I'm going to let you live. For now. Try anything and you die, understand?"

Tori nods.

"You go first," I tell her, "and remember I have the gun on you."

Tori turns away and heads to the door. She holds it for me. "Which way?"

A quick glance around doesn't help. The harsh overhead lighting, linoleum floors, and white walls tell me we're somewhere at the back of the house. I spot another set of doors with a sign: 'Grand Ballroom Kitchen'. A balloon of relief puffs me up. From the ballroom, there's one flight of steps to the casino and then we're out.

"Go through that door and into the ballroom."

She nods and takes off. The doors bounce back on me, typical of industrial kitchen doors that swing to make pushing heavy carts of food in and out much easier.

"They left this kitchen fas–"

An axe swings from behind a column, cutting deep into Tori's neck. Time slows as Tori's lifeless body remains upright momentarily before collapsing in a heap.

Chapter 37

"Oh, that felt good. I've been waiting so long to do that." My mom steps out from behind the column, dragging a fire axe next to her. "I only wish I could've done it to her parents first."

My arms tremble as I aim the gun at her.

Mom laughs. "Isn't that cute. But can you actually pull the trigger?"

"I can and will," I say as I step over Tori's body and slowly inch deeper into the kitchen and towards the ballroom.

"Why are you trying to run? You can't escape this."

I scan the kitchen, taking slow, deliberate steps backwards. People fled in a hurry. Equipment is scattered everywhere, burners left on, some with large pots still boiling.

"Our Dark Lord is bound to you. He's with you everywhere you go." She takes a few steps toward me, the metal of the axe grinds on the kitchen's tile floor.

I shoot, and the bullet lodges in her thigh. *How can my aim be so bad?*

She looks down at her leg. Her eyes widen, jaw clenches, and lips curl into a snarl. "How dare you! That's going to leave a scar."

The air pressure changes. The metal pots on the stove rattle, the doors slam open and shut.

Mom cackles. "Oh dear, you've made him angry."

"Stop," I scream. "Stop! Stop!"

My mom picks up her pace, lifting the axe into a ready position. I plant my feet, aim for her heart, and pull the trigger. Click. I pull again. Nothing.

"You will be queen. You should be thanking me." Mom charges.

I hurl the gun at her. It bounces off her head, splitting open the skin above her left eye. Her head rocks back, and she stumbles. When she raises fingers to her head, they come back bloody.

"My face! I'm doing this because it's what's best for you!" A primal scream erupts from her as she lunges.

I sprint down the closest aisle, right by the carving station where a massive cut of rare meat still bleeds, waiting to be carved. A huge knife sits next to it, and I snatch it up. When I spin to face my mother, she's swinging the axe like a baseball bat. I duck, feel it cut the air above my head.

"Darling, you are making this so much harder than it needs to be," Mom says breathlessly. "It will only hurt for a moment."

"Never." I back away, knife held firm, and bump into a counter.

"I didn't want a child, but then you were born and the thought of ever losing you drove me literally mad. When you were chosen as a candidate for this, I knew it's what you were born to do. Now, I will never have to lose you. We will spend eternity together." She holds the axe with both hands, ready to take another swing.

"What are you talking about? You're trying to kill me." I scream as a take a few more steps back.

"Just temporarily."

"You murdered dad!"

"Yeah." She pauses her forward aggression and rests the head of the axe on the ground. "So, he could be with you while you were waiting to make your grand return as queen."

"You should be the one that burns in hell."

"Darling it's not like that. All Father wants is freedom of the flesh."

"He's pure evil."

She rolls her eyes and shakes her head. "You have spent too much time with Tori, thank Lucifer, that's over." She laughs. "You are so misguided. What kind of god gives you these incredible bodies then tells you everything that brings you pleasure is wrong. *That* is sadistic abuse."

"You've lost your mind. You can't just murder people." I start to back up again.

"Semantics. I'm tired of talking. You'll understand soon."

"NO!"

"You are going to do this one way or another. This is what you were born for. You don't have a choice."

"Yes, I do."

My mother swings the heavy axe.

I feint back then slash forward with the knife before she can counter the momentum of the axe. It slices deep through the flesh above her elbow.

She drops the axe, grits her teeth, and opts for a knife. "Let's make this fair." Mom lunges again, the tip of her knife catching my forearm, leaving a thick line of blood.

My mom licks the remnants of my blood off her knife. "My blood is your blood, Darling," she says, "Now, I taste him, too. His blood is already mixing with yours. He's part of you. It's too late."

"Never." I maneuver towards the stove, and prepare for her next attack.

It comes quickly, but I pivot, hook her ankle with my foot, and send her toppling into the industrial burner with a massive pot of still-boiling soup.

She tries to arrest her fall with her hands, screams when they hit the hot stove top. Momentum carries her forward, bouncing off the huge pot before she drops to the floor.

The pot teeters a moment before it falls. Gallons of boiling blood soup pour over her face and body. Her skin immediately bubbles and blisters. She screams, writhing in pain.

I know I can kill her, know I should. It would be a mercy . . . but I'm not feeling merciful. This is what she *deserves*. A blur of movement pulls my attention and I scan the kitchen. No one else is here, but waves of heat eat at the walls. The fire consuming the top floors has worked its way down, heating the floors above. The paint blisters and bubbles and then flames erupt along the wall.

I don't look at my mom when I leave. Knife in hand, I dash through the empty halls and down a single flight of stairs to the casino.

The fire alarm blares against a cacophony of slot-machine sound effects that drill into my skull. With no one in sight, I wind through the aisles. The slot machines throb like living organisms, their lights flicker and taunt with a strange mechanic heartbeat.

Out of nowhere, Tony's disembodied cry, "Duck!"

I drop to the ground. Something heavy slices through the air above me. It crashes down with an explosion of sparks and lodges itself in a line of slot machines—the axe. Still stained with Tori's blood. The air moves and a soldier in a World War II uniform walks across the aisle in front of me, he looks more like a sepia-toned projection. He stops for a moment and points behind me. Amon is there, charging.

There's no point running; he's too close. I take a runner's ready position, knife carefully tucked away. I can't tell if Amon's heading for me or his axe. Have to time it perfectly. When he's a foot from me, his right leg drags. *He's going to kick me.*

Gripping the knife handle, blade against my forearm, I prepare to take the force of his kick.

I brace my legs against the slot machine bank. Waiting. Waiting. At the last second possible, I raise my arms, flip the blade edge so that it's facing out, and try to turn out of the hit. The knife connects but so does his foot. White hot pain explodes through my arms as the knife hits flesh and is wrenched from my hand. I smash back against the slot machines, wind blown out of me. I gasp for air, stumble away. A pool of fire licks along the high ceiling.

Spots invade my vision as I fight for consciousness. If I don't, I'm dead. I plant every ounce of focus on Amon as he stumbles backwards; the knife lodged in his calf. I think he's screaming but can't hear anything over the fire alarm.

I still hear Tony. "Run! Now. Head to your left."

Using the slot machines as my brace, I make a tight turn down a weaving aisle. I'm grabbed from behind and I come to a violent stop. When I spin back, the loose bodice of my dress is hooked around a slot machine handle.

As I writhe, frantic to free myself, the fabric of my dress becomes more knotted around the machine and it pulls me closer. Tightening its grip, unable to break free, I twist to face the slot machine; the handle is beginning to break off. Using all my strength, I grab the handle and wrench myself free, the force of my effort throwing me to the carpet. The handle still dangles from my bodice.

Glancing around the bank of slots, I lock eyes with Amon, face contorted, lips peeled back in a demonic grin. He pulls the knife from his leg.

I run.

The sharp shards of the slot machine lever cut my skin as it bounces off my body. I awkwardly pull the broken handle out from my bodice and grip it tight. The edges are jagged and sharp. It's not heavy but it is solid.

I take twists and turns down the aisles, avoiding Amon but keep moving towards the exit. Drenched in sweat, the fire has not reached the floor, but its closing in. My skin feels like it's burning, and my lungs ache. Heat has blackened the ceiling tiles, and the flames will burst through the ceiling any moment.

Hiding just inside a row of slots, I stop to look for Amon. He's nowhere. Over the blaring alarm and slot machines comes that odd ragtime tune I'd heard on the second floor, and again in the Lede's party. Knowing what this building is, the trauma of every experience I had at The Golden Sands detonates, sending white-hot sparks of panic through every fiber of my being, and I make a run for it through the table games pit.

"Duck!"

Before I have time to process this, Amon tackles me. We hit hard, and in the impact, he loses his grip. I roll free, scramble to my feet.

The main entrance is just up ahead.

The bright red glare of emergency lights casts a crimson hue on the lobby. A chair sails over my head to crash in front of me. I stumble, giving Amon enough time to catch up. He throws me into a blackjack table, pins himself on top.

A thought rolls through me with such force, I gasp for air. But it's not my thought . . . it's Amon's. I know it is. When he touched me, it was like a static exchange. Electric. I saw into him through his shame.

Amon lifts the spear high above his head.

"You loved me," I scream. "I know you did, and you were ashamed. You, the stupid, weak brother. You loved me."

"Who's the stupid, weak brother now? They're dead and I'm the one that's going to see this through. The Order has more power than you can imagine. It's part of everything and I am its savior!" Amon lifts the spear a little higher but holds it there.

"Eyes," Tony's voice cuts through the noise. To reach his eyes I will have to move towards the spear aimed at my heart, and I don't want to.

"Now!" Tony yells.

I surge upward, dig my thumbs into Amon's eye sockets. He twists his face away, but my right thumb manages to dig into his eye. I feel his eyeball and try to hook it, but he pulls away. Amon stumbles backwards with a roar, one hand on his eye and the other holding the spear.

"Move," Tony says, his voice flat and quiet. Chips scatter as I skitter off the blackjack table.

Amon blocks my way toward the exit.

"Hide," Tony says, and I'm forced to run deeper into the casino.

Stooping behind a ticket redemption kiosk, I wait. A loud boom echoes from the other end of the casino. An explosion of red-hot flames crawl across the ceiling.

"Come here, little lamb, so I can rip your heart from your chest! Or stay hidden and let the flames devour you." Amon winds through the aisle. Over the alarm, I hear him scraping his spear against the metal slot machines. "Either way, I win, you stupid bitch!"

He's so close. I'm done.

The alarm shuts off. The slot machines flicker out. Harsh, emergency lights cast eerie, demonic shadows into the casino. The roar of fire, once hidden by the din, quickly becomes deafening.

Amon steps around the corner.

In one swift move, he stabs. The spear lodges in my shoulder. For a moment, it's like I'm watching this happen to someone else. Instead of pain, an odd numbness melts down my arm. My arm goes limp, and I worry he hit something vital. My throat tightens with panic and blood pours from my wound to soak, crimson and warm into my white dress.

Amon's face twists into a horrific smile, as he yanks the spear shaft, slicing through the muscle and sinew as it tears free. He rises up to drive the spear into me as though he wishes to pin me to the floor. I steady myself, draw in a deep breath and prepare for the end. But it's not the end he wants.

He begins his deadly descent, the point of the spear driving towards my heart. I skewer him right through his side with the broken lever, twisting and driving it deeper for good measure.

Amon stumbles back. Blinks once, twice, three times. He grips the steel shaft protruding from his gut, gurgles and yanks the slot handle out. A thick spurt of blood follows. He looks at me and laughs. Tossing the handle to the side, he readies himself to kill me.

"Run!" Tony yells. His voice is distant, softer.

I hammer into Amon with my good shoulder and then duck past him. I don't look back as I race for the exit. But, he's close. I can feel him.

I'm almost to the lobby when a sharp crack thunders through the air—like a massive tree splintering. A jagged fissure lightning-bolts across the doorway between the lobby and casino floor. I dive and roll across the hard marble as the entire structure collapses, sending burning lumber crashing down where I stood seconds before.

Like a crab, I scramble back on my ass. Amon is still there, staring at me, his gaze spells my death. I will myself to move, but my eyes lock with Amon's holding me still.

And he changes, shifts. Not physically . . . but something. His gaze softens. "I'm sorry, Lilly. This isn't what I wanted. They forced me to do this. You're right. Let's run away from it all. You and me." he steps closer to the burning blockade, and his eyes widen. It's the first time I've ever seen him afraid. "Please, Lilly, you must help me! Please, Lilly! Hurry!" Tears glisten in his eyes. "I love you."

I want to believe him. But it's all bullshit. He's all bullshit. I struggle to my feet beneath the flaming heat. "Liar. You were ashamed to love me."

Amon's eyes narrow, and all his hatred flashes there. He's a murdering psychopath and I'm on his hit list. His arm shoots through the burning timber, and he roars as he tries to reach for me. "You fucking bitch! This isn't over."

"Burn in hell!"

"You can't kill me!" A maniacal laugh erupts from him before seamlessly morphing into a furious howl. "I will hunt you down!"

Spittle flies from his mouth. "I will find you and squeeze every ounce of life from you with my bare hands!"

What he doesn't realize is he's on my hit list too.

All the anger and humiliation and fear melts away, and all that remains is revenge. He may have had a full house, but I raise him two middle fingers. "Looks like I won this hand, asshole."

Spinning on my heel, I push through those beautiful, imposing front doors where all this had started. I take a deep breath and rotate on my heel to gaze at the blazing destruction. Firemen and EMTs race over and try to pull me away. But, I push them off.

I strain to see through the glass as fire takes over the casino floor. In the pit of that conflagration, I see Amon. Perfectly still and watching me through the wall of flames. Behind him are Tony and other shadowy figures.

Amon turns and disappears into the burning building. Tony and the others watch him but remain perfectly still. Grateful for their help, I wonder what will become of them. They seem to fade in the growing flames—nothing more than smoke. *Were they ever even there?*

The world spins.

I stumble back, fall, but never hit the ground.

Lost to utter darkness.

Chapter 38

A heavy blanket of darkness holds me still. An incessant beeping somewhere in the distance begins to penetrate the covers. Eventually, I force my eyes open. Bright light floods my vision, burns. I squeeze my eyes shut. It's too bright. I want to go back to sleep, but that beeping won't stop. Awareness slowly returns.

Someone is moving nearby.

"Tuuurrn." My mouth is so dry, my tongue feels fat when I try to speak. "Turn it ooofffff." I try to say again.

"You're awake," a female voice says, confirming her presence.

"Make it stop," I croak.

"Make what stop?"

"Bright. No. Beep."

"I'm not sure what you're asking for?"

Blinking furiously, I try to clear the glaze that's plastered to my eyes. It doesn't work; everything is so blurry. I can make out a wavy figure standing nearby and squint to focus. "I want to sleep. Make the beeping stop."

"You've been sleeping for nearly forty-five hours. You need to try to wake up. But I can quiet the beeping for you."

"The light. Too bright."

"Your eyes will adjust," she says.

I pull my eyes shut again.

"Here drink this. It's water, it will help."

I reluctantly open my eyes and make out a white Styrofoam cup held in front of me. Parting my lips, I take a pull on the straw. The cold liquid soothes my mouth and throat. A bitter antiseptic smell punches my sinuses, pulling me from the rest I so desperately want. The film clears from my eyes and the white-on-white walls slowly come into focus. *Hospital.*

"Better?" the nurse asks.

"Thank you," I say, and she sets the cup on the bedside table, then wheels it in front of me. Pain erupts from seemingly every part of my body when I try to pull myself into a better sitting position. Once the pain settles to a tolerable level, I take a quick inventory of my body. My left arm is bandaged in a tight sling. An IV line holds my right arm hostage. The rest of my body is covered by a white blanket.

"Try to take it easy," she says.

"What . . . ?"

"You have three broken ribs on your right and two on your left. You also have a fractured ankle, a concussion, and a severe laceration to your left shoulder which required surgical repair."

"Where am I?"

"ACMH."

I just look at her.

"Atlantic City Medical Health Center . . . in *Atlantic City*," she adds.

"Yeah, I figured."

"I'm Amanda, your nurse. The rest of your care team is written here." She points to a whiteboard on the wall of my room where names are written. "You're in the trauma unit. Have been for two days."

"Two days?" I try to pull the blanket off, but agony punches my chest, and I cough, releasing a tornado of pain that tears through my entire torso from the inside out. I pull my eyes shut, grit my teeth, and wait for the storm to subside.

"Please, try to relax." Amanda pulls the blanket up again. She's both firm and caring. "I can give you something for the pain."

As her arm brushes mine, I'm hit with an overwhelming sense of guilt. It's not mine, it's Amanda's. I know why she became a nurse. She was supposed to give her best friend a ride home from a party in high school, but Amanda wanted to stay. Her friend got a ride home from someone too drunk to drive and ended up a quadriplegic.

"No, I need to get out of here," I say as the memories of the ceremony come flooding back.

"You can't. Not yet at least. You're on IV antibiotics for another three days. Like I said, your laceration was severe, and you're pretty beat up."

"No, you don't understand."

"I know you've been through a traumatic event, but right now you need to try to relax. Are you comfortable?"

"Comfortable?" I let out a dark chuckle. "What's that?"

"What?"

"Never mind." I'm not sure if I want to scream or laugh at the irony of being comfortable. *My stupid mantra.* The 'comfort zone' I was trying to break out of was just the jail of lies in which my mother imprisoned me. I bark another laugh; the walls burnt down along with her.

"A social worker and our intake manager are on their way. They need to talk to you. You had no ID when you were brought in, so technically, you're a Jane Doe."

"Technically?"

"I should leave this conversation—"

"Perfect timing," says a husky voice from the doorway. "Thanks, Amanda. We'll take it from here," A woman, well into her fifties, wearing a smart suit strides into my room.

Amanda nods. "I'll be at my station if you need anything."

The older woman leads a younger woman and a man into my room. They push the door closed behind them.

"I'm Ava Adler, Senior Director of Operations at ACMH, this is Martha Fernandes, our Director of Social Services, and Agent Tom Parker of the Federal Bureau of Investigations. Can you confirm your name?"

"Lilly."

"Full name?" Ava asks.

I clear my throat. "Lilith Layne Umbra."

"Do you know what happened?"

"There was a fire."

Ava nods. "Yes, the most devastating fire in this city's history."

"Ms. Umbra," Martha says, "we figured out who you, or who we thought you were earlier today. We attempted to contact your parents—"

"My parents?"

"Yes, but were not successful. Do you have any other family we can contact for you?"

"No."

"Were your parents at The Golden Sands?" Martha asks.

I nod.

"We were afraid of that. There's no one else we can contact?"

"No." I lift my good arm to reach for my water, but gasp as a sharp pain stabs my ribs. Martha pushes the tray close enough so that I can guide the straw into my mouth and take a slow pull of water.

Agent Parks steps forward. "What do you remember about Saturday's events?"

I clear my throat. "It was supposed to be a big weekend, a grand reveal for press and VIPs. We had several parties planned and a show."

"The show in the thirteenth-floor theater?"

I nod.

"Do you know who was in that show? Was it the VIPs and press?"

"That was the plan."

"The plan?" he asks.

"Yes, we had the entire weekend planned and the show was intended for Golden Sand's highest-level VIPs and press."

"Why weren't you in the show?" he asks.

"I've seen it," I say before taking another drink of water. "I was trying to catch up on some work and prep for the afterparty while I had a bit of free time." I clear my throat and take another quick sip of water. "What's going on?"

"We suspect a terrorist attack," Agent Parker says.

"What?"

"An act of terrorism."

"Yeah, I heard you, but I don't understand. You think this was intentional?"

"Sadly, yes. While still not confirmed, this attack seems to have killed several high-profile individuals and been perfectly planned out."

"So, you think the Golden Sands was targeted?" I open my eyes wide.

"We know it was."

"But . . . why?"

"That's what we're investigating. As of now, you seem to be the only executive that survived or that we've located."

"Really?"

"Can you tell us what happened and how you got out?" Agent Parker asks.

I close my eyes like I'm trying to think. "I was in my office. There was an explosion, I think. I vaguely remember fire alarms and running down the stairwell and out through the casino. I saw the fire and a doorway collapsed. It's all very fuzzy."

"Where was your office?"

"The eighth floor."

"You were very lucky," Agent Parker says. "Your recollection is consistent with your injuries. We suspect the explosion caused your injuries and knocked you out briefly. When you came to, you were able to get out just in time."

"Why do you think it was a terrorist attack?" I ask.

"Did you hear any gunshots?"

"Gunshots? I don't think so. I just remember an explosion."

"We found several bodies that died from gunshot wounds near the theater."

"That can't be right," I lie. "What about the people in the theater? My parents . . . Did you find them?"

"No, I'm sorry," Martha says. "The remains of ninety-three people were found trapped in the theater. At the moment, they're . . . difficult to identify. If your parents were in the show, it's likely they did not make it out."

I drop my head and close my eyes, grateful there are ninety-three less Order of Mu members.

"Ms. Umbra, there's not much left of The Golden Sands, other than the shell and Mr. Asra's apartment," Agent Parker says. "He appears to have installed living quarters that were essentially a fireproof safe. From our intel, we know he was a collector and intended it to keep his prized collection safe."

"Was he in there?"

"No one was in there. We believe he was trapped in the theater."

Clenching my jaw, I look down. "That's impossible."

"I know it's difficult to fathom. However, several items seem to have been removed from the apartment, so we suspect this organization specifically targeted Mr. Asra and his network. They seem to have had at least one person on the inside. This attack was incredibly well planned. But don't worry, we will find them. I promise you that, and I'm hoping you can help us."

I nod but continue to look down.

"I wanted to see if you can help us identify a few people, in particular those we found with gunshot wounds."

I pretend to wipe my eyes with the blanket then look up at Parker. "Okay."

He pulls an eight-by-ten photo out of a manilla folder and holds it up.

"That's Buddy," I say. "He's harmless. He was part of a homeless outreach employment program. There's no way he was involved; he had some severe mental health issues. Not violent or anything, from our brief interactions he seemed to have the mind of about a seven-year-old."

"What about him?" Parker holds up another picture.

"That's Amon's brother, I think. I can't remember his name."

"Amon Asra, the owner?"

"Yes."

"What about him?" Agent Parker holds up a picture of a security guard.

"No, sorry."

The next few pictures are all men, some of whom I recognize as security officers, but I shake my head to all of them. "I'm pretty sure they're all security, but I'm not completely sure. Did Peter make it out?"

"Who's Peter?"

"Golden Sand's Head of Facilities, he knows everyone and everything about the property."

"What's his last name?"

"I don't know."

Agent Parker pulls another paper out of his file and begins scanning it. "This is a complete list of every employee that worked at Golden Sands. There's no one by the name of Peter in the facilities department. Are you sure his name was Peter?"

"Yes, I'm sure . . . I . . . I'm pretty sure."

"Well, everyone from the Facilities department has been accounted for. They had never met any of the executives and were as surprised by all of this as you. Perhaps you're thinking of someone in another department?"

"Maybe."

"You had a bad concussion. I'm sure things are still a little fuzzy."

"I guess." I close my eyes for a moment and picture Peter clearly. I know I'm not confused.

"We'll let you get some rest," Agent Parker says. "Thank you for your help. Here's my card. I'll be in touch." He sets his card on the table.

"Is there anyone we can contact for you?" Martha asks.

I shake my head. "I recently moved here. I only knew people that I worked with and my parents."

"Here's a list of support groups in the area. We have a trauma counselor on call, I will send them up."

"No. Please. I'm not ready for that."

"Okay, let me know when you are." Martha sets her card on the table alongside Parker's.

"Ms. Umbra, before we leave, can you confirm your birthdate?

"January 27, 1992."

Ava nods. "We understand you've been through a lot. If you need anything, let us know." Ava turns to leave.

"Wait, how many people got out?"

Parker answers, "Luckily, the explosion and fire burned from the top floors down so close to three-thousand people were able to escape."

"Were there bodies found anywhere else in the casino or only in the theater?"

Parker looks at me for a moment. One eyebrow lifts and I worry that I've pushed too far. "No, not really. There were a few bodies found on the Thirteenth floor and a nearby stairwell, but that's it. Are you remembering something?"

"No, I'm trying to piece together how I made it out. I don't remember seeing anyone."

"You were the last survivor out. Get some rest, Ms. Umbra." Agent Parker nods to Ava and Martha, gesturing for them to leave.

Ava opens the door and is followed by Martha. Parker pauses before he crosses the threshold. "Oh, Ms. Umbra, I nearly forgot. Have you ever heard of a group called The Knights of the Solar Temple?"

"Knights, as in like medieval knights?"

"Yeah, that's what they call themselves."

"No, I haven't. Why? Is that the group you think did this?"

"It was just a question. We have no suspects yet. Thanks for your time." Parker nods to me before disappearing.

As the door clicks behind him, a cocktail of dread and pain crushes me. The weight of the blanket becomes suffocating. Everything from my toes to my crown seems to scream in pain. Gritting my teeth, I press the call button on the remote attached to my bed.

"Yes?" A voice quickly answers.

"I'm in a lot of pain."

"Okay, I'll send your nurse right in."

Moments later, there's a soft rap on my door. It slowly opens. It's not a nurse but a young priest with a mop of glossy-black, curly hair.

"Lilly?"

Discomfort stokes my irritation, and I blatantly roll my eyes. "Let me guess, if I just have faith everything will be fine, right?" A laugh escapes before my ribs scream in pain and I close my eyes.

"Don't be silly, this is important." The priest closes the door behind him. He pulls a chair very close to my bed and sits.

"I told them I don't want to talk to anyone right now."

"This won't take long," he says. "I'm Father Chris."

"Your magic won't work on me, Father. Please leave me alone. I'm in a lot of pain and not in the mood to talk to a trauma counselor." My head drops and my eyes sink to his black combat-booted feet. I remember those boots.

"I'm not a trauma counselor. I was—"

"I know who you are. I'm not talking to you. You were at Golden Sands when Tony was killed."

He leans closer. "Yeah, how do you think Sharp got the information to pass on to you. We were trying to warn you."

"You knew Sharp?"

Holding my gaze, his bright-blue eyes are stunning. "Yeah, and I was also very good friends with Xander. We were working together. You knew him as Buddy."

The intensity in my gaze equals his, but I remain silent.

"I know everything. I can help you. You need me."

"You don't know everything. I'm sorry. I . . . I . . ." My eyes sink back to his boots; they've clearly seen their share of wear and tear. Father Chris is no ordinary priest.

"Xander knew what he was up against. It's not your fault."

"It is my fault. He was trying to help us."

"Shh. We'll have time to talk, but this is not the place," he whispers.

I nod slowly then look directly into his eyes. "I'll talk to you. For Buddy. But from here on out, I'm working alone."

"You're going to need my help, trust me. You'll be safe while you're in here, we've made sure of that. Once you've been cleared, I'll get you out of this area and into hiding."

"Hiding?" I wince when I try to pull myself up.

"Shush." Chris gestures for me to calm down. "There's a lot you don't know. I'll explain everything in a few days. Try to get some rest."

"You don't understand. I can't hide—"

A quick tap on the door interrupts me. Amanda sticks her head in. "I have the pain medicine you requested."

Father Chris waves Amanda in then places his hand on my shoulder. "I *understand*. You will be in my prayers, Lilly. I'll check in on you in a few days. Remember, as Ecclesiastes 3:7 says, there's a time to keep silent, and a time to speak. Now, dear Lilith, is your time to keep *silent*." He squeezes my shoulder. "Let yourself rest and heal."

Epilogue

The string of pearls appear,
Hope held in every breath.
Liquid memories, forgotten names,
A culture of false promises and hidden dreams.
When dawn breaks and beckons her awake, hope is found.
Fore she will not drown,
If only she chooses to play.

The roar of traffic sooths me, almost lulling me to sleep—something I've struggled with since leaving the hospital. Father Chris convinced me to spend a few torturous months in a safe house in the mountains of West Virginia. Other than Chris, I didn't see or speak to another human being for months. He filled me in on the histories of the different organizations we'll be up against. As it turns out, there're several that will be a threat to us.

Regardless of which side you stand, there's more than just The Order of Mu and The Knights of the Solar Temple that want what I have to offer. There's the Final Judgement or Second Coming of Christ, Al-Malhama Al-Kubra or Islam's Armageddon—the greatest battle, or The Four Horsemen of the Apocalypse. Though as far as Chris knows, none has ever come this close.

Chris has also trained me in several self-defense techniques, including firearms. I'm quite the sharpshooter. While Father Chris says this is the safest place for me, it's only prolonging the inevitable. We have to find a way to undo this. Thankfully, we've since moved into the next phase—hiding in plain sight.

I'd never spent much time in New York City, just the occasional day trip. Now that I'm living here, it certainly seems like the best place to disappear. Giving up on sleep, the twin bed screeches as I kick my legs off the side. I slip my feet into slippers as a cockroach scurries from under the bed. Its guts shoot out from under my heel as I step on it. There's something oddly satisfying about the crunch of these armored insects.

Grabbing the jeans and the flannel draped over the chair, I dress quickly in yesterday's clothes. Then throw an oversize sweatshirt on. The outside chill easily creeps in through the poorly sealed windows and I pull a beanie over my head. Lace up my boots and pull open the thin door to my efficiency.

The halls in my building are always busiest at night. Most of the bulbs have been smashed out so there's only a dim haze of light. I squeeze past a group of hunched-over bodies resembling zombies in their drug-induced stupor.

A hand grabs my elbow. "I got tootsie rolls, cotton, bars, blues, candy, butter. I even got a few fry daddies already rolled," a gravely man's voice says from behind a dark hood. He's new to this hall.

"No thanks." I jerk my arm away.

"Why you here if you don't wanna play?" He puts his arm around my shoulder.

A fuse ignites in my chest, and I slam this dealer against the wall, cornering him. I look into his eyes, my lips pull back in a snarl, and I can smell his fear. "What would Auntie B say if she saw you here, pushing your dirty, dirty drugs? The same drugs that killed your uncle." Tears form in his eyes, but I can't stop myself. "You found him, collapsed in a dirty alleyway, dead, sitting in his own piss and shit. You were only eight. You made a promise to Auntie B, didn't you?" I look at him for a moment and inhale his fear. "They raised you. And now, look at you. You're disgusting. Turning loving family members into addicts." The color has drained from his tear-soaked face.

"I'm sorry. I'm sorry." He collapses into a crying heap as I walk away.

I'm sick to my stomach as the bolt of fury settles into a steady rain of guilt. I've had a hard time controlling my anger lately, though I'm getting used to knowing things about others that I shouldn't. When people touch me, I know things about them. Not good things. Even more troubling, I'm learning how to use it to serve my own intent.

No one else bothers me as I weave through the dark hall and down the single flight of steps. The desk attendant is drinking a beer and watching his phone; he doesn't even look up through his plexiglass window as I walk by. The lock on the main door is permanently jammed so that a little tug is all it needs to click open.

Even late at night—or early in the morning, depending on your perspective—the streets in this neighborhood are busy. Night-crawlers still work their corners while the early-morning shift prepares for the day. This is my favorite time to walk; it's such an interesting mix and I'm easily lost in it. No one notices me. No one even looks at me. This is when I'm most comfortable.

Someone grabs my shoulder from behind. As I spin, my hand goes to my belt. Ready.

"Hey—"

"Shit! Chris. Don't do that."

"Sorry," Father Chris says, lifting his hands in mock surrender. His charming, dimpled smile makes it extremely hard to stay mad. He's wearing his clerical collar, which he only wears doing 'outreach.'

"What are you doing here? *Working*?" I roll my eyes.

"I'm not spying on you, if that's what you're insinuating. I—"

"This is the safest place for me. No one will look here. I blend in."

"I know. I know. That's not why I'm here. I have an official meeting later this morning, which I need to talk to you about."

"What kind of meeting?"

"I'll buy you breakfast."

"I'm not hungry."

"Coffee then. Come on."

We head towards the twenty-four-hour corner coffee shop we visit at least twice a week. The only reason I agreed to work with Chris is because he works alone. Every parish in the Catholic Church has one priest who's in charge of exorcisms, but their identity is kept secret. He's also responsible for monitoring any dark organization's activity. Technically, Chris has been ordained in the Catholic Order of The Malum Interfectorem. There're thousands of priests in this order, well 221,703 to be exact—one for every parish in the world. A handler maintains communication between the church and the priest, but that's it. Chris doesn't know the identity of anyone else in the Order. This way, they could never organize and become corrupted, like the Knights of the Solar Temple, previously known as the Knights Templar, but more on that later.

Chris opens the door to the coffee shop for me. "Thanks, Harry Potter." I wink as I walk in.

"I should've never told what order I'm in."

I chuckle. "It sounds like something you'd say before whipping out your wand."

Cindy, the overnight waitress, is sitting at the food bar on her phone. She doesn't seem to notice us as we enter, and we duck into our usual booth in the back corner.

"What's this about?" I ask.

Chris just lifts his eyebrows and moments later, Cindy is pouring coffee into our mugs.

"Thanks," I say.

"Thank you, Cindy," Chris says.

"Can I get you anything else, Father?"

"Just coffee for now."

"What about you?" She scowls at me.

"Just coffee," I say with a smile.

Cindy glowers for a moment before looking at Chris and smiling. "Call me over if you need anything," she says before shuffling back to her post.

Sometimes, I'm sure people can sense something in me, like they're automatically afraid or don't trust me.

"So?" I ask.

"We're going to an art auction."

"What?"

"The upcoming Sotheby's auction just added an illuminated Book of Hours, rumored to have been done by Jan van Eyck."

"The Ghent Altarpiece guy?"

"Yes," Chris says.

"A Book of Hours?" I rub my temples as if that might help Chris get to the point.

"It's a book that holds prayers to say throughout the hours of the day and night. Wealthy people would commission artists to make them."

"Does it have to do with the Altarpiece?"

"I'm not sure. But here's the thing. It was recently discovered by Rodrigo Alvarez. He's a notorious art and relic hunter, for lack of a better word. He's been searching for the missing panels and other lost works for years." Chris sips his coffee.

"Now he's just selling it?"

"Yeah."

"And?" I ask, throwing my hands up. Chris takes another sip of his coffee. "It must be worthless, right?"

"Don't jump to conclusions. I'm getting there, relax. So, Rodrigo found it in 2021, it should be priceless and now he's in a rush to unload it for somewhere between twenty-five and fifty-thousand dollars. Rumor has it this piece made him go crazy. The wife thinks it's cursed."

"I'm confused."

"My source told me Rodrigo began talking to this book and thought he was speaking to God. His wife freaked out and had him committed. Now she's selling it, claiming they found out it was just a copy."

"So, you think he's talking to God through this book?"

"What? No." Chris looks at me with one eyebrow raised. "That's not how God works."

"Then what?"

"It's a bit of a gamble, but I think it holds some clues that will point us towards the lost panels."

"And you're sure the lost panels hold the key to undoing this?" I hold my hand to my chest.

"As sure as I can be till we get our hands on them."

"No one has been able to find them for the better part of a century."

"This book may be our first step."

"You make this sound easy." I sigh. "Where are we going to get the money? And how are we going to get into the auction?"

"I put in a request for the funding, which we received plus travel expenses." Chris slides a packet across the table. "Here're our invites to the auction as well as our numbers and our new passports."

I remove the passport and flip it open. "Heidi von Sant, blonde hair. Are you kidding me?"

"You can't go to the auction looking like that. And you're in hiding." Chris lets out a huff of frustration, his shoulders caving towards the table. "I shouldn't have to remind you of this every day."

"All I'm saying is that I would've preferred being a red head."

"Oh, um—"

"I'm joking."

Chris looks at his watch. "I have to run, meet me at my place at noon."

"When's the auction?"

"This evening. Then we board our flight to Rome with the book."

A tingle runs down my spine and I sit up straight.

"So?" Chris asks.

I hold out my hand to Chris. "Heidi von Sant, nice to meet you."

"How's your German accent?"

My eyes narrow and I open my mouth to protest, but he cuts me off.

"I'm joking." Chris winks as he stands. "See you in a few." He drops a twenty on the table before leaving.

ROLL THEM BONES . . .

www.ingramcontent.com/pod-product-compliance
Lightning Source LLC
Chambersburg PA
CBHW030358180626
46812CB00005B/1836